The Widow of Rose Hill

Book Two

The Women of Rose Hill Series

by

Michelle Shocklee

SMITTEN
HISTORICAL ROMANCE
LIGHTHOUSE PUBLISHING of the CAROLINAS

THE WIDOW OF ROSE HILL BY MICHELLE SHOCKLEE
Published by Smitten Historical Romance
an imprint of Lighthouse Publishing of the Carolinas
2333 Barton Oaks Dr., Raleigh, NC 27614

ISBN: 978-1-946016-40-9
Copyright © 2018 by Michelle Shocklee
Cover design by Elaina Lee
Interior design by Karthick Srinivasan

Available in print from your local bookstore, online, or from the publisher at:
ShopLPC.com

For more information on this book and the author visit:
http://www.michelleshocklee.com/

Brought to you by the creative team at Lighthouse Publishing of the Carolinas (LPCBooks.com): Robin Patchen, Pegg Thomas, Brian Cross, Judah Raine, and Lucie Winborne

Library of Congress Cataloging-in-Publication Data
Shocklee, Michelle
The Widow of Rose Hill / Michelle Shocklee 1st ed.

Printed in the United States of America

Praise for *The Widow of Rose Hill*

Michelle Shocklee not only writes about history, she puts the reader right in the middle of it. With characters so real they feel as if they are going to step off the page, this novel is one you won't be able to put down. From the first page until the last, the reader will be drawn in to a story that keeps the pages turning. If you love history, especially the Civil War period, do not miss this novel!

~**Kathleen Y'Barbo**
Best-selling author of *The Inconvenient Marriage of Charlotte Beck*

The Widow of Rose Hill illuminates the turmoil of a nation in the aftermath of war and creates a portrait of healing, restoration and hope.

~**Allison Pittman**
Author of *Loving Luther*

Praise for *The Planter's Daughter*

Shocklee's novel carried me to a past time, a unique culture, and held me captive. Its realistic setting, believable characters, and gripping storyline—told honestly yet never wallowing in ugliness—came together into a beautiful tale about following one's conscience regardless of the cost. Kudos to Michelle on a lovely, heart-stirring debut.

~**Kim Vogel Sawyer**
Award-winning author of *My Heart Remembers*

Dedication

For my sons, Taylor and Austin

My joy. My pride. My heart.

The LORD is my rock, and my fortress, and my deliverer.

Psalm 18:2

CHAPTER ONE

Williamson County, Texas
June 1865

"I declare, Carolina, I believe we will positively melt before the day is finished with us."

Seated on the swing on the wide front porch that graced the big house of Rose Hill plantation, Natalie Langford Ellis cooled her face with her favorite lace fan until the muscles in her arm cramped. Not even the uppermost branches of the great oaks near the house stirred in the sultry afternoon air. Nary a cloud floated in the clear blue sky to offer a brief respite.

"Yes'm." Carolina mopped her ebony skin with a damp cloth. From her place in a worn wicker chair near the rail, the young servant leaned forward to catch the whisper of a breeze that might venture past. "Summer jest gettin' started, but we's already feeling the misery. Don't 'spect it'll get better 'til after harvest."

With the toe of one slipper, Natalie lazily propelled the swing back and forth, the groan from rusty chains blending with the song of dozens of cicadas high in the tree branches. Childish laughter drew her attention to the sun-scorched lawn just down from the house where two small boys—one white and one black—played with a reddish-brown dog, the three of them rolling and chasing and generally doing what little boys and dogs do best.

Natalie smiled despite the uncomfortable trail of sweat trickling down her back. She loved to watch Samuel play, all innocence and goodness, free of the heavy burdens his mother carried. "I believe my son will require two tubs of water to wash the filth from him tonight."

Carolina chuckled. "Master Samuel shore don't take pleasure in bath time. Says if Isaac don't have to bathe, why should he?"

"Moses bathes his son in the creek, only he calls it swimming, so Isaac is none the wiser." Natalie glanced toward the vast cotton fields west of the house. "Speaking of Moses, he should be here by now."

Dozens of slaves dotted the rolling green landscape, busy at their tasks in spite of the warm afternoon. Reflected sunshine glinted here and there as workers used hoes to attack ever-present weeds. Harvest was still many weeks away, so it was vital the unwanted plants remain under control lest they choke out the cash crop. Assuming, that was, she could market the cotton this season.

Scanning the horizon and not finding Moses, she frowned. "I would like to know what he thinks about the beetles the workers discovered in the cornfield yesterday."

"Ain't right you has to worry your pretty head about such things, Miz Natalie. You need a man to run this plantation." Carolina punctuated her statement with a nod.

Familiar ire tugged Natalie's brow. The sixteen-year-old was much too outspoken. George would roll over in his grave if he knew she let the slave speak to her in such a forward manner. Her husband had never treated their Negroes as anything other than property. But George wasn't there. He had decided the Confederate cause was more important than staying home with his wife and son, and he had paid the ultimate price.

"Even if I agreed with you," Natalie said, "which I don't, the only men who aren't away fighting that dreadful war are either too young or too old."

Wisely, Carolina didn't comment further.

A thin line of dust near the edge of the cotton fields caught Natalie's eye a few minutes later. Squinting, she made out Moses' large form lumbering up the trail to the house. With the spring rains long gone, every road and footpath on the property was caked with powdery dirt that filled the air and clung to shoes and clothes.

"Finally, here comes Moses now." She stood, noting a larger cloud of dust on the horizon some distance behind him. Perhaps the slaves were plowing a fallow field, although it seemed an odd time for such an activity. "Fetch a cup of water, Carolina. I'm certain he'll be thirsty."

While the servant disappeared into the house, Natalie walked to the corner of the wide covered porch. Gratitude for the big slave welled up within her breast, though she could never let anyone know the extent of it. Rose Hill had been without an overseer for most of the war. She'd feared a revolt, or at the very least, an exodus of slaves once they realized no one would stop them from leaving. A few did escape, taking their chances with the patrols. They disappeared into the night, no doubt headed for Mexico. Moses had taken charge of the remaining workers then, seeing to it they planted, tended, and harvested the crops as though nothing had changed. She knew it was their respect for the big man and not a sense of loyalty toward her that kept them on the plantation.

"Miz Natalie." He panted as he reached the bottom of the steps. Rivers of sweat rolled down his face from beneath a floppy hat and soaked his homespun shirt. "I got news." He bent over and placed his hands on his knees to catch his breath.

Alarm washed over her. "I hope you're not here to tell me those horrid beetles are destroying the corn." How would she feed the slaves all winter if they lost the corn? "We haven't the seed to replant if we lose the crop."

Moses straightened, his leathery brow tugged in a deep frown. "No, ma'am. That ain't the news I has. The corn be fine. Look yonder." He pointed to the large cloud of dust hanging in the still air. It was closer than it had been minutes before. "So'diers is comin'. Bluecoats, all."

Natalie gasped. "Bluecoats? Here?"

"Yes'm. They's comin' real slow like they been travelin' for a time, but they's comin'."

Indeed, the shapes of many horses and riders emerged through the dust, making their way slowly up the long poplar-lined road.

Carolina arrived on the porch and handed a tin cup of water to Moses, who downed the liquid in one swallow. She looked at the approaching swirl of dust. "Who that comin'?"

"Soldiers. Yankee soldiers." Natalie's heart twisted with dread. The war couldn't be going well if Yankees were in Texas. With no access to newspapers the last few years due to a statewide shortage of paper, word of mouth was the only way to keep up with the battles. It had been several months since she'd received any significant word on the war.

Natalie spoke with a trembling voice. "Moses, get the rifle. Carolina, run inside and close the windows. Then go upstairs and hide my jewelry. Hurry!"

Wide-eyed, the slaves ran to do her bidding while Natalie watched the riders approach, her stomach knotting with fear. Why were Yankees in Texas? The answer didn't bode well.

Moses returned to her side as the forms of sixty or more horsemen in blue Union coats became clear. The line of soldiers rode through the open whitewashed gate and entered the yard.

"I's put the gun next to the door inside," Moses said, keeping his voice low and his eyes on the strangers. "I's prayin' we don't gots to use it."

Natalie nodded. What could one gun do to protect them from these armed men? She had heard stories about homes across the South being pillaged and burned by vengeful Yankees. Was that what they were here to do? Burn her home and leave her destitute?

The sound of a barking dog stilled her racing thoughts.

Samuel!

"Where is my son? Moses, where are the boys?" Horses and men blocked her view of the lawn where the children had been playing.

"They be yonder, Miz Natalie." He pointed to the far edge of the grass where Samuel and Isaac knelt beneath the branches of an ancient black walnut tree, clinging to the big dog to keep it from charging toward the soldiers.

Though he was safe for the moment, she desperately wanted to call him, to tell him to run and hide in the barn. She remained mute lest she draw attention to the boys. Shadows from thick branches overhead made it difficult to see them, but the incessant barking of that mangy dog surely wouldn't go unnoticed by the soldiers.

As the men dismounted, a young Negro soldier separated himself from the group and approached the bottom of the steps. Natalie held her shock in check. She'd heard rumors both armies had begun to allow black men to join their ranks, but to see one in uniform was nothing less than startling.

"Ma'am. Sir." He gave a polite nod to include Moses. "The colonel requests permission to speak with the man in charge of this plantation."

Fear kept Natalie silent. To admit she was in charge would reveal her vulnerability. If only her father-in-law were still alive, no matter how unpleasant and cruel he'd become in those last years.

"You may state your business and move on," she said, her chin rising, though she felt little of the bravado she hoped she displayed. "We haven't many provisions and no money to speak of. You will waste your time searching for either."

From the corner of her eye, she saw a tall man with a thick dark beard approach. While she'd never seen a Yankee officer before, he looked like she might have imagined. Broad shoulders filled out the dusty blue coat that reached nearly to his knees, giving way to equally dusty high black boots. A long saber hung from his belt, the handle tied with gold cord, while the emblem of two crossed miniature sabers on his hat reflected the afternoon sunshine. His very stride exuded power and confidence, and his dark eyes, when they met hers, sent a chill coursing through her.

"Ma'am." The deep timbre of his voice held no warmth. "I am Colonel Levi Maish, commander of this company. Let me assure you we have no need for your provisions or your money. There is, however, a matter of great importance which I must insist on discussing with the man in charge of this plantation. We will not leave until I have spoken to him."

For a brief moment, Natalie thought to tell the bearded man a lie. That her husband was simply away for the day, but upon his return, she would gladly relay any information the colonel wished to impart. But what if the Yankee chose to wait for the nonexistent husband?

In the end, his words and forceful tone left little choice but to reveal herself as the owner of Rose Hill. All she could do was pray he would treat her and the slaves with compassion. Squaring her shoulders, she met his gaze without wavering.

"As I said, sir. You may state your business, and then you may remove yourselves from *my* property."

CHAPTER TWO

Admiration stole over Levi at the blond beauty's defiant attitude. He kept his expression stony, but he couldn't help but be impressed that she'd stood up to an entire company of Union soldiers. He didn't know whether to believe her or not. She looked far too young to be the mistress of a large cotton plantation, with her long curls flowing down her back and tied simply with a ribbon. But he knew the war had forced many women into roles they never would have assumed otherwise.

He asked, "Your name?"

"Mrs. Natalie Langford Ellis, mistress of Rose Hill plantation." Her blue eyes sparked with pride.

"Mrs. Ellis." He gave a slight nod before turning to Corporal Banks. Without a word, that man offered Levi a folded piece of paper, having played out similar scenarios multiple times over the past week as they'd traveled north from the port city of Galveston, stopping at farms and plantations along the way. After studying the map and reading the notation regarding this particular location, Levi returned his attention to the woman. "My records indicate this plantation is owned by Luther Ellis. You are his wife?"

"I was married to his son George."

"Was?"

A long moment passed before she responded. "My husband was killed in the war. As for my father-in-law, Luther succumbed shortly after news of George's death reached us. So you see, Colonel, Rose Hill is my property. I haven't the time to stand on the porch, wasting away the day. You may state your business before you ride back in the direction you came from."

If his mission hadn't been so serious, he might have chuckled at her feisty attitude. Instead, he inclined his head. "Very well, Mrs. Ellis. If I might have a word with you privately, I am to make you aware of a proclamation from the Executive of the United States to all Texas slave owners." Corporal Banks handed him a second folded sheet of paper.

A frown creased her smooth brow. "A proclamation?"

"I believe you will understand once I read it to you. In the meantime, my men need to water their horses."

She glanced to the big Negro beside her. Levi hadn't acknowledged the man before, simply because a slave was not the person in charge. But now he noticed how the man stood near her, legs braced, powerful arms stiff at his side as though ready to slay anyone who dared come near his mistress. When he gave a slight nod, Mrs. Ellis faced Levi again.

"Please join me in the parlor, Colonel. Your men may take their horses to the creek, just past the quarter."

Natalie Ellis disappeared into the house with the big slave trailing behind. Inside, voices echoed in the foyer, though he couldn't make out the words.

Levi turned to Corporal Banks. "Have the men take the horses to the creek, then I'd like you to join me inside. Once we're certain Mrs. Ellis understands and complies with the orders, we should have plenty of daylight left to get to the abandoned plantation and set up camp. Hopefully, the supply wagons will arrive ahead of us."

"Yes, sir." Banks' brow furrowed. "Colonel, wasn't the plantation where we're to make camp owned by a man named Langford?"

Levi glanced at the map in his hand and found the marked area where he'd been ordered to set up his command. Notes were written off to the side. "Yes. Calvin Langford. But according to the information we received, he and his wife died of yellow fever a few years ago. The place has been abandoned ever since."

"It may just be a coincidence, but Mrs. Ellis introduced herself as Natalie Langford Ellis. You think she might be related?"

How, Levi wondered, had he not noticed the similar names when the blond-haired, blue-eyed woman revealed her identity? He would like to blame it on fatigue from the long journey from Galveston, but a need for honesty prevented him from lying, even to himself. The truth was, he'd felt an immediate attraction to the woman, despite her being everything he loathed—a southern slave owner. Her delicate appearance awakened long-dormant feelings deep inside, feelings he'd thought dead and buried like the thousands of men he'd seen perish in battle. That he had allowed himself to be distracted by a pretty face reminded him he wasn't the eager soldier he'd been four years ago when the war had broken out.

"Good observation, Banks. I expect we will learn the answer to that question soon enough." He turned to mount the steps, but the approach of a barking dog, with two little boys chasing after it, stilled him.

"Ebenezer, come back here!" called the white boy. Levi guessed him to be four or five years old, close to the same age as Levi's own nephew back home in Pennsylvania. The boy's companion, dark skinned and of similar size, hung back, his eyes round and fearful as they neared the soldiers.

The dog made a beeline for Levi. Before he could decide what the best course of action was to avoid an attack, Corporal Banks, who hadn't gone far, removed his revolver from his holster and leveled it at the charging dog.

"Don't shoot!"

Levi turned to see Mrs. Ellis rush onto the porch, her bell-shaped skirt swinging as she dashed down the steps.

"Ebenezer, no!" The big dog skidded to a stop at her command, mere feet from Levi. His spotted tongue lolled to one side, and his tail swished in a friendly manner. Mrs. Ellis turned angry eyes to Levi. "He wasn't going to hurt you. He'd probably lick you to death before he'd think to bite." Her fury settled on Corporal Banks next, who was still aiming his gun at the dog. "Put that thing away. There are children present."

Levi nodded to Banks. The young man replaced the gun in its holster then proceeded to take his and Levi's horses by the reins and follow the others toward the creek.

"Mama, was that so'dier really gonna shoot Ebenezer?" The white boy ran to Mrs. Ellis and grabbed a handful of her skirts. She received him in a warm embrace, her features softening.

"No, Samuel, he wasn't. He didn't understand that Ebenezer was welcoming them." She smoothed his sandy hair then glanced at Levi. "Isn't that right, Colonel?"

Levi met her gaze. Banks most certainly would have shot the dog. The men were trained to protect their commander, no matter the enemy. But Levi understood her desire not to upset the child. He looked down at the boy. "Corporal Banks just wanted to keep me safe. Is Ebenezer your dog?"

The boy nodded.

"Well, he is a fine watchdog. With a little training, he'll learn to mind you when you give him an order. Keep working with him."

Samuel offered a shy grin.

"You and Isaac go on to the kitchen now," Mrs. Ellis said, giving the boy a little shove toward the black child, who'd stopped some distance from them. "Harriet found a jar of peaches in the cellar this morning. Tell her I said you and Isaac may have some. Take Ebenezer with you."

"Yes, Mama." With one last peek at Levi, Samuel scampered off to the back of the house with his companions in tow.

"Thank you, Colonel." Her softened voice drew his attention. "A dead dog would be of no consequence to the Union Army, but my son's heart would have been broken. He has experienced enough loss in his short life to last through the ages. I appreciate you sparing him another."

Her sincere gratitude surprised him. "You're welcome. My brother's son is about the same age as Samuel. I can imagine how Lucas would feel if his pet were killed right in front of him."

Her expressive blue eyes studied him for a long moment before she turned away. "If you will join me in the parlor, we can attend to business so you may be on your way."

Levi followed her into the airy foyer of the big house, taking notice of the marble floors, grand staircase, expensive furnishings, and a rug he guessed came from the Orient. A large vase containing roses of various colors sat on a polished table, filling the space with a sweet aroma.

The parlor was situated to the right off the entry, and she led the way into it. Several sofas and horsehair chairs graced the spacious room, while four large windows let in an abundance of outdoor light. Artwork filled the walls, and a sizable hand-painted medallion on the ceiling circled the base of a crystal chandelier. Dominating the wall between two windows was a fireplace adorned with an ornate mahogany-and-marble mantel that held porcelain frippery, silver candlesticks, and two framed photographs.

Levi's ire rose as he took in the room, far more lavish than any he'd seen in Texas thus far. Any compassion he may have felt toward the widowed mother evaporated at the sight of such luxuries, all bought with proceeds earned from the labor of enslaved men and women. How could a woman so concerned about her child's dog justify keeping human beings in bondage, all for the sake of maintaining her excessive lifestyle, fully on display in this room?

When his observations ended, he found Mrs. Ellis seated on the edge of a sofa, watching him. Her gaze flicked to the trinkets on the mantel, and alarm swept her features. Did she think he meant to steal her valuables?

"You mentioned a proclamation of some sort," she said, a tremor in her voice as she nervously smoothed the striped material of her skirt.

Good. He hoped she felt uneasy. People like Natalie Ellis lived their lives in undeserved comfort at the expense of others less fortunate. With both his parents active in the abolitionist movement for as long as he could remember, Levi's understanding of right and wrong where the Negro was concerned had been established at a very early age.

He would enjoy these next few minutes immensely. "I'll get to that in a moment. Are you aware, Mrs. Ellis, that the war has ended?"

Her eyes widened. "It's over?"

A gasp came from the hallway, though the person from whom it emitted remained out of sight.

After he and other Union troops landed in Galveston on June nineteenth, they'd been astonished at the number of Texans who hadn't heard the news regarding the war's end or of President Lincoln's assassination.

"It is." The desire to gloat over the Union's victory lasted only a second. Too many lives had been lost on both sides to resort to schoolyard antics. "General Lee surrendered to General Grant in Virginia on April ninth." The memory of that historic day flashed through Levi's mind. He'd been with General Sheridan's cavalry the last year of the war, taking part in the downfall of the Confederate Army of Northern Virginia. When they'd learned Lee had accepted Grant's offer of surrender, Levi's company rode hard to reach the house where the two generals met in order to witness the South's final defeat.

She seemed stunned by the news. "We heard that President Lincoln had been killed, but no one said anything about the war ending."

"President Johnson, Lincoln's successor, has issued orders for a proclamation to be read to all Texas slave owners." Levi removed his gloves and took the folded sheet of paper from his pocket. He'd read these same words to slave owners many times over the past week, but each time they brought a sense of satisfaction to his very soul. This was what he'd fought for. This was why men had died. He cleared his throat. "The people of Texas are informed that in accordance with a Proclamation from the Executive of the United States, all slaves are free."

Another gasp came from the hallway while Mrs. Ellis sat wide-eyed and silent.

Levi continued. "This involves an absolute equality of rights and rights of property between former masters and slaves, and the connection heretofore existing between them becomes that between employer and free laborer. The freedmen are advised to remain quietly at their present homes and work for wages. They are informed that they will not be allowed to collect at military posts and that they will not be supported in idleness either there or elsewhere."

He let the words sink in. Clearly, from the shocked expression on her face, she had not expected this. "Do you have any questions?" he asked after several long moments.

She blinked. "I ..." She glanced out the window then back. "You mean to say *all* the slaves are free?"

"Yes." Levi tucked the paper back into his pocket. "They have been free since President Lincoln issued the Emancipation Proclamation in eighteen sixty-three. But with the same lawless attitude that drove states to secede from the Union, the South refused to acknowledge that freedom."

"What ... what happens now?"

The frightened, almost childlike tone in her voice cooled Levi's indignation. It wasn't this woman's fault the South seceded and started a war. It wasn't even her fault she'd been raised to believe slavery was a legitimate means of labor. She, like the Negroes themselves, was victim to the misguided and selfish beliefs of men who had been placed in positions of authority for far too long.

"It is now your responsibility as owner of this plantation to gather all of the slaves and inform them of their freedom." He waited for her to meet his gaze. "Once they've been informed, it's up to them whether they stay or not."

Myriad emotions played across her face. She glanced to the doorway, then out the window, then back to Levi. "How am I supposed to manage the plantation without them?"

"As the proclamation states, you will become their employer. At least for those who choose to stay." He tempered his tone. "Mrs. Ellis, you need to be aware that the majority of the slaves will most likely leave. Even with no place to go, freedom offers them choices they have never had before."

"This has taken place throughout the South already? Slaves walking away from plantations, free?"

He nodded. "It has."

After another long period of silence, she slowly rose. "Very well. Moses?" She raised her voice slightly. The large black man appeared in the doorway.

"Yes, Miz Natalie?" His stony expression hadn't changed since Levi had first seen him on the porch.

"Is Carolina with you?"

A slender young black woman joined him, her dress similar in style to the one her mistress wore. Her rounded eyes were full of concern as she wrung her hands. "I's here, Miz Natalie."

"I'm sure you heard everything." At their murmurs of affirmation, she continued, "I suppose I should have said these words to you long ago, but Papa and George ..." Tears sprang to her eyes. "Well, never mind about them. You heard what the proclamation said. You are free."

The two slaves stood rooted to the hardwood floor, staring at their mistress.

Moses' dark gaze flicked to Levi then back to Mrs. Ellis. "What that mean, Miz Natalie? That mean we has to leave Rose Hill?"

When she didn't answer, Levi did. "Not unless you want to leave. It's your decision. If you choose to stay, Mrs. Ellis will become your employer. You and she would work out the details of your employment, including wages, to your satisfaction."

The astonishing information, Levi knew, took time to fully grasp. Both for the slave owner and for the slave. Freedom and choices were things the Negroes at Rose Hill and other plantations like it had never experienced.

"Moses, please gather the others and have them meet me in

the yard. I would like to be the one to tell them, so keep this to yourself, if you would." She took a wobbly step forward. Moses moved to her side, offering his strong arm for balance.

"You don't look so good, Miz Natalie. Why don't you sit down a spell?" Concern rang in the man's deep voice. She did look rather pale.

She waved him off. "I'm fine. Go on now and get the others. Carolina, please gather the house servants."

As Moses and Carolina exited the room, Corporal Banks entered. For a brief moment, the soldier stared at the young black woman's retreating back before he seemed to remember Levi awaited him. "The men are in position, sir."

"Thank you, Corporal." He turned to Mrs. Ellis, who now had tiny beads of moisture dotting her forehead and upper lip. The room was definitely stuffy, but he wondered if it wasn't the sheer shock of learning her slaves were free that had her ill. "Ma'am, we will escort you outside so you may address your people when you're ready. My orders are to have you read the proclamation to them yourself."

She simply nodded.

They made their way to the porch. Nearby, a teenage boy tugged on the rope of a large cast iron bell, the resounding noise calling to workers throughout the property. Negroes began filling the yard. More arrived from the fields and barns, hurrying toward the house. When it seemed all had arrived, Mrs. Ellis stepped to the rail. Levi noticed Moses stood off to the side of the group with one arm around a stout woman and little Isaac hoisted in the other. Samuel stood beside them. His dog was nowhere in sight.

"I am sure you're all wondering why the soldiers are here," Mrs. Ellis said, her voice wobbly as her legs had been. She grasped the porch rail with both hands, her knuckles turning white. "They have brought news. The war is over."

Gasps followed by cheers went through the crowd. "Who won?" someone called out.

"The Yankees."

A low murmur rose and fell.

"They also brought a proclamation that concerns you."

All eyes focused on Mrs. Ellis. Levi almost felt sorry for her. Her world was changing at a lightning-fast pace, and there was nothing she could do to stop it. He stepped forward and handed her the printed paper.

With hands shaking, she read the remarkable words. When she came to the end, she looked at the people in the yard. "You are free men and women."

It only took a moment before the group erupted. Hats flew in the air amid whistles and shouts. One man cried, "Free, my Lord! Free, free, my Lord!" Some knelt on the ground and wept while others hugged their neighbors. Moses simply held the woman and the boy close, tears streaming down his face.

"If you will excuse me, Colonel." Mrs. Ellis' subdued voice pulled his attention away from the boisterous celebration. Her face looked like a sun-bleached sheet when she handed back the paper. "I would like to be alone now. I have much to consider."

He bowed slightly. "I understand. My men and I will depart shortly."

She nodded and moved toward the doorway. She hadn't taken more than a few steps when her legs gave out. Before Levi could react, she collapsed into a puddle of blue-and-white fabric.

CHAPTER THREE

"Mama? Mama!"

Samuel's frightened voice penetrated the fog that gripped Natalie.

"Your mama is going be fine, son. Let's get her inside." The deep voice seemed very near.

As Natalie became aware of being lifted in strong arms, she forced her eyelids open only to find herself face to face with Colonel Maish. "What ...?"

"You fainted."

His muscles flexed beneath her as his grip on her tightened.

Horrified to find herself in the man's arms, Natalie glared at him. "I did not faint, sir. I simply became overly warm. Please put me down." Her stocking-clad calves were exposed in this position, and she tried in vain to smooth her voluminous skirt and crinolines into place.

A shade of humor gleamed in his deep brown eyes. "Call it what you will, ma'am, but you hit the porch fairly hard. Let me get you inside and make certain you aren't injured."

Helpless to argue, Natalie let the Yankee carry her into the parlor and settle her on the sofa. The fact that she did feel a bit lightheaded irked her further. She took a steadying breath.

"Mama, you fell down." Samuel crawled up beside her, his cherub face showing curiosity rather than concern. "Why?"

She smiled at her son and drew him to her side. "Mama had a silly accident. I'm fine now. Did you and Isaac enjoy your peaches?"

"Mmmhmm. Why was all the slaves crying and hollering?"

She glanced at Colonel Maish, who stood nearby, watching.

The explanation she gave her son regarding the slaves' freedom was none of his concern. She would have a long talk with Samuel later and explain what it meant. Right now, she simply wanted the Yankee officer out of her home and off her land.

"They're happy the war is over, like I am. It means the soldiers can all *go home*." She gave the colonel a pointed look.

"My papa can't come home."

The sad words tugged at her heart. Samuel rarely spoke of the father he had never known. "No, love, he can't."

Samuel looked up to Colonel Maish. "Will you go home?"

The colonel nodded. "As soon as I have completed my orders."

"Is your home in Texas?"

The man's dark beard twitched. "My home is in Pennsylvania. But I've been ordered to stay in Texas for a while, so I guess you could say it's my home for now."

Seemingly satisfied, Samuel bounded off the sofa. "Mama, can I go play with Isaac? We were gonna go rock hunting down by the creek, but Moses said we had to go stand in the yard and listen to you."

Natalie hesitated to answer. Nothing in their world was the same as it had been a mere hour ago. She wasn't certain any of the slaves would still be on the property, considering they were now free. There was also the fact that a company of Federal soldiers remained outside her door.

"Not right now, Samuel. I need you to go to your room and play. I'll come up and tell you a story in a bit."

Her son's bottom lip poked out, but he obeyed and trudged into the foyer and up the stairs. Oh, how she loved that boy. What did the future hold for him now that everything had changed?

"Why didn't you tell him the truth? That the slaves are happy because they're finally free?" A hard tone edged the colonel's voice.

"I didn't lie to my son." She glared at him. "I will explain things in a manner he can understand when we're alone. I certainly don't need an audience to dissect every word I choose trying to explain something very complicated in a way a four-year-old can comprehend."

After a tense moment, he acquiesced. "I apologize. I have no right to question what you tell your son."

His contrite words gave her pause. He didn't seem the type to admit to being wrong about anything. George certainly never had. "Apology accepted. Samuel won't understand freedom any more than he understood slavery, but I will do my best to explain it all."

"Are you feeling better?"

Embarrassment washed over her. She had never fainted in her life and was mortified she had done so in front of the Yankee and his men. "Yes, thank you. I'm not sure what came over me."

"You had some rather shocking news. All in all, I'd say you handled things quite admirably."

Once again, his kind words were unexpected. If she weren't mistaken, he had just given her a compliment. "You may not believe this, but I am happy for them. I never really thought about the plight of the slaves until my husband's sister helped several of our people escape, my favorite maid included."

"That event changed your mind?"

"Not at first," she admitted, recalling the morning after Adella and Seth left Rose Hill, taking four slaves with them. She shivered, remembering Luther's wrath. If not for George's reasoning that the plantation couldn't operate without slaves, she felt sure her father-in-law would have sold them all that very day. "After Adella Rose left, she wrote explaining why she'd done it. She described how Jeptha and Zina and Aunt Lu were free, living in Mexico, and how happy they were. I suppose someone from the north can't understand this, but that was the first time I realized Negroes were simply people, just like us."

"And yet you kept them in bondage."

She looked away, his words reminding her of the guilt—and fear—she'd lived with since the responsibility for the plantation fell into her hands. "As I said, someone from the north wouldn't understand."

A long silence followed.

"What will you do now?"

"I have no earthly idea, Colonel. I suppose it will depend upon whether or not any of the slaves—I mean, free men and women—stay or not." She glanced to the window. The ruckus had died down, and she wondered if her people were even now packing their meager belongings to leave Rose Hill.

"You do realize if some choose to stay, you will be required to pay wages. And"—he almost sounded apologetic—"Confederate currency is worthless. Only gold or United States currency is being accepted."

Any shred of hope of keeping Rose Hill operating evaporated with his words. "I haven't any money, Confederate or otherwise. We've been without an overseer for three years because I couldn't pay the salary, though the only men who hadn't gone off to war weren't the type I would hire anyway."

"Some planters are giving a share of the harvest to their workers as payment. Others, free room and board. There are ways to pay someone without cash."

Natalie considered his words. "I suppose those are options."

"I am curious how you managed to keep your slaves on the plantation without an overseer."

"Moses." She gave a sad smile. Aside from Samuel, Moses, Harriet, and Carolina were the closest thing she had to family these days. It hurt to think of them leaving. "Moses saw to it the fields were planted and tended. He tried to arrange the sale of the cotton, too, but the markets were closed. Your Union blockades were quite effective, Colonel."

"War is an ugly thing. People in the south as well as in the north have suffered. I, for one, thank God it is over."

His sincerity touched her. "That is something we can agree on."

He gave her a long study before he tugged on thick leather

gloves. "My men and I will take our leave now. I'm setting up a command post not far from here. We've been ordered to help Texans in the reconstruction of the Union and see that free Negroes are treated fairly. If you find yourself in need of anything, send word to the old Langford plantation."

Natalie gasped.

"Are you acquainted with the previous owner, Calvin Langford?"

She stood, practically sputtering. "Of course. He was my father. Langford Manor is my home."

He appeared taken aback by her outburst. "As I understood our information, the plantation was abandoned after an outbreak of yellow fever a few years ago. Langford and his wife succumbed to the disease. Is that not the case?"

"There was an outbreak, and I lost my parents, but the property has not been abandoned. I simply reside at Rose Hill instead."

His thick, dark eyebrows drew into a frown. "Is anyone living there? Do slaves still work the land?"

"No. My husband feared the outbreak would spread, so he sold off the remaining slaves after so many had died."

The colonel's shoulders relaxed. "I'm sorry for your loss, ma'am, but with no occupants, the plantation is indeed abandoned."

Natalie held back a very unladylike snarl. "No sir, it is not. The house may be closed and the fields fallow, but it is still very much my property."

Several ticks from the mantel clock filled the strained silence.

"I'm afraid you'll have to take the matter up with the Union officer in charge, General Gordon Granger. I believe he's in Austin presently. In the meantime, I have orders to follow." With a nod, he turned to leave.

"You cannot mean to seize my property after I have just informed you it is not available." Natalie stared at him, aghast at the very thought of a company of Yankees living in her childhood home.

He turned. "Mrs. Ellis." He took a deep breath, as though

forcing himself to remain civil. "I have my orders. If you would like—" Something outside the window caught his eye. A grave look swept his features, and he returned his gaze to her. "I fear you have more important things to worry over than an abandoned plantation."

Hurrying to the window, Natalie covered her mouth with her hands, choking down a wail that threatened to come forth.

A line of slaves, bundles on their backs and in their arms, made their way down the long drive toward the road.

The exodus had begun.

A wave of compassion washed over Levi as Mrs. Ellis stared out the window. Hearing her story, seeing the pain and fear in her eyes, he couldn't imagine what was going through her mind now. Although she seemed to be a strong woman—she'd kept the plantation going all alone when others in similar circumstances could not have—he had glimpsed vulnerability in her eyes.

"Miz Natalie?"

They turned to find Moses in the parlor doorway, his hat held with both hands.

"Moses." The whispered sob spoke volumes. Tears glittered in her blue eyes as the big Negro approached. "I suppose you're here to tell me you're leaving too."

"No, ma'am." He nodded toward the window. "Them folks ain't got no place to go, but freedom done called their name. Harriet and me, we figure on stayin' at Rose Hill, if that be to your likin'."

She nodded as tears slipped down her cheeks. "Of course it is to my liking." She cast a wary glance at Levi then back to Moses. "I can't pay you. I am not sure how ..." Her words trailed.

"Don't you worry none 'bout that, Miz Natalie. We work that out later."

"Thank you, Moses." Looking toward the window again, she asked, "Has everyone else gone?"

"Not everyone, but most. We has 'bout two dozen left in the quarter."

Carolina appeared in the doorway and gave a slight shrug. "I stayin' too, Miz Natalie, if that be all right. I got no place to go."

Levi thought Mrs. Ellis might crumple to the floor again from sheer relief.

"I promise I will pay you somehow." She included both servants in her gaze. "It will all depend on whether or not we can bring in the harvest. Without workers though ..."

There was no need to finish the statement. Without workers, how could she get the cotton harvested, baled, and shipped to the markets in Galveston?

"My men and I will take our leave now," Levi said, offering a slight bow. He had a camp to set up and orders to see about. The plight of a widow—albeit a beautiful one—was not his concern.

Her worried frown turned into a scowl. "And do you still intend to occupy my property without my permission?"

"I will send word to General Granger and let him know that although the plantation is abandoned, the owner resides nearby. Until I hear from him, I have my orders, and my men need a place to camp."

"Colonel, Langford Manor is a home. My home. It's filled with family heirlooms and personal belongings. I will not have your men rifling through my property, taking what little there is left of value and ruining the furnishings with muddy boots and dirty bodies."

They stared at each other, neither willing to concede defeat. She crossed her arms and arched one fine brow, almost daring him to proceed with his plans.

"I assure you," he said, "my men are not thieves. Besides, they will stay in tents on the property." He glanced down at his boots covered in trail dust. "However, I will occupy the house. I also require use of a room for an office. Other than the kitchen, I do not foresee a reason to disturb the rest of your home."

She seemed to measure his earnestness through narrowed eyes. "Do I have your word you will contact your superior regarding the matter immediately? And that you will vacate the premises the moment he informs you a grave mistake has taken place?"

Levi held back a chuckle. General Granger was not likely to consider the use of an unoccupied plantation a grave mistake. The man had far more important matters to concern him, the most pressing being the liberation of more than two hundred fifty thousand Texas slaves.

"I will deliver his response to you personally, Mrs. Ellis."

"Very well." Although she agreed to the plan, her tone was anything but compliant. "You may make use of the downstairs guest room as well as the adjoining sitting room. They have their own entrance, thus you will have no need to venture into the rest of the house." She glanced at Moses then back to Levi, her gaze challenging. "I will have Moses drive me over in the morning to see that all is well."

Levi met the challenge with his own unflinching stare. Did she think the threat of her arrival the following day could prevent his men from ransacking the place if they chose, as other Union companies had done all across the South? His men knew they would face severe punishment if they stooped to such ignoble levels.

"That is your choice, Mrs. Ellis." He inclined his head. "Until tomorrow."

He made his way to the porch and down the steps to his waiting horse. The men were already on the move.

"I take it things went well with Mrs. Ellis." Corporal Banks handed him the reins to his horse before swinging up onto his own mount.

"Why do you say that?" Levi looked back to the two-story white house. Mrs. Ellis stood at the parlor window.

"I haven't seen you smile in days."

Was he smiling?

He made a conscious effort to appear straight-faced and settled into the saddle. "I'm just glad to finally be on our way to make camp."

Corporal Banks glanced at the woman in the window then chuckled. "Yes, sir. Setting up camp sure is something to smile about."

Glaring at the young man's back as he rode away, Levi kicked his horse into motion.

The smile, however, gradually crept back to his lips and remained there for some time.

CHAPTER FOUR

D espite getting very little sleep, Natalie arose before the sun. The dawn-drenched world she found out the window looked much the same as it had each morning since she'd come to Rose Hill six years ago. Yet, everything had changed. Not even the deaths of her husband and parents had left her feeling as forsaken as the events of yesterday had. Simply putting one foot in front of the other took more effort than she dreamed possible.

After the departure of the slaves and soldiers, she'd gone upstairs to Samuel's room and never left. Harriet had brought up a light meal for both of them at some point, a worried look in her eyes when she found Natalie sitting on a child-sized chair, staring at nothing. Natalie somehow managed to keep Samuel from asking too many questions and then put him to bed early. She'd crawled onto the small goose-down mattress with her son and wrapped him in her arms despite the muggy evening air coming through the open windows. More than anything, she'd needed his nearness, inhaling his little-boy scent, whispering quiet prayers throughout the night that God would not take him from her too.

Birdsong greeted her now as she made her way to the detached kitchen wing. Absent were the voices of dozens of servants bustling about, carrying breakfast dishes, sweeping the porch, or filling lamps with kerosene. There was no blow of the ram's horn to call workers from the quarter, no jingle from wagons carrying slaves to fields, and no laughter of children from the double row of cabins down from the manor house. Instead, a strange, unsettling stillness hung over the entire plantation.

As she'd expected, Moses, Harriet, and Carolina were seated

at the long work table. Mugs of chicory root coffee sat in front of each of them, though no one seemed interested in the bitter-tasting brew they'd sunk to drinking after Union blockades prevented coffee beans from entering through the ports. The other house servants, including Clara, the young woman who cared for Samuel when Natalie was occupied, had joined the majority of field hands in their departure yesterday.

Moses stood. "Mornin', Miz Natalie."

Harriet, too, jumped up. "I get you some breakfast straightaway."

"There's no need," Natalie said, exhaustion already in her voice even though the day had barely begun. "I couldn't eat a thing. I need to get to Langford Manor, if it's still standing." She turned to Moses. "I fear what those Yankees may have done last night." Tears threatened, but she blinked them back.

"Now, don't go borrowin' trouble." Moses took his hat from the chair post and plopped it on his graying head. "That Yankee colonel seemed like a decent fellow, from what I could tell. He say they wouldn't do nothin' to your house, and I believe him."

Although she appreciated his calming words, the knot in her stomach would not unwind until she knew her childhood home remained safe and intact. "I pray you're right. It still infuriates me how that man defied my wishes, as though they were of little consequence compared to those of the great Union Army."

Recalling Colonel Maish's unflinching dark eyes as he'd stood his ground, Natalie shivered. Though the man had seemed sincere, she would be foolish to trust a Yankee. They cared little for Southerners. His scornful tone when he'd accused her of lying to Samuel about the slaves' celebration was evidence. It didn't matter to him that their entire way of life had changed in an instant. It didn't matter that Samuel's very future looked bleak and uncertain now. What legacy could there be in a plantation with no one to work the land? Her concern wasn't for herself but for her son, yet did the Yankee colonel care?

"I get the wagon hitched."

Natalie watched Moses leave the kitchen. What would she have done if the big man had heeded the call of freedom and walked off the plantation with the others? She didn't deserve his loyalty, but she was grateful for it nonetheless.

"You want me to fix yo' hair before you go yonder to Langford Manor, Miz Natalie?" Carolina's scrutinizing gaze had Natalie looking down at the rumpled dress she'd slept in. She touched her head and felt matted curls. "Wouldn't want you meetin' with that Yankee soldier lookin' like somethin' ol' Ebenezer found in the woods."

Natalie almost smiled at the candid words. It was good to know some things never changed.

"Yes, please. I would also like you to accompany us to the plantation. I may need your help inside the house." She looked at Harriet. "Would you see to Samuel while we're gone? I don't want him venturing too far from the house today."

If something happened to Samuel …

She tamped down the fear rising inside, refusing to give it a foothold. Today of all days, she needed her wits about her.

"When he wakes up, I'll put him an' Isaac to work makin' molasses cookies." Harriet chuckled. "Them two can eat more sweets than a growed man."

Natalie left the kitchen, knowing Samuel would be well cared for in her absence. Harriet doted on her white master's son as much as she did on her own.

Shame pricked her. Neither she nor her family deserved the woman's kindness.

Memories swirled, taking her back five years.

After Harriet and Moses lost their youngest children to yellow fever, George sold their two oldest sons, along with the remaining Langford slaves, for fear the disease would spread to Rose Hill. Harriet had grieved nearly unto death. Yet in those dark days, Moses never said a word against George or against God. Natalie was expecting her first child, and though the baby was months away from making its appearance, she couldn't imagine the pain of losing one child, let alone all five. Not long afterward, Harriet confessed she too was expecting. When the baby arrived, both she and Moses laughed and cried, naming the little boy Isaac, which, according to the preacher Moses had belonged to years ago, meant *laughter*. Like the biblical couple Abraham and Sarah, they'd trusted God to bring them joy in their old age. Though she'd never expressed it aloud, Harriet seemed at peace after Isaac was born. George was gone to war by then, and the two women raised their babies side by side. Freedom hadn't come in time to save Harriet's other children, but Natalie was grateful the Negro woman would not lose Isaac at the hands of a white master.

In her room, Natalie pulled a grass-green silk day dress from the back of the wardrobe, having kept it from becoming threadbare as most of her other gowns had grown. The wide collar buttoned at her throat and gave way to delicate ruffles across her chest while larger side-panel ruffles on the skirt fell in gentle waves to the floor. Luther had always called her the Mistress of the Manor when she wore it and gave mock bows when she entered a room.

Carolina arrived to help her get dressed. Natalie had the servant cinch her corset tighter than usual, frowning into the mirror when she noticed that despite being overly thin, her hips had most assuredly broadened since giving birth to Samuel. Vanity seemed silly in the face of all her troubles, but she couldn't help wanting to look her best when she met with Colonel Maish. She was, after all, Calvin Langford's daughter and the widow of George Ellis. She had a responsibility to their memories.

"That Yankee colonel shore gonna see what a lady you is, dressed in yo' finery with yo' hair done up all nice." Carolina finished buttoning the dress and started to work on Natalie's hair. The servant combed, teased, and pinned curls in place, expertly fashioning Natalie's hair into a becoming style. "He think twice 'bout taking charge of yo' property like you some silly addlebrained woman who cain't think fo' herself."

Natalie sighed. "I fear I may have no choice in the matter. Even if he does send word to his superior, I doubt that man will care about my wishes any more than Colonel Maish does."

"Maybe Señor Lopez could help you get them soldiers off yo' land," Carolina said. "He seem to be an important man. Has all them cows an' rides a fine horse. He always treat you nice, too."

The swarthy face of Alexander Lopez came to mind. A few years older than George, the attractive man claimed his Mexican roots prevented him from taking sides in the war, conveniently keeping him safe in Texas while men like her husband went off and got themselves killed. Being in the cattle business, Señor Lopez—Alexander, as he'd asked her to call him—had approached Natalie a year ago, interested in leasing Rose Hill pastures. With most of their cattle long since slaughtered or sold, and with bank notes overdue and no way to market her cotton, she had agreed. *Vaqueros* arrived shortly afterward with the first herd of cattle, staying to allow the stock to graze on Rose Hill grasses a few weeks at most. Not long after they departed, another group of Mexican cowboys arrived with more cattle, and so began a routine. Alexander, too, made an appearance at the plantation every few weeks with his interest being not only in the land but, as became obvious after a few visits, in Natalie herself. He had hinted more than once at a possible union between them.

In the reflection of the mirror, Natalie watched Carolina carefully place a stiff green bonnet with lace edging on her styled hair, leaving the ribbons dangling. Throughout the restless night, weighing the decisions she had to make and the few options available, she had not considered enlisting Alexander's help. She knew very little about him, considering all the time he'd spent at Rose Hill the past year. He was always rather vague when she inquired about his business and family, but his manners and speech were impeccable. She'd never had cause to believe he was anything other than a gentleman rancher.

"If Señor Lopez should stop by, I'm sure he would lend

assistance. However, that does not help me today." Natalie stood, giving herself a critical study in the mirror. She did look more mature with her hair coiffed. Her gown, too, was more akin to what the mistress of a large plantation would wear than the sheer summery dress from the previous day. Would the Yankee colonel, as Carolina had suggested, see her as such and give her the respect due her position?

Outside, Moses helped her onto the wagon seat while Carolina settled in the bed for the hour-long journey. The fancy carriages she would have preferred to arrive in had long since been sold to pay creditors, leaving a farm wagon as their only choice.

When Moses turned the team in the direction of the long drive, Natalie was surprised to see a dozen or so workers out in the fields. "I admit I hadn't expected to see anyone at work today." She looked at Moses, knowing he had to be responsible.

He glanced at her, then back to the road. "Them folks is employed by you now, Miz Natalie. Just 'cuz freedom come don't mean the weeds is gonna stop growin'. Critters still need tendin'. Garden still needs waterin'. I tells them you is workin' on how to pay them, whether it be in cash money or crops or some such."

"Thank you, Moses." Looking out to the handful of laborers, Natalie felt like weeping. While she was grateful they were willing to stay and work, she knew it was pointless. Two dozen people could not do the job it took sixty or more slaves to accomplish. Even if they only harvested half the crop, it would still take far more able-bodied workers than she could afford.

For one brief moment, she wished the soldiers had never set foot on Rose Hill, bringing with them the shocking proclamation of freedom. The thought was selfish, she knew. Though the slaves had no choice but to stay on the plantation all these years, none had been mistreated since George left for war. Luther was too far gone in his anger over Adella's betrayal and then his grief over George to give much consideration to the slaves, especially after his Negro driver, Monroe, mysteriously disappeared. Rumors in the quarter suggested someone murdered him, but his body was never found. Moses took charge after that, and life on the plantation for the slaves became more pleasant. Yet when the majority had chosen an uncertain future yesterday rather than choosing to stay and help bring in the crop ... well, that said more than words ever could.

Heaving a sigh, Natalie squared her shoulders. Harvest was still several weeks away. She could only worry about one problem at a time. Today, she was David facing Goliath. Colonel Maish and his Northern troops had taken possession of her property, establishing the battlefield. Now she had to figure out what she could use for a slingshot and stones.

They arrived at Langford Manor before she came up with a plan. That it was still standing left Natalie weak with relief.

"Thank heaven," she whispered as they drove across the yard to the big house. Not quite as grand as Rose Hill Manor, the home she grew up in held a special place in her heart. It, like Rose Hill, was her son's inheritance, his future. She would do everything in her power not to lose either.

"Guess that Yankee colonel tellin' the truth," Moses said. "Look yonder at all them tents."

Indeed, across what used to be fallow cotton fields lay a sea of white canvas tents, one neat row after the other. A roped off area held more horses than she could possibly count, and empty wagons formed a long line that disappeared behind the tents. Obviously, more men than she had seen at Rose Hill were encamped on her property. Any hope she'd held for their immediate evacuation vanished like a mist in the breeze.

"No wonder them Yankees won the war," Carolina said, balancing on her knees in the wagon bed to get a better look at the spectacle. "They done built a town overnight."

Moses drove the wagon to the front of the house. Several men in uniform stood on the porch, deep in conversation. A hush fell over them when Moses stopped the wagon mere feet from the steps, just as he'd always done over the years.

Natalie's stomach twisted when the men's curious gazes landed on her. What had Colonel Maish told them about her? That a foolish widow owned the plantation and thought to prevent the Union Army from doing as they pleased? Briefly, she wished Alexander Lopez were there. Perhaps the colonel would not be so arrogant if he had to face a man.

"I help you down, Miz Natalie," Moses said in a lowered voice before setting the brake. When he came around to her side of the wagon, she noticed he appeared as apprehensive as she felt. "Does you want me to come inside with you?"

As much as she longed for his steady presence, Natalie knew she had to handle this on her own. "Thank you, Moses, but no." She allowed him to assist her down from the high seat. It wouldn't do to fall flat on her face in front of the Yankees who now lined the porch rail, watching. "You and Carolina wait here while I speak with the colonel."

"Yes'm."

Gathering what little courage remained within her, Natalie brought her chin up and mounted the steps. Ignoring the men's bold stares, she headed for the front door. A familiar voice stopped her.

"Good morning, Mrs. Ellis."

Natalie turned to her right and found Colonel Maish standing at the far end of the wraparound porch, admiration in his dark eyes as they traveled over her attire. That her stomach did a strange flutter under his perusal startled her.

"Good morning, Colonel. I see you and your men have settled in." She looked out to the canvas city, mostly to prevent him from observing how his apparent appreciation for her laborious toilette left her flustered. If she had any hope of insisting he listen to her concerns, she couldn't display the slightest form of weakness.

"We have, but I've also kept my promise," he said, dismissing the other men with a nod as he joined her at the railing. The soldiers descended the steps, with one taking a last curious peek at her before they headed in the direction of the tents. "I sent a message to General Granger yesterday evening apprising him of your situation. I expect to hear back from him in a day or two."

This news surprised her. "I appreciate you handling my interests in such a prompt manner, Colonel."

His dark beard twitched. "Shall I assume you did not believe I would?"

Natalie offered a small shrug. "I admit I wasn't entirely convinced."

"And now?" His eyes glinted. Was he making fun of her?

She lifted her chin again. "Now I will make certain my belongings are where they should be. The Rose Hill house servants have cleaned Langford Manor every month since we closed it. There has never been anything missing or out of place."

The challenge in her voice was unmistakable even to her own ears. Any humor the colonel may have felt vanished as he narrowed his gaze on her.

"As I stated yesterday, Mrs. Ellis, my men are not thieves. Corporal Banks and I are the only ones who have been inside the house. When we first arrived, we walked through it, ascertaining it was indeed unoccupied." He quirked a dark eyebrow. "You are not the only one with doubts as to whether or not certain statements can be believed."

"I'm sure you found all exactly as I said."

He inclined his head. "I did. However." He folded his arms across the double row of brass buttons on his long blue coat. "The plantation itself is not being used. I sincerely doubt General Granger will order an evacuation."

Natalie scowled. "Surely the owner of the plantation should have some say in whom to allow on her private property." She indicated the fields, now full of men, animals, and tents. "I certainly did not expect this when you said your men needed a place to camp. There must be two hundred men living here."

"Your plantation is centrally located between San Antonio, the eastern communities, and the frontier. There are still thousands of slaves across Texas who have not learned of their freedom and slave owners who have not heard they are breaking the law by keeping people in bondage. The army needs a central command post from which to send companies to deliver the proclamation." He unfolded his arms. "Once every slave in Texas is free and all Texans are complying with the law, *then* the Union Army will depart."

Natalie met his steady gaze for a long, tense moment, but defeat forced her to be the first to look away. "It appears I have no choice in the matter."

"It appears you don't."

The softer tone of his voice tempered the harsh truth. When she turned back to him, Natalie thought she saw a hint of compassion in his dark eyes. "Must I seek your permission to remove a few keepsakes, Colonel?"

For the first time since meeting the man, he smiled. "I'm not an ogre. I have seen for myself that this *is* a home full of family mementos. You may take anything you wish. Corporal Banks will assist you."

"Thank you," Natalie said, the flutter in her stomach once again making itself known. The Yankee was devastatingly handsome when he wasn't being difficult. She looked away. "There is no need to bother the corporal. Moses and Carolina will help me." She started to move away, but his hand on her arm stopped her progress.

"Nevertheless, Banks *will* accompany you into the house." When she met his gaze again, she noted the smile was gone and the hard edge had returned. "I want a record of every item you remove. Banks will compile a list, and you will sign it before you leave the property."

Annoyed by his authoritative tone, she stared at his hand until he lifted it from her arm. "Is that really necessary? What will compiling a list accomplish? I already own the items."

He leaned ever so slightly toward her. "The list is not for you,

Mrs. Ellis. It is for me. We wouldn't want any items to suddenly go missing, leading to, shall we say, *false* accusations."

His meaning was infuriatingly clear.

The intruder occupying her land without her permission didn't trust her.

CHAPTER FIVE

Levi attempted to work at the small desk in the sitting room that adjoined the guest bedroom he'd commandeered, but voices from deep inside the big house carried through his open door, distracting him. The low rumble of Moses. The high-pitched squeak of the female servant—Carolina, wasn't it? But it was the soft voice with a slight Southern drawl that had him adding the same column of numbers on the supply manifest for the fourth time.

He blew out a breath and tossed the list onto the desk.

Natalie Langford Ellis.

What was it about the woman that so captivated him? Since leaving Rose Hill yesterday afternoon, the look of abandonment in her blue eyes had haunted him. It shouldn't matter that a slave owner felt the sting of loss when the majority of her slaves walked off the plantation. It shouldn't matter that she had no money and no one to help her rebuild. But for reasons he didn't understand, Levi couldn't bring himself to feel pleased over her suffering the way he'd felt every other time he'd ridden away from a Texas plantation or farm, knowing he'd played a part in freeing human beings from slavery.

Soft laughter floated down the stairs. He closed his eyes and strained to hear the words that followed. What was she saying? Something about when she was a little girl—

"Sir?"

Levi looked up to find Banks in the doorway. "Are you finished?"

A sheepish expression filled the young man's face. "I need another sheet of paper, sir."

"Another sheet? You mean to say she is taking so many items with her you have filled an entire sheet already?"

"No, sir. Mrs. Ellis wants to compile a list of her own."

"A list of her own? And what would that list be comprised of?"

"The items she *isn't* taking, sir."

Levi stared at the corporal. She intended to make a list of everything left in the house? Of all the ridiculous …

He stood. "I will speak to her."

Corporal Banks followed him down the hallway to the narrow set of stairs tucked at the back of the house. They'd most likely been used by servants, leaving the grand staircase in the foyer for the white residents and their guests.

"They're in the master's bedroom."

Levi recalled where the room was located and headed in that direction. When they reached the open door, the three occupants fell silent. Natalie had removed her bonnet, revealing stylishly coiffed hair. For one unguarded moment, Levi envisioned himself taking the pins out to free the blond locks, knowing the thick tresses would feel like silk in his fingers.

Natalie lifted one delicate eyebrow. "May I help you, Colonel?"

He ignored her question and took stock of the room, mentally chastising himself for such a foolish thought. Furniture covered with sheets filled the space, but a mahogany bureau had been uncovered and its drawers left open. Several objects lay on the bare mattress, including a small framed painting and some jewelry. Moses held two rifles, one in each hand, with a look of determination that would have terrified many southern white men.

Levi returned his gaze to Natalie. "Corporal Banks informs me you wish to document the contents of the house. May I ask why?"

"I imagine my reasoning is the same as yours, Colonel." She swept the room with her eyes. "I can't take everything of value with me. In the same way you wish to ensure my trustworthiness with a list of what I take, I feel compelled to do the same. It seems only fair."

As much as he hated to admit it, she had a point. Scrutinizing the small pile of belongings, he conceded. "I find that I agree with you, Mrs. Ellis."

Blue eyes rounded. "You do?"

"I do." Levi allowed the trace of a grin. "However, it would take too long and too many sheets of paper to document everything. I believe the simplest solution is for me to accompany you into each room where together we will observe the items of value you are leaving behind. Your servants and Corporal Banks will act as our witnesses."

A long moment passed. She seemed to weigh the offer. Finally, she inclined her head. "Very well. We have already removed most of what I wish to take with me." She gazed about the room, sadness filling her countenance. "Mama would be aghast to see her room like this." Her eyes grazed Levi. "With a Yankee standing in it, no less."

Ignoring the slight, Levi looked about the space. "Is there anything worth noting in this room, or shall we move on?"

Walking around the large bed, Natalie pointed out a few pieces of art, an ornate lamp, and a chair said to have come from King George II's summer palace.

Levi made a mental note of the items, enjoying her narration of her family's history. For the next hour, the group went from room to room while Natalie pointed to portraits, porcelain vases, small tables, and one very old, very large, and very ugly embroidered face screen near the main parlor's fireplace that she seemed to think was quite valuable. Levi thought it would make good kindling.

When they arrived in the kitchen wing, the last room on their tour, she rattled off the name of the fine china dishes and noted a silver tea service and silver utensils, all in desperate need of polishing. That people spent vast amounts of money on everyday items like plates and cups left him dumbfounded. Give him a tin of beans and a mug of hot coffee, and he was happy.

In the middle of her speech, Natalie gasped, her eyes wide.

Drawn out of his woolgathering, Levi feared she had discovered a crystal goblet or brass candlestick missing. "Is something wrong?" He followed her gaze to a long table in the middle of the room. His men had stacked crates of food supplies there. Was she upset that he was making use of the kitchen?

"You have an entire crate of … *oranges*." The last word was spoken with near reverence.

It took only a moment for him to understand. "I gather you haven't seen a fresh orange in some time."

She looked at him as though he were daft. "Colonel, it has been over three years since any shipments made it into the ports. Lemons, oranges, grapefruit. It has been an age since we had any."

Levi walked to the crate, picked up an orange, and handed it to her. "For you." He smiled as her gaze went from him to the fruit then back. "Please, take it. A shipment arrived from Florida before we set sail for Galveston. My men have had their fill."

The tip of her pink tongue moistened her lips before she accepted the fruit. "Thank you."

But she didn't remove the peel. Instead, she tucked it into a hidden pocket in her gown, the bulge making one of the large ruffles stand out.

"You are welcome to enjoy it now, Mrs. Ellis. As you said, it's been some time since you've tasted one." For some reason, he wanted to see her reaction when the sweet juices first touched her lips. To know that something he had given her brought her pleasure was suddenly important.

"I appreciate the offer, but I'll take it home and share it with Samuel and Isaac."

Her son. How could he have forgotten the little flaxen-haired boy and his companion?

"Of course." Without another thought, he reached for two more pieces of fruit. "Here, take one to each of them." His glance captured the servants watching the exchange, and an idea sprang to life. "In fact," he said, picking up the crate, "take them all." He handed the load to Moses, whose hands were free after leaving the rifles near the front door during their tour. That man looked startled now to find a box of sweet fruit in his arms.

Every occupant in the room, including Corporal Banks, stared at Levi.

"While that is very generous of you, we can't take all your oranges." Natalie cast a longing look at the fruit then back to Levi. It was obvious she wanted them.

His mind made up, Levi gave a slight bow. "Consider it a small token of the Union Army's appreciation for allowing us use of your home."

Natalie seemed to struggle with the offer. When her questioning gaze met Moses', he simply lifted his brow. Finally, she faced Levi again.

"I appreciate your generosity."

Satisfaction swelled his chest as he looked into eyes the color of the sky. "You are welcome."

The group made their way to the front porch. While Moses carefully descended the steps to the wagon with the crate of oranges balanced on one broad shoulder, Carolina and Corporal Banks carried the remaining items that had been stacked near the door. Levi noticed Banks sneak surreptitious glances at the young servant. Carolina, in turn, giggled and ducked her head when he came near.

"I will be waiting anxiously to hear news from your commander, Colonel."

Levi turned to find Natalie focused on him from a few steps away. Standing on the porch in all her finery, Negro servants doing her bidding, she was very much a Southern lady. It would do well for him to remember she had been a slave owner just one day ago. And would be still had Union troops not forced her to set them free. He could not allow a beautiful face to detract him from the truth.

"As soon as I receive word from him, I will bring it myself. You may rest assured that we will not occupy your land even one day longer than necessary." When she made to speak, he held up his hand. "But knowing General Granger as I do, it would be prudent for you to simply accept that you will have to deal with me and my men indefinitely."

A pretty glower creased her forehead. "We shall see, won't we?" With that, she flounced down the steps, green skirts swishing. Moses helped her onto the high wagon seat.

Once she was settled, Levi thought she might turn to send him one last glare, but much to his disappointment, her gaze focused ahead. The wagon lurched forward, and only Carolina sent a shy wave goodbye from her seat in the crowded bed. Levi looked away in time to see Banks return the gesture, a wide grin on his face.

Levi cleared his throat. The young man jerked to attention, though his smile remained in place.

"See to it that the house is closed up. I want all the doors locked except the one leading to my rooms."

"Yes, sir."

Levi glanced at the retreating wagon, then back to the soldier. "We won't have time to fraternize with the locals, Banks. We have a mission to accomplish."

"Yes, sir." The young man opened his mouth, then closed it. He'd been Levi's right-hand man for over a year now, and Levi always knew when Banks had more to say.

"What?"

Banks gave a slight shrug. "I'm just thinking that I'm not the one who gave a pretty lady a crateful of oranges, sir."

Levi dismissed the soldier with a wave of his hand.

Banks was too smart for his own good.

❧⚬❧

"Tell me the story again, Mama."

Samuel sat on Natalie's lap on the porch swing, his hands and face covered with sticky orange juice as he leaned back against her chest to watch the dusky western sky fade to twilight. She would need to scrub her son well before tucking him into bed this night.

"Samuel, you've heard it three times already." She ran her fingers through his thick, sweaty hair. "It's nearly time for bed."

"Please." He moved his head so he could look up at her with pleading eyes the same color as her own.

She bent to kiss his nose. "One last time."

He nestled against her again. "You went to Grandfather Langford's big house 'cuz you forgot to get somethin'."

"Yes." She smiled. He often asked to hear a story then proceeded to tell it himself.

"But when you and Moses and Carolina got there, the so'diers was there already."

"They were indeed."

"But they aren't mean, and that nice so'dier that carried you when you fell down was there too."

Natalie nodded, her mind inadvertently conjuring the image of Colonel Maish standing on Langford Manor's porch. How had she not noticed how handsome he was when he was here at Rose Hill? Surely the shocking news he brought prevented her from noticing the deep brown of his eyes and the fullness of his lips. When those lips curled in smile—

"Mama?"

She looked down to find Samuel studying her.

"What comes next in the story?" she asked, shaking loose the image of the Yankee. She certainly didn't need to entertain thoughts of a man who'd been her enemy only the day before and who refused to vacate her property.

"The nice so'dier gave you the or'nges 'cuz he wanted to say thank you for letting his men sleep in tents in the fields."

Natalie smiled and clapped her hands. "Very good. Now, young man, it is off to bed."

"Aw, can't I have 'nother or'nge?"

She laughed, scooped him up in her arms, and headed for the door. "You've already eaten three. You only have a few left, and you'll want to save them for a special treat on a hot afternoon."

Earlier, when they'd returned to Rose Hill, Natalie gave Moses and Carolina several oranges and then instructed Moses to give one to each of the remaining workers. She would have gone to the quarter and passed them out herself, but she didn't want the freed slaves to be suspicious of her motives. The truth was, it felt good sharing the sweet fruit with them. Wasn't that what Adella Rose had tried to tell her years ago? Natalie's mother-in-law, Martha Ellis, had apparently been generous with the slaves over the years, and Adella had tried to follow in her mother's footsteps, as much as her father would allow. She'd advised Natalie to do the same once she became mistress of Rose Hill, yet Natalie hadn't taken the advice to heart. Had she shown more of an interest in the slaves' well-being, perhaps the majority of them would not have left.

With Samuel tucked into bed, she went to her room. Carolina would be in soon to help her out of her dress and corset. She stood at the open window. A soft evening breeze stirred the curtains. Night sounds filled the air, and stars twinkled in the darkening sky.

She glanced to the east, in the direction of Langford Manor. Was Colonel Maish settling into the guest room after a long day? Perhaps removing his high black boots and coat and stretching out on the quilt-covered bed? Heat rose to her cheeks at her scandalous line of thought, but she couldn't prevent the image of his thick brows and long dark hair from stirring something deep inside her.

Shaking her head, she turned from the window. Had she been alone so long that an infuriating man like the Yankee colonel could now appropriate her mind? Although she'd been a wife for two years before George went off to war, their marriage had left much to be desired. George had shown himself more like his father with each passing day, especially when she was not with child soon after the wedding. In his impatience to produce an heir, his approach to her in the bedroom grew callous. She shuddered, remembering one terrible night in particular. He'd had too much to drink and demanded to know why she wasn't pregnant, bragging that he'd fathered several children in the quarter, the latest being the infant girl his sister Adella stole the night she and the overseer ran off. The child's mother had been killed during the escape, yet George laughed, declaring his sister had done him a favor when she took the brat with her. While Natalie reeled with the knowledge that her sister-in-law was raising George's illegitimate child, he'd grabbed her and pinned her to the bed, ordering her to give him a legitimate heir.

Samuel was conceived soon after.

Annoyed with herself for allowing her thoughts to stray to such unpleasantness, she didn't wait for Carolina and began unbuttoning her gown with impatient fingers. The fact that the handsome Union colonel had her mind dredging up memories she had no desire to visit made one truth very clear as she tugged off the dress she'd purposefully worn today.

The sooner the Yankee left her land, the better.

CHAPTER SIX

The message arrived shortly before noon the following day. Levi read the brief note twice, making sure he understood General Granger's orders. His frown deepened with each word.

"Bad news?"

Levi glanced up to find Corporal Banks standing in the doorway to the sitting room. "General Granger has ordered us to remain here, but he wants us to find a way to *compensate* Mrs. Ellis for use of her plantation. Preferably using the least amount of Union funds as possible."

"I'm guessing a box of oranges isn't enough?"

Levi sent the young man a look of warning. "He has left it up to Mrs. Ellis' discretion, of all things. I can't imagine what that woman might demand."

Corporal Banks remained silent, which was probably for the best.

"We'll ride over to deliver the news in an hour. Please have the horses ready."

After Banks exited, Levi heaved a sigh. He wasn't sure why the general's vague orders left him so surly. Natalie Ellis deserved compensation while the Union Army occupied her property. He could understand her unhappiness with the arrangement, but he also couldn't let go of the fact that she was in the position of plantation owner because slaves had worked the land up until two days ago. Why should she receive payment when it was the slaves who deserved reimbursement for all their years of labor?

He leaned back in the chair, surveying the small room. It wasn't decorated as grandly as the front parlor, but the furnishings were comfortable and well made. Since the war began, Levi had seen plenty of southern plantation owners lose everything, often at the hands of angry Union soldiers ready to set fire to homes and outbuildings for the fun of it. Although Levi didn't participate in the unruly behavior, nor did he allow his men to, he couldn't blame those soldiers for wanting to inflict hardship on the people whose unyielding ownership of Negroes forced a nation into war. Justice, the soldiers had called it, and he agreed.

Now the Union Army would compensate a plantation owner for use of her property, leaving it to said owner to determine how it should be handled. After all the years slaves had lived in bondage on Langford land, it seemed a slap in their faces to reward their former owner. Granted, Natalie only came into ownership a few years ago when her parents passed, but she had benefited from slave labor all her life. A little hardship, it seemed to Levi, would do her some good.

A knock at the door drew his attention. First Lieutenant Ridley stood in the entry. He'd ridden in with the private who'd delivered the general's message earlier.

"Colonel. The general asked me to brief you regarding some trouble that has come to his attention."

"Trouble?" Levi stood, glad for a diversion. He hoped there hadn't been more freedmen murdered. When Union troops first landed in Galveston and began spreading the message of freedom, some white slave owners hadn't received it well and took matters into their own hands.

"Yes, sir. It appears someone has been stealing cattle and horses throughout the region."

Levi's brow rose. "The general is concerned about a horse thief?" After four years of devastating war where thousands of men died, and with thousands of slaves still in bondage in Texas, surely a horse thief was the least of their worries.

"The numbers are significant, sir."

"How significant?"

"At least five thousand head of cattle. Maybe more. The number of horses is also considerable, although many of them were unbranded Mustangs."

Five thousand missing cows? Levi couldn't imagine a cattle-stealing ring big enough to take that many animals without being caught. He waved toward the sofa, which Lieutenant Ridley settled on. Levi returned to his seat. "When did the general learn of this?"

"Reports of missing cattle and horses have been coming in steadily since we set up the Austin command post." The lanky officer shrugged. "At first, we thought people were simply trying to take advantage of the Army, hoping for some sort of reimbursement for their missing animals."

"Could the freed slaves be responsible?" Levi had been witness to hundreds of free men and women walking away from plantations and farms. It would not be a stretch to imagine them stealing in retaliation as well as for survival.

Lieutenant Ridley shook his head again. "We don't think so. The owners of the missing animals, mostly women left in charge of property, state this has been going on for well over a year. But without the manpower to investigate, there was little anyone could do."

A picture of the crime began to form in Levi's mind. Women, like Natalie Ellis, were left to run farms and plantations while their men went off to fight the war, leaving them vulnerable.

"Are the numbers accurate?" Levi asked, wondering where the thief could keep so many animals without someone becoming suspicious.

"They appear to be. Some farms and ranches were hit multiple times over the course of the year."

"What does the general expect us to do about it?"

"Keep your eyes open for anything unusual. Large herds of cattle where they shouldn't be. That sort of thing."

"I'll report any findings."

After the lieutenant left, Levi went to his quarters to retrieve his hat and gloves, mulling over the information. A passing glance in the mirror atop the bureau revealed his hair and beard were in desperate need of a trim. Rubbing a hand over his bristly whiskers, he couldn't recall the last time he'd visited a barber let alone cared about such things. The past four years had been full of death and survival with little time for anything else. Yet now, with news to deliver to a lovely widow, Levi couldn't suppress the desire to clean himself up a bit.

A half hour later, he strode across the porch toward the steps where Corporal Banks waited with two saddled horses. If the corporal noticed anything different about him, he wisely kept it to himself. Besides, Levi noticed the younger man's uniform had been brushed, his boots shined.

It seemed Levi wasn't the only one looking forward to their trip to Rose Hill.

❧ ☙

Natalie grimaced at the sight in front of her.

"Them plants shore look sorry," Carolina said, shaking her head. She wore an old baggy homespun to work in the garden rather than risk dirtying one of Natalie's castoff gowns. A red kerchief covered the young woman's hair, a change from the knitted hairnet she'd taken to wearing when she'd become Natalie's personal attendant. Natalie couldn't help but think Carolina looked more like a slave today than she had before the soldiers arrived with their freedom proclamation.

The large garden behind the main house spread out before them. In the two days since Federal soldiers had ridden into the yard and the majority of her slaves had walked off the plantation, the rows of tomatoes, cucumbers, carrots, and other vegetables had been sorely neglected. Without daily watering, the plants had quickly wilted under the relentless Texas sun, although the weeds didn't seem affected in the least.

"They'll perk up once we get some water on 'em," Harriet said, already heading for a row of beans, the bucket in her hands sloshing precious drops of well water over the sides. "Jest remember not to give 'em too much. Too much water jest as bad as too little."

"I'm helping." Isaac followed his mother carrying a small pail.

"Me too." Samuel hurried to catch up to his friend, but when a butterfly distracted him and he lost his balance, he splashed most of the water from his pail onto his clothes.

If their situation weren't so dire, Natalie might smile at the sight of her son barefoot and golden haired, romping through the garden. But as it was, seeing him working—or at least attempting to work—alongside former slaves served as a stark reminder that everything in their world had changed.

Earlier, she'd overheard Moses tell Harriet he couldn't spare any field workers to tote water to the garden. He hated that his wife would have to take care of the strenuous chore herself, but there wasn't any other option. As the couple discussed the desperate need to keep the produce alive, Natalie, sitting outside the window on the porch with a glass of water and a fan in hand, came to the startling realization that if she hoped to survive all the changes taking place around her, she was going to have to change too.

Now, she grasped the handle of a heavy bucket full of water, already feeling the burn in her muscles even though all she'd done was carry it from the pump near the house to the garden. Heaving a sigh, she said, "We best get to work."

"I still don't think it right for you to be out here helpin' us, Miz Natalie." Carolina surveyed Natalie's outfit with a frown. Although she'd worn an old straw bonnet and the most faded gown she owned, she still managed to appear overdressed for the task. "You gonna get your pretty yellow dress dirty."

"Then I suppose I will have to learn to do laundry as well." At Carolina's wide-eyed reaction, Natalie chuckled. "I'll water the tomatoes. You water the peas and carrots."

The women worked nearly an hour in the afternoon sun, toting bucket after bucket from the well pump to a garden Natalie was certain had grown in size since they'd begun. The boys laughed and played in the mud far more than they actually watered any plants, but every so often they would announce they were helping. At least five blisters sprang up on Natalie's hands, smarting each time she refilled her bucket. Sweat trickled down her face and neck, but she trudged on. If Harriet and Carolina could do the hard work, so could she.

Ebenezer's barking drew her attention a short time later. It came from the front of the house, and she wondered if he'd cornered the barn cat again. She'd scolded him that very morning for chasing the poor thing up a tree.

"Samuel, please go see about Ebenezer. We may have to tie him up if he continues harassing the cats."

"Yes, Mama."

Samuel hopped up from where he and Isaac were digging for worms. Mud caked his hands and knees, and a large smudge crossed his face. Watching him scamper off around the corner of the house, she thought she'd let Moses bathe her son in the creek tonight along with Isaac. It would certainly save her from heating water to fill the tub, and he would enjoy it far more.

The dog's barking didn't stop. In fact, it seemed to grow more urgent. She'd almost decided to go see for herself when Samuel came charging around the corner, Ebenezer fast on his heels. But as her son ran to her, the dog stopped, turned, and gave a ferocious growl.

"What is wrong—"

"Señora Ellis? Are you there? I cannot move another inch, else your dog will take a bite of my leg, I am sure."

Was that Señor Lopez?

"Ebenezer, come."

The dog bounded to her, tongue hanging out of his mouth, tail swishing happily. He sat, looking up at her expectantly. A moment later, Alexander rounded the house, dressed in his usual impeccable style. Considering the man dealt in cattle, he always looked more like a banker. Ebenezer growled again, but Natalie shushed him with a snap of her fingers.

"Señora." Alexander moved cautiously toward her while his gaze flicked from her to the dog and back. "I came as soon as I heard Federal soldiers were in Texas and the slaves had been freed." He looked behind her to where Harriet and Carolina stood. "I am glad to see you have kept some of yours from running away."

"Señor Lopez." She glanced at the women, who looked as worn out as she felt. "Harriet and Carolina are free women now. They chose to remain at Rose Hill and work for me."

Alexander's forward progress halted when the fur on Ebenezer's neck stood. A low growl rumbled in his throat. What had gotten into the dog? When she pointed to the ground, he plopped down again.

"And what of the others?" Alexander asked, glancing at the empty cotton fields closest to the house. Where most days found dozens of slaves working each field, none could be seen now.

"Twenty-five men remain in the quarter."

He nodded, then his eyes travelled over her, seeming to just now notice where she was and what she was doing. His brow arched. "Señora Ellis, surely it is not necessary for you to do such strenuous labor. It is not fitting for the lady of the manor to work alongside the servants. Come, let us sit on the porch and enjoy some refreshments while we talk."

Annoyance at the man's presumptuous attitude rose to the surface, but manners instilled in her from the time she could walk kept her from voicing it. She turned to the women, who were back at work. "Please, take a rest while I see to our guest."

Both of the women nodded, but Natalie didn't miss the brief look that passed between them. She could guess at what it meant. She'd never before invited them to rest nor had she tended to a guest on her own. Well, nothing was the same as it had been. They all might as well get used to it.

"Samuel, come with me, and we'll share one of your oranges with Señor Lopez." She stretched out her hand, expecting her son to take it enthusiastically, especially if it meant getting to eat one of the treasured treats.

But Samuel scowled, his dark gaze landing on Alexander. "I don't wanna share my or'nge with him. I don't like him."

"Samuel! That is not polite." She turned to Alexander, embarrassment heating her already warm face. "I must apologize. I'm sure he didn't mean it."

"It is all right, Señora," he said, presenting a tight smile to Samuel. "He can stay here with the servants while we discuss business." He held out his hand to her. "Shall we?"

Although she needed to speak to Samuel about his rude behavior while it was fresh, she didn't want to offend the man further. To be sure, her son would get a firm lecture on manners the moment Alexander left. Accepting his hand, she allowed him to lead her toward the front of the house.

"When I heard the news of Yankees in Texas," he said, tucking her hand into the crook of his arm, "I had to be certain you were safe. Have they been here to Rose Hill?"

"A company of soldiers brought news of the proclamation two days ago." They rounded the corner of the house and ascended the steps. Sweat continued to trickle down her neck and back, and she desperately wished she could go inside and mop her face with a cool cloth.

"It is astonishing, is it not? All the slaves, free. I rode past dozens of them lining the roads, heading to Austin and San Antonio. It was a sight I did not think to ever see."

Natalie settled on a wicker chair. "I can't say I'm surprised. President Lincoln vowed he would set them free. It is a pity he didn't live to see his wish lived out."

Alexander's brow creased as he leaned against the porch rail. "You do not sound disappointed to no longer own slaves."

She gave a slight shrug. The past few days had her emotions

and thoughts whirling to the point she wasn't sure what she felt or believed anymore. "I'm happy for them to gain their freedom from slavery, but I would be lying if I said I didn't wish them back. I don't know how we'll bring in the cotton crop in a few weeks with barely two dozen people."

"Your government has put you in a difficult position." He wore a grave look. "To take away the slaves is to take away your livelihood."

She pondered his statement. George's father had always declared Rose Hill would go bankrupt if they had to pay the slaves a wage, yet hadn't he faced bankruptcy anyway because of his own mismanagement of Rose Hill funds? Luther Ellis struck a bargain with Marshall Brevard, a fellow planter, to save the plantation, practically selling his own daughter to the man. But when Adella ran off with Seth Brantley, thus nullifying the arrangement, George had to step in and increase the profit shares Marshall would receive over the next decade in order to save the deal. The one and only reason Natalie no longer had to do business with Marshall was that he was dead. Southern sympathizers had hanged him when they discovered he was supplying Union troops with beef.

"The plantation hasn't seen a profit in nearly four years, yet we survived." She forced confidence into her demeanor, though doubts and fears threatened to overtake her. "We will get through this. If I have to, I'll pick the cotton myself."

His dark eyes surveyed every inch of her face. "You amaze me, Señora. When I rode into the yard, I thought I would find a helpless widow weak with worry, but instead I find a beautiful woman full of fire and determination. Such a woman is worthy of admiration."

The intensity of his gaze made Natalie uncomfortable. She looked away. "Thank you, but it isn't as though I have much choice."

He moved to the seat next to hers. "Ah, but you do." When she met his gaze again, he reached to take her hand in his. "I had hoped we would have time to properly court, but it appears I cannot delay in discussing a matter of great importance with you."

Natalie's eyes widened. Surely he didn't mean to propose! She must stop him before they were both embarrassed. Marriage was the last thing on her mind. "Señor Lopez, I—"

Whatever she hoped to convey to him was lost in Ebenezer's barking. The dog rounded the corner of the house, but instead of charging toward Alexander, he passed in front of them and headed straight for the open gate, which usually meant visitors were coming. Curious, Natalie stood, causing Alexander to release her hand. He rose as well. A moment later, two riders came up the lane, Ebenezer yapping at the horses' legs.

The men's blue uniforms were unmistakable.

CHAPTER SEVEN

Disappointment washed over Levi when he spotted Natalie on the front porch of the plantation house with a well-dressed man by her side. Although he reminded himself it wasn't any of his business whom she entertained, he hadn't counted on finding her with a man, certainly not one scowling at them like the stranger was right now. Levi brushed his fingers across the holster on his hip, making certain his revolver was at the ready. Southern sympathizers were known to create trouble from time to time.

"Colonel Maish," Natalie said, her face flushed beneath a wide-brimmed hat. "I hope you come bearing good news."

She looked slightly disheveled, a first since he'd met her. Was that dirt smudged on her cheek?

"Ma'am." He nodded a greeting. "I do have a matter to discuss with you." His glance shifted to the dark-haired man. "In private." The man's scowl deepened.

Natalie looked between the two men. "Colonel, may I introduce Señor Alexander Lopez. Señor Lopez, this is Colonel Maish. The colonel and his men brought the proclamation regarding the slaves' freedom."

Lopez regarded Levi a long moment before inclining his head ever so slightly. "Colonel."

Levi returned the gesture, wondering who this man was and what he meant to Natalie.

Barking at his heel drew his attention away. When he looked down, he found the rust-colored dog—Ebenezer, of all names—carrying on like Levi was a squirrel he'd just treed.

"Sit," he commanded. The dog quieted and plunked his back end on the ground, his tail stirring up a cloud of dust. Levi smiled. "Good boy." The cloud grew bigger.

When he turned back to Natalie, her face registered surprise while the scowl of Señor Lopez had grown darker. Levi disregarded the man. "As I said, Mrs. Ellis, there is a matter I must discuss with you."

She glanced at Lopez. "I really must speak with the colonel. He and his men are encamped at Langford Manor"—she shot Levi a little frown—"although I hope it won't be for much longer."

A look of pure shock flashed across Lopez's face. "Union troops are camped nearby?" He looked at Levi, then Banks, his eyes filled with what Levi could only describe as alarm, making Levi all the more wary of the stranger.

"Yes." Natalie appeared startled by his reaction. "Is something wrong?"

Lopez stared at her. "Why would you allow them to camp on your property?"

His hard tone didn't sit well with Levi. He may not feel any sympathy for Natalie's predicament, but she was still a lady and deserved to be spoken to with respect.

Ebenezer let out a low growl. Apparently, the dog agreed.

"Sir," Levi said, gaining Lopez's attention. "Mrs. Ellis had no choice in the matter. However, as this is between her and the Union Army, I would ask that you take your leave."

Lopez obviously did not appreciate the request. "I will not leave her alone with two strange men." He faced her. "Natalie, I do not believe you should meet with these men without a proper chaperone and someone to protect your interests."

His use of her given name told Levi more than he wanted to know.

"I appreciate your concern," she said, her tone kind yet firm. "But I am the mistress of Rose Hill. You will find no one more determined to protect the interests of the plantation than me."

"What about your safety?" Lopez tossed a scowl at Levi. "You don't know these men. They were your enemies until recently."

Levi didn't like the man's insinuation. "You may rest assured, sir, the lady is perfectly safe." When Natalie glanced at him, he added, "If you wish, your servant can attend the meeting."

"That won't be necessary." When Lopez made to protest, she interrupted. "Thank you for coming to see about me. I'm afraid, though, that we will have to continue with our visit another day."

Frustration flashed across Lopez's face before the man finally yielded. "As you wish, Señora," he said, taking her hand in his. "But I must insist on returning soon to see for myself you are well." He kissed her knuckles.

"I will look forward to it." She withdrew her hand and stepped away.

Without a glance or word to Levi and Banks, the man descended the steps and strode to his mount tied nearby. Levi noted the horse was one of the finest animals he'd ever seen. The midnight-black beast must possess the bloodline of a Texas thoroughbred. Watching Lopez ride off on the magnificent animal made Levi wonder at the man's occupation as well as his purpose for being at Rose Hill. Turning to find Natalie's eyes on Lopez's retreating back, Levi could guess the latter.

When she faced him, she offered a tight smile. "I hope you've brought promising news, Colonel."

"I suppose that will depend upon you, Mrs. Ellis, and whether you willingly accept or fight against what cannot be changed."

Though he hadn't intended to sound harsh, even Banks glanced at him with a quizzical expression. Levi ignored the corporal and dismounted, his mood significantly darker than when they'd first set out for Rose Hill.

"I take it the Army has no plans to vacate my property?"

He met her angry gaze with one of his own. "No, they don't. However, General Granger sent an offer you may find beneficial."

Her brow puckered. "I don't see how. I don't need anything from the General. What I need is the peace of knowing the Union

Army is no longer encamped on my land."

"Do you want to hear the General's terms or not?" When Banks sent him another look, Levi tempered his testiness. "Trust me, the Union Army will do as they please, so it would behoove you to comply with whatever they want, for as long as they want. It will go much easier for you in the end."

They stared at one another, each unhappy with the situation but for very different reasons. Levi could pinpoint the rise in his ire to the moment he'd seen Lopez on the porch. That he was obviously jealous of the *Tejano* galled.

"Very well." She indicated a grouping of wicker furniture on the porch. "Please, come in out of the sun. Would you and your corporal care for something to drink?" Her stiff good manners revealed her displeasure, but he had to give her credit for them nonetheless.

"We would, thank you." He ascended the whitewashed steps, Banks behind him, while Natalie disappeared into the house. Removing his gloves, he remained standing. This was no social call. The sooner they determined how she wished to proceed with the compensation, the sooner they could leave. Coming to Rose Hill had been a mistake. From now on, he'd let Banks handle the delivery of any messages for Mrs. Ellis.

Several minutes ticked by before Banks broke the silence. "When we were in Louisiana, I heard someone say they paint the ceilings of their porches blue to keep ghosts away. It doesn't make sense to me. Why would a ghost care what color the ceiling was painted?"

Levi turned to find Banks staring upward. He glanced at the painted planks above them, boasting a coat of soft blue-green paint. He'd heard similar stories during the war as the Northern army had worked its way south. He was about to tell Banks the stories were stuff and nonsense when Natalie returned, her hair freshly combed and free of the hat, bearing a tray with two glasses of water and a plate of dark cookies. That she carried the refreshments herself surprised him. He'd expected her to fetch a maid for the task.

"Harriet baked a batch of molasses cookies yesterday," she said, setting the tray on a small table. Settling on the sofa, she looked up at the men. "She's a master at turning the simplest ingredients into something quite delicious. Please, help yourselves."

Banks looked like a kid, all big-eyed and licking his lips, but he kept himself in check, waiting for Levi to give permission to indulge in the sweets. When Levi gave a nod, the corporal snagged a large cookie, grinning.

"Thank you, ma'am," he said before he stuffed the entire thing in his mouth.

"I couldn't help but overhear your comment regarding our blue porch ceilings." She looked up, as did Banks. "Supposedly the restless spirits—haints, as some folks call them—see the blue color and are fooled into thinking it's water. Haints, it is said, cannot cross water."

Banks gulped down the cookie.

Levi nearly chuckled. He didn't believe for a moment someone as sensible as Natalie Ellis fell for such superstition. "If the two of you are finished telling tales, I would like to get to the matter at hand."

Natalie and Banks exchanged a brief look, and if he wasn't mistaken, a small smile passed between them too.

"General Granger's orders are clear. The Union Army will remain at Langford plantation indefinitely." When Natalie opened her mouth, Levi raised his hand. "Hear me out, Mrs. Ellis. While the Union Army is occupying your land, you are to be compensated."

Her fine brows shot to her hairline. "Compensated?" She blinked several times before a look of interest sparked in the blue depths. "Are you saying the Army will pay me to use my property?"

The hopeful tone in her voice was unmistakable. "I am saying the Army will compensate you in some form, but I would not expect a large sum of cash, if that is what you ultimately demand."

"If not cash, then what could the Army possibly offer?"

Levi had anticipated the question. General Granger was tight-fisted when it came to Union funds, so handing over a fair amount of cash to a widow wasn't something he'd expect to happen. But just as Natalie and other plantation owners could find creative ways to pay newly freed slaves for labor without cash on hand, the Army could do the same.

"While I don't know what your plans are for the future, I believe we can help with your immediate needs."

"And what might they be?" Skepticism rang loud and clear.

"Your fields are full of cotton plants that will require harvesting. The Army would hire free Negroes to bring in the crop. Some of my men are accustomed to farming and could oversee the endeavor, all the way to market if you so choose. By order of the president, all southern seaports will resume trade on July first."

Levi watched as her eyes narrowed in thought. She glanced out to the emerald fields, which extended far beyond what they could see from the house. When her gaze met his once again, the gleam of interest he'd seen earlier had turned to one of eagerness.

"And you believe I will be able to sell the cotton once the blockades are removed?"

"I do. The price of cotton is at an all-time high. With so many southern plantations not producing, those with a crop in the field stand to make a decent profit. More, I believe, than what the Army would pay you in cash."

A rooster crowed from somewhere nearby while Natalie contemplated the offer. After several moments, during which various expressions crossed her face, she seemed to come to a decision. She stood and faced Levi. "Very well, Colonel. I would like our agreement in writing, if you will. I would like to know how many men you will hire and how many soldiers you will provide."

Levi bit back a chuckle. This wasn't the first time she'd asked for something in writing. It probably wouldn't be the last before it was all said and done. Considering she'd lived her entire life as a pampered daughter and wife, she seemed to have a keen understanding of business. "As you wish. I will have the papers drawn up and sent over for your signature."

A pleased smile curled her lips. "Thank you. I would have never dreamed something good could come from having the Union Army camped on Langford land, but it appears I was mistaken."

For a moment, Levi was captivated by the delight on her face. The same feeling he'd experienced when he'd given her the box of oranges washed over him. *Pleasure*. It was pure pleasure making this woman smile.

The screen door screeched open, and out bounded Samuel, covered in dried mud from head to toe. He ran to Natalie. Levi thought for certain she would keep him at arm's length to protect her gown, but he was wrong. When Samuel reached her and wrapped his dirty arms around her skirt, she smiled down at him.

"Did you finish watering the garden?" she asked, using her fingers to comb his sweaty hair from his face.

"Yes, Mama. Harriet 'n Carolina are still working." Samuel peeked up at Levi. "Is that the man that gave us the or'nges?"

Natalie met Levi's gaze, humor in her blue eyes. "It is. Would you like to thank him?"

"Thankee, sir."

Levi turned his attention to the boy. "You're welcome. Have you been working with Ebenezer to get him to obey your commands?"

Samuel shook his head.

"Well," Levi said, glancing to where the dog lounged in the shade of the house. "If you want him to mind you, you'll have to teach him his lessons."

Carolina came through the door then. "There you are, Samuel. Don't run off like that without tellin' me or Harriet where you goin'."

"I wanted to find Mama," the boy said, eyeing the cookies on the plate. "Can I have a 'lasses cookie, Mama?"

Natalie nodded. "Yes, you may." She glanced at Levi. "Why don't you share one with the colonel, the way he shared his oranges with you."

Samuel looked up at Levi then back to the cookies. With a pudgy finger, he silently counted the remaining cookies on the plate. Three were left. Apparently deciding that was enough to share, he carefully picked up the china plate with both hands and held it toward Levi.

"Want one?"

Levi grinned, wondering if his nephew Lucas was anything like Samuel. The boy had been born shortly before the war began. Levi hadn't seen him in several years, but thankfully, his brother had survived the battles and was even now home with his family in Pennsylvania. Seeing Samuel's cherub face looking up at him reminded Levi of his own deep longing to return home.

"No, but thank you. You can eat mine."

Samuel's eyes brightened. He wasted no time returning the plate to the table and reaching for a cookie.

"We will take our leave now," Levi said to Natalie, tugging on his gloves. "Corporal Banks will return tomorrow with the papers. Once you've signed them, we can begin hiring workers." He glanced at Banks. Instead of finding the corporal attentive to the plan, however, the young man's gaze was fastened on Carolina, who, when Levi glanced in her direction, wore a shy smile, lashes fluttering as she snuck peeks at Banks.

Levi heaved a sigh. The last thing he needed was a lovesick corporal. There was still far too much work to be done in Texas to waste time on flirtation and silliness.

He cleared his throat, gaining Banks' attention. That man drew his shoulders back and gave Levi a firm nod.

"Thank you, Colonel," Natalie said, falling in step beside him as he moved to the stairs. "With so many changes taking place, I didn't know how we would get the harvest in. I would have never believed it, but you and the Union Army are an answer to prayer."

Her comment dogged him all the way back to Langford Manor. While Natalie Ellis might be pleased with the turn of events, he was not. He'd come to Texas to free Negroes still in bondage, not help the very people who had kept them enslaved.

CHAPTER EIGHT

"Miz Natalie, that corporal is here to see you. I told him to wait on the porch."

Natalie breathed a sigh of relief at Carolina's announcement. If she'd had to stay on her knees pulling weeds from around her mother-in-law's prized rose bushes one minute longer, she was certain her legs would never unbend. All morning she'd labored over the fragrant bushes that bordered the house. First pruning and cutting away dead flowers and leaves, then pulling weeds that sprang up overnight, it seemed, despite the lack of rain. The work was hot and tiresome, but she felt a measure of pride with her accomplishment, bleeding fingertips and weary muscles notwithstanding. She hoped Martha Ellis would be pleased should she be given an opportunity to look down from heaven and see how Natalie was faring as mistress of Rose Hill.

"Thank you, Carolina." She unfolded her legs with a groan. Painful prickles filled her feet when she stood, and she nearly tumbled forward when she took a step. She grabbed hold of the kitchen porch post to keep her upright and flinched when the blisters on her palms from the previous day's labor rubbed against the rough wood.

"You shouldn't be down on the ground, Miz Natalie. Someone else can see to them roses."

Natalie wiped perspiration from her brow with the back of her hand while wiggling her toes to get the blood flowing again. "You know as well as I there is too much work for you and Harriet to handle alone. I must do my part, although I fear I will never be very useful." She held up her hands, which sported dried blood on several fingers. "I had no idea a rosebush could be so ornery."

Carolina giggled.

"Please see that our guest has some cool water while he waits," Natalie said, moving slowly toward the back door to the house. Her toes still tingled, but thankfully, the initial pain had subsided. "I'd like to wash up before joining him."

"Yes'm." Carolina's smile broadened, and she hurried away.

Natalie shook her head as she made her way to her room. She'd seen the sly looks Carolina had exchanged with Corporal Banks yesterday. Colonel Maish had seen them, too, and hadn't appeared pleased. She supposed his dislike for her colored his view of everyone associated with her. He'd made it perfectly clear how he felt about former slaveholders. That he now had to assist her with her harvest surely irked him further.

She entered her room and cringed at her reflection in the tall mirror near the window. Her long braid was a wild mess, several strands escaping the ribbon she'd tied to the end. Now that Carolina had taken on more household chores, Natalie dismissed the young woman as her personal maid. While she still required help into her corset and gowns, she declared herself able to bathe, arrange her hair, and finish her daily toilette without assistance.

Studying the bedraggled woman in the looking glass, Natalie wondered what George would think if he could see her now. Gone was the elegant and poised lady he'd courted and married. Four years of war had taken its toll on her, worry and responsibility weighing heavily. Yet not until the slaves were freed had she realized how much work went into the running of a plantation. And not just the fields, barns, and livestock. The grand house alone required hours of labor to maintain.

Going into the bathing room adjacent to the bedroom, Natalie came to a decision. She would close off most of the rooms in the house. There was no need for Harriet, Carolina, or herself to bother dusting and cleaning rooms that no one used. Perhaps she would talk to Moses about doing the same in the barns. Surely they could move all the remaining animals into one barn, thus eliminating the need to clean dozens of stalls and corrals.

With her face and hands washed in cool water and her hair freshly combed, she felt more herself as she descended the stairs and made her way to the porch. Male laughter floated through the open doorway, followed by soft female giggles. When she appeared on the threshold, she found Corporal Banks seated on a wicker sofa while Carolina stood nearby holding a plate of Harriet's molasses cookies. Neither of them noticed Natalie until she cleared her throat.

"Oh, Miz Natalie." Carolina practically jumped away from the corporal. "I didn't hear you." When Natalie's gaze took in the cookies and the corporal's apparent comfort on the sofa, Carolina looked guiltily down at the plate of sweets in her hand. "I … I thought the corporal might like some refreshment." Her declaration ended feebly.

The corporal stood, his face bearing a little guilt as well.

"Thank you, Carolina," Natalie said. While it was strange to come upon a scene that never would have occurred had Carolina still been a slave, times had changed. "Please, Corporal Banks, have a seat."

He did. "I'm much obliged for the cookies, ma'am." He glanced at Carolina but didn't let his gaze linger. "Miss Carolina was good enough to bring some when I asked about them."

Natalie appreciated his honesty. "Help yourself, Corporal." She indicated Carolina could set the plate on the small table near him. Carolina did, then disappeared into the house, stealing one last peek at the corporal as she went.

"I take it you have the papers I am to sign." She moved to the chair near the sofa. When Banks rose in a gentlemanly fashion while she settled herself, she once again realized how everything in her world was altered. She had never entertained a Negro man on the porch in all her days.

"I do." He produced a folded sheet of paper from inside his

coat. "The colonel made two copies, so you could keep one here at the plantation. That way, should anyone have questions when the colonel isn't around, you'll have proof of the agreement."

Surprised, Natalie noted he did in fact have two sheets of paper. That Colonel Maish had thought of her well-being pleased her far more than such a simple act should. She took the papers and read over the terms. The Union Army would hire and pay thirty freedmen of color to tend, harvest, and bale all of the cotton on Rose Hill. If she required their help getting the cotton to market, she could extend the agreement. Two Union soldiers would accompany the workers to ensure her crop was properly handled and harvested in a timely manner. Colonel Maish's neat signature already graced each of the documents.

"My, it seems the colonel has thought of everything."

Corporal Banks smiled. "That's the kind of man he is, ma'am. Always thinking ahead."

Clearly, the young corporal held his superior in admiration. "Were you with him during the war?"

He nodded. "We were in Virginia mostly, right up until the day General Lee surrendered."

She heard the pride in his voice. He, a black Union soldier, had fought to free people of color like himself, and he no doubt had celebrated all the more when Lee conceded the Confederate Cause. Looking at Banks now, happily eating a molasses cookie made by a woman who had been a slave less than a week ago … well, it was most definitely a new and different world.

"Where is your home, if you don't mind my asking, Corporal?"

"I don't mind." He grinned. "I'm from Massachusetts. Prettiest state in the union, my mama always says."

Natalie smiled, his cheerful attitude contagious. "Well, if your mama said it, it must be true."

His grin grew. "The colonel doesn't agree. He and I argue from time to time which state is prettier. He, of course, says Pennsylvania is. Having never been there, I don't know if he's right, but I know

I wouldn't want to live anywhere but Massachusetts."

"The colonel is from Pennsylvania?" she asked, oddly pleased at discovering something personal about the serious man without his knowledge. She thought he might have mentioned his home the day he and his troops arrived at Rose Hill, but many of the details of that day had been lost in the events.

"He is. Has a big family back home, from what I can tell."

As Corporal Banks went on about his own family, Natalie sat in stunned silence. Why had it not occurred to her that the colonel might be married and have a family? *It doesn't matter*, she reminded herself, ignoring the rush of disappointment that settled over her. His marital status had nothing to do with their business agreement, which was the only reason they had any cause to interact. But it made sense that he would have a wife, considering he was handsome and strong and—

"Ma'am?"

Startled, she found Banks looking at her. "I'm sorry. What did you say?"

"I asked if you were ready to sign the papers. The colonel is eager to get the men hired so they can begin tending the crops."

Yes, he would be impatient to get Natalie's cotton harvested and wash his hands of her and Rose Hill.

She stood. "If you will excuse me, I'll get a pen and ink."

Corporal Banks stood politely. "Yes, ma'am."

When she returned, she signed her name opposite Colonel Maish's on both papers. After blowing on the ink to keep it from smearing, she handed one sheet back to the corporal. "How soon should we expect the men to arrive?" she asked as they both stood.

"Within the week, I would say. There are hundreds of freedmen looking for work, so it shouldn't be too hard to round up a crew."

How odd, Natalie thought as she watched the corporal mount his horse and ride away. The men who worked cotton fields as slaves would now work those same fields as freedmen, earning wages this time. She couldn't help but wonder if they were better off or not. Rose Hill slaves had always had plenty to eat and a roof over their heads. Now they had to find work and pay for food, clothes, and housing. A pang of guilt washed over her, knowing her former slaves were woefully unprepared for life away from the plantation.

Carolina appeared on the porch, her gaze trained on the departing man. "Guess we'll have more o' them so'diers around once they tote them free Negroes back to work the cotton."

"I suppose we will." Natalie eyed Carolina. "I'm sure you wouldn't mind if one soldier in particular spent time at Rose Hill." When Carolina's wide gaze met hers, she couldn't help but laugh. "It is as plain as the nose on your face you're partial to the corporal."

After a moment's hesitation, Carolina's face melted in a gooey smile. "Ain't he handsome? I ain't never see'd a Negro man so sure of himself. And that uniform look mighty fine on him, even if it is a bluecoat."

"My, Carolina, I do believe you are smitten." A hint of envy tinged her words. Romance and flirtations, it seemed, were not her destiny.

"I might be, Miz Natalie." She shrugged, a shy look in her eyes. "My stomach gets all wiggly when he look at me."

Ever since Luther Ellis sold Carolina's mother and sisters, Natalie felt protective of the girl. She wouldn't want the Union soldier to break Carolina's heart. "Well, mind you don't do anything foolish when it comes to Corporal Banks. He and all the other soldiers will eventually leave Texas and go home."

Carolina sobered. "I know."

After Carolina retreated into the house, Natalie stood on the porch, looking east. The warning she'd given Carolina rang true for herself as well. She had no business mooning over a handsome Yankee colonel, especially one with a family waiting for his return. Oh, that the Union soldiers had continued north the day they stopped by Rose Hill instead of settling on her property nearby. Life hadn't been easy before their arrival, and most certainly would not have been after they departed, but the days had passed with a sameness she'd found comforting.

Now, nothing felt familiar.

Not even her own heart.

CHAPTER NINE

Levi stood on the porch of Langford Manor evaluating the thirty former slaves milling about the yard. Corporal Banks and several of his men had gone to the surrounding communities and found hundreds of men willing to work. The settlements, they said, were overwhelmed with free men and women looking for employment. Many towns were already experiencing problems due to the lack of jobs for the newly freed Negroes. Thefts were on the rise, as were the tempers of local residents unsure how to handle the influx of unemployed workers. A solution, however, was slow in coming. There simply weren't enough jobs to go around nor citizens financially able to hire all the former slaves.

Studying the group, one man in particular caught Levi's eye. He was large and well-muscled, but what captured his attention was the man's face. Raised scars were clearly visible on both cheeks, their lighter color standing out against his ebony skin. When the man looked toward the house, Levi realized the marks were not simply scars from an injury of some sort. They were letters. Letters that had been branded on his face the way one brands an animal.

Disgust for the slave owner who'd done such a despicable thing rolled through him. Thank God Negroes were no longer in danger of such inhumane treatment by their white masters. Seeing the former slave standing there, ready to earn wages like a man should, brought a sense of pride to Levi. He had played a small role in this man's freedom.

"Sir, the men are ready for your instructions before we depart for Rose Hill."

He looked down to Corporal Banks, who was approaching the

base of the steps. "Thank you, Corporal. They appear to be a good group."

"Some of them are former Rose Hill slaves."

Levi's brow lifted. "Really?" He looked over the group again. He'd watched the line of slaves leave the day they were given their freedom. Frankly, he hadn't expected any to return. At least not so soon. "We can hope their familiarity with the plantation will be beneficial."

Levi noticed a small group of women and a few children some distance away gathered near the road. Even from this vantage point, he saw they had packs and bundles with them.

"What are those women doing here? I specifically asked for men only. Strong men, at that. They'll be doing the work of twice as many field hands."

A look of helplessness came over Banks. "Sir, they followed us here. I told them over and over we couldn't hire them, but …" He shrugged.

Levi blew out a breath. What was he supposed to do with women and children? "Bring them over. I'll have a word with them."

Corporal Banks walked to the group, motioned toward Levi, then led them over. When the gathering reached the yard where the freedmen waited, he noticed each of the women went to stand next to a man.

Ah. Now he understood. These were not women looking for work. They had relationships with some of the men Levi intended to hire. He hadn't counted on that.

"I am Colonel Maish, commander of this post. I understand Corporal Banks informed you we are only hiring men at this time. You women will need to go back to town with your children."

Fear and uncertainty registered on many of their faces. One man, tall and reedy, put his arm around the waist of a woman holding an infant. A small girl stood next to her, clinging to her homespun dress.

"Colonel, suh, if I might speak freely," he said, meeting Levi's gaze.

Levi nodded. "You may."

The man glanced at the woman at his side before returning his attention to Levi. "My name's Wash Ingram. This here my wife, Ruth. We come from a plantation south o' here. We got family up in Missouri we's hoping to get to, but we ain't got no money to get there." He glanced at the men around him. "Heard the Army payin' ten dollars a month to work cotton, with food and a place to stay. I shore am in need o' the job, suh, but what my Ruth an' chillens s'posed to do whilst I's workin' if you don't 'llow them to come on along?"

Several others in the group murmured agreement.

Obviously, Levi, as an unmarried man responsible for no one but himself, had not thought this through. That the men he hoped to hire would bring families along had not occurred to him. Had he considered the situation beforehand, he would have stipulated the need for unmarried men only.

But he hadn't. And it didn't seem fair to change the requirements after men like Wash Ingram had already been told they had the job. Splitting up families was something slave owners did, and Levi was loathe to stoop to those levels. He counted the women. Five, plus a half dozen or so youngsters. Surely a group so small wouldn't put a strain on the rations the Army would provide the workers. The women could earn their share by working in the house or garden or wherever Natalie deemed necessary.

The silent group continued to stare up at him.

"Because you men have already been hired by the Union Army, I will allow those with families to bring them to Rose Hill. However, the women who choose to come along will be required to work for food and shelter. No wages in cash will be paid to the women."

Whispered discussions took place between husbands and wives. Wash approached several men, speaking in lowered tones, nodding from time to time. Finally, he stepped forward.

"We 'ppreciate you understanding, Colonel. We that has families here accept yo' offer."

"Very well. Corporal Banks will need the names and ages of each person coming with us before you will be allowed onto a wagon. Those who can sign their names will do so. Anyone who can't is required to make their mark. Are there any questions?"

No one spoke up. Banks herded the group in the direction of the line of awaiting wagons, some loaded down with supplies. Earlier, he'd set a small desk and chair nearby in anticipation of recording the freedmen's names before departing for Rose Hill. Now, women and children of various ages would be added to the register.

Mounting his horse, Levi wondered what Natalie would say when she saw the group. He didn't think she would mind the extra help, but he felt he should give her warning before they actually arrived.

Starting out ahead of the wagons, he viewed the landscape around him. Fallow, overgrown fields filled the Langford property before gradually blending into land that had never seen a plow. Groupings of trees dotted the landscape, along with clumps of low shrubs, cactus, and rocks. Although he hadn't known what to expect when he arrived in Texas two weeks ago, he had to admit there was a beauty in the land. From the sandy coast with its swampland and marshes to the rich farmland surrounding him now, he could see why settlers chose to come here. Men like Stephen Austin, who was still called the Father of Texas in some circles, saw potential in the wild land and fought hard to attain it. Many lives had been lost securing Texas for the United States. That her citizens voted to secede from the very country they'd embraced only a few short years before still baffled Levi.

His thoughts strayed to Natalie. A daughter of Texas. A slave owner until recent events put an end to it. How different her life would have been had her family come from the north. In a way, he almost felt sorry for her, growing up in ignorance when it came to people of color. While she could blame her parents and even her husband for purchasing and keeping slaves, those same people had been her responsibility the past five years. Only a few days ago, she'd been the owner of more than eighty Negroes, despite her recognition of their humanity after her sister-in-law helped several escape. He understood her fear for survival, but why couldn't she have seen the benefit of freeing her slaves and offering to let them stay on the plantation and earn a share of the cotton profits? Why had it taken force to get her to do what any decent person would have done ages ago?

Rose Hill came into view. The grand house sat on a slight rise, gleaming white in the morning sunshine. Huge oak trees sheltered it from storms while a row of tall poplar trees lined the long entrance. Thin trails of smoke rose from two or three dying cook fires in the quarter, although that area of the plantation was quiet. The few people who had remained after freedom was announced were more than likely already hard at work in the fields.

Incessant barking greeted him as he neared the whitewashed gate. Ebenezer bounded toward him, tail wagging.

"Hush, you mangy mutt," he said, grinning when the dog did just that.

The barking, however, had done its job. Natalie stepped onto the porch looking fresh and lovely in a lavender gown, the skirt wide and bell-shaped. Her hair was held in a simple braid that lay over her shoulder, yet she appeared as elegant and poised as if she were greeting guests arriving for a gala. For a moment, Levi could only stare at the scene of her standing on the porch, the white of the house as backdrop. No painter could have come up with a more southern yet perfect portrait.

"Good morning, Colonel." Her soft voice washed over him like warm sunshine. Former slave owner or not, she was beautiful.

"Good morning, Mrs. Ellis."

She glanced toward the empty road behind him then back. "I

understood the workers would arrive today."

Grateful for a solid conversation topic, Levi gave himself a mental shake. "They are. We've hired thirty strong men, all eager to earn wages."

She smiled. "That is wonderful news. Moses believes the crop is ahead of schedule despite the lack of rain the past few weeks. We had good soaking rains shortly after planting, so the crop is well established. He thinks we should be ready for harvest by the end of July."

"That is good to hear. It seems some of the men we've hired have families. Admittedly, I did not issue instructions that only unmarried men should be offered jobs. I hope you understand that I had to make a decision regarding the women and children without your approval."

She frowned. "I hope you didn't send them away. We certainly have room in the quarter for them."

Pleasantly surprised, he smiled. "I did not send them away. They'll be arriving shortly with the men. I did stipulate that the women are to be put to work to earn their portion of the provisions the Army will supply. You may, at your discretion, assign them to tasks as you see fit."

Her brow rose. "Truly?"

"Yes, truly," he said with a grin.

"My goodness, Colonel. You do come bearing good news today. Harriet and Carolina will be pleased. They are exhausted trying to keep up with everything."

While Levi dismounted, he couldn't help but wonder if Natalie were still playing the part of pampered mistress while the two remaining female servants worked themselves to death. The thought caused a frown to take the place of his grin.

Moses arrived and came toward him. "Morning, Colonel, suh. I take your hoss on into the barn if you like."

Although Levi hadn't intended to stay, it did seem appropriate that he remain and see that the free men and women were settled in their new living quarters as well as given their assignments of work. He didn't foresee any problems, but one could never tell what might arise. The situation was all very new to everyone involved.

"Thank you, Moses." He handed the big man the reins. "Mrs. Ellis tells me you believe the crop will be ready for harvest earlier than expected. I'd like to discuss this with you when you have time to determine a course of action for the next few weeks."

The black man seemed hesitant to reply, glancing at Natalie then back to Levi. "I's glad to speak with you, suh, if that's what Miz Natalie wants."

"Colonel," Natalie said, crossing the porch to the railing directly above where he and Moses stood. "I trust you remember this is still my plantation and my cotton crop. I would like to be involved in any discussions regarding such matters."

For a moment, Levi stiffened. He didn't appreciate taking orders from a woman, plantation owner or not.

Her eyes sought Moses then, and her face softened. "However, Moses is my trusted employee. Whatever he believes best in regards to the crop and the harvest, you may rest assured he speaks for me."

A look of pride glistened in Moses' eyes. He gave Natalie a slight nod, which she returned.

"Very well," Levi said, glancing between them. "Perhaps the *three* of us can sit down and discuss how and when certain things need to happen in order to gain the most profit for Rose Hill."

"I would like that." Natalie smiled, seeming quite pleased.

Moses took the horse to the barn.

Glancing down the road, Levi saw no sign of the wagons. He guessed they would arrive within the half hour. What could he do to fill the time?

"Colonel," Natalie said, gaining his attention. "Since you will be a frequent visitor here at Rose Hill in the coming weeks, perhaps you would like a brief tour of the grounds."

He inclined his head. "I would." Especially, he grinned, with the lovely mistress as tour guide.

As she descended the steps, Samuel, Isaac, and Ebenezer rounded the corner of the house.

"Co'nel!" Samuel said upon spying Levi. "I didn't know you were here." The boy hurried to him, all smiles and bright eyes. That the child was happy and healthy despite so much uncertainty and sadness in his young life spoke of his mother's great care. Whatever disagreement Levi had with Natalie over her treatment of the slaves, even he could see she was doing a good job raising her son.

"Hello, Samuel." He looked at Isaac, whose eyes held a touch of fear as he hung back. "Who is your friend?"

Ebenezer meandered over, begging for a scratch on his head, which Levi willingly offered.

Samuel turned to the other boy. "That's Isaac. Me an' him are going fishin'." He looked up at Levi, squinting in the morning sunshine. "We have to catch us some dinner on account o' the war bein' over and the slaves leaving. Mama says we have to help now. But I like fishin', so I don't mind helping."

Levi held back a grin. "I'm glad to see you boys are doing your part." He included Isaac in his gaze. The black child gave a shy grin.

"Samuel, be sure to stay along the creek where I can see you. And no wading." When Natalie reached to cup his cheek, Levi noticed a strip of cloth wrapped around the middle of her hand. A quick glance at her other hand found one there too.

"Yes, Mama."

With that, the boys and the dog scampered off. It seemed odd to see the two youngsters of different color, raised as master and slave until recently, enjoy such obvious companionship. What would their lives have been like a decade from now had emancipation not come? Would their friendship have stood even after Isaac was sent to the fields and Samuel assumed his role as head of the plantation? Levi shook his head. The paradoxes of slavery never ceased to amaze him.

Returning his attention to Natalie, he found her blue gaze on him. A slight flush filled her cheeks at being caught, and she turned away. "Are you ready to begin our tour?"

"I am." He fell in step beside her. "When was Rose Hill built?" he asked, hoping to alleviate her embarrassment, although he had to admit to being pleased by the attention.

"My father-in-law came to Texas in eighteen thirty-six with dreams of building the largest cotton plantation this side of the Mississippi." She glanced at him as they walked the beautiful grounds in front of the manor. Ancient oaks shaded a large expanse of lawn, and views of the extensive cotton fields were visible in all directions. "While it is large compared to others in the state, he never achieved his dream. Several plantations south of us began as land grants from Mexico. One, I heard, was well over sixty thousand acres."

"I can only imagine the number of slaves it took to work a property that size." Disapproval rang loudly, even to his own ears.

She stopped and faced him. "I understand your aversion to slavery, but not all of us had the benefit of being raised in the north where slavery is not the custom. The changes will take some getting used to. Surely you can empathize with us as we adjust."

"Mrs. Ellis," he said, fighting to keep his tone tempered. "One should not have to be raised in the north to understand keeping men and women in bondage is wrong. The vileness of owning another human being speaks for itself. Where was this empathy you speak of when eighty slaves were under your ownership?"

"My, my, Colonel." She glared at him. "I suppose you Yankees have never done anything wrong. Burning homes and leaving women and children to starve is perfectly acceptable behavior in your opinion, I take it?"

He stiffened. "There are those who believe such activities were justified. That the South brought it on themselves when they chose to leave the Union in order to protect what they like to refer to as the *peculiar institution* of slavery."

"Justified?" She looked at him as though he'd sprouted horns. "How can someone who preaches freedom and equality for all find justification in the ill and often brutal treatment of others for any reason? If you truly believe in that type of justice, sir, you are as contemptible as any slaveholder."

CHAPTER TEN

Several heated moments ticked by before regret took hold of Natalie. She had no right to accuse the colonel. While she didn't know if he had participated in the burning and pillaging in the South, it wasn't her place to condemn him. Oh, but the man could rile her like no one had in a very long time.

"I apologize," she began contritely at the same time he said, "You're right."

When he inclined his head, she offered a slight smile. "I should not accuse anyone of things I know little about."

"As I should not assume all slave owners are of the same ilk."

The deep brown of his eyes held hers as they faced one another. When she could bear their intensity no longer, she looked away. "Since you are a military man, perhaps we can agree on a truce during the time you're at Rose Hill. I don't believe we'll see eye to eye on the subject, but arguing serves little purpose."

A moment passed before she looked up and found his gaze still on her.

"A truce then." He bowed, a half-smile on his mouth. "If Generals Grant and Lee can come to agreeable terms, I am certain you and I can as well."

The humor of his words eased the uncomfortable tension. He could be quite charming when he put his mind to it.

Resuming their walk, Natalie gave him a brief tour of the quarter and the barns. As they made their way back to the house, she stopped to admire a pale pink rose in full bloom.

"My mother-in-law, Martha Ellis, brought cuttings of these bushes when they came from Virginia. Luther named the plantation in her honor." She bent to smell the fragrant flower, inhaling deeply of its heady scent. When she straightened, she found the colonel's attention not on the flower but on her hands. Too late she remembered to keep them hidden.

"Might I inquire about the bandages?"

Embarrassed, Natalie held out her hands, both wrapped with strips torn from an old chemise. She'd doctored the painful sores herself, not wishing for Harriet or Carolina to see them. Both women had asked after her, but she'd declared herself fine. The pain was excruciating when she'd hauled water to the garden that morning, but she wouldn't let it keep her from doing her fair share of work. "It's nothing. Just a few silly blisters."

He raised his brow.

Ashamed at her ineptitude at plantation chores, she tried to wave him off. "I was helping to water the garden. A few blisters were my reward."

"May I see them? You wouldn't want the wounds to become infected."

"Truly, they are fine, Colonel." As she spoke, a line of wagons entered the yard. Corporal Banks and several other soldiers accompanied them on horseback. She turned back to the colonel, glad for the interruption. "We best see to the new arrivals."

She started to move away, but he clasped her arm.

"Mrs. Ellis, I would very much like to see the wounds for myself. Even something as small as a blister can become a larger problem should infection take hold."

A long moment ticked by as she considered his words. "Very well," she said, unhappy to remove the bandages yet fearful he might be right. The cloth stuck to one of the open sores, and she grimaced when she gave a slight yank on it, tearing the tender skin. She opened her palms as much as she dared to reveal four giant blisters on one hand and three on the other. Stretching the wounds, she'd discovered, was nearly as painful as carrying a bucket.

With a touch far more gentle than she'd expected, the colonel took her hands in his and examined the sores. "You say these are the result of watering the garden?"

"Yes." She tried to tug her hands free, but he wouldn't release them. "Harriet and Carolina and I must carry water from the well to the garden. I never realized a bucket of water was so heavy."

He continued to study her hands for a long moment, his thumb lightly caressing her skin. When he met her gaze again, she thought she saw a hint of compassion in the brown depths rather than the scorn she'd anticipated. "I'll have Corporal Banks attend your hands. He served on a medical detail the first years of the war."

Without another word, he strode toward the wagons. Natalie felt foolish for allowing him to look at her sores. After years of watching men fall in battle, a few blisters were obviously not worth fretting over. Replacing the cloths, she was surprised when he returned to her side a few moments later.

"Here." He held something out to her.

Looking down at his offering, she gasped. *Gloves!*

When she met his gaze, a question surely shining in her eyes, he shrugged. "You need to protect your hands if you insist on carrying heavy buckets of water."

After accepting the gift, she watched him stride away again, her emotions a whirl of confusion. Why had he shown such compassion toward her? Especially when he'd made his dislike of her obvious, despite their truce?

"Miz Natalie," Carolina said, coming down the steps, a puzzled look on her face. "What them folks doing back here?"

Thankful for the distraction, Natalie glanced at the people in the yard. "These are the workers the Army hired to help us with the crops. Some of the men had families, so the colonel allowed them to bring them along."

"That un' over there, and them two back there ... they's all Rose Hill slaves."

Astonished by the news, Natalie turned back to the group. Several of the men and at least one woman did look familiar.

Carolina made her way over to the woman and gave her a hug, tousling the curly head of a small boy standing next to her. They talked for some time before Carolina returned to Natalie's side, wearing a smug look.

"Ol' Adline there says they's had it hard since they left Rose Hill," she said, her voice lowered so only Natalie could hear. "Says they ain't eaten much since freedom come. When her man heard the Army hirin' out to work Rose Hill's cotton, they jumped, wantin' to come back. Them others done the same."

Colonel Maish and Corporal Banks approached with Moses on their heels. "We'll need a place to store the supplies where no one will have access to them but you or whomever you put in charge of distributing them."

Natalie looked to Moses for a suggestion.

"The bachelor's quarters ain't been used in some time," he said, nodding toward the long one-story building behind the kitchen yard. "Figure the colonel's men can bunk in one room, the supplies in the other."

"Bachelor's quarters?" Levi asked.

Natalie smiled at the bewildered look on his face. "It is a guest house now, but when my husband was a teen, he lived there. It was also used when the plantation received male visitors who were unmarried, since they were not allowed to sleep in the main house for propriety's sake."

"The bachelor's quarters it is then," the colonel said, an amused look in his eye. "I have six men who will rotate in and out as needed over the coming weeks. They'll see to their own meals, assuming there is a fireplace or stove they can utilize."

"There is," Natalie said, secretly wishing he would join his men in the guest house. Even with their disagreements over slavery, his presence brought a calmness that permeated the air around him. His men seemed fond of him, showing him a level of respect she sensed had been earned as opposed to the sort simply given because of his rank. Even Moses, who'd grown decidedly guarded toward strangers once the war had begun, had warmed up to the colonel.

Corporal Banks issued orders to the new men to unload the wagons while Colonel Maish had Carolina take the women and children to the quarter to get settled. Everyone bustled about except Natalie, who felt rather useless in spite of being the mistress of the plantation.

Samuel—drawn by the noise, no doubt—ran to the yard from the creek, the lower portion of his pant legs damp despite her instructions not to go wading. Fearing her son would be in the way and might get hurt, she was about to call to him when Colonel Maish knelt beside the boy. A conversation ensued, although she couldn't make out their words with all the clattering of boxes and barrels and the calls of the workers. A moment later, the colonel stood, put his hand on Samuel's shoulder, and walked the boy toward her.

"Mama," Samuel hollered. He broke free of the colonel and ran the short distance. "So'diers gonna live in the bach'lor house. They got lots of food."

Natalie smiled at her son. "Yes, they do, but they'll share it with the new workers."

"I'm gonna be a so'dier like my papa when I get big."

Her eyes shot wide at the startling announcement. Samuel had never said such a thing before. She glanced at Colonel Maish, who watched as though waiting for her response. Had he said something to her son to put this idea in his head?

"I'm sure you don't need to decide just now what to be when you grow up," she said, forcing a smile. The thought of her son perishing in battle like his father sent a tremor of terror through her. "Being a soldier requires a great deal of hard work. You wouldn't have time to go fishing or play with your friends. It isn't much fun being a soldier."

Samuel seemed to contemplate her pronouncement then looked up to Colonel Maish. "Co'nel, do you think so'diering is fun?"

The colonel glanced to Natalie momentarily, then returned his attention to Samuel.

"I wouldn't say soldiering is fun." He knelt on one knee to get eye level with the boy. "But if that is what you want to do, it is a noble occupation." He reached out to chuck Samuel under the chin. "Your mama is right, though. You have lots of time to decide what you want to be."

Samuel grinned at the colonel. "I a'ready decided. I'm gonna be a sol'dier, like you and my papa." With that, he ran off, headed back to the creek where Isaac and another Negro boy played on the bank. Their fishing poles were nowhere in sight.

When Colonel Maish stood, she glared at him. "I would appreciate it if you wouldn't encourage Samuel with this silly idea of his. I realize he's far too young to truly consider joining the army someday, but suffice it to say I would rather he didn't even speak on such things, lest it take root in his mind."

"Mrs. Ellis." His words and expression conveyed surprise. "Joining the army is not a silly idea. I was not much older than Samuel when I knew I wanted to be a soldier." Giving her a thoughtful look, he added, "I would think you'd be proud your son wants to follow in his father's footsteps. While it is regrettable he fought for the wrong side and lost his life, I'm sure he believed it his duty to serve. There is nothing shameful in that."

His answer didn't please her. Not in the least. She didn't wish her son to ever believe it his duty to put on a uniform and leave his family, never knowing if he would see them again. That was not the life she desired for Samuel, and she would do everything in her power to see that he stayed safe, preferably right here on Rose Hill lands. Clearly, she needed to establish boundaries where her son was concerned while the soldiers were in residence.

"Colonel, once again we find ourselves in disagreement." Glancing toward the bachelor's quarters, where several uniformed men stood on the porch, she knew she had to be firm. Returning her attention to the colonel, she squared her shoulders. "While you and your men administer my agreement with the Union Army,

I forbid you speak to my son without my permission. Is that understood?"

❧ ☙

Levi leveled a stare at the widow. Was she a mite touched in the head? Her ridiculous edict would make it seem so.

The chuckle started deep in his gut. It rumbled in his chest, moved upward to his throat until, finally, his shoulders shook as laughter burst from his lips. When her face mottled with outrage, he laughed all the more.

"I do not see what is so funny, Colonel." She crossed her arms, a storm gathering behind her blue eyes.

"You are," he said, chortling. "You *forbid* me to speak with a four-year-old boy?" She scowled while he continued to chuckle. He had the strongest desire to grab her in a fierce embrace and kiss that pout right off her lovely face. Sobering, he pushed the foolish thought away. Kissing her was as ill-advised as trying to explain a man's call to soldiering.

"I am perfectly serious about this. I don't want you or your men speaking to him about the army or war or anything of that nature."

As his amusement subsided, he glanced in the direction of the creek. Samuel, Isaac, and the new boy were clustered together, looking into a can that more than likely held worms. They had yet to put their hooks into the water.

Returning his attention to Natalie, he chose his words carefully. "Mrs. Ellis, I understand your concern for your son. Raising the boy without his father can't be easy. But the truth is, he will grow up one day, probably sooner than you wish. Trust me when I say, you don't want to raise a boy to become a man who hides behind a woman's skirt."

She continued to glare at him, unyielding. But after a long moment, ever so slowly, her rigid posture softened, and her arms fell to her sides.

"Of course I don't want my son to be that kind of man." She watched the boys chasing each other, a look of longing in her eyes. "I want Samuel to be strong and confident, but I also want him to have compassion for others." She turned back to Levi. "I don't want to lose my son, Colonel. Although Texas was spared the worst of the fighting, the effects of war have changed our lives forever. I pray he never has to experience battle firsthand."

"That, Mrs. Ellis"—Levi looked into her troubled eyes—"we can agree on."

She studied him, measuring his words. "Thank you. That means a great deal, coming from a man such as yourself."

Whether she intended a compliment or criticism, he wasn't sure. Either way, he understood her fear for her son. He hoped to have children of his own one day when God brought a woman into his life he couldn't live without. But even though he wasn't a father yet, he held much the same sentiment as Natalie. After what he'd seen and experienced the past four years, he wouldn't wish war upon anyone's children.

He grinned, hoping to lighten the mood. "Am I still forbidden to speak to Samuel without your permission?"

Her pert mouth twitched until she finally lost the battle and smiled. "I suppose my decree was a bit melodramatic."

"A bit."

Her eyes held him captive for a time. They were the same color as the summer sky above, bright and full of life, looking up at him with far more vulnerability than he'd seen in her before. If he lost himself in their depths, would he discover a woman vastly different from the one she appeared to be on the surface?

Long lashes fluttered downward under his perusal, and a pink flush filled her pale cheeks. "I'm sure you have many things that need your attention, Colonel. Don't let me keep you."

The dismissal served its purpose. He had no intention of discovering the woman's secrets. Nor did she seem willing to reveal them. At least not to him.

The image of Señor Lopez flashed across his mind's eye as he strode toward his men. Had the *Tejano* uncovered the womanly mysteries Levi felt certain were hidden behind those blue eyes?

The unanswered question left him in a foul mood.

CHAPTER ELEVEN

"**M**iz Natalie, you don't need to tote them buckets to the garden no more. These gals can see to it."

Natalie had just set her bucket under the nozzle of the pump, dreading the chore ahead, when Harriet approached with two of the new female servants following. Although Corporal Banks had tended her blistered hands, they were still tender. He'd given her a salve for the sores, but still, the flesh beneath the blisters remained red and painful.

Eyeing the three women, Natalie straightened. "I don't mind helping."

The two new women glanced at each other, astonished expressions on their faces.

"There be lots'a chores you can he'p with that ain't so wearing on ya," Harriet said. "Ruth and Adline here is used to workin' in them fields. Totin' water be easy on them."

Natalie turned to the newcomers. She offered a hesitant smile. "Thank you. I truly appreciate the help."

The younger woman named Ruth smiled shyly, but Adline's eyes remained wary.

Leaving her bucket for the women, Natalie followed Harriet to the kitchen wing. Yesterday, after the soldiers had departed, she and Moses and Harriet discussed where to put the women to work. Colonel Maish was adamant that they were not to work in the fields, and she found herself agreeing with him. Slave women may have been forced to labor alongside the men, but free women would be assigned much less strenuous tasks. With Harriet knowing far more about the needs throughout the plantation and house, Natalie put

Moses and his wife in charge of the new employees.

Laughter came from the quarter. Natalie glanced in that direction to see Samuel playing with Isaac and several Negro children. One of the new women stood nearby, tending to the youngsters while their parents worked. Natalie recalled how the ancient Mammy cared for the Negro babies up until she passed on to glory a few years ago. "It's nice to have more children on the plantation again. Things were much too quiet after they all left."

Harriet nodded. "Ain't nothing as sweet as the sound of happy chillens."

Following the woman into the kitchen, Natalie inhaled the aroma of baking bread. She glanced around the neat room. Despite the early hour, everything was in its place. The breakfast dishes were washed and put away, the floor was swept, and errant crumbs had been removed from the table.

Watching the stout woman bustle over to the pantry, Natalie asked, "Is there something I can do to help you in here?" She'd given the idea of learning to cook some serious thought the past few days.

A brief look of alarm swept Harriet's face before she masked it. "Nothin' much needs doin' in here, Miz Natalie."

Natalie kept her annoyance in check. She could guess why Harriet didn't want her help. Just that morning, Natalie had accidentally spilled a pot of chicory root coffee when the hot handle burned her blistered hand. She'd reached for a towel to mop up the mess, but she hadn't realized the edge was caught beneath a stack of dishes, and she sent them crashing to the floor.

"Surely there must be something I can do." As odd as it sounded, she didn't want to go back to simply sitting on the porch while the others labored around her. She didn't relish hard work, but it no longer seemed right to expect everyone else to contribute to keeping the plantation running while she read or sewed. "With the new women helping in the garden and doing laundry and working in the house, I find myself free to try something different."

"Well." Harriet glanced about the spacious room. Finally, her gaze landed on the basket near the door. She seemed pleased. "You could gather the eggs an' feed the chickens."

"Feed the chickens?" What did chickens eat?

"The pigs need their slop, too."

Slop? The word sounded … smelly.

Natalie squared her shoulders, sending her squeamish thoughts packing. "Very well. If you'll tell me where to find the chicken feed and the … slop, I will tend the animals."

Uncertainty flashed in Harriet's eyes, but she nodded. "The chicken feed is in the grain barn closest to the coop. A few big handfuls ought to do it. Just scatter it on the ground. You can leave the gate open so's they can run out in the yard once they done eatin'. They help keep the bugs an' grasshoppers out'a the garden. The slop barrel be just outside the pigpen. Give 'em three or four bucketfuls, but take care not to get it on your clothes."

The warning reinforced her initial assessment of the word *slop*.

With the basket in hand, she headed for the barn. When she passed near the quarter, she called to Samuel. He came running.

"I'm going to feed the chickens and the pigs. Would you like to help?"

"Yes, Mama!" He skipped ahead of her to the smallest of the three barns. "I've seen Harriet feed the chickens a'fore."

"Good," she said, following him into the dim interior. "You can teach me."

Samuel was already at the bin, peering inside. "Harriet puts the food in her apron and carries it to the chickens." He looked up to Natalie. "How you gonna carry it, Mama?"

Hmm. She hadn't realized she needed a vessel to carry the feed in. The weave of the egg basket was too loose to contain the bits of cracked corn and small seeds. A quick inspection of the surrounding area revealed nothing adequate for the task. Looking down at the pale blue skirt of her dress, she shrugged. "I suppose I can put it in my pockets." Surely that would suffice.

A few minutes later, the pair headed toward the chicken yard, Samuel's nonstop chatter filling the morning air. At least three dozen full-sized birds hurried toward the gate when they arrived, noisily clucking their welcome. Another group of smaller, scraggly looking chickens hung back, watching.

"Those are the babies," Samuel said, rushing into the fenced yard as soon as Natalie unlatched the gate. "Ain't they funny lookin'? Harriet says they don't lay eggs yet on account of them just hatchin' not long ago."

Natalie nodded, pleased to have her wise son along to provide information. She watched him try to catch one of the smaller birds, sending the entire group into a run. The larger chickens clustered around her feet, pecking at the material of her skirt, clucking their impatience.

"They certainly are eager," she said, setting the basket on the ground. Immediately, several chickens went over to investigate. Reaching into her pocket, she pulled out a small handful of feed and tossed it on the ground around her. "Here you go."

The group of birds near the basket hurried over to join the others pecking at the food, their beaks snatching the pieces of corn faster than Natalie could have imagined. "My, you *are* hungry." She reached into her pocket again, but before she could pull out another handful of food, a large red hen flapped her wings and flew at Natalie.

"Oh!" She whirled out of the way to avoid getting feathers in her face and backed into the open gate. The hem of her skirt snagged on a sharp edge, leaving her stocking-clad ankles exposed. Afraid the soldiers or someone near the barns might see her, she worked to get the material free without tearing it. All the while, cracked corn spilled from her pocket, attracting the chickens.

"Shoo," she said when they ran under her skirt and between her feet. "Go away."

Samuel stood watching from a safe distance, a curious look on his face.

When a large black rooster with colorful tail feathers got too close, she flicked her skirt to scare him off. The bird, however, did not appreciate the sudden movement. Instead of running away, he let out a fierce screech, leaped at the skirt, and dug his sharp claws into Natalie's leg.

With a screech of her own, she sprang forward, the material of her skirt ripping from where it had been snagged. Startled by the commotion, the chickens scurried to the opposite side of the yard while the rooster strutted nearby, making angry noises.

Samuel ran over, his eyes big. "Harriet says we shouldn't make the rooster mad 'cuz he's mean."

This news had come a bit too late.

Lifting the hem of her skirt, she was dismayed to see a trail of blood staining her torn stocking. Tossing a glare in the rooster's direction, she headed out the gate. "Come, Samuel."

They exited the chicken yard. Harriet had instructed her to leave the gate open, but Natalie feared the rooster might attack again, so she closed it, securing the latch. After sticking her tongue out at the strutting bird, too late she realized the egg basket lay toppled over on the ground inside. She had yet to gather the eggs.

"Let's feed the pigs," she said, putting her hand out to her son, who grasped it. "We'll come back for the eggs later."

The pigpen was situated behind the largest barn. A foul odor greeted them as they rounded the building, and Natalie wrinkled her nose.

Samuel released her hand and climbed up on the bottom rung of the low fence. "Moses said one of the mama pigs has babies." He gasped, then giggled. "There they are. They sure are little."

Natalie joined her son at the fence. A large sow lay in the far corner of the muddy yard nursing nine or ten pink piglets. Seeing Natalie and Samuel, she grunted but otherwise remained where she was. Several of the other pigs, covered in filth, meandered in their direction.

Glancing about, Natalie spied a large barrel pushed up against the three-sided shed the animals used to get out of the sun or rain. "I suppose that's the slop." She cringed. If what was inside the barrel smelled as bad as the air in the pig yard, she feared she might lose her breakfast.

Moving to it, she eyed the covered container. Dried drips of something ran down the sides, and a horde of flies buzzed around it. Rolling up her cuffs so they wouldn't get soiled, she took a deep breath and held it in her lungs. She opened the lid.

Her eyes shot wide at the sight that met her. Slamming the lid down, she quickly backed away from the barrel, her breath swooshing out.

"Oh! It's horrible." A shiver slid up her spine with a picture of the watery mixture of vegetable scraps, stale bread, corn, and who knew what else firmly planted in her mind. She eyed the pigs that had followed her across the yard, obviously waiting for their breakfast. "You enjoy eating that mess?"

They stared back.

With a frustrated sigh, she weighed her options. If she went back to the house and begged Harriet to finish the job, the servant would do just that without saying a word about Natalie's ineptness. But Natalie couldn't do that. She may not be strong enough to tote water to the garden or handy in the kitchen, but surely she could feed a few animals.

Determined, she marched back to the barrel. Holding her breath, she removed the lid, picked up the pail sitting next to it, and dipped it into the slop. The pigs grunted, squealed, and jockeyed for position at the trough as Natalie dumped the slimy contents over the fence into the wooden crib. Splashes of the mess flew into the air, much of it escaping through the fence slats and landing on her skirt.

She repeated the process three more times, oddly satisfied to see the pigs gleefully gobbling down their nasty meal. After replacing the lid on the barrel, she spied a pump near the barn door.

"I'm going to wash my hands, Samuel." Her son had climbed to the top rail of the fence while she distributed the slop. He happily watched the pigs enjoy their food.

"All right, Mama."

It took several minutes of rinsing her hands in the cool, clear water before she felt they were clean again. A look at her skirt revealed flecks of foodstuffs there. She grimaced. Well, perhaps today she would learn how to do laundry.

Returning to the pigpen, Natalie came to an abrupt stop. "Samuel!"

Her son stood in the middle of the muddy pig yard, ankle deep in the smelly muck.

"Come out of there this minute." She hurried to the fence. Although the pigs were still busy with their meal, the sow with the piglets was on her feet, looking at Samuel.

"My shoe is stuck, Mama."

Natalie opened the gate to the pen. Mud, manure, and bits of straw filled much of the space.

"Try to work it free," she said, watching her son struggle to lift his foot. His thin arms flailed while his face scrunched up. Suddenly, his foot popped out of the shoe, which stayed planted where it was, sending him backwards into the muck. A look of startled surprise washed over him.

His laughter rang out a moment later, and even Natalie had to chuckle.

The sow, however, was not pleased. She grunted angrily, glancing between her babies and Samuel. She took a menacing step forward.

❧

Levi tied his horse to the hitching post in front of Rose Hill Manor, feeling foolish for coming. He'd told himself the entire ride over that he simply wanted to check on the new workers and make certain they were settled in their temporary home. It was, after all, the exact thing he'd been commissioned to do when he'd arrived on Texas' shores. The newly freed men and women across the state would need help gaining independence after a lifetime of bondage. With the thirty men and handful of women he'd hired to work on Rose Hill being his first attempt at fulfilling that commission, it made sense he would want to have a role in its success.

But he couldn't fool himself with such thoughts. He'd left two capable privates in charge of the new workers, and he knew Moses was there to supervise and offer instructions specific to Rose Hill. They certainly didn't need a man with no farm experience giving advice regarding things he knew nothing about. Now, ask him about building cedar chests or bentwood rockers and the like, then he could teach them a thing or two.

He glanced about and found no one around, although he'd seen field workers laboring over the cotton plants as he'd ridden up the lane. Harvest was still several weeks away, but the crop needed careful tending, lest bugs and weeds interfere with healthy plants. He'd instructed his men to assist with the work rather than sitting on their horses as an overseer would. Neither of them seemed bothered by the order, and Levi was again grateful for the farm boys in his command. They were used to the hard work of tilling, hoeing, and picking, and they would provide the experience Levi lacked.

Childish laughter sounded from down the hill, near the barns. Wondering if it was Samuel—and guessing the lad's mother wouldn't be far if it were—he headed in that direction. Voices led him to the back of the barn to the pigpen, but he was not prepared for the sight that met him.

"Co'nel!"

Samuel, covered in smelly mud, ran to him. He noticed the boy was missing a shoe. But it was Natalie, sprawled in the middle of the pen, who rendered him speechless. When she jerked her head around to look at him, surprise in her eyes, her face reddened. She looked away, struggling to get to her feet.

"My shoe got stuck in the mud. Mama tried to get it out, but she fell down." Samuel giggled.

Natalie's slippers were covered in the slimy mess. She held what appeared to be Samuel's mud-covered shoe in one hand, but getting up from the awkward position seemed to be proving difficult.

An angry grunt sounded. Levi had been so shocked to find Natalie in the pen that he hadn't taken notice of the animals whose home she'd invaded. While most of the pigs didn't seem bothered by her presence, a large sow with a litter of babies nearby had her eyes fixed on Natalie.

"Would you like some help?" He approached the gate. His instinct was to rush in and carry her to safety, but the last time he'd done that, she hadn't been pleased.

"No."

The clipped word said it all.

Samuel climbed up the fence and sat on the top rung. "Me and Mama fed the pigs. And the chickens."

Levi's brow rose. He'd been curious what these two were doing at the pigpen. Shaking his head in wonder, he continued to watch Natalie struggle. The sow did too.

"I'd be happy to help." He leaned against the fence next to Samuel. The boy looked at him, and they exchanged a grin.

"I don't need help."

Her thrashing in the mud said otherwise, but he kept that to himself. After a long moment, she managed a wobbly stance. But when she tried to lift one foot, it refused to give way, and back she fell on her behind.

Her squeal, along with the sudden movement, was apparently too much for the sow. The big animal let out a fierce snort and charged. Levi reacted as though he'd heard the call to battle. He rushed into the pen and yelled at the sow. Waving his arms, he herded her back to where her piglets cowered in the corner.

When he felt the animal was no longer a threat, he turned to Natalie. "We need to get you out of here before she decides to take a bite out of us both." With that, he bent down and scooped her into his arms, the squishing sound of wet suction releasing its prey and eliciting a giggle from Samuel. Levi carried her beyond the gate and set her down before he realized she was missing both of her shoes. Looking back to the pen, he could make out the shapes of two small slippers.

Samuel hopped down from the fence and came over. He looked his mother up and down, looked at Levi, and let out a belly laugh.

"Samuel, this is not funny." She scowled at her son.

When her angry gaze turned to Levi, he attempted to remain straight-faced. But a streak of mud across her nose did him in. A snicker shook his shoulders.

"Surely you are not laughing at me too!"

"No, ma'am." His shoulders bounced slightly as he fought to control himself. Her scowl darkened.

"I could have been mauled by that beast."

Samuel's little-boy giggles filled the air with merriment. Levi couldn't contain it any longer. He laughed. Harder than he'd laughed in years.

At first, Natalie seemed outraged. But when Levi and Samuel's hilarity persisted, her lips twitched. Soon, she burst into girlish giggles Levi found irresistible.

After a time, she looked down at herself. "Oh," she said, sobering. "This is awful. I thought getting splashed with slop was bad." She glanced at his coat and boots, also covered in muck. "I hope you haven't ruined your uniform."

"I'm sure it can be cleaned."

She smiled into his eyes. He got lost in the pools of blue until Samuel piped up.

"Mama, what about your shoes?" One pig nudged the slippers around with its snout.

She laughed. "The pigs can have them."

"I'd be happy to carry you to the house," Levi said, itching to have her in his arms again, smelly muck and all.

Natalie's brow rose at his suggestion. She glanced at her son, who seemed interested in the conversation. "That isn't necessary, Colonel. I'm sure I can walk just fine."

They began a slow trek toward the manor, her watching the path, stepping carefully over small stones and sticks.

"I admit my surprise at finding you in the pigpen." When she flashed him a scowl, he clarified. "I mean, Samuel informed me the two of you were feeding the pigs. That surprises me. I would think the servants would tend the animals."

Samuel ran ahead of them, chasing a dragonfly, his gait comical with one shoe on and one shoe off.

"They normally do, but I volunteered to help." She shrugged. "I suppose I'm not very good at any plantation chores."

"We fed the chickens, too," Samuel said, skipping back to her side. "But Mama made the rooster mad. She got blood on her leg."

"It attacked you?" Levi asked, concerned.

A faint blush filled her cheeks. "I'm fine. Just a scratch, is all."

Recalling the blisters she'd received from toting water, he felt a wave of sympathy for the muck-covered widow as they reached the bottom of the porch steps. "That may be, but it is best if we clean it properly. Especially considering where you've just been. If you'll sit, I can see about the wound."

Her blush deepened. "As I said, Colonel, that isn't necessary, but I appreciate the offer. Thank you for your assistance at the pigpen." With that, she hurried up the steps, leaving muddy footprints on the whitewashed wood, and disappeared into the house.

Levi watched her go, amused by the whole affair. When he looked down at Samuel, the boy was grinning up at him.

Together, they shared a good laugh.

CHAPTER TWELVE

A slight breeze teased Natalie's hair as she and Samuel sat on the grass in the shade of the ancient black walnut tree with Carolina and Moses' family. Thick branches and lush foliage overhead offered a respite from the sweltering weather now that July had arrived with the promise of sunny days and little rain.

"Did the others say they's comin'?" Harriet asked her husband, fanning herself with an unhemmed square of cloth.

"They said they is." Moses glanced in the direction of the quarter. "Told 'em we don't meet in the chapel when it get hot like this. I 'spect the Lawd don't mind where we meet on His day, 'long as we get together an' say a word or two of praise."

The couple exchanged a smile.

Natalie looked away, not wanting to intrude on a private moment. The love the pair had for each other was evident. As far back as she could remember, they'd been together. Even before Natalie married George and moved to Rose Hill, Moses and Harriet had lived on the Langford plantation. When Natalie married, Papa gave Moses to her as a wedding gift. After Aunt Lu ran away with Adella, leaving Rose Hill without a cook, Papa gave Harriet to Natalie too.

She heaved a sigh. That seemed a lifetime ago. So much had happened since then. Mama and Papa were gone. The war came. George's death, then Luther's. And now freedom for the slaves. Nothing of her old life remained.

Lately, though, a quiet question stirred strange thoughts in her mind, usually in the dark of night as she lay in bed. A question she had yet to answer. If time could rewind, would she *want* things to remain as they'd been?

Voices drew her attention. Some of the new workers and former Rose Hill slaves came toward them. When they reached the shade of the tree, Ruth was the only one who smiled timidly in Natalie's direction before settling down next to a tall man who held a fat baby. Adline and the others simply ignored her and Samuel.

"Welcome, folks. Glad you could join us." Moses stood near the massive tree trunk as the newcomers sat on the grass. "We don't got a fo'mal preacher that comes Sundays, but we do all right. The Lawd ain't particular. He just say come in His name, so that's what we do."

He nodded to Harriet. She began singing a soulful song in her rich alto voice. A few of the others joined in, softly at first. Little Isaac tried to keep up with his mother, his high soprano squeaking, with him often mangling the words and the tune, though no one minded.

Natalie closed her eyes, enjoying the peaceful gathering. She didn't know the hymn, but it didn't matter. It washed over her like a warm blanket on a cold winter's night. Comforting. Soothing. The first years of her marriage, she hadn't joined the slaves in the small chapel behind the quarter. George didn't approve of the meetings, and for a time, after Jeptha and the others escaped, he'd banned the services altogether. Eventually, however, things fell back into their normal routine, including the worship gatherings. By then, though, she'd learned it was not wise to cross George, and she stayed away from the little chapel. After he died, there was nothing to keep her from attending.

With a glance toward Harriet, she recalled the first time she'd stepped foot in the small building. The singing had started before she'd worked up the nerve to enter. An awkward silence washed over the crowded room as everyone stared at her. Just when she thought she would turn and leave, Harriet stood, baby Isaac in her arms, and walked down the aisle between the crude benches. With every eye on them—and a collective intake of breath, it seemed—

they waited to hear what the slave, who'd suffered so much loss because of Natalie's family, would say to her mistress. But Harriet didn't utter a word. She simply took Natalie by the arm and led her to the seat next to hers.

In that moment of acceptance—and undeserved forgiveness—Natalie encountered her first glimpse of grace.

When the singing quieted, Moses took in the crowd. "It shore has been a week we ain't soon to forget." He smiled broadly. "We is free." His sweeping gaze included Natalie and Samuel. "All of us." He paused to wipe a tear from his cheek. "I been thinkin' on what freedom means. One thing I know it don't mean is we's all o' sudden our own massa." He shook his head. "No. We still has a Master."

"I ain't got no massa." The man with the branded cheeks stood at the edge of the gathering, arms crossed, and glared at Moses. Natalie had only seen him from a distance and hadn't realized the scars on his face were letters. A large "R" filled one cheek while a large "N" filled the other. She didn't need to be told he'd received them after attempting to run away from his owner.

"Well, Jezro, maybe we ain't got a white massa no more, but ever'body got a Master," Moses said. "The Lawd be our Master. He done made us, so I 'spect He has the right to tell us what to do and what not to do. Long befo' I come to know Him by name, He already know mine. Long befo' I come to love Him, He already love me. Same be true for you." His gaze swept the group. "Same be true for us all."

Jezro remained silent, frowning.

Moses picked up a cloth bundle lying on the ground next to him. Carefully, he unwrapped the covering. Natalie was not the only one to gasp when he revealed a black leather-bound book, its edges worn and ragged.

Holding it as though it were a delicate china dish, a soft smile settled on his face. After a moment, he looked up. "This here ... is the Holy Bible."

The group remained wide-eyed, staring first at Moses and then at the book. Natalie, too, could not hide her shock. Slaves were not allowed to own books. Their masters feared if slaves learned to read and write, they might start an uprising and demand their freedom.

She glanced at Harriet. Her eyes shimmered with pride. Even little Isaac watched his papa with wide-eyed interest.

Samuel, who had been leaning against Natalie with drooping eyes, got to his knees so he could see the book better.

"Some o' you know my massa some years back was a preacher man. He a good man. Loved the Lawd. He talked 'bout givin' me my freedom papers from time to time. We's livin' in Lu'siana back then, and it weren't a good place for a Negro to be turned loose, so I stays with him." Moses gazed out to the fields with a thoughtful look, perhaps reliving the past in his mind.

"Just befo' Rev'rend Adams passed on, he says to me, 'Moses, I wants you to have my Bible when the Lawd takes me on home.' He'd taught me my letters, and I could read a few words here and there." A frown tugged his brow. "After he die, they put me on the block down in New O'leans, fixin' to sells me. I had this here Bible fastened to my leg with rope, under my trousers." He glanced briefly at Natalie. "Them traders sometime make the slave take off their clothes, so's a buyer can see what they gettin'. I's prayin' they don't ask that of me, otherwise they find the Bible."

Natalie had never heard such candid talk from a slave—former slave—about the markets. Shamefully, she'd never considered what they must've gone through before her father or father-in-law or some other buyer purchased them and took them home. She peeked at the others in the group, their rapt attention on Moses. Had each of them experienced the disturbing scenario he'd just described?

"Massa Boyd buys me lickety-split, so I's not have to worry no more 'bout them findin' my book. He brings me an' some others to Texas, plannin' to put us to work in the cane fields. I's glad when

Massa Langford buys me from Massa Boyd to drive his carriage."
His gaze landed on Harriet. "I's had me a good life since I come
here."

After a moment, he turned his full attention to Natalie. "Miz
Natalie, I want to 'pologize for bein' dishonest 'bout having this
here Bible all these years. I know it was against the rules to have a
book, but this one be mighty special to me. I hope you can forgive
me for keepin' it hidden."

The earnest request caused moisture to spring to her eyes.
Here was her former slave, asking for forgiveness for owning a
Bible when it was she who had claimed ownership of him. It was
her husband who'd sold his sons. Why wasn't he demanding an
apology from her instead of seeking her pardon?

"There is nothing to forgive, Moses," she finally said, her voice
thick with emotion.

An understanding passed between them.

He flipped through its pages. "I cain't read most o' these words,
but they is two that is my fav'rites." He smiled broadly. "God …
and Jesus. When I come 'cross one o' them, I tells ya, my heart skip
with joy. Don't matter that I don't know what the words 'round
them say. Only matter that they's in this book, and they's in my
heart."

The service ended a short time later. Carolina and several others
rushed forward to look at the treasured book. Unless they'd been
house servants, most had probably never held one in their hands,
though even house servants were forbidden to learn to read.

Making her way back to the manor, Natalie couldn't help but
wonder what would have happened to Moses had George or his
father learned the Negro had the book.

She shuddered. The thought was too awful to imagine.

❧ ❧

Natalie retreated to the privacy of her sitting room, desperately needing the quiet to sort through the tangle of confused emotions swirling through her mind and heart. She hadn't been there long when Ebenezer announced the arrival of visitors. Her open window faced north, so she wasn't able to see who was coming, but the dog's incessant barking didn't stop. Alexander Lopez had sent word through one of his *vaqueros* that he'd hoped to visit her the coming week, so she didn't expect to see the *Tejano* today.

Could it be Colonel Maish, arriving to check on his men?

The flutter in her stomach sent her racing to the long mirror in her bedroom. She smoothed her hair, wishing she'd spent more time fashioning it that morning rather than resorting to the simple braid she'd taken to wearing lately. Perhaps she could quickly pin it in a coil. At least she'd chosen one of her better gowns in honor of the Lord's Day. The sheer fabric was not only cooler than her silks and cottons, but the pale green set off her complexion in a way Mama had always told her would be the envy of other women.

A thread of conscience worked its way into her thoughts, recalling Corporal Banks' comments about the colonel's family. She'd wondered many times since that day if he referred to the man's wife and children, or simply parents and siblings. While freshening her appearance for a visitor was not unusual, she certainly wouldn't want to attract the attention of another woman's husband.

Her hands stilled, and she gazed at her reflection. Was that what she hoped to do? Attract the Yankee?

"Miz Natalie!" Carolina called from the foyer, something she would not have done had she still been a slave. "A wagon is comin'. It's wearin' one o' them canvas coverin's."

Natalie frowned. A covered wagon? Colonel Maish rode his horse when he came to Rose Hill. Unless he was bringing additional supplies or men, she had to assume the Yankee was not their visitor. Disappointment washed over her as she put the last pin in her hair and exited her room. Carolina and Moses waited at the bottom of the stairs, the latter holding a rifle.

"We shore is gettin' our fill o' strangers lately," Carolina said when Natalie joined them.

They moved to the porch to await the vehicle.

"That look like women drivin' that rig," Carolina said, moving her head from side to side as though she could get a better view.

"I believe you's right," Moses said. He turned and leaned the gun against the wall inside the open door.

As the wagon stopped in front of the porch amid a cloud of dust, Natalie saw that two women, one black and one white, sat on the high driver's seat, with the black woman holding the reins. The wide brim of their bonnets hid their faces, and Natalie couldn't begin to guess who the company might be.

The white woman stood after the brake was set, revealing a rather rotund figure. She removed her bonnet, her graying hair plastered to her head, and met Natalie's gaze with a glare. "Natalie Langford Ellis, I have a bone to pick with you."

Although her aging face seemed vaguely familiar, Natalie could not place the woman. "I beg your pardon? And who might you be?"

Annoyance mottled the woman's plump cheeks. "Well, that's a fine way to greet your cousin."

Cousin?

"Mrs. Eunice Porter, wife of the late Judge Porter from Shelby County. For pity's sake, you stayed in my guest room on your honeymoon trip. And this is the thanks I get? Forgotten, in my greatest time of need."

Cousin Eunice, her mother's cousin.

"Forgive me, Cousin Eunice." Natalie descended the steps while Eunice none too gracefully climbed down the wagon wheel. "I fear my memory isn't as good as it should be. You've caught me quite by surprise." She embraced the large woman, assaulted by the odor of sweat and dust clinging to Eunice's clothes.

When they parted, Eunice glanced up at the manor. "So, this is Rose Hill. I've certainly heard many tales about it. That husband of yours was mighty proud of it. I heard he was killed early on in the war." She sent Natalie a sour look. "'Course I had to learn that information from Sally Porter since you didn't have the decency to write to us and let us know. That woman loves to lord it over me that she knows more about my own family than I do, what with her daughter living right here in Williamson County."

Her loud voice and scolding words transported Natalie back to the night she and George had stayed with the Porters. Mama had insisted the newlyweds stop in Shelby County and stay with her favorite cousin on their way to New Orleans. The farmhouse was modest, as was the guest room, but it would have been a perfectly pleasant stay if not for Eunice's nonstop gossip and the judge's overindulgence from the liquor decanter. When they retired to their room, George had nothing good to say about the entire visit. They'd avoided Shelby County on their return trip.

"What brings you to Rose Hill?" She glanced up to the young Negro woman who remained seated on the driver's bench. The poor thing looked exhausted with droopy eyes and slouched shoulders. Upon closer examination, Natalie realized she was heavy with child.

"The Yankees," Eunice spat, her upper lip curled in a snarl. "Those no-account devils burned us out."

Natalie gasped. "They burned your home?" She could hardly believe such news.

"It's all them Negroes' fault." Eunice looked up at the servant, who stared straight ahead as though she hadn't heard the accusation. "Ever since Judge Porter passed on two years ago, I've barely managed to keep food on the table. Then those Yankees showed up on my doorstep, demanding I set my slaves free. Well, you can be certain I refused. How was I to get along without my slaves?"

Natalie had asked the same question when Colonel Maish and his men arrived at Rose Hill. She couldn't imagine where she'd be now if the Army hadn't supplied her with workers.

"They threatened to burn the house if I didn't comply. I told the lot of 'em to get off my property. 'Them Negroes are mine,' I said, 'bought and paid for. If you want 'em, you can pay me for 'em.'" Her eyes filled with moisture. "That hateful captain said I had ten minutes to get what I wanted out of the house before they torched it. And that's just what those devils did." She sniffled loudly.

Natalie didn't know what to say. She'd heard of homes burned to the ground across the South over the last few years of the war, but the war was over now. It seemed beyond heartless to burn out a widow because she wasn't immediately in compliance with the proclamation. Surely the soldiers could have set the slaves free and left Eunice's home standing. What difference did it make who delivered the proclamation Natalie herself had read to her people?

"I'm so sorry." She wondered what the woman planned to do now.

"And that's why I could not believe my eyes when we arrived at Langford Manor and saw a sea of Yankees on your land!"

"I had no choice." Natalie felt like an errant child. "They declared the plantation abandoned. Nothing I said made any difference."

"Your mama would be sick at heart to see those Bluecoats making themselves at home in the very house where you were born." Perspiration dotted her upper lip, and she used her stiff bonnet as a fan. "A terribly arrogant colonel directed us to Rose Hill when I demanded to know what he'd done with you."

Colonel Maish, no doubt.

"Please, come sit on the porch and have some refreshments. It's much too warm to stand here in the sun. Your servant may join us as well."

Eunice harrumphed. "Lottie there can take that wagon to the barn and tend the animals, is what she can do."

The young woman's tired eyes met Natalie's. Far be it from Natalie to tell someone how to treat her servants, but Lottie looked as though she could topple from her high perch any moment.

"That won't be necessary. Moses can see to the wagon and the animals." She turned to Carolina. "Please bring some cool water for Cousin Eunice. You may take Lottie with you to the kitchen and offer her some as well."

The three servants followed her instructions while Eunice ascended the steps, out of breath when she reached the top.

"I see you managed to hold on to some of your slaves, what with the Yankees trying to turn 'em all loose every which way." She shook her head as she practically fell onto a wicker sofa. "It t'aint right, I tell you." She fanned herself, wafting her pungent scent toward Natalie. "The judge would have something to say to those northern devils were he alive. He paid good money for those slaves, same as your pappy."

"I was sorry to hear of his passing." Natalie was already weary from the woman's grumblings. She knew she should invite Eunice to stay overnight, but she couldn't help hoping the travelers were simply stopping to rest before continuing to their destination.

Carolina arrived with a glass of water, which Eunice gulped down. After wiping her mouth with the back of her hand, she said, "I'm glad my husband didn't live to see this day." The sound she made spoke her disgust. "Yankees swarming Texas, setting all them Negroes free. These are sad times for our state, I tell you."

"You are of course welcome to stay the night with us." Natalie hoped her true wishes weren't detectable in the invitation. "Although I'm sure you are anxious to continue your journey. Where is it you're going?"

Eunice stared at Natalie as though she'd been out in the sun too long.

"Where am I going? Why, *here*, of course!" Eunice let out a high-pitched cackle, as though Natalie's question were beyond silly. "My dear, I have come to live at Rose Hill."

CHAPTER THIRTEEN

With the sun barely topping a rosy eastern horizon, Levi and Banks made their way to Rose Hill along rain-rutted roads. A fierce storm had blown through during the night, damaging many of the tents where his men slept and leaving debris scattered throughout the Langford plantation. Although he knew Natalie had ample help with Moses, his men, and the new field workers, Levi felt the need to see for himself that all was well with the widow. Her property was, for the time being, the responsibility of the Union Army.

"I thought we might get blown all the way down to old Mexico last night," Banks said as they maneuvered their mounts around several fallen branches from a copse of live oak trees. Leaves littered the road until it was almost indistinguishable from its surroundings.

Levi surveyed the mess. "I don't suppose riding out the storm in a tent was much fun."

"No, sir. I'm sure I heard a few of the boys crying for their mamas at the worst of it."

Levi chuckled. "It'll take the better part of the day to get things in order back at camp. I'd hoped to send units to the farms north of here, but I suppose that'll have to wait."

He let out a frustrated sigh. Bringing news of freedom to Texas slaves was their first priority. The joyful cries of hundreds of Negroes who'd heard the proclamation still echoed in his memory, but there were many more who had yet to receive the good news. The unexpected delay brought on by the storm meant one more day in bondage for those men and women.

Despite the damage around them, the rain-washed countryside

looked fresh and bright, bathed in early morning sunshine. Sweet air filled their lungs while birdsong met their ears. Although he wasn't pleased about the delay in their mission, he couldn't help acknowledging that a valid excuse to visit Rose Hill—and its mistress—had been delivered to him during the night.

"I remember a bad storm rolled through while we were waiting to attack Fort Wagner," Banks said, gazing off toward the east, a solemn look on his face. "Some said it was a sure sign we were going to lose."

Had someone else been listening, they might have thought the comment strange. But Levi knew memories from the war often sprang up at odd times, as this one just had for Banks. Sometimes he and his fellow soldiers shared them, sometimes they didn't.

Levi knew the battle he spoke of. The Fifty-Fourth Massachusetts, an all-black company, penetrated the fort after a brigade of Federal troops unsuccessfully assaulted the strongpoint guarding Charleston Harbor a few days prior. Their victory, however, was short-lived. Reinforcements were slow in coming, and the Confederates retook the fort. Banks' unit suffered enormous losses. Levi could only imagine the carnage the corporal witnessed in the surgical tent.

"Colonel Shaw was a good man," was all Levi said. He'd never met Shaw, the son of an abolitionist who'd organized and led the Union's first black regiment, but he'd heard much about the man. Shaw fell during the battle for the fort. The newspapers said the Confederates stripped his body and threw it into a grave with dead Negro soldiers in a mark of contempt for this white officer's championing of blacks. But Shaw's father said it best when he declared he could imagine no holier resting place for his son, nor better company.

Neither said any more about the battle, but unspoken memories of the war hovered on the edge of the silence, always there. Levi wondered how many years it would take to forget what they'd seen and done the past four years. Perhaps they'd never forget.

The gleaming white plantation house came into view, but even at a distance, Levi saw that Rose Hill had undergone far more damage than the Langford place. Pieces of roofing were scattered throughout the yard, and tree branches lay about. A giant oak had fallen, barely missing the barn and leaving its tangled roots exposed. Farm equipment that usually sat in neat rows was now a jumbled heap. The two soldiers he'd left at Rose Hill stood with Wash Ingram and a group of hired workers, but no one seemed to know where to begin the cleanup.

Banks gave a low whistle. "They sure got hit."

Levi scanned the chaos, already formulating a plan of action, but first, he had to make sure Natalie and Samuel were safe. He galloped the rest of the way and drew up in front of the porch. The main door stood open, but silence came from inside the house. He dismounted and took the steps two at a time.

"Natalie?" His voice echoed in the empty foyer. Too late he realized he'd used her given name in his worry.

The hasty tread of footsteps sounded from the floor above. A moment later, she appeared at the top of the staircase.

Relief washed through him. She was safe.

"Colonel Maish." Her voice revealed her astonishment. Descending, she paused to glance behind her before hurrying down the remaining steps. "I'm surprised to see you here so early this morning. I hope you haven't brought news that Langford Manor was damaged by the storm."

"It's minor compared to what I've seen here."

They walked onto the porch. In the brief time Levi had been inside, Banks had assembled the men. They stood in the yard awaiting instructions.

"We hid in the cellar during the worst of it," she said, looking at the destruction. "Moses feels certain it was a tornado. He's gone to check on the crop."

"A tornado? I hadn't thought of that." He whispered a prayer of thanks the damage wasn't worse.

"They aren't terribly common this time of year, but it is possible. Everyone in the house is still asleep since we stayed in the cellar nearly until dawn."

A smile inched its way to his face. "I must say, Mrs. Ellis"—he remembered to address her properly—"your calmness in the face of such a frightening experience is … unexpected."

"I will take that as a compliment, Colonel." Her blue eyes sparked with teasing.

He bowed slightly. "If it suits you, I'll have my men assign the field workers to cleanup details. From the looks of things, the roof of the house, as well as those of some of the outbuildings, will need repair. Preferably before another storm rolls through."

She frowned. "The only carpenter we had departed the day you brought the proclamation. I'm not sure Moses or the others know how to make the repairs, and I haven't the funds to hire someone."

Levi weighed his next words—and the consequences they would bring—before speaking. "As luck would have it, I possess some carpentry skills. I'd be glad to assist Moses and show him what needs to be done."

She stared up at him, her eyes searching his face. "That is very kind of you, Colonel. Thank you."

Their gazes held a long moment before she looked away, a faint blush staining her cheeks.

Corporal Banks approached. He nodded politely to Natalie before addressing Levi. "Sir, we're ready for your orders."

Before Levi could respond, however, the barrel of a rifle poked out the open doorway behind Natalie. Ever so slowly, the rotund woman who'd stopped at Langford Manor the previous day emerged from the shadowed room, her narrowed eyes on him, the weapon trained on his gut.

※ ❧

"Don't move a muscle, Yankee. The judge taught me how to shoot, and I'm not afraid to pull this trigger."

Natalie whirled around to see Cousin Eunice step onto the porch in her dressing gown, her nightcap askew, holding a gun pointed at the colonel. "Eunice, put that down," she exclaimed, fear causing her pulse to race. A sideways glance revealed Corporal Banks already had his revolver out of its holster and aimed at her cousin.

Eunice's gaze flitted to Natalie. "Why are these Bluecoats here?" She used the barrel of the rifle to indicate Colonel Maish. "He's the one I found making himself at home in Langford Manor."

Terrified the woman might accidentally shoot the colonel, Natalie took a careful step toward her. "Cousin Eunice, this is Colonel Maish. He and I have a business agreement that involves the use of Langford Manor." She took another step. "Now, put the gun down before someone gets hurt."

Several tense moments passed before Eunice lowered the weapon. Her glower, however, remained fixed on the colonel. "What kind of business could you possibly have with a Yankee? They aren't to be trusted." She looked at Natalie. "I am disappointed in you, Natalie Ellis. If your mama and daddy could see you now, cavorting with the enemy ..." She *tsk-tsk'd*. "Well, it seems I have come just in time. Whatever your agreement is with this man, we'll end it immediately. The judge taught me a thing or two about the law, too."

With the gun lowered, Natalie stole a peek at the colonel. She found him as she'd expected, his gaze narrowed on Eunice and his fists in tight balls. They twitched several times before his eyes flicked to her.

"Mrs. Ellis." The words were said through clenched teeth. Had she only imagined him using her given name when he arrived, his voice full of concern? "Kindly inform your *relative* that it is against the law to point a weapon at a Union officer." He returned his glare to Eunice. "If she so much as looks at that gun in my presence, I will have Corporal Banks arrest her. Is that understood?"

Natalie nodded.

The colonel turned and stomped down the steps. He and the

corporal made their way to the waiting men, who'd all witnessed the incident.

Eunice muttered a foul word before turning to Natalie. "What on earth has gotten into you? You said the army took over your land without your permission, but you never said anything about an agreement with them."

Inhaling a deep breath, Natalie fought to remain civil. "Langford Manor and Rose Hill are my property. I am doing everything I can to see that they remain so. If allowing the Union Army to set up their camp in a fallow field keeps us fed and clothed, then that is my business."

Eunice's eyes widened. "You dare speak to me in such a tone! Your mother and I were practically sisters growing up."

"I don't mean to be disrespectful." Natalie tempered her frustration. "I'm simply doing the best I can to manage the plantations and see that my son's inheritance remains intact."

The older woman seemed mollified. For the moment, anyway. "You would be wise to keep your eyes on them—especially that arrogant colonel. You mark my words. Thieves and miscreants, all." With that, she huffed noisily and disappeared into the house.

Natalie closed her eyes. Could things get any worse?

A glance toward the men told her they'd received their instructions from Colonel Maish and were now setting about cleaning up the debris left from the storm. He and Corporal Banks stood apart from the group, talking. At one point, they both looked in her direction, and heat rose to her face. What must they think of her outlandish cousin?

She turned to go inside.

"Mrs. Ellis, a word, please."

Colonel Maish's deep voice stopped her. He strode toward the house, an unhappy look on his face.

Before he could commence with his scolding, which surely was his intention, she shook her head. "You needn't subject me to your chastisement, Colonel. I apologize for my cousin's behavior. It was ill-mannered and completely inappropriate of her to point a rifle at you. But you must understand, she's been through a great deal at the hands of unscrupulous men wearing Union uniforms."

He'd reached the bottom of the steps but didn't make to ascend. "How so?" Skepticism reverberated from the two simple words.

"They burned her home before she was allowed to think through the consequences of arguing against the proclamation. It was unnecessary. I am certain she would have, like the rest of us, come to terms with giving the slaves their freedom. Now she, a childless widow, is homeless. Surely you can see how she would be distrustful of anyone wearing a blue coat."

He eyed her a long moment. "While I am sorry your cousin's home was burned—for that has never been something I approve of—it is no excuse for endangering people who had nothing to do with her loss. I may need to confiscate your weapons while she is in residence."

Natalie's back stiffened. "Sir, you would leave us completely defenseless because of an inconsequential incident? I apologized for her behavior. That should be sufficient."

"I don't find having a gun leveled at me inconsequential." He glanced into the house then back to her. "How long will she stay with you?"

She shrugged. "I don't really know. Her arrival took me by surprise. She retired early last night, claiming exhaustion from the long journey. Then the storm arose. We haven't had much opportunity to discuss it." For certain, she *would* discuss it with Eunice. While she wanted to help her cousin as much as possible, the idea of Eunice remaining at Rose Hill indefinitely was simply too unbearable to consider.

His dark gaze narrowed. "Then my advice to you is, keep your eye on her. And your guns. She isn't to be trusted." He turned and strode away.

The warning was nearly identical to that of her cousin's regarding him.

CHAPTER FOURTEEN

With afternoon sunshine beating on his back, Levi stopped to mop his brow with his rolled-up shirt sleeve. High on the roof of Rose Hill Manor there wasn't an ounce of shade or even a lone cloud to offer a respite from the oppressive heat. July in Texas was not for the faint of heart—that was for certain. He hoped his men were following the instructions he'd left with Banks and his staff and not taking advantage of his absence. The hot days made it all too easy to get lazy, especially for the younger men who weren't as disciplined as he'd like.

Glancing at Moses, who continued hammering shingles into place, he marveled at the older man's stamina. They'd been working the better part of the day, measuring and cutting pieces of wood to replace the damaged ones. Climbing up and down the ladders, first onto the kitchen wing roof, then up to the main house, where the two buildings were joined by a covered walkway. Levi wasn't ashamed to admit he was worn out, but Moses kept right on going.

Sitting back on his haunches, he gazed at the view around him. From their lofty vantage point, he could see for miles. Fields, woods, and plains. Far in the distance, following the sun's path, the landscape gave way to gently rolling hills covered in trees. He'd been told they weren't far from the edge of the frontier, where various Indian tribes still made their home. Years ago, he'd longed to head to the wildernesses to seek adventure and excitement. But after four long years of war, boyhood dreams seemed part of another lifetime.

Gazing at the landscape, Levi felt the tug of home pull on his heartstrings. Like many soldiers, he had yet to return to his family despite the war's end. He'd been ordered to Texas soon after Lee surrendered, although skirmishes had continued west of the Mississippi until mid-May and delayed their arrival in Galveston. His brothers, Matthew and Joshua, had both returned to their wives and children. Matthew would have to learn how to walk with only one leg, but he was alive, for which they were grateful. Letters from Ma and Pa and his sisters and brothers all spoke of their eager desire to have Levi home, but that would have to wait until his mission in Texas was complete.

Looking down to the tools that surrounded him, he couldn't help but smile. He'd always had an interest in carpentry, but it hadn't been more than a hobby before the war. Soldiering was what he'd believed he was destined for. His time at West Point only served to confirm it. Now, with the world such a different place than it had been four years ago, even his dreams had been altered. All he wanted was to buy a piece of land not far from his parents and brothers and set up a carpentry shop. He'd build dining room tables where families could gather over meals and laughter, or cradles for newborn babies whose innocence would help heal a nation torn by hatred and war. A simple life, far from the battlefields, was what he yearned for.

The kitchen door hinges squealed from below. A few moments later, Natalie entered his view, walking toward the chicken coop with a basket swinging from her hand. Samuel ran after her. When he caught up with his mother, he held something out, to which Natalie gave a little shriek. She shooed it away. Levi saw a toad leap from the boy's hands and hop across the dirt, Samuel chasing after it. Natalie said something to her son, although Levi couldn't hear the words, and the boy left the toad and followed her around the corner of the coop, out of Levi's view.

He took up his hammer once again and banged a shingle into place, his thoughts not on the roof but on the widow who owned it. Natalie Langford Ellis. The woman was confounding. One minute she was helpless and needy, the next she was standing in defense of her shrewish cousin. One day she was a pampered slave owner, the next she was feeding chickens and hogs. He didn't know what to make of it. Of her. He admired the tenacity it must have taken for her to keep the plantation operating during the war. Despite his deep hatred for the institution of slavery, he had to admit only a strong-willed woman could have accomplished such a feat without a husband or male relative to oversee things.

He glanced at Moses. Natalie had freely admitted the slave—former slave—was the reason the plantation hadn't fallen into ruin. That he'd seen to the planting, harvesting, and upkeep of things for four years, despite there being no person of authority to keep him on the property, baffled Levi. That the man continued to serve Natalie, now as a paid employee, further confused him.

"I 'spect I's gonna need a few mo' shingles cut, Colonel," Moses said, wiping his face with a handkerchief. He removed his hat and ran the cloth over his short-cropped graying hair. "After that, this section o' roof be just like new."

"You've done well, considering you've never patched a roof before."

Moses' smile revealed his pride. "I 'ppreciate that, suh. It's good to learn to do somethin' new, even when you's as old as the hills."

They climbed down the ladder and headed to the barn. Using a fallen tree practically outside the door, they'd taken a two-man crosscut saw and created several drums of timber that morning. While Moses had worked on removing the bark, Levi'd located the tools they'd need to slice the hunks into shingles.

He watched the other man take the froe and mallet to the wood, as Levi had taught him earlier, and his curiosity got the best of him.

"How long have you been at Rose Hill, Moses?"

Without glancing up from his task, Moses said, "Been at Rose Hill six years, but I's at the Langford place 'fore that."

Levi hadn't anticipated that revelation. Had Natalie or her husband purchased the slave from her family? There wasn't a tactful way to ask.

Moses finished the shingle and looked up. "Miz Natalie's papa give me to her when she married Massa George." He handed the shingle to Levi for inspection. "She done asked him to."

"And were you pleased about that?" Levi knew it was none of his business, but the fact that the former slave continued to serve his mistress intrigued him.

Moses seemed to contemplate the question. "I wasn't pleased to leave my family over to the Langford's, but it weren't so far away that I couldn't see them from time to time. 'Specially when Miz Natalie went to see her mama. My Harriet come to be the cook here at Rose Hill a few months later, but our young'uns has to stay at Langford's."

"How many children do you have?" Levi asked, recalling he'd only seen the one little boy.

A pained expression filled the big man's face. "The Lawd blessed us with six chillens. He done took three home, from the same yellow fever that took Miz Natalie's folks. Massa George sold my two oldest boys after that. I wanted them here, o' course, but he feared the fever might spread over to Rose Hill. Ain't seen them since."

A swift stab of remorse struck Levi. "I'm sorry, Moses. I shouldn't have pried."

"It ain't prying to ask a man 'bout his family. The Lawd giveth, and the Lawd taketh away. That just life. We's blessed with Isaac after all that sadness." He smiled. "That boy bring us as much sunshine as the sun itself."

Levi watched Moses return to cutting out shingles. Now more than ever he wanted to ask how the former slave could stay with Natalie, especially after the tale he'd just told. Her husband had sold away his sons, for pity's sake. It was unthinkable that Moses remained on Rose Hill land despite having the freedom to leave, yet there he stood, cutting shingles for her roof. Levi had heard some slaves were so attached to their white owners they couldn't imagine living anywhere else, but he didn't think that applied to Moses. He had a suspicion the man's reasoning went deeper than that.

The sun sat low on the western horizon by the time they finished patching the damaged roof. There were still two barns and several quarter houses that would require repairs in the coming days.

After climbing down from the ladder, Levi stretched his back muscles, cramped from hours of bending over.

"I wondered if you two were going to work into the night."

He turned to find Natalie standing on the kitchen porch. The aroma of roasted turkey wafted out the open door, reminding Levi that their noon meal of sliced ham sandwiched between thick slices of bread had been hours ago.

"We wanted to finish the main house." Levi was torn between feeling aggravated with her after hearing Moses' story and finding her breathtakingly beautiful in the waning light. "Moses did excellent work. You should have no fear of a leaky roof come the next storm."

She sent a warm smile to the big man, who in turn grinned under the praise.

Samuel arrived on the porch. "Can we eat now? I'm hungry."

"Is that turkey I's smellin'?" Moses asked, ruffling the boy's hair as he moved to the doorway.

"Yep!"

Samuel and Moses disappeared through the open door. When Levi's gaze met Natalie's again, she chewed her bottom lip.

"Colonel," she said, a note of uncertainty in her voice. "We would be honored if you would join us for supper. After all your hard work on our behalf, we can't let you leave without showing our thanks."

The invitation took him by surprise. The thought of riding back to camp on an empty stomach did not appeal, but to sit in Rose Hill's grand dining room, making polite conversation with Natalie and her rude cousin, was something his tired brain and body were not up for.

"Cousin Eunice has already retired for the evening," she said, guessing his hesitation. "The others wanted to wait for Moses."

He frowned. "The others?"

"Harriet, Carolina, and Lottie. Samuel and I have taken our meals with the servants in the kitchen ever since you brought the proclamation." She grinned. "Eunice was horrified, of course, and demanded her dinner brought up on a tray."

He couldn't help but chuckle. The woman was a paradox, to be sure. "I accept your invitation then."

They entered the kitchen, where the four servants, Samuel, and Isaac, all gathered, talking and laughing. Seeing Levi, Moses smiled and gave a nod of approval. The long table in the center of the room was set for eight. That she'd planned for him to join them all along sent a wave of pleasure coursing through him.

"There's a wash stand there"—she indicated the basin near the door—"if you'd like to make use of it."

He did, gratefully. While he washed his hands and arms, the others took their places at the table. He joined them and saw that the seat at one end had been left vacant. Moses sat at the other end with Natalie to his right and Harriet to his left. Samuel and Isaac, he noted, would flank him.

When everyone was seated, Moses stood. "A few weeks ago, this here turkey made the mistake of comin' onto the plantation." The amusement of those around the table must have satisfied him. He grinned and continued. "I hung him in the smoke house, thinkin' we'd save him for somethin' special. Well, today ain't Thanksgivin', but we shore is thankful tonight. The Lawd done spared us durin' the storm, and He sent us a helper to get things back to right."

All eyes turned to Levi. He gave a nod of acknowledgment, meeting Natalie's unreadable expression last.

The big man bowed his head, and everyone followed suit. The blessing he prayed was more eloquent than Levi had heard from any preacher back home. After the "amen" was said—Samuel and

Isaac adding their own shouted version amid giggles—and the food was passed around the table, Levi took in the odd gathering. From former slaves to their white mistress to her son to him, an officer in the Union Army and an abolitionist. All seated at the same table, sharing a meal.

A few months ago, this would have been an impossibility.

Perhaps, he thought as he stabbed a tender piece of roasted turkey, there was hope for their country after all.

❧

From the front porch, Natalie watched the new dawn arrive. With her legs tucked beneath her on the sofa, a cup of chicory root coffee in hand, she wondered what the day had in store for them. So much had happened in the past week, it was difficult to know how to prepare her emotions.

Surveying the area, she was pleased to see much of the debris from the storm had been cleared. The fallen tree near the barn lay in pieces, and she'd learned over supper last night that the colonel and Moses would chop the rest into firewood once all the new shingles were in place.

Warmth spread through her as she recalled the evening meal. While Moses and the colonel worked long hours on the roof, she'd grown increasingly nervous. An invitation to join them would be the polite and mannerly thing to do, but to have a Yankee officer at her table … well, there were simply too many reasons why that was not a good idea. Cousin Eunice being one. Samuel another. Both had suffered loss because of the Yankees. Samuel was too young to understand that Colonel Maish had been their enemy until recently, but someday he would ask questions Natalie dreaded answering. The less confusion in the boy's mind about the war and whose side was right or wrong, the better.

But Colonel Maish had been the perfect guest. He'd easily conversed with Moses and the others, discussing a variety of topics as though he dined with former slaves every day. When he mentioned his home in Pennsylvania, at Carolina's inquiry, Natalie nearly choked on her bite of turnip. She held her breath, listening for reference of a wife, but if he had one waiting for him, he didn't reveal it. He only spoke of his brothers, and that was simply to state they had returned home from the war safely.

Voices from the quarter drifted across the dawn. Several people milled in front of the small cabins, starting cook fires and preparing for the day. With harvest still a few weeks away, they weren't required to rise as early as they would be soon enough. Then, they would work sunup to sundown, toiling in the heat over the prickly pods that held the tufts of cotton captive. She wondered, not for the first time, if they had enough workers for the laborious job. But she'd signed an agreement with the Union Army to provide thirty workers. They, plus the two dozen Rose Hill former slaves who'd chosen to remain on the plantation, would have to suffice.

Standing, she gazed at the vast fields. When the harvest was in, the hired workers would move on. Though she would receive payment for her cotton this year, she owed money to the bank, owed more for taxes. If there were anything left over, it wouldn't go far, especially now that Moses and the others were employees, requiring wages. She could barter with them for food and housing, as Colonel Maish suggested, but eventually, they would want cash payments for their labor. How could she keep the plantation running without money to pay workers? The situation seemed impossible.

Looking west, she wondered, not for the first time, if she should accept her sister-in-law's invitation to come to Oregon. After Luther had passed, leaving Rose Hill and all its vast responsibilities to Natalie, Adella wrote and begged Natalie to bring Samuel and come live with them. That Samuel's half-sister also lived with Adella was a concern, mainly because Natalie wasn't sure how to feel about the child her husband had fathered with a slave. Yet despite the hardships and fear she faced if she remained in Texas, this was their home. Rose Hill and Langford Manor were Samuel's inheritance. She couldn't simply give them up.

But everything had changed. Samuel might lose his inheritance after all. With slave labor, there had always been plenty of people to complete the work necessary to plant and harvest the cotton, corn, and wheat. Without them, she didn't see how the plantation could continue to operate.

Luther had been right all along, she realized. Rose Hill could cease to exist without slaves.

Two riders rode up the lane toward the house. Her heart tripped over itself when she recognized Colonel Maish's blue uniform. She had to admit she looked forward to his presence on the plantation today, continuing with the repairs to the barns and other damaged roofs. She frowned when she glanced at the second rider, though. She'd assumed it was Corporal Banks, but as they came out of the shadows, she saw it wasn't the Negro soldier.

Alexander Lopez entered the yard, a dark scowl on his face.

CHAPTER FIFTEEN

"Señora Ellis, I am relieved to see you are safe."

Levi watched Lopez swing out of his saddle before his mount had time to come to a full stop. He rushed up the steps to Natalie and took her hand in his, grazing her knuckles with his lips.

"I arrived in town late last night with plans to visit you this morning. In the café, before I could even order breakfast, I heard talk of the storm. I came as fast as I could."

Annoyance coiled in Levi's belly at the man's familiarity. While Natalie didn't appear overly joyful to see Lopez, she didn't withdraw her hand from his grip.

"As you can see, the storm did some damage, but nothing that can't be repaired."

Her gaze flitted to Levi. It didn't go unnoticed by the *Tejano*.

He turned unfriendly eyes to Levi. "I met the colonel on the road to Rose Hill. He informed me he is helping with the repairs." A chilly smile lifted his lips. "Neglecting the Union Army's mission in order to help a beautiful widow, eh, Colonel? My, how one's priorities can change with the wind."

Levi dismounted, ignoring the barb. He directed his attention to Natalie, who withdrew her hand from Lopez before looking at him. "Mrs. Ellis." He nodded politely even as he wished to snatch her away from the man. "I will keep several workers on cleanup detail today, but the others can return to the fields. My men will supervise, as I'll need Moses' help again with the shingles. He became quite adept at cutting them yesterday."

"Very well, Colonel."

"Natalie, what is this all about?" Lopez said, his Spanish accent thick. "I understand the army's need to camp on your family's land, but what purpose do they have here at Rose Hill?"

She glanced between Levi and Lopez. Levi couldn't tell if she was annoyed by the question or hesitant to reveal the business agreement she had with the Union Army.

Before she could answer, however, her outlandish cousin bustled through the open door. At least she wasn't wearing her nightclothes or carrying a gun this time.

"Natalie Ellis, what are you doing entertaining men at this hour?"

Levi saw Natalie's fist clench briefly at her side before she released it.

"Cousin Eunice, I'm not entertaining anyone. May I present Señor Lopez, a friend. He heard about the storm and was concerned for our well-being. Señor Lopez, this is my mother's cousin, Mrs. Porter. She's staying at Rose Hill."

The rotund cousin eyed Lopez. "I take it you're Mexican."

Lopez inclined his head. "I was born in *Tejas*, but of course that was when *Tejas* belonged to *Méjico*."

"My late husband, Judge Leftwidge Porter, was a congressman in Shelby County." Pride practically dripped from the statement. "He had many friends who were Mexican. I told him frequently to stay on their friendly side after that scoundrel Santa Anna stopped causing trouble and went back to Mexico. 'It won't do us any good to keep enemies,' says I. The judge agreed."

Levi held in a chuckle when he saw the look of uncertainty pass over Lopez's face as he studied the odd woman.

"Well, don't keep your company standing on the porch, Natalie," Eunice said, retreating into the house. "Invite him in for breakfast."

Natalie closed her eyes for a moment before offering a polite smile to Lopez. "Señor, please, won't you join us for breakfast? Especially if yours was interrupted on my behalf."

"I would be delighted," he said, bowing. He sent Levi a

triumphant look.

"Colonel?"

Levi switched his attention back to Natalie. "You are welcome to join us as well."

The smug look vanished from Lopez's face, much to Levi's satisfaction. "Thank you, Mrs. Ellis, but I ate before leaving Langford Manor."

Was that disappointment in her eyes?

"Come, Natalie," Lopez said, extending his arm. "I'm sure the colonel has work to do."

Levi watched Lopez escort her inside. He'd never been jealous of another man his entire life, and he certainly wasn't about to start now. So why did he have the insane urge to race up the steps and knock the *Tejano* into the next county?

"Mornin', Colonel."

He turned to find Moses standing at the corner of the house. How long had he been there?

"Good morning, Moses. I hope you're ready for another long day."

Moses chuckled. "Is there any other kind?"

"Before we get started"—Levi glanced in the direction of the bachelor's quarters—"I could use a cup a coffee. You're welcome to join me."

A wide smile filled Moses' face. "Yessuh, Colonel. Thank ya."

They made their way to the small building. His men were already in the field, but the coffee pot sat on the stovetop and was still quite warm and at least half full. Levi poured two cups and handed one to Moses. They carried their drinks to the porch. Moses seemed to savor the coffee, almost as though he'd never tasted the pungent drink before. Levi was poised to ask him about it when Natalie exited the house under the covered walkway, headed to the kitchen. When she spied them, she came to a stop. Her brow rose in question.

"We thought we'd enjoy a cup of coffee before we get to work."

Levi held up his cup.

Her gaze went to the cup in his hand then to the one Moses held. "Coffee? Do you mean … *real* coffee?"

Levi grinned. "Yes, *real* coffee. Would you care for some? I think there's still a bit left in the pot."

Her pink tongue moistened her lips. She glanced back at the house then at Moses, who looked as happy as a kid with a new slingshot. A sly grin crept up her face. "Yes, I would love some coffee."

She stepped off the wooden walkway and crossed the grassy yard that separated the two buildings. Levi went inside and poured the remains of the coffee into a cup, chagrined to see grounds in the bottom. Maybe he should make a new pot.

"We haven't had real coffee in several years."

He turned and found her standing in the doorway. "I'm afraid this is the bottom of the barrel," he said, handing her the cup. "I can make a fresh pot if you'd like."

"That isn't necessary, Colonel." She lifted it to her face. Closing her eyes, she inhaled the aroma. "Oh, my." Her eyes opened, sparkling with merriment. Taking a dainty sip, she sighed. Her gaze met his. "It sounds so silly now, but I think, of all the supplies we could no longer purchase after the blockades were put into place, I missed coffee most."

Now he understood her and Moses' reactions. He turned, dug through a box of supplies sitting next to the stove, and found a container of coffee beans. "Here," he said, offering it to her. "The men have plenty. They won't miss this."

Her eyes widened as she looked at the metal container and then at him. "I … I couldn't accept it, Colonel. You've already given us a crate of oranges. Not to mention the repairs to the plantation … and the gloves."

"I would not be able to enjoy my morning cup of coffee now that I'm aware of your suffering," he teased, pleased to see her smile. "If you don't accept this, you will henceforth be responsible for ruining my day."

She giggled. "Well, we wouldn't want that." She accepted the coffee tin.

They exchanged satisfied smiles. Hers for the coffee. His for bringing pleasure to her once again.

"There you are, Natalie." They turned to find Eunice standing in the doorway to the main house, hands on her ample hips. "You went to get butter and never returned." The woman's eyes narrowed on Levi as though he had detained Natalie on purpose.

"I'm coming." After gulping the remaining coffee in the most unladylike fashion, she handed the empty cup to Levi. "Thank you, Colonel." She hurried toward the kitchen. A moment later, she whooshed past again, this time carrying a small plate of butter, and followed her cousin into the house.

When the door closed behind her, Levi glanced at Moses. The man's lips twitched, though he seemed to fight off a full-fledged grin.

"Women are strange creatures, Moses."

The other man nodded gravely. "Yessuh." He took a sip of his drink and smiled. "But this shore is good coffee."

Levi couldn't agree more.

❧❧

"Tell me, Señor Lopez, what is your business?"

Cousin Eunice eyed the man sitting across the table from her. She had monopolized the conversation throughout the meal, regaling them with stories from Shelby County and her colorful life as the wife of Judge Porter, a man who, according to Eunice, could do no wrong. Now it seemed she was determined to interrogate their guest.

With a quick glance at Natalie, Alexander said, "I prefer to be involved in various enterprises rather than settling for only one to take all my time."

Eunice squinted. "That sounds like an excuse to flit from one fancy to another. The judge always said you could ascertain a man's dependability by how long he'd been at his occupation. Whether farmer or store owner or however one chooses to make his living, steadfastness is a sure sign you can trust the man."

An uncomfortable silence followed her pronouncement. Natalie cleared her throat, hoping to bring the meal to an end. "I'm sure Señor Lopez is a fine man of integrity, Cousin. He and I have done business for over a year now, and I've always been able to depend upon him."

She glanced at Alexander, whose warm smile said he appreciated her confidence.

"And what business is that?" Eunice's heavy brows arched.

"Señor Lopez has leased Rose Hill pastures for his cattle."

"Cattle, you say. Well, that is a fine business, indeed. The judge knew many cattlemen. I suspect with the war over and the ports opening soon, you should turn a nice profit." Eunice gave Natalie a pointed look. "A successful man would be a fine catch for a widow left to run a plantation all alone."

Natalie refused to acknowledge the blatant hint. She addressed Alexander. "My brother-in-law is raising horses in Oregon, but in Adella's last letter, she said the desperate need for beef in the northwest has convinced him to try his hand at cattle. Perhaps you have some advice I can pass along to Seth."

Before he could reply, Eunice *tsk tsk'd*. "Such a disgrace, Adella Rose running off with that overseer. And taking a Negro baby with her. Why, whatever was she thinking?"

The clock on the mantel ticked in the awkward silence.

"I am sure your relative will do well," Alexander finally said, as though Eunice had never spoken. "Grass and water are all cattle need." He stood, much to Natalie's relief. She certainly did not wish her cousin to continue her remarks regarding the Negro baby Adella was raising. No one, to Natalie's knowledge, knew the truth about Mara's parentage, but one could never be certain.

"Ladies, I wish to thank you for the delicious meal." He came around to assist first Natalie with her chair and then Eunice.

The plump woman seemed pleased by the gentlemanly gesture. "I hope you will stop by again, Señor. I should like to get to know Natalie's suitor."

Natalie's eyes widened. "Cousin Eunice, you are mistaken. Señor Lopez is a friend, that's all."

Alexander reached for Natalie's hand and dropped a kiss on the back of it. "I confess I hope to change that." He let go of her hand and turned to Eunice. "My sincere wish is to court your cousin. It would be my honor to get acquainted with you when I visit."

Eunice's stubby lashes fluttered under the handsome man's attention. "Of course, Señor, of course." She faced Natalie. "My dear, as your mother's closest relative, I give you permission to accept this man's request to court. I will act as chaperone, of course. A woman widowed after only two years of marriage is more vulnerable to temptation than a maiden, I should think."

Heat flooded Natalie's body. Whether it was brought on by fury or mortification, she knew not. Turning to Alexander, she didn't meet his gaze, too embarrassed over Eunice's insinuation. "Thank you for stopping by to check on us. I need to see to Samuel now. Good day, Señor."

She fled the dining room knowing she'd been incredibly rude and wishing she could find the nearest hole and crawl inside.

A few minutes later, while she sat with Samuel at a small table in his room, she heard the sound of a horse galloping away from the house. She could only hope her cousin hadn't humiliated her further after she'd escaped their presence, but she wouldn't put it past the meddlesome woman. She had yet to find an opportunity to sit Eunice down and discuss the future, but suffice it to say, Natalie was considering taking drastic measures to rid herself of her relative. She just didn't know exactly what those measures would entail.

"Mama, what's this letter?"

Natalie looked down to where Samuel's pudgy finger pointed to the letter *K* in his primer.

"That is the letter K. If you were a prince, you would grow up to be a king. King starts with the letter K." She made the sound a *K* makes.

Samuel watched her mouth. "Like cat."

"Yes, they make a similar sound, but cat begins with the letter C. Do you remember how to spell it?"

With slow, careful strokes, Samuel set out to write the word they'd practiced on his slate. She smiled, full of motherly pride. Her son was growing up so fast. These were bittersweet days for her. While she wanted him to keep his childish innocence and his need for her intact, she couldn't help but marvel at the growth that had taken place in the last few months, not only in his stature but in his independence. Colonel Maish's words reminding her that her son would be a man before she was ready pushed forward. Once again, she wondered if he spoke from a father's perspective.

A movement at the open door drew her attention.

Carolina stood in the hallway with her lips pressed together and an odd look on her face. Natalie could only guess what mischief the young woman had found. "Yes, Carolina?"

She took hesitant steps into the room. "Miz Natalie, I's wonderin'…" She bit her bottom lip.

"About?"

"I's wonderin'…" Her eyes darted to Samuel, who continued to work on forming the letter A, his small tongue poking out the corner of his mouth. When Carolina met Natalie's gaze again, she brought her shoulders back. "I's wonderin' if you would teach me to read."

Natalie stared at the servant. The request was certainly not what she'd expected. In all her days, it had never entered her mind to teach a Negro to read. She had a suspicion her sister-in-law had defied the rules and taught Jeptha—a Rose Hill slave until he ran away—but Natalie hadn't seen the need to tempt fate with such an act. Slaves had no reason to learn their letters anyway. It wasn't as though they needed that knowledge to pick cotton.

Shame pierced her conscience.

Wasn't that the mentality that kept people in bondage? A mentality she herself had subscribed to until recently? An entire war had been fought, thousands of lives lost, because of that sort of thinking. She considered Moses, in possession of a Bible all these years with no way to read the precious words. She glanced at her son, who was busy drawing the childish image of a cat's face next to his correctly spelled word. Why shouldn't Carolina and Moses and the others have the same opportunity as her son to learn their letters? In their newfound freedom, who knew what prospects might come their way if only they could read and write?

"I would be proud to teach you to read, Carolina," she finally said, her voice full of emotion.

Carolina's eyes rounded. "You would?"

"Yes, I would." Natalie smiled. "We can begin this afternoon if you like."

A smile wider than Natalie had ever seen before filled Carolina's face. "I would, Miz Natalie. I shore enough would."

After the servant departed, Natalie stared out the window, half listening to Samuel's chatter about kings and princes. A warm tear trailed down her cheek, and she wiped it away. Six years ago, she'd come to Rose Hill a spoiled, self-centered young woman who never gave a second thought to the slaves or to anyone else. Adella tried to talk to her about it on more than one occasion, but Natalie wouldn't listen. It had taken war and hardship and pain to pry her eyes open so she could see herself for the first time. Oh, how she prayed God approved of the woman she was becoming, one hard-fought struggle at a time.

"Mama, do you like my cat?"

She smiled at her son. "Very much." She snagged him into a ticklish embrace and planted a kiss on his soft cheek as he snuggled against her. "Your mama is going to be a teacher, Samuel," she whispered into his hair, contentment rising up from somewhere deep, practically filling her to overflowing. "What do you think about that?"

CHAPTER SIXTEEN

Laughter and happy voices drifted to where Levi and Moses worked on the final repairs to the barn roof. Although Moses hadn't at first been keen on being up so high, more than once, Levi found the man staring off into the distance. The view *was* amazing.

"It doesn't sound like much work is getting done down there," he said, lifting the canteen of lukewarm water to his lips. With the barn roof being far more difficult to access than those of the house and quarter cabins, they'd limited the number of trips up and down the steep ladder by bringing all their supplies, water, and even their lunch in the first few trips.

Moses grinned. "I's thinkin' the same thing, suh. Thought at first it just the chillens, but I fairly certain I heard my Harriet and Carolina, too. Don't know what they's doin', but it shore sound joyful."

Joyful. Yes, it did sound joyful. Levi suspected the former slaves hadn't had much opportunity to experience that feeling. What joy was there in bondage? In being owned by another human being?

He recalled the day Pa had handed him the book *Uncle Tom's Cabin,* hailed as the greatest book of the ages. Levi had been eighteen years old, full of himself and his dreams and eager to start his military career at West Point. Slavery was an evil institution, to be sure, but he couldn't see that it had anything to do with him. His future was in the frontier, where slavery wasn't permitted. Pa was insistent, however, that Levi read it, and the book very nearly changed the course of his life.

Glancing over to Moses where he carefully fit a new shingle into place, Levi wondered what that man would think of the sensational book. Levi suspected every slave could relate to the trials and tribulations the book's characters experienced. Even President Lincoln, it was said, credited Harriet Beecher Stowe's work as being a catalyst for the war. With the horrors of slavery exposed, the people in the north became incensed. Levi himself had considered abandoning his plans to attend West Point and instead join the abolitionist movement and help slaves attain freedom through the Underground Railroad. Pa declared Levi could do more good for bondsmen as a statesman or lawyer, careers that many military men chose after serving. He'd heeded Pa's advice to continue with his plans, but the fire in his belly to help slaves gain their freedom had never waned.

Levi hammered several more shingles into place and surveyed their work. "I believe that should do it, Moses. You'll know when the next rainstorm comes if you have a few gaps here and there, but I feel certain we've patched it well."

"Yessuh, I think you's right. I 'spect I'll go down yonder and take a look to see if daylight comes through, just to be sure."

They carefully made their way to the ground. While Moses entered the cavernous building, the laughter coming from the side of the main house had Levi curious. Not wishing to disturb whomever he found enjoying themselves, he quietly made his way to the end of the porch and peered around the corner.

Just down from the house in the shade of a giant tree, Natalie sat on the grass with Harriet, Carolina, and Lottie, whom Levi recalled was Eunice's maid. The three servants' backs were to him, but he could clearly see Natalie. Samuel and Isaac lay on their stomachs nearby, their knees bent and bare feet waving in the air, obscuring from Levi's view whatever it was they were looking at.

Natalie held up a child's slate. "This is the letter B," she said, making sure each woman noted the large, handwritten letter. "Remember, it is the second letter in the alphabet. A, *B*, C, D, and so on. Book begins with the letter B. Boy. Baby. Bird. B. Buh. Now, try to find the letter B in your book."

Levi watched, stunned, as the women each took a book from her lap and began searching the printed words for the letter. Every so often, someone would look up to study the slate, then bend her head back to the book.

"Here it is," Carolina shouted a few moments later. The others cheered and laughed. She handed the book to Natalie, pointing to the letter.

Natalie smiled and nodded, speaking in tones too low for Levi to make out the words.

"Well, I'll be." Moses' incredulous voice sounded from behind Levi.

He turned to find a matching expression on the man's face. "I take it you didn't know Mrs. Ellis was giving reading lessons."

"I shore didn't. No, suh, I shore didn't."

They watched a while longer. After Natalie showed them the letter C, the women searched for it. When Harriet was the first to shout that she'd found it, moisture shone in Moses' eyes.

"Praise the Lawd! Praise the Good Lawd," he said, unashamedly wiping the wetness away. "I done asked the Lawd to send us some he'p with our letters, and here He done sent Miz Natalie."

They retreated behind the house.

"I once had a massa who taught me a few letters years ago," Moses said as they walked back to the barn toward the workshop. "He a preacher man and give'd me his Bible when he passed on. I cain't read but a word here and there, so it don't make no sense. I's askin' the Lawd just this mornin' iffen He want me to share the Good News in that book, He gonna have to send me some he'p." He grinned. "Guess He shore 'nough did."

Levi watched the man put the tools away. While he knew it was none of his business, he couldn't keep the question that had bothered him since coming to Rose Hill from slipping past his lips.

"I don't understand why you and Harriet and Carolina stay here with Mrs. Ellis." He planted both hands on the workbench. "You are free to go, to leave the place where you were enslaved. Are you so loyal to your former owner that you can't envision living anywhere else?"

Moses hung a hammer on two nails in the wall. He heaved a sigh and looked at Levi. "I don't 'spect you to understand, Colonel, suh. You ain't never been a slave. But best I can explain it, even though I's a slave here at Rose Hill before freedom come, it still my home. Miz Natalie, she just a little chile when her pappy buys me. It not her fault I's a slave."

"But she could have freed you after her husband and father-in-law died."

"Shore she coulda, but then what? What's a free Negro gonna do here in Texas? Ain't no white person gonna hire 'em. Can't buy land to farm. Weren't no Union Army to he'p us. Them patterollers just as soon kill a free Negro as they would a slave. Don't make no never mind to them."

These were realities Levi had not considered. The problems the free men and women faced today were the same problems they'd have faced before the war started. Perhaps more so, given the facts Moses had just laid out. Simply having freedom handed to them did not mean all their problems would go away.

"I think I'm beginning to understand." Levi glanced toward the grassy area, but he could no longer hear the happy voices. It was nearly the supper hour, so they'd probably stopped the lessons for today.

"Don't misunderstand me, Colonel," Moses said, a solemn expression on his face. "I's thankful for freedom. Wouldn't never want to belong to nobody again. My Isaac can grow to be a man and do anythin' he want to make a livin'. Some o' them Negroes you brung in to work them fields is fearful the gov'ment gonna change their mind and make us slaves again. That boy with the brands on his face ..." Moses shook his head. "He trouble. He say he gonna get hisseff a gun and kill any white man who try to make him a slave again."

Levi didn't like the sound of that. "Maybe I should speak to them. Assure them the government will never allow slavery again."

Moses shrugged. "I 'spect it can't hurt. But you got to understand, we was slaves 'cuz the gov'ment said so. Now we not slaves 'cuz the gov'ment said so. What's to stop them from changing it back again?"

He could see their point. "Too many men died fighting to end slavery. Our country will never go back to the way things were."

"That's good to hear, Colonel, suh."

Levi followed the big man from the barn, realizing he didn't know as much about slavery and freedom as he thought he did.

※ ※

Natalie carried a stack of dirty dishes from the table to the washtub. Behind her, Colonel Maish arm-wrestled Samuel while Isaac and Moses had their own arm-wrestling match at the opposite end of the table. Their laughter, grunts, and groans filled the kitchen.

"Miz Natalie, Lottie here will do them dishes," Carolina said, carrying a serving dish that now held only traces of the delicious beef stew Harriet had made for supper, along with cornbread and greens from the garden. Colonel Maish, she'd noticed, had enjoyed three helpings of stew, much to Harriet's satisfaction.

Lottie offered a smile. "I happy to do 'em, Miz Natalie. Since we come to Rose Hill, I been grateful not to have to cook meals for Miz Eunice. I don't mind cleanin' up."

Cousin Eunice had again refused to join them in the kitchen for the evening meal, especially when she learned the colonel would be their guest once more. No one seemed too upset over her absence.

"Thank you, Lottie." Natalie glanced at the young woman's protruding belly. "We don't want you on your feet unnecessarily, though." She lowered her voice so only the two other women could hear over the ruckus coming from the table. "I remember how my feet would swell in the evenings when I carried Samuel. When is the baby due?"

Lottie smoothed a hand over her big belly. "I 'spect it gettin' close. Seem like it be 'bout Christmastime when I suspect I's carryin' this little one."

Natalie didn't ask about the father. Such questions were better left unasked.

"You go on to the porch and sit a spell, Miz Natalie," Carolina said, tying on an apron to cover her red plaid skirt. She cast a quick glance toward the colonel. "I 'spect the colonel might enjoy sittin' out yonder in the swing 'fore he has to ride back to Langford Manor."

The competition between Samuel and the colonel had ended—Samuel won, of course—and the man turned toward the women, obviously hearing Carolina's enthusiastic suggestion. Heat filled her cheeks under his gaze.

"Did I hear something about a swing?" he said, a teasing tone in his deep voice.

"Yes!" Samuel jumped up and down, tugging on the colonel's hand. "Come on. I'll show you."

Merriment glittered in Levi's brown eyes when he looked at Natalie. "Mrs. Ellis, won't you join us?"

With the others in the room pretending to be busy—of course, she knew they were all listening—she chose her words carefully. "A few minutes on the porch would be nice before I ready Samuel for bed."

As she went out the door, Samuel tugging the colonel along behind her, she heard sniggers that sounded very much like they came from Carolina. Frowning, Natalie decided she would have to teach the sassy young woman how to spell *decorum* and learn its meaning.

The three walked around the porch to the front of the house. Samuel ran to the swing and crawled up, his dirty, bare feet sticking out with no hope of reaching the floor.

"Come on, Co'nel. Swing with me." He grinned as Colonel Maish settled next to him, the rusty chains groaning under his weight. He glanced up as if to make certain the swing wasn't in danger of collapsing.

From her place near the railing, Natalie watched as he gently pushed them into motion. Samuel giggled then snuggled up to the colonel's side. Natalie wasn't the only one surprised by the action. The colonel looked up at her, uncertainty in his eyes before he glanced back down at Samuel. The little boy yawned and snuggled deeper into the colonel's arm.

"Maybe I should take him on to bed now." She didn't want the big military man to feel uncomfortable. Playing with the little boy was a nice gesture, but having a child make himself at home on you was another matter entirely.

"No," both Samuel and the colonel said.

When they grinned at each other, she knew she'd lost that battle.

"Come swing with us, Mama. There's room." Samuel gathered his legs up, inadvertently squishing into the colonel.

She sent him an apologetic look, but he didn't seem to mind the closeness of the sweaty little boy.

"Please, join us." The warmth in his voice sent chills racing up her arms.

Once she was settled on the other side of Samuel, the colonel put them into a soothing back and forth motion. With the sun setting the western horizon ablaze with color and the night creatures beginning their unique songs, she couldn't think of a more perfect end to an extraordinary day.

"Moses and I saw you teaching the women their letters," he said, his voice gentle. When she turned to him, the tenderness in his eyes nearly took her breath away. "That is a remarkable gift you're giving them."

Samuel yawned again. Curling into a ball, he lay his head on the colonel's lap and closed his eyes. Embarrassed, she reached to remove him, but the colonel stopped her with a hand on her arm.

"He's fine. Let him sleep."

She leaned back against the swing, very aware of the warm

place where his hand had touched her. They sat in silence for a while before she responded to his comment.

"I see now how selfish it was of us to forbid the slaves to learn to read and write," she said quietly. "I'm ashamed I never thought of it before." She looked up and found him watching her, the details of his face shadowed in the waning light. "I'm also ashamed to admit it wasn't my idea to teach them. Carolina asked to learn to read. When Harriet heard what we were doing, she and Lottie asked to join us."

"Moses said some of the freed people are fearful the government is going to change their minds and reinstitute slavery."

Her eyes rounded. "That isn't possible, is it?"

He shook his head, looking down at a sleeping Samuel. "No. Neither our children nor our children's children will ever have to fight a war because of slavery."

While his assurances brought a measure of peace, they conjured an image of a wife and children waiting for him in Pennsylvania.

"I'm sure you must be eager to return home to your family." If he did indeed have a wife, she was certain Mrs. Maish would not appreciate him sitting on the porch with Natalie. Best to remind him of his responsibilities and have it out in the open.

"I am," he said, a smile lifting the corner of his mouth. "I miss Ma's cooking and Pa's corny jokes."

Natalie smiled, but his answer did nothing to relieve her anxiety over whether or not a wife waited for him.

"And your children?"

He glanced at her, confusion tugging his brow. "I don't have children." He looked down to Samuel. "I always thought I'd be a soldier and wouldn't have time for a family. But now, after four years of war, I'm done with the military. As soon as I'm finished in Texas, I plan to go back to Pennsylvania and open a carpentry shop." His eyes met hers. "And hopefully, one day I'll fall in love with a beautiful woman, and we'll have a dozen children."

Relief burst from her lips in the form of a laugh. "A dozen

children! My, I hope your future wife doesn't plan on getting any sleep for two decades."

His hearty laugh made her laugh all the more. Samuel stirred, and they shushed each other, shoulders still shaking.

"Will you ever remarry?"

The quiet question caught her off guard. "I … I don't know." Señor Lopez came to mind. If he and her cousin had their way, the *Tejano* would come courting soon. But marriage to him? She simply couldn't imagine it.

"Samuel will need a man in his life, to teach him those things a father teaches a son."

She knew he was right. Samuel didn't like Alexander, though, which didn't bode well for a father-son relationship.

Her eyes drifted from her sleeping son to the handsome face of the colonel, a man Samuel clearly adored. From what she'd seen of the way he interacted with the boy, he would make a wonderful father someday. Warmth swirled in her belly with the thought.

"Do you mind if I ask when your husband was killed?"

The question doused her romantic musings like a bucket of water to an errant flame. She was a Confederate soldier's widow, and her son's father had been killed by a Union soldier very much like the one sitting on the swing. It would do well to remember such truths before she allowed her heart to do something foolish.

"George rode away from Rose Hill believing the war would only last a few weeks. He joined the Confederate Army of Northern Virginia because he'd been born there and wanted to defend his birthplace against the Yankees." She looked down at Samuel to be certain the boy was asleep. She didn't want him to hear the sad end his father had met. "He died in the battle at Manassas Junction," she said softly. "Luther wrote to everyone he knew in Virginia, desperate in his grief to learn the details of what happened. We eventually received a letter from one of the soldiers George served with. He said a Union officer on horseback shot George, but when he didn't die right away, the officer dismounted and ran him through with his saber."

She closed her eyes, a slight shudder coursing through her. Though she hadn't loved George, nor had they been happy in their marriage, she wouldn't have wished such a horrible death for him. Luther had gone insane after reading the letter and had passed away a few months later. Those dark days were not ones she desired to revisit.

The colonel departed a short time later, acting almost as though he could not get away quickly enough. Had he been offended? With no way to answer the question, she carried Samuel up to bed, his arms wrapped around her neck and his legs around her waist. She'd been quite candid in her description of George's death, but it wasn't the colonel's fault George fell in his first battle. The colonel had most likely been far from Manassas Junction when her husband's end came. Perhaps he simply didn't like being reminded of the atrocities that took place under the guise of war.

It would do well, she decided, to avoid such talk with Colonel Maish from now on.

CHAPTER SEVENTEEN

Levi exited General Granger's office in Austin, stepping into the Texas sunshine after too many hours of sitting through meetings and discussions with the general and a dozen of his top officers. They'd accomplished a great deal, including plans to institute the Freedmen's Bureau, the organization Congress had established in March to help the former slaves acclimate themselves to their newfound freedom. Once in place, the bureau would open branches in all the inhabited areas of the state, bringing relief to the thousands of refugees, both black and white, who were homeless and jobless. The bureau would provide rations and protection and would even administer land abandoned by Confederates. The key to promoting peace and goodwill throughout the state, General Granger and others believed, depended upon the creation of a new labor system followed by the education of the Negro. Both would take time.

Levi headed toward his tent, sobered by how much work still remained. *Reconstruction*, the government called it. In reality, it was simply helping people live out their daily lives. Stories of free Negroes being beaten, robbed, and murdered continued to come in. There was also the real problem of too few jobs across the state to support the influx of wage-earning workers. White men, especially those who'd owned slaves, didn't take kindly to having to compete with them for jobs now.

But amid the ongoing difficulties and adjustments were also stories of hope. Schools for the children of former slaves were already popping up. Levi thought of Natalie teaching her servants their letters. He couldn't help but feel a sense of pride, knowing how difficult her life had become because of the slaves' freedom, yet she was making a valiant effort to change, not only her way of doing things but her way of thinking as well.

Recalling their time on the porch swing two nights ago, he now recognized the hope he'd allowed to build up in his heart unawares. With Samuel's head resting on his lap, the lad's beautiful mother inches away, the homey scene had convinced him to explore his attraction to the widow. Though their differences were many, was it so far-fetched to imagine a life with Natalie and Samuel? He'd tested the waters when he'd asked if she would consider remarriage. Her uncertainty was expected but not off-putting.

Then she'd told him of her late husband's death at Manassas. The grief on her face over his loss, the knowledge of all that little Samuel had lost, too … Levi knew then a future with the widow would be impossible.

"Maish, a moment of your time."

First Lieutenant Ridley exited the general's office and strode toward him. The man saluted Levi before offering his hand.

"It's good to see you again, Lieutenant." Levi nodded toward the building behind them. "Congratulations on your appointment to the Freedmen's Bureau. I believe much good will come of it."

"Thank you, sir. I'm eager to begin work." A frown tugged the tall man's brow. "However, until we have it organized, the general wants me to continue investigating the cattle thefts. We've received more complaints, mainly from landowners near the Mexican border. Apparently, the disappearances are fairly recent."

"It isn't hard to imagine someone stealing cattle for their own use or to sell locally, but none of the evidence seems to indicate that is what we're dealing with." Levi looked toward the south, wondering just how big this cattle rustling ring was and, more importantly, who was responsible. "The mystery lies in where someone could keep hundreds of stolen head of cattle and not draw suspicion."

"If you can spare the men, I'd like to establish patrols in your area. We're doing the same throughout the region."

"Of course," Levi said.

A glint of humor flashed in the lieutenant's eyes. "Rumor has it you've taken up cotton farming."

Levi chuckled. "The Union Army requires much of its men."

"The Widow Ellis is said to be a beauty." Ridley lifted his eyebrows. "I don't suppose it is too much of a hardship to assist the lady."

Gossip through the ranks was not new, but Levi didn't appreciate having his or Natalie's names attached to it. "Mrs. Ellis has a business agreement with the Union Army, Lieutenant," he said, his tone terse, causing the other man to jerk his relaxed posture upright. "An officer should never stoop to passing rumors, especially when another officer—a higher-ranking officer—is involved."

Ridley's Adam's apple bobbed as he swallowed hard. "Yes, Colonel."

After dismissing the lieutenant, Levi strode toward his tent among a sea of canvas on the outskirts of Austin. A river lined with towering cypress trees flowed nearby. He had some time to himself before his next meeting. The thought of spending it on his bunk in a stuffy canvas cave did not appeal, but his conversation with Ridley had soured his mood. Avoiding others was probably for the best. Eyeing the grassy bank of the river and seeing no one about, he changed his course and headed there instead.

Settling against the thick trunk of a very old tree, Levi set his hat on the ground next to him. Why Ridley's offhand comment about Natalie rankled so, he couldn't say. She *was* beautiful, and it *wasn't* a hardship to help her. So why had he nearly taken off Ridley's head for the harmless banter?

Recalling his time with her from two nights past, he shook his head in disgust. He'd been a fool to toy with the idea of a future with her. Not only was she a former slave owner, but she was a Confederate widow. A widow whose husband he may have killed.

Images from the battle along the Bull Run hovered on the edges of his memory. As a captain, he'd been in charge of a company of men under General McDowell's command. They'd advanced from Washington, thirty thousand troops strong, with more confidence than anyone should possess in war. The Confederates were encamped at Manassas Junction, twenty-five miles to the southwest, and President Lincoln wanted them removed from that important rail-crossing point.

But most of Levi's men and the majority of the others were green, three-month volunteers and militia who possessed little drill and marching skills. Their slowness and inexperience gave the Confederates time to call in reinforcements, a miscalculation the Union general would later regret.

The battle, Levi recalled, quickly turned into a free-for-all. He lost most of his men in the first hour, and McDowell's strategy—feint to the left, attack on the right—soon fell apart. Riding his horse amid the chaos, firing his gun and swinging his saber, Levi remembered the eerie, shrill wail that came from the Confederate side. The Rebel yell, he would later hear it called, did nothing but ignite a fire in his belly to drive the Southerners into the ground. He lost count of the number of men in gray uniforms he cut down, their faces and screams blurring together. By the end of the struggle, hundreds of dead bodies littered the ground, and he was covered from head to toe in blood. Though the Union lost the battle and had to march back to Washington in defeat, Levi's boldness had not gone unnoticed. He was promoted to colonel two days later.

But what of George Ellis? Was he one of the soldiers Levi killed? The same saber he'd worn in battle still hung at his side. Looking at it, a sick feeling in his gut, he wondered if it had been plunged into the heart of Natalie's husband, Samuel's father. How could either of them forgive him for things done in battle that may have altered their lives in the most profound way?

The answer was simple.

They couldn't.

❧ ☙

Alexander Lopez arrived at Rose Hill shortly after noon with his magnificent horse hitched to a carriage. Natalie stood while Cousin Eunice gushed over the man when he came to a stop in front of the manor.

"Señor, how good of you to come for a visit," she said, giving Natalie a satisfied look as they waited in the shade of the porch to greet their visitor. That Ebenezer had not announced the arrival of the man more than likely meant the dog had found some sort of mischief to keep him occupied. Thankfully, she knew her son and Isaac were in the kitchen with Harriet baking sugar cookies. One of the privates assigned to help supervise the new field workers had bartered a bag of sugar for a batch of the sweet treats. Harriet was all too pleased to make the trade.

"The judge had a horse very much like that one," Eunice continued as Alexander approached the steps, looking perfectly groomed considering the long and dusty drive from town. "He had it brought all the way to Texas from a farm in Tennessee. 'Best horse I ever owned,' says he, more than once."

Alexander bowed politely. "Ma'am." His dark gaze found Natalie, and the corners of his eyes crinkled with his smile. "Señora Ellis. You look lovely, as usual."

Eunice cackled with pleasure. "My, my, you certainly are a charmer. Well, don't just stand there. Come. I'll have Lottie bring us some refreshments."

Natalie nearly groaned. Her cousin's meddling knew no end. Not an hour ago, Natalie had been forced to intervene when Eunice had Carolina cornered in the dining room, berating the servant for washing her white underskirt in the same tub of water as Samuel's indigo trousers. While Carolina certainly should have anticipated the results, Natalie reminded her disgruntled cousin that everyone was learning new skills, and mistakes were bound to happen. Eunice was not appeased, but she hadn't followed when Carolina dashed from the room.

"Actually, I hoped to invite Señora Ellis for a ride." Alexander indicated the carriage. "Perhaps we might enjoy the refreshments when we return."

"While that is a fine idea," Eunice said with a frown, her hands on her generous hips, "without a chaperone, it is highly improper. I don't see room in that fancy rig for the three of us."

Natalie had no desire to ride with Alexander, especially in the heat of the day, but if it afforded her even one hour away from her cousin, it would be worth the discomfort. "Cousin Eunice, you needn't worry. Señor Lopez has visited at Rose Hill for over a year. If anyone cared about the impropriety of our friendship, it is long past."

Eunice's brow went up. "Why, I am surprised to hear you say such a thing, Natalie Ellis. Just because you are a widow does not mean—"

"I will get my hat, Señor," Natalie said, leaving her cousin openmouthed.

She hurried inside, not because she was eager to be alone with the *Tejano*, but because she could not bear another moment in the presence of her cousin. Reaching the entrance to her bedroom, she thought she heard someone in the adjoining sitting room.

"Carolina, is that you?"

Silence met her. Perhaps it was the rose-scented breeze coming from the open window, stirring the curtains. She removed a forest-green bonnet from the bureau and tied it beneath her chin. Surveying her reflection in the long mirror, she was satisfied with her appearance. It wasn't as though she hoped to gain the admiration of Alexander.

Memories of primping for a certain colonel brought a flush to her cheeks. One of his men informed Moses that Colonel Maish had been called away to Austin. The void the colonel's absence left on the plantation—and in her—was more than a little surprising, being that he'd only spent two days with them making the repairs after the storm.

Descending the back stairs, she alerted Harriet to her plans, kissed Samuel's sticky face—he scowled when she mentioned her escort was Alexander—and proceeded to the foyer, where she heard Eunice regaling Alexander with more stories. She was tempted to delay her entrance onto the porch, but the sooner they took their drive, the sooner she could return. She'd promised the women they would continue their reading lessons before supper, much to everyone's delight.

"Shall we go, Señor?" She breezed through the open doorway. Eunice sat on one of the wicker chairs while Alexander leaned against the porch rail.

"Indeed." He extended his arm. When she placed her hand on it, he turned a pleasant smile to Eunice. "You may be assured, dear woman, I will take fine care of your cousin. You need not worry."

Eunice fluttered her lashes. "I trust you, Señor."

Alexander helped Natalie into the carriage, climbed in on the opposite side, and took up the reins. "I know a shady spot near the creek not far from here."

Natalie nodded, vaguely wondering how he was so familiar with Rose Hill lands. The pastures where his cattle grazed were in the opposite direction. But simply getting away from Eunice had her willing to go to the frontier if it meant she didn't have to listen to her cousin's prattling.

"Your cousin is an … *unusual* woman," he said. When he lifted his brow, she couldn't help but chuckle.

"That is a polite way to put it." She sighed, looking out over the countryside. She couldn't remember the last time she'd simply ridden through the plantation for enjoyment. Alexander steered the horse down a path she had never noticed before. "I must say, this is nice, taking a drive purely for pleasure."

"Ah, that is what I hoped to hear."

A few minutes later, he guided the horse off the little-used road to a shady glen. The creek gurgled nearby, although the wild grasses were in need of a good rain shower.

He helped her down then retrieved a blanket from beneath the seat. "I thought we could rest in the shade of the trees." He offered his arm once again.

They walked the short distance, and he spread the blanket on the ground.

Natalie settled on it, keeping her skirt over her feet. "How did you know about this place? I've lived at Rose Hill six years, but I don't believe I've ever seen it."

He sat beside her, looking slightly out of place in his neat vest and tie. An image flitted across her mind—Colonel Maish working one end of the two-man saw with his coat removed and his shirtsleeves rolled to his elbows. Far more often than she cared to admit, she'd created reasons to go near the barn the day he helped Moses cut up the fallen tree, mesmerized by the play of muscles across the colonel's back and arms.

"I mistakenly took this road one afternoon when I was trying to return to the pastures." He smiled. "I thought that day how nice it would be to bring you here."

While she appreciated his kindness, she did not want to encourage him. "Señor—"

"Alexander. Please."

She inclined her head. "Alexander, I hope you understand that I am grateful for our business partnership ... as well as our friendship."

"Ah, Natalie." His eyes roamed her face with more familiarity than she cared for. "Surely you must know I desire more than friendship. As I told your cousin, I wanted us to court properly, but I have changed my mind."

"You have?"

"Yes." He positioned himself to face her. "I do not wish to court. I wish to marry you. We have known each other over a year now. That's enough time to keep tongues from wagging, as you

Americans say. Natalie Ellis, do me the honor of becoming my wife."

She stared at him, fearful of what might come out of her mouth if she opened it. Had she known this was what he intended when he invited her for a drive, she would have declined. There were so many reasons to say no …

"I … I can't—"

"Please." He grasped her hand and put it to his warm lips. "Please, do not say you cannot marry me. Let me take care of you, Natalie. You are alone. Even the slaves are gone. I fear for you with no one to see to the plantation. The Army will use your property as long as they wish, but then they too will leave." He put her hand against the hard muscles of his chest, shocking her with the intimate gesture. "My heart is yours. Together we can make Rose Hill prosperous again. I have the means to hire workers for the fields and for the house. You will want for nothing as my wife. Please," he said, his dark eyes pleading. "Say you will."

"There are many things to consider, Señor." She withdrew her hand. "There is Samuel."

"He needs a father." His words echoed Colonel's Maish's.

Her son did need a father. A father he adored.

"Rose Hill and my family's land are Samuel's inheritance. If I remarry …" They both knew the property would become Alexander's the moment she married him. "I can't risk losing what is rightfully Samuel's."

"Of course, your son would still inherit your property." He looked grave. "But the truth is, you may lose the plantations anyway. You no longer own slaves. How can you pay workers after the Army leaves? How will you plant, harvest, and market your crop with the few Negroes who might stay? And if they leave because you cannot pay them? What then?"

A queasiness clenched her midsection. Everything he said was true. Hadn't her own fearful thoughts come to these same conclusions?

"I don't know what to do." She felt more confused than ever. She didn't want another loveless marriage, but was his offer the solution she'd prayed for? For a fleeting moment, she wished it were Colonel Maish proposing marriage, but he would return to his home in Pennsylvania soon. Even without a wife waiting for him, a life with him was still impossible. Her home was here, in Texas.

Alexander took both her hands in his. "I will wait, *mi pequeña*. Please say you will consider my proposal, hmm?"

She looked into his eyes, such a deep brown they almost appeared black. He'd been her friend for many months now, and she had never had cause to fear or mistrust him. He'd offered to be a father to Samuel and to help keep Rose Hill running. Perhaps marriage to the handsome man would not be such a terrible thing.

"Very well, Alexander." His obvious satisfaction at her use of his name brought a hint of pleasure. "I will consider your proposal."

CHAPTER EIGHTEEN

Natalie entered the kitchen after breakfast the following day carrying a basketful of fresh garden produce. Carolina's giggles met her, but the wide-brimmed hat flopping over her eyes made it difficult to see what the young woman thought so funny.

"Carolina, what are you—?" Natalie lifted her head and found Corporal Banks seated at the long work table sipping from a cup. Carolina stood nearby, the coffee pot in her hand. None of the other servants was nearby.

Corporal Banks stood. "Good morning, Mrs. Ellis. Let me assist you." He took the basket. Without asking, he carried it to the sink and set it where the carrots, tomatoes, and onions could be rinsed before being taken to the cold pit or chopped up for a meal.

"Thank you, Corporal," Natalie said. Was Colonel Maish also at Rose Hill, perhaps waiting for her on the porch? Her heart fluttered at the thought. "What brings you to see us today?"

"The colonel asked me to check on the men while he's in Austin." A look in Carolina's direction set off another giggle.

Disappointment washed over Natalie. "I see."

"He also asked that I make certain the fallen tree is chopped into firewood. Miss Carolina volunteered to assist me if that would be all right with you. It sure would save time if I had someone to help pick up the pieces of wood and stack them while I do the splitting."

Natalie almost snickered at the absurd request, but one look at Carolina's hopeful face told her she would crush the young woman's heart if she refused. "What chores do you have this morning?"

Carolina's shoulders slumped. "Harriet said I's to beat the

rugs in the parlor, dining room, and hall." Her voice held little enthusiasm. "After that I's to dust and polish ever'thing in those rooms."

The chores would definitely take the remainder of the morning. Natalie glanced between the two young people. Corporal Banks did seem genuinely interested in Carolina, but she didn't want the servant hurt when Banks returned home, as he surely would. Yet looking at them, with their surreptitious glances and obvious attraction, who was she to keep them from exploring the possibilities?

"Very well," she said. "You may assist Corporal Banks this morning."

The young woman squealed.

"But you'll need to return to your chores this afternoon."

"Yessum." The young woman beamed brighter than the sun when she met Corporal Banks' happy grin.

From the kitchen doorway, Natalie watched the pair head down to the barn, Carolina chattering like a magpie and Banks grinning like a fool, hanging on every word.

"Now ain't that a sight." Harriet came toward her from the main house, her gaze on the young people. "That Yankee be all that girl can talk 'bout these days."

Natalie sighed. "I keep reminding her he will return home soon."

"I think she hopin' she gonna go with him."

Shocked by the revelation, Natalie looked at Harriet. "Do you think she would?"

The woman shrugged. "We ain't never had no choice to stay or go before. Some think the grass is greener up no'th, so to speak. Say there be more jobs and such for us Negroes. Others say Texas just as good as any place to start fresh." She shrugged again and entered the kitchen.

While Harriet set to work washing the produce, Natalie sat at the table to mull over the possibility of Carolina leaving. She would miss the sassy young woman. Somewhere along the way, she'd come to care about Carolina, not simply as a servant but as a friend. The realization was astounding.

She watched Harriet peel and slice the carrots into a pot on the stove. Though they still had awkward moments between them, Natalie found she would like to consider Harriet a friend as well.

"Harriet," she said, "I don't know if I've told you this, but I appreciate you and Moses staying on at Rose Hill. I know you could have gone with the others. It means a great deal to me that you stayed."

The older woman met Natalie's gaze. "Moses say this is our home. Don't have no place else to go. Goin' just because you can ain't smart when you got no way to make a livin'." She paused, seeming to measure her next words. "But that ain't the only reason we stay."

"Oh?"

Harriet glanced out the window, and Natalie thought she saw a tear trail down the woman's cheek in the silent moments. "We stay," she said, her voice thick with emotion, "because this is where our boys knows where to find us … if they still alive."

The words cut to Natalie's soul.

Their sons. Sold off by George. Of course Harriet and Moses would stay at Rose Hill, hoping and praying the boys—men, now—would come in search of their parents. It struck her then that Negroes all across the South must hold similar hope, desperate to reunite families torn apart by slavery.

She closed her eyes, shame piercing her once again at the cruelties her own family had inflicted on two of the dearest people in her life.

"I'm sorry, Harriet," she whispered, the words woefully inadequate.

The woman simply nodded and went back to work.

Natalie left the kitchen, the uncomfortable distance between her and Harriet as strong as ever. Laughter drifted up from the area near the barn. Natalie watched Corporal Banks swing the ax, easily splitting a log in two. Carolina sashayed over, picked up the pieces, then twirled her way to the bin situated against the barn wall and tossed them in. The young people chatted and laughed and repeated the process.

Were they the image of hope for the country's future? A former slave and a Negro Yankee, forging ahead, determined to find happiness in the aftermath of so much pain?

She went into the house and found it blessedly silent. Eunice and Lottie had gone into town after breakfast, and she could only hope their errands took the better part of the day. Ruth and Adline had stripped beds and were now paddling the sheets in a huge caldron behind the kitchen. She'd waved to Ruth when she returned from the garden, and the timid woman waved back. Adline continued to ignore Natalie. She couldn't blame the woman. While Ruth had been a slave on a distant plantation, Adline had been a Rose Hill slave. It would take time, she was sure, to earn the woman's trust, if she ever did.

With Carolina otherwise occupied, Natalie decided she would beat the rugs herself. She'd never done the chore, but she'd seen servants at it often enough that she knew it wasn't difficult. She started with the smaller rugs, carrying one to the backyard and draping it over the sturdy wooden rack that had been built for this very purpose. The rug beater hung on a peg. She took it in hand and gave the first rug a solid whack. A puff of dust floated out.

"Well, what do you know." She looked around to see if anyone bore witness to her accomplishment. The yard was vacant. Feeling silly, for it wasn't as though she had done a great service for the world, she set out to attack the rug with gusto.

❧

"Ohhh." Natalie groaned as she trudged up the stairs to her room. Her arms, legs, shoulders, neck, and back ached more than she knew was possible. Her gown and hands were filthy, and she imagined she looked worse than some dead something Ebenezer might find in the woods and drag home. But the parlor, dining room, and hall rugs were clean, by gum.

"Mama!" Samuel and Isaac ran from his room when she reached the landing. They each held wooden farm animals in their hands. "We're playing." He cocked his head and looked her up and down. "What's wrong with you?"

Natalie chuckled. "Nothing that a good soak in the tub won't cure. Does Harriet know you two are up here?"

"Uh-huh. We found a toad and was gonna scare Carolina with him, but she's busy helpin' that so'dier with the wood. He said we ought not scare girls 'cuz they get all willy and might cry. When is the nice so'dier gonna come back? I like him." He didn't wait for an answer. "Moses said the mama cat that lives in the barn has babies. Can Isaac and me go see 'em?"

The running discourse finally came to an end. "Yes, you may, but don't try to pick them up just yet. It will be a few weeks before they'll be big enough to play. Let Harriet know you're going outside."

"Yes, Mama." The boys briefly disappeared into the bedroom and came back empty-handed.

Natalie watched them run past her and stomp down the back stairs out of sight, their excited voices fading as she envisioned them hurrying from the house and racing to the barn. Little had changed for the two boys, despite everything in their lives being different. They'd been the best of friends before the Union Army brought the freedom proclamation to Texas shores, and they continued to be friends even as the people around them struggled to find a new balance in a world that seemed frighteningly unstable under their feet.

She trudged toward her bedroom at the opposite end of the hall, wondering if all the adults in the country should take a page out of the boys' book of life. Their approach to the questions of black or white, rich or poor, seemed so much simpler.

Finding her door closed, she turned the glass knob, entered, and headed toward the bathing room.

Jezro, the field worker with the branded cheeks, stood next to her bureau. Martha Ellis' pearl-drop necklace dangled from his hand.

She gasped.

Fear flashed across Jezro's face, but it quickly vanished, replaced with a steely-eyed glare. "Don't you make a sound. I don't want to have to hurt nobody."

Natalie swallowed, her mouth gone dry. "What are you doing in here?" The answer was terrifyingly obvious, but her mind could not seem to grasp the scene before her. A Negro man stood in her bedroom, rifling through her belongings. Was this part of the new world Colonel Maish and the northern abolitionists wanted her to accept?

"I's gettin' me a little extra pay for all my years o' service to you white folks." His sneer made the scars more pronounced.

"You were not a Rose Hill slave." What should she do? The open door was only two steps away, but she feared if she tried to escape, he'd be upon her before she could get away. Thank goodness Samuel and Isaac were outside.

"Don't matter if I weren't your slave, *Miz* Natalie. Your kind thought they could own me, mark me up with a hot iron, an' make me bend to them." He spat on the carpet. "I done with white people tellin' me what to do."

"I'm sorry for what you endured," she said, working to keep her voice calm. Surely if she reasoned with him, the man could see the error of his ways. "Things are different now. You're free. Free to make your own choices." She glanced at the open drawers of her bureau. "Stealing is not the way to begin your new life. The Bible says it's wrong."

He laughed coldly. "What does some uppity white woman know about right an' wrong? You ain't never gone hungry because yo' white massa won't give you food. You ain't never had an iron fresh outta the fire pressed against your face, the smell of yo' own burnin' flesh making you sick. You ain't never been strapped to a tree and had yo' white massa take the skin off your bones with a whip, cursin' you with every swing 'cuz you done tried to get that *freedom* you white people give and take away whenever you please."

His voice and his eyes hardened with each horrible description.

Trying to reason with the angry man was foolishness. His hatred went too deep. He blamed her for all the sins imparted upon him by his masters. And though she was guilty for keeping Rose Hill slaves in bondage the past four years, she had done nothing to this man.

She took a step backward, her eyes wide with fear. "Take the necklace and go."

Run! a voice in her mind commanded.

A silent, tense moment passed before they both sprang into action.

Natalie whirled to flee the room. Jezro lunged to keep her inside. A struggle ensued. His sweaty body odor filled her nostrils as he pressed her against the wall. She fought and struggled, but her tired muscles were no match for his powerful arms. Terror washed over her. Would she be violated in her own bedroom by a newly freed slave?

Voices sounded from below stairs.

"Help!" she cried. "Help me!"

Jezro stilled, listening.

"Miz Natalie? That you makin' all that ruckus?"

She had never been so happy to hear Carolina's voice.

Footfalls on the stairs forced Jezro to release his grip on her. With a curse, he flung her from him and sprinted through the adjoining sitting room then into the hallway. The back stairway would allow him to escape, but she didn't care. She wanted him gone.

Tears clouded her vision as Carolina and Corporal Banks

entered the room.

"Miz Natalie!" Carolina rushed to her. "What happened?"

Natalie trembled and her breath came in such hard gulps, she couldn't speak.

Carolina shot the corporal a concerned look.

"Jezro," Natalie finally gasped, wrapping her arms around her body. "He was here … in my room."

"Just now?" Carolina shrieked, horror widening her eyes. She turned to the corporal. "He must've gone out the back."

Corporal Banks tore from the chamber.

Carolina took Natalie by the arm. "Come sit down, Miz Natalie. You safe now." She led Natalie to a chair near the cold fireplace. When Natalie was settled, Carolina knelt beside her. "You want some tea to calm yo' nerves?"

Natalie shook her head and closed her eyes. "I just need to know that man is long gone." Her eyes flew open again. "Samuel!" She moved to stand, but Carolina gently pushed her back into the chair.

"He fine, Miz Natalie. He and Isaac are with Harriet up in her room over the kitchen. They lookin' at that picture book you give Isaac."

Relief washed through her, but her body would not stop trembling.

"I get some water heated for yo' bath." Carolina stood. "A nice soak do you good. I tell Harriet and Moses to be on the lookout for that no-good Jezro, but I 'spect he hightail it outta here and won't never come back. Not with Yankee so'diers lookin' for him." A hint of pride sounded in her voice.

Carolina left, closing the door behind her. Natalie rose on shaky legs and turned the key in the lock. She went into the sitting room and locked the door that led to the hallway. With her forehead pressed against the wood and tears slipping down her cheeks, she let out a sob. Surely God had sent Carolina and Corporal Banks at just the right time. Had it also been His voice in her mind, telling her to run?

"Thank you," she whispered, weak with gratitude.

Only then did the tremors in her body begin to subside.

CHAPTER NINETEEN

Langford Manor had never looked so good.

The sun was dipping below the western horizon as Levi rode into the yard. All he wanted was a bath and a good night's sleep. Not even a meal tempted him, tired as he was. The two-day journey from Austin wasn't hard riding, but long hours in the saddle left him worn out these days. It was yet another reason he found himself dreaming of his carpentry shop more and more.

"Welcome back, Colonel."

Corporal Banks crossed the yard to take the reins of his mount. A group of men played a game of horseshoes nearby, and the twang of a shoe hitting the metal stake resounded in an otherwise tranquil camp. With their days starting long before the sun came up, most of the men were ready to crawl into their bunks the moment it grew dark.

"Thank you, Banks. I don't mind confessing it's good to be back." With stiff movements, he climbed from the horse. "I'll brief you on my meetings in the morning. Our orders haven't changed, but there is new information to discuss."

"Yes, sir." Banks didn't turn toward the barn. The play of expressions across his face told Levi something was amiss, but he was too exhausted to deal with any new challenges just now.

"I'm going to bed, Banks." He strode to the steps of the manor. "Whatever has you fretting like an old lady can wait until morning."

"It's about Mrs. Ellis, sir."

That stopped Levi. He turned and retraced his steps. "What about Mrs. Ellis?"

A look of guilt washed across the corporal's face. "There's been an incident."

Levi didn't like the sound of that. "Out with it."

"One of the new field workers—the man with the brands on his face—attacked Mrs. Ellis in her bedroom. Miss Carolina and I were just coming in when we heard her call for help."

The blood drained from Levi's face. "Attacked her? Is she …?" He couldn't finish the question.

"It shook her up, but she's all right. At least, she said she was when I left there a little while ago."

"Are you telling me this happened today?"

Banks nodded. "Around noon. I had our men and Moses search the plantation for Jezro, but we didn't find him. I suspect he's long gone by now."

A sick feeling swirled in Levi's gut.

He'd felt sorry for Jezro. He'd wanted the branded man to know there were white people whom he could trust, but Levi had never considered whether or not he could trust Jezro. Or any of the others, for that matter. He'd simply assumed the Negroes' gratitude would keep them in line. What a fool! His carelessness had put Natalie in danger.

"I need to see her." The words were out of his mouth before he realized it.

Banks nodded. "I'll get you a fresh horse."

As the sun disappeared, Levi raced away from Langford Manor. He gave his mount the lead despite the growing darkness, flying over the dirt road and turning everything around them into a blur. He berated himself the entire way for not providing more soldiers to watch the workers, for hiring unsuitable men, for not being there when Natalie needed him most.

Rose Hill came into view over the next rise, bathed in the silvery glow of a half-moon.

He slowed the horse as he entered the long tree-lined drive, not wishing to alarm anyone with a wild entrance. From this distance, the house looked dark, and it occurred to him Natalie might have turned in already, especially after such a harrowing day. Even so, he needed to have a talk with his men—one they would not soon forget. Jezro should have never made it to the main house without someone noticing.

His heart lurched.

What if Banks and Carolina hadn't gone inside? What if …?

An urgent need to see Natalie filled every corner of his mind. He nudged his horse. "Let's go, boy."

Dark house or not, he intended to speak with Natalie tonight. He wouldn't leave Rose Hill until he knew she was safe.

꽃 ꙮ

The night sounds, normally so familiar and soothing, kept Natalie on edge as she sat motionless in the swing, too afraid the creaking chains would prevent her from hearing other more sinister noises. She'd thought to come out to her favorite spot to help calm her nerves after a trying day, but the shadows and sounds did exactly the opposite.

Was Jezro still out there? Corporal Banks, Moses, and even Carolina didn't believe so, but something in Natalie could not rest until she knew for certain he was not coming back. The cold look in his eyes when he'd listed the sins of his former owners made his hatred for white people ominously clear. There was no trusting a man like that.

Her thoughts turned to Corporal Banks, as different from Jezro as night was from day. He'd searched the plantation for hours in the heat that afternoon, doing his best to offer Natalie reassuring words each time he came back to check on her before riding off in a different direction. When Cousin Eunice eventually returned from town, he'd dealt with her hysterics with more patience than Natalie knew was possible. Eunice vacillated between accusing him of conspiring with Jezro—"they're all the same, you know"—and demanding that he stay to guard them, declaring they would all be murdered in their sleep otherwise. The judge, she'd said at least a half-dozen times, would have hunted down Jezro and put a bullet between his eyes. She advised the corporal to do likewise then proceeded to barricade herself in her room.

Stifling a yawn, Natalie knew she should turn in, but the thought of going up to her bedroom sent a wave of panic coursing through her. Moses had quietly locked all the doors leading into the main house before he'd turned in. Since he, Harriet, and Isaac slept in the room above the kitchen, they wouldn't need inside the house until morning. She knew he'd done it to help her feel safe, but her mind's eye still saw Jezro standing in her room, his hands on her belongings.

On her.

She shivered and glanced at the rifle leaning against the wall next to the swing.

Maybe she would sleep in Samuel's room tonight. He'd gone to bed upset with her because she wouldn't let him run down to the barn to see the kittens. With Jezro's whereabouts unknown, she'd kept him inside the remainder of the day. Rarely did she raise her voice to her son, but his whining had pushed her taut nerves too far this evening. She would apologize to him in the morning and make a special trip to spend time with the new cat family.

A noise came from the trees lining the lane.

Natalie stood, listening, poised to grab the gun and dash inside.

"Mrs. Ellis, it's Colonel Maish." His hushed call came through the darkness.

Colonel Maish?

Her body practically sagged with relief when he came into view. It truly was him. As if dreaming, she watched him dismount, tie the reins to the porch rail, and then climb the steps, his eyes never leaving her.

"Corporal Banks told me what happened." His voice was gentle and full of concern. "I came the moment I heard."

She nodded, not trusting herself to speak. More than anything, she wanted to fall into his arms and let him hold her, protect her, love her. She was tired of being strong. She was tired of being alone.

"Is there anything I can do for you?" When she shook her head, he glanced around the dark yard. "We will assign more men to your plantation tomorrow. I don't expect Jezro to return, but I will feel better when there is a stronger military presence on the premises. At least until the man is caught."

"You plan to pursue him?" This news surprised her.

"Of course. He assaulted you, Mrs. Ellis. The Union Army will do everything possible to ensure your protection."

"Corporal Banks was incredibly helpful. I hope you'll convey my appreciation to him. I'm afraid between my own emotions and those of my cousin, he had his hands full."

"I'm sorry. We should have taken more care to keep an eye on the workers." He shook his head. "This is my fault."

"You couldn't have known something like this would happen."

"I should've anticipated it and taken measures to prevent it. That's my job. You and everyone else at Rose Hill are my responsibility while the Union Army works here."

The words stung. Was that how he saw her? A temporary responsibility?

"Why did you come?" She turned away, hurt and vulnerable. "You could have waited until morning to check on your *responsibilities*."

He closed the gap between them with purposeful strides. She saw his feet just inches from the hem of her skirt. When she didn't look up, he gently lifted her face until their eyes met and held.

"I came because I had to know you were safe."

The softly spoken, honest words washed over her like spring raindrops, filling her with hope. "I am now," she whispered.

With more tenderness than she dared imagine, he lowered his mouth to hers. Her eyes closed, savoring the feel of his lips, tasting, then possessing hers. When his hands moved to capture her face, she leaned into him, aware of only her desperate need to be in this man's arms.

Far sooner than she wished, he lifted his head, separating their lips but still cradling her face with his warm hands. She opened her eyes to find his dark gaze studying her.

"That was unexpected," he said, his voice husky.

With reluctance, she nodded and took a step back. His hands fell away. "Very."

The corner of his mouth tipped. "But nice."

"Very." Her face warmed with his smile.

Looking out into the starlit night, he sighed. "It gets complicated from here."

When he looked at her again, she saw his longing ran as deep as her own. "Yes, but it doesn't have to be impossible, does it, Colonel?"

His eyes crinkled. "After a kiss like that, don't you think we should dispense with formalities, *Natalie*?"

"I quite agree … *Levi*." She couldn't keep the smile from her face.

He cupped her cheek, his thumb smoothing her skin. "Are you willing to explore this? To see where it leads? If you are, there are things you need to know."

Before she could answer, a distant noise in the still night—was that glass shattering?—made Levi straighten. Had it come from the quarter? The barns?

"What was that?" Natalie asked, her heart thrumming against her ribs. Had Jezro returned?

He shook his head. "I don't know, but I'll find out." Reaching for the lantern, he said, "I'm going to wake my men. You go inside and lock the door."

"I'd rather come with you," she whispered, suddenly more afraid of the dark than she'd been as a child. "We can wake Moses and Harriet. She can stay with Samuel."

"All right."

Levi reached for her hand. When his strong fingers closed over hers, he gave them a squeeze. Together they hurried along the porch that surrounded the lower floor of the house. When they arrived at the walkway to the kitchen, Levi stopped. He jerked his head up and sniffed the air.

She did the same. Smoke! Far stronger than a simple cook fire in the quarter would produce. Something was burning.

"Get Moses!" He pushed the lantern into her hands and sprinted to the bachelor's quarters.

While he roused his men, Natalie hurried to the kitchen. Thankfully, Moses had not locked that door.

"Moses! Harriet!" she hollered up the narrow stairs. "There's a fire! Come, quick!"

She didn't wait to see if the couple awoke but rushed back outside. The smoke was heavier now and hung in the still night air.

"It looks like one of the smaller barns is ablaze." Levi ran toward her. "Have Moses wake the others and bring buckets. We'll lose all the barns if we can't put out the fire."

He was gone an instant later, tearing across the lawn with the two privates trailing, both tugging on shirts as they ran.

"Miz Natalie!" Moses hurried from the kitchen, Harriet following close.

"The grain barn is on fire. Levi and his men have gone to put it out. We'll need everyone's help and all the buckets you can find."

Moses tore off toward the quarter.

"We got buckets out by the garden," Harriet said, already on the move in that direction.

Natalie flew into the house. She had to see Samuel's sleeping face and know he was safe before she could help.

The second floor loomed dark and quiet. Shouts and voices from those fighting the fire drifted through the open window at the end of the hall. She hurried to Samuel's room, tiptoeing across the floor so as not to wake him.

Desperate to see his sweet face, she held the lantern aloft. But his bed was empty.

Samuel was gone.

CHAPTER TWENTY

Smoke from the fire penetrated the wet bandana Levi had tied over his nose and mouth. His throat was already scratchy, and his eyes wouldn't stop watering, yet no relief could come until the fire was out. While flames shot up from the back of the small barn, the men concentrated their efforts on tossing bucket after bucket of water through the open doorway and onto the walls. Although no animals were housed in the structure, no one had to tell Levi that losing it would be disastrous. All the feed grains, corn, and seed for planting were stored here.

Wash Ingram pushed a bucket of water into his hands. Levi turned and passed it to the man in front of him. Three more men handled it before Moses, at the front of the line, tossed it onto the burning building. The process repeated, over and over, amid shouts to move faster.

Carolina stood at the pump, her thin arms working the handle continuously to keep up with the demand. Her rounded eyes spoke of her fear, but she kept working. Other women struggled to get skittish plow horses and milk cows out of the larger barn nearby, lest an errant spark ignite that structure as well.

Amid all the chaos, Levi was keenly aware that Natalie was not among the people frantically laboring to save the building. What if Jerzo had broken into the house and even now had Natalie in his clutches, finishing what he hadn't been able to the first time?

He had nearly convinced himself to leave the bucket line and race up to the house when he saw her rush into the glow the flames created. His relief was short-lived when he saw her face.

"Samuel," she cried, nearly collapsing into Levi's arms when he hurried to her. Her panic-filled eyes met his. "Samuel isn't in his room. I've searched the house. He isn't in the kitchen or the quarter or anywhere."

Sobs shook her body. Levi cradled her against his chest. As vital as the grain barn was, the boy was far more important. "We'll find him," he said, soothing her even as his mind whirled. Where could Samuel be? Surely Jezro hadn't harmed the child.

"Mama! Mama!"

Natalie gasped and pulled away from his embrace. All eyes looked upward. Samuel's tiny form, still dressed in his nightclothes, was silhouetted in the opening of the hayloft of the blazing barn.

"Samuel!"

Natalie's terror-filled cry sent chills coursing through Levi. A murmur ran through the crowd.

"Get that water comin'! Hurry!" Moses shouted, frantically tossing a full bucket onto the wall beneath Samuel.

Levi tore off the bandana and ran to the barn, stopping under the loft opening. Heat radiated around him. "Jump to me, Samuel." He stretched out his arms. "I'll catch you."

But Samuel shook his head. "Noooo. I'm scared." His bony shoulders shook, and he disappeared from view.

"Samuel!" Natalie rushed over, coughing and covering her mouth. Tears flooded her face. "Samuel!"

Levi pulled her away from the fiery building. She fought his grip.

"My son! Levi, I have to get my son!"

He grasped her by the shoulders and gave her a shake. "I'll get him, Natalie. Trust me. Stay here." Harriet hurried over and draped her arm across her mistress' trembling shoulders. He met the servant's wide-eyed gaze, and she nodded in understanding.

With no time to spare, Levi ran to the trough and jumped in. Carolina shrieked, but he paid no attention to her or the others who looked at him as though he'd gone insane. Dripping with water, he charged past the line of men. Moses grabbed his arm.

"Colonel, it be too dangerous." Fire glow reflected in the man's worried eyes.

"If it were Isaac, would you go in after him?"

The man didn't hesitate. He shoved a blanket someone had soaked in water into Levi's hands. "Lord, protect this man and our Samuel ..."

Levi didn't wait to hear the end of the prayer. He rushed into the burning structure, ducking low to keep out of the worst of the smoke. The bottom rung of a ladder was visible a short distance from the door. Throwing the blanket over his head, he scaled the rough wood.

"Samuel!"

The boy didn't answer, but Levi could hear him coughing.

"Samuel, come to me. I'm at the ladder. I'll take you to your mama."

The roar of the fire echoed in the narrow space. Shouts continued outside. Finally, Samuel emerged through the smoke on his hands and knees, his face streaked with soot and tears.

"Come to me. We need to get you out of here."

"But the kittens and the mama cat," Samuel said, looking behind him. "They're scared too."

A crash sounded behind Levi, but he didn't turn to see what it was. Samuel started to cry. It was foolhardy to risk their lives for a barn cat, but the boy might fight Levi if he tried to make a grab for him. "Show me where the cat is," he said, crawling onto the wooden platform built for hay storage.

Tucked in the corner against the wall, the mother cat and four new kittens crouched. A child's blanket lay next to them. With a swift move, Levi scooped the animals into it, then hoisted Samuel onto his back, covering them both with the wet blanket. "Hold on to me and don't let go."

With the boy's scrawny arms looped around his neck, choking him almost as much as the smoke, Levi descended the ladder as fast as his cumbersome passengers would allow. Though thick smoke completely obscured the entrance, he knew it was to his left. Hurrying in that direction, another deafening sound came from above.

The roof was about to collapse.

❦

Natalie stared at the opening to the barn, her eyes stinging and watery, but she would not look away. Black smoke billowed out, and terrible noises came from within. Still, Levi and Samuel did not appear.

"Oh God, oh God," she whispered over and over.

Harriet stood beside her, her own mutterings beseeching the Lord to spare Samuel and the colonel. A woman who'd lost children of her own, her prayers for the life of another's innocent child surely reached heaven and God's ear.

The minutes dragged by.

Finally, Moses shouted.

Natalie gasped, holding her breath, her hands clasped against her heart.

Like an apparition emerging from swampy fog, a blanket-covered form came through the smoke. Levi stumbled, and Moses kept him upright, leading him toward her. She couldn't move as she watched them approach. He held a small bundle in his hands, but it was too small to be her son.

"No!" She covered her mouth with her hands. Harriet's arm tightened across her shoulders, offering strength.

When he reached her, Levi dropped to his knees and placed the bundle gently on the ground. She recognized Samuel's blanket, and a silent wail began in her heart. When the soft material flopped open to reveal a cat and several kittens, she could only stare, confused. He'd saved a cat family but let her son perish?

"Mama!"

The lump on Levi's back wiggled. The blanket dropped to the

ground, and there was her son, clinging to Levi's neck.

"Samuel!"

The boy slid down Levi's back and ran to her. She sank to the ground, enveloping the precious child in a fierce embrace. She wept, and so did he. "Thank you, Lord," she sobbed into his smoky hair. "Thank you."

When she lifted her eyes, she met Levi's steadfast gaze. How could she have doubted him?

A crash behind him drew their attention. The roof of the barn gave way, sending flames and sparks high into the night air. Shouts for more water rang out, and Levi, after one last look at her, hurried back to the line of men.

Natalie carried Samuel to the house, leaving the noise and commotion behind.

"Stay with me, Mama," he whispered when they reached the porch, his arms tightening around her neck.

"I will, love." She might never let him out of her sight again.

They settled on the swing, Samuel curling into a ball next to her. Tomorrow she would find out why he'd been in the barn and if he were responsible for the fire. But not tonight. Tonight, she would hold him and comfort him and reassure herself that he was safe.

Eventually, Samuel fell asleep, leaving Natalie to stroke his hair as his head lay in her lap. She listened to the sounds of people fighting the fire until a large group of riders entered the yard. One of the soldiers must have gone to Langford Manor to get help, for men in uniform were suddenly everywhere.

Closing her eyes, tears rolled down her cheeks. God had given her back her son. When all seemed lost, He sent Levi. Strong, courageous Levi. He'd risked his own life to save Samuel. Even now, he battled to save the other barns. *Levi*. The man who'd kissed her with more tenderness and passion than she knew existed. A man her son adored. A man she knew she could trust without a shadow of doubt.

A man, she joyfully admitted, whom she loved with all her heart.

✺ ✺

Soldiers were milling about the yard, cups of strong coffee in their hands, when the sun peeked over a cloudless eastern horizon. The acrid smell of smoke hung heavy in the air, but thankfully, the fire was no longer a threat. They'd been able to contain it to the one barn, although Levi doubted any of the grain and corn would be salvaged. Between the smoke, flames, and water, it had doubtless all been destroyed.

"Mo' coffee, Colonel?"

He glanced up from his place on the porch steps to see Harriet come toward him, a blue enamel pot in her hands. She looked as tired as he felt. "I believe I've had my fill, but thank you."

She nodded, her serious gaze resting on him. "You runnin' in after Samuel 'bout the bravest thing I ever saw, Colonel." Tears sprang to her eyes. "Losing a chile the worst heartache a person can go through in this world. You done saved Miz Natalie's life, I 'spect, just as shorely as you saved little Samuel. Don't know that she would'a survived iffen somethin' happen to that boy. You done a good thing for this family, Colonel. A mighty good thing."

He watched her walk away, thoughtful. While the praise was appreciated, saving Samuel was not something he'd done to be heroic. The truth was, sometime between the day he and his men had arrived at Rose Hill and last night, he'd fallen in love with Natalie *and* Samuel. Seeing the boy in the opening to the hayloft, flames licking the walls behind him, Levi felt he was looking at his own son. The danger hardly crossed his mind.

"She's right, you know."

Natalie's soft voice came from behind him. Levi turned. She stood in the doorway, an expectant look shining in her eyes. He stood, muscles aching from fighting the fire most of the night, and

✺ 190 ✺

went to her. There hadn't been an opportunity to talk after he'd carried Samuel out of the barn. Harriet said she was resting when he and the men came looking for coffee after the last bucket of water had been tossed onto the smoldering embers. Several of his men continued to watch what remained of the structure to make certain it no longer posed a threat.

Now, with her mere inches away, he didn't know where to begin. He loved this woman. He wanted to spend the rest of his life protecting her and Samuel. That she'd returned his kiss, sweet and promising, ignited a hope deep in his heart.

"How is Samuel?" He was overcome by a powerful desire to pull her into his arms, yet he knew he could not with so many people nearby.

"Sleeping. He confessed to sneaking from the house to see the kittens after I tucked him into bed." She looked toward the barns, though the burned-out remains were not visible from the porch. When she met his gaze again, tears pooled in her eyes. "I nearly lost him, Levi," she whispered, her chin trembling. "How can I ever thank you enough for saving him?"

By marrying me.

The words were on his tongue, but he knew now was not the time to speak of such an important and complicated matter. Later, when she'd had time to recover from the shock and fear of nearly losing her son, he would tell her of his involvement in the battle at Bull Run. Then he would confess his love for her and for Samuel and beg her to marry him.

"You don't need to thank me. Knowing Samuel is safe is all that matters."

The look of love she gave him was nearly his undoing. If Eunice had not appeared in the doorway at that exact moment, he would have swept Natalie into his arms and proposed right there in front of the world.

"The last time I saw this many Yankees was the day they burned me out." Eunice turned a narrowed glare to Levi. "And now we've lost all our grain to a fire. Seems suspicious, don't you agree, Colonel?"

Her implications were clear.

"Cousin Eunice." Natalie turned abruptly to face the woman. "I hope you're not suggesting the soldiers had anything to do with the barn catching fire." Natalie glanced at Levi. "Samuel has already admitted he was there. Perhaps he tried to light a lantern."

"Pfft." Eunice eyed Levi. "I wouldn't be so fast to put the blame on the boy. Not when you have a yard full of Yankees. It was certainly fortunate that you happened to be at Rose Hill when the fire started, Colonel. Whatever would have become of poor little Samuel had you not arrived for a visit well after dark when most of us were already abed?"

Levi's ire rose, but he would not sink to the woman's level. Ignoring her, he turned to Natalie. "The embers will stay hot for several more hours. My men will remain to make certain no other fires pop up."

She nodded. "Thank you"—she glanced at Eunice then back to him—"Colonel."

He tried not to grin. "You're welcome, Mrs. Ellis."

The secret smile on her lips reminded him of how soft and yielding they'd been under his own. He hoped to get another chance—soon—to kiss them again.

He turned to leave.

"Co'nel!"

Harriet carried Samuel onto the porch, his hair a wild mess and sleep still in his eyes. The boy wiggled out of her arms and hurried to him.

"Mama says you're a *he-ro*. That means you were brave." He grinned up at his mother. Natalie smiled at him, smoothing the unruly locks into place before lifting her gaze to Levi. That she considered him a hero, he had to admit, puffed his chest a bit.

"How are you?" He knelt on one knee so he'd be eye level with the boy.

Samuel's little brow tugged into a frown. "I was scared before you came and got me." A smile melted it away. "The mama cat and her babies are in the kitchen. Harriet put 'em in a crate so me and Isaac don't have to go down to the barn to see 'em."

Levi rustled Samuel's hair, leaving it messy again, and stood. "That's a good idea."

"Did you catch the bad man?" Samuel peered up at him.

"The bad man?" He looked to Natalie for explanation, but her expression echoed his confusion.

"The one with the marks on his face. Moses said he was a bad man and I should stay away from him." Samuel grabbed a fistful of Natalie's skirt, inching closer to her. "He was in the barn, too, but he didn't know me and the cats were there."

When Levi glanced at Natalie, her eyes had rounded with alarm. Kneeling again, Levi kept his voice calm. "What was he doing in the barn?"

Samuel shrugged. "He wanted some corn, I guess. He was diggin' in all the bins and spilled some on the ground. I was gonna tell him Moses would be mad, but one of the kittens was sleepin' in my lap, and I didn't want to 'sturb it."

Levi frowned, trying to piece together the story. Why would Jezro still be at Rose Hill, searching grain bins? "And then what did he do?"

"He found one of Mama's candlesticks in the corn and put it in a bag. He put something else in too, but I couldn't see what it was." Samuel frowned. "I don't think he was s'pposed to have Mama's candlestick. She says they aren't to play with."

"No, he wasn't," Levi said, smiling at the boy so he wouldn't sense the fear that swept the adults on the porch. "But you were a very brave boy to stay quiet. Now, why don't you go check on the kittens? I imagine they miss you."

Samuel grinned and looked up to his mother. "Can I?"

"Of course. Harriet will take you." Though she smiled as she spoke, Levi heard the tremor in her voice.

Once Samuel and Harriet disappeared around the corner, Natalie's wide eyes met his. "Jezro started the fire, I know it."

Eunice, unusually silent and rather pale, put her arm around Natalie's waist.

"I fear you may be right." Levi glanced to the dozens of soldiers in the yard, preparing their horses to return to camp. "I will have the men search every inch of the plantation, but Jezro is most likely long gone."

"That's what Corporal Banks said yesterday, but look what happened. My son nearly died because of Jezro!" Natalie's eyes blazed.

Levi understood her fear. "He came back last evening to get the items he'd stolen. There is no reason for him to stay around."

"We need to alert the patrollers," Eunice said, giving her head a firm nod. "They have dogs trained to track Negroes. The judge—"

"Please, Cousin Eunice," Natalie said, exasperation echoing in the firm words. "Now is not the time for a story about the judge."

Eunice's eyes widened with indignation. "Well, how do you like that? I am simply trying to help, but I can see I am not wanted here." She shot a glare at Levi and marched into the house.

Natalie closed her eyes for a long moment. "I'll apologize to her later. For now"—her gaze held Levi's—"I'm frightened."

Her vulnerability tore at Levi. Throwing caution to the wind, he reached for her. Without hesitation, she folded herself into his embrace.

"I won't let him hurt you or Samuel," he said, smoothing her hair as her cheek rested against his chest. "If he is anywhere near Rose Hill, we'll find him." Although Eunice's suggestion to use the patrols and their dogs wasn't how Levi would like to handle the situation, it might be the only option. Jezro needed to be found before he hurt anyone else.

"Will someone tell me what the devil is going on here?"

Levi and Natalie sprang apart, startled to hear Alexander Lopez's angry voice. The man sat astride his huge mount, immaculately dressed, glaring at them.

"What are all these soldiers doing at Rose Hill," he said, leveling a threatening look at Levi, "and why is my fiancée in the arms of another man?"

CHAPTER TWENTY-ONE

Alexander's loud voice drew the attention of everyone in the yard, much to Natalie's dismay.

"Your fiancée?" Levi's gaze shot to her, confusion in his voice.

Frustrated, she turned to the man on the horse. "Alexander, you and I are not engaged. We simply—"

"I asked you to be my wife, and you agreed to consider it. Surely an understanding such as ours would prevent you from seeking the attentions of another man." His cold eyes grazed Levi. "Especially one who was so recently your enemy."

A gasp from the open door revealed Eunice had returned. She sent Natalie a reproachful frown. "You didn't tell me Señor Lopez proposed."

She had no time for Eunice's pouting. "Colonel Maish was comforting me, Alexander. We have experienced a number of upsetting incidents over the course of the past twenty-four hours."

"Oh, Señor," Eunice said, barreling between Levi and Natalie, forcing them to step farther apart. "You have come just in time. We are desperate for one of our own men to protect us."

Alexander dismounted and joined them on the porch, his face a dark scowl. "You are in danger?" He glanced at the soldiers.

Eunice nodded enthusiastically. "As you recall me saying, Señor, the Yankees burned us out down in Shelby County, and I had to flee the only home I'd known since I was a young bride. The judge … er …" She glanced at Natalie, seeming to remember her recent reprimand, then continued. "Well, never mind that. We have had a fire here, Señor. The grain barn was destroyed." Her glower found Levi. "I felt sure the Yankees had something to do with it, but as it turns out, one of the Negroes they hired is responsible. He attacked poor Natalie and nearly killed our Samuel, too."

Alexander turned his startled look to Natalie, obviously astonished by the tale he'd just heard, while Levi stood silent, hurt and uncertainty in his dark gaze. Cousin Eunice appeared poised to launch into another speech, which Natalie simply could not endure.

"Please, everyone." Natalie closed her eyes and took a deep breath. "The fact remains that Jezro must be found. That is most important." She looked at Levi, wishing she could explain the situation with Alexander, but this was not the time nor the place.

After a long moment, he acquiesced. "I will have my men begin the search immediately." With a slight bow, he turned to descend the steps. His voice had held none of the warmth from minutes ago.

"Natalie, my dear," Alexander said as soon as Levi joined his men in the yard. "Please, tell me all that has happened."

She allowed him to lead her to a wicker sofa, where she explained about finding Jezro in her bedroom, the fire, and nearly losing Samuel, keeping her eyes averted when she described Levi's heroic rescue of her son. She didn't want anyone to guess her love for the colonel. "So you see, Alexander, we are very grateful for the soldiers. We might have lost all the barns had we not had their help."

"That may well be," he said, frowning at the group of men in blue uniforms receiving instructions from Levi. "But wasn't it the colonel who chose the new workers? He should have taken more care in who he allowed onto a plantation where a widow and her small son reside."

Levi's own admission of that very thing echoed in her mind. "No one could have predicted something like this would happen."

"I daresay an officer in the Union Army should have," Eunice said, adding a firm nod to punctuate the forceful words. "That man is too arrogant for his own good, and now that arrogance put you and little Samuel in danger. As your mother's dearest relative, I advise you to end your agreement with the army posthaste before something else happens."

"I must agree with your cousin." Alexander exchanged a satisfied look with Eunice. When he met Natalie's gaze again, his face turned grave. "I have learned some troubling information about Colonel Maish. In fact, that is the very reason I came this morning, as it is rather alarming."

Natalie stared at the man. "What sort of information?"

"The kind that leads me to believe you are in far more danger with that man on Rose Hill land than you were with a former slave who turned out to be a thief."

She stood, angry that he would say such a thing. "Alexander, Colonel Maish has been nothing but a gentleman in the time I've known him. He risked his life to save Samuel. I doubt anything you might have learned through gossip is even true."

Carolina and Corporal Banks rounded the corner of the porch, their smiles fading when they took in the serious faces of Natalie, Alexander, and Eunice.

"Miz Natalie," Carolina said, hesitation in her voice. "Harriet wants to know if she ought to make up some sandwiches for the soldiers befo' they head out."

"Of course not," Eunice said before Natalie could answer, her tone indignant. "We can't spare a morsel of food now that the grain barn has been destroyed." Her accusing eyes landed on the corporal. "I'm still not entirely convinced those Bluecoats didn't have a hand in it. It would not surprise me if they bribed that Jezro to do it, just to keep the attention off the true culprits."

Corporal Banks' brow furrowed, but he remained silent.

"Carolina," Natalie said, determined not to let her overbearing cousin make decisions that were hers alone to make. "Please ask Harriet to use the bread she baked yesterday and what's left of the ham in the smoke house to feed the soldiers. While Cousin Eunice is correct—we will need to begin rationing immediately—we also can't neglect the very men who helped save the barns and who are even now going in search of the man responsible."

Natalie watched the couple retreat in the direction they'd come from.

"Perhaps we should go inside to discuss the news I have discovered," Alexander said, glancing at the handful of soldiers who still remained in the yard. Levi was nowhere to be seen.

Exhausted by everything that had happened, Natalie agreed, needing the tranquility of her favorite room in Rose Hill Manor to help sort things out. She allowed him to lead her inside, wishing she could send Eunice away while Alexander revealed whatever it was that had him upset. She couldn't imagine anything he'd learned about Levi would change her feelings. She loved him. When the dust settled from all the events of the past twenty-four hours, she would explain about Alexander and her fears for the future, and, if she were brave enough, admit her love for him.

When the two women were settled on the parlor sofa, Alexander stood near the ornate fireplace and took a deep breath.

"I am sorry I must bear such disturbing news, Natalie." His dark eyes conveyed his distress. "Suffice it to say, my concern is only for you."

"Please, Alexander." Natalie was ready to have this conversation over with. "Tell me."

He nodded, frowning. "I have just come from Austin, where I ran into an old friend. We enjoyed a good visit, discussing the many changes in Texas. When he learned I had business at Rose Hill, he shared a most interesting tale."

Natalie's patience thinned. "Such as?"

"Because he is a *Tejano* and a respected business owner, the Union Army General—Granger, I believe his name is—has sought my friend's advice on many occasions over the last weeks. Just a few days ago, Colonel Maish met with the general, and my friend was there. Later, when he asked about the colonel, he was told of the man's fierceness in battle, and how countless Confederates died by his hand."

Natalie shuddered. She didn't want to hear stories from the war. She and everyone else in the country still struggled to put the pain it wrought behind them. "He fought for the North, Alexander. That is no secret. What he did in those battles is between him and God, the same as any other soldier, including my husband. I don't see how this information has anything to do with me."

"You once told me your husband died at Manassas Junction at the hands of a Yankee officer on horseback."

"Yes." A knot of trepidation began to form in her belly.

Satisfaction flashed across his face before he grew sober again. "Maish was in that battle, as a captain. He received his promotion to colonel because he boldly rode into the fighting, killing dozens of Confederate soldiers with his saber as he went."

The implications of the story settled over Natalie like a dark, ominous cloud.

Alexander knelt before her and took her hands in his, his eyes showing his deep concern. "There is a strong possibility, my dear Natalie, that Colonel Maish is the very man who murdered your husband."

She stared at him, unable to believe it. Surely Alexander's friend was wrong. Of course, Natalie knew Levi had killed men, Southern men. War forced a man to do things he would never do otherwise. She thought back to the night they sat on the porch swing together. He'd asked about George's death, and she'd conveyed to him the same details she'd disclosed to Alexander several months ago. If Levi had been in that battle, he would have mentioned it, she was certain.

A sound from the foyer drew her attention.

Levi filled the parlor doorway a moment later. When she met his solemn gaze, what she saw in his eyes sent a chill racing through her, ending when it reached her heart and the tender shoot of love that had just begun to blossom.

He'd heard Alexander's accusations.

And he wasn't there to deny them.

❧ ❧

Levi hadn't intended to eavesdrop, but when he'd come in search of Natalie and heard Lopez use his name, he'd stood outside the parlor, listening. Everything the *Tejano* said was true, of course. When he'd learned how and where George Ellis died, he'd wondered the same thing Lopez seemed certain of. Had he killed Natalie's husband, Samuel's father? They would never know, but the look of betrayal shining in her eyes now, staring at him as though he'd slain Ellis there in the parlor, sufficiently snuffed out any hope he had of explaining himself.

"Is it true?" She stood, her voice full of distress.

Lopez rose to his feet, a sneer on his face when Levi glanced at him.

"That I was in the battle at Manassas Junction? Yes, I was there."

"Why didn't you tell me?"

Lopez and Eunice stared at him, satisfaction in their eyes.

"I believe this is a conversation we should have in private."

"Absolutely not." Lopez stepped closer to Natalie. "I will not allow the man who may very well be responsible for making her a widow to come anywhere near her again."

"I agree." Eunice stood on the other side of Natalie, as though she needed their physical protection from Levi. "Indeed, little Samuel will never know his father because *you* killed George Ellis."

Levi seethed at the charge, fighting to remain calm. He'd had about enough of the accusations, and he was preparing to challenge them when Samuel brushed past him, staring up at Levi with wide, troubled eyes.

"Did you hurt my papa?"

Levi's indignant wrath evaporated at the sight of the fatherless child. What could he say? "I … I don't know, Samuel." The truth sounded pathetically inadequate.

"Samuel," Natalie said, breaking free of her protectors and coming to kneel in front of her son. "I need you to go play in your room while I talk to the grown-ups. Then I'll come up, and we'll talk about your papa."

Samuel's frown deepened, and he put his pudgy hands on either side of Natalie's face. "Did the co'nel hurt Papa, Mama?"

She gathered him into her arms and carried him from the room. "I don't know, Samuel," she whispered as they went out the door. Samuel's head was on her shoulder, but his teary eyes landed on Levi.

They disappeared, leaving Levi with the strongest urge to follow and capture them both in his embrace. He'd never intended to hurt them. To hurt anyone. War, they surely must understand, left lives broken, even those who never saw a battlefield.

"You are not welcome here, Colonel." Eunice drew herself up to her full, rounded height. "You need to leave."

The officer in him refused to budge. He didn't take orders from the woman. Besides, he had to talk to Natalie. Between her supposed engagement to Lopez and his involvement in the battle where her husband had perished, they had plenty to discuss. But one look at Lopez's stony face told Levi he would not have an opportunity to speak with her alone. Not now, anyway.

Without a word, he spun and exited the house. The yard was devoid of soldiers and horses, every available man off searching for Jezro. He'd put Banks in charge of the details, knowing the corporal would make certain every inch of the plantation was searched. Moses felt the field workers should not be involved in the hunt since there was no way to know if Jezro had been working alone or not. Levi agreed. Looking to the cotton fields now, he made out the shapes of people at work.

"Colonel, suh?"

Moses strode toward him.

"I done searched all the buildin's like you asked, suh. Didn't find no stolen things anywhere. Thought I might look in the quarter houses whilst the others are out in them fields."

"I'll join you," Levi said, glad to have something to occupy his mind besides the debacle between Natalie and himself. "Until Mrs. Ellis is able to ascertain what's missing from the house, I want to be certain Jezro doesn't have more goods stashed somewhere."

Together, they walked down the sloping lawn to the quarter, passing a larger cabin that had probably once served as the overseer's home. When they reached the two rows of small houses, he and Moses entered the first one. Though it had plank floors and a fireplace, there wasn't much else to offer comfort. Two sagging rope beds, several straw pallets, and a few crude furnishings occupied the cramped space. Unwashed dishes were stacked in a bucket, and a few items of clothing hung from pegs on the wall. There were very few personal belongings, despite the cabin housing a half-dozen people.

"This here the cabin where Jezro was stayin'." Moses glanced around the area that wasn't even as big as Rose Hill's parlor. "I'll look over here." He indicated the bed farthest from the door.

Levi nodded, trying to imagine where Jezro might have hidden the treasures he'd stolen from Natalie. That the Negro had been in her bedroom, going through her things, and then attacked her ... well, that man better be long gone. If Levi got his hands on him—

"I feel responsible for all this mess with Jezro, Colonel."

Levi looked up to find Moses' troubled gaze on him.

"How so?"

"I shoulda been more careful, keepin' a better eye on them boys."

The same guilty thoughts plagued Levi. "I suppose we've all learned a valuable lesson, especially when it comes to keeping Mrs. Ellis and Samuel safe."

"Yessuh, I 'spect we has."

They continued their search. A few minutes later, Moses tapped the floorboards with the toe of his stiff-looking leather shoe.

"What are you doing?"

"I's listening for a holler spot underneath them boards. Makes a good place for hidin' things you don't want found."

Levi got the impression Moses knew this from experience. A few more taps, and Levi's curiosity reached its limit.

"Did you ever hide something in the floor you didn't want found?" He expected a guilty expression to fill the other man's face, perhaps from stealing something from his master and keeping it secret, so he was surprised when Moses grinned.

"Shore did. I hid my Bible under them boards. First while I's at the Langford's then after I come to Rose Hill, up over the kitchen." He smiled. "I shore am pleased I don't got to hide that book no more. I got it sittin' on the table there in our room, as proud as can be."

Levi nodded, and they both went back to work. The old Negro was a puzzle—that was for certain. He never seemed angry at Natalie or her family for keeping him in bondage all those years. Even telling a story about having to hide his Bible brought a smile rather than righteous anger.

They went through each cabin but found no stolen items. Exiting the last one, they walked into hot afternoon sunshine. Levi glanced over and saw a small shack off by itself. Although a horde of flies buzzed around it, it wasn't an outhouse. Those were in the opposite direction. Too small to be of much use for storage or animal care, he wondered at its purpose.

"Should we check inside that building? Jezro may have used it as a hiding place."

A grave look washed over Moses' face. "That there *the shed*. When a slave disobeyed or got into mischief, Massa Ellis had him thrown in there."

Levi looked back to the small structure. Moses' tone alone told Levi how bad it must have been to be put inside. "I'll check it. You don't have to."

Moses took hold of Levi's arm when he started toward the building. "Colonel, suh, that place nastier than anythin' you can imagine. Not even Jezro go anywhere near it."

He contemplated the information for several moments. "Is it still used?"

"Not since ol' Massa Ellis die."

"Why don't you tear it down?"

Moses shrugged. "Don't guess I ever thought to."

"Would Mrs. Ellis care if you got rid of it?"

"No, suh, I don't believe she would."

They both turned to study the shed. When Levi met Moses' gaze again, the glint of eagerness he saw there matched his own. It would feel good to destroy something as hateful as that shed. Especially after such a vexing day.

"We'll need a sledgehammer."

A grin stretched across Moses' face. "I'll bring two."

CHAPTER TWENTY-TWO

It had been a full week since the fire. Gratefully, Samuel didn't appear traumatized by the event. He played with the kittens and with Isaac, ran around the yard with Ebenezer, and curled up in Natalie's lap for stories each night before bedtime. Everything would seem back to normal if it weren't for the shadow of sadness in his eyes whenever Corporal Banks or one of the many soldiers residing at Rose Hill passed by.

Gently pushing the porch swing with her toe, Natalie broke open a pea pod and let the small green balls roll into the bowl in her lap, thinking of the day they'd learned Levi had been at Manassas Junction. Samuel shed huge tears because the colonel hurt his papa, or so he believed. She soothed him as best she could, trying to explain that no one knew what happened the day George died. When her son finally quieted, he didn't ask about his papa or Levi again, and Natalie didn't press him.

She sighed. Levi hadn't been back to Rose Hill since that terrible day. Corporal Banks was very tight-lipped about it, and not even Carolina could get information from him about the colonel's whereabouts. Natalie vacillated between the need to see him and talk things through and silently railing at him for his role at Manassas. Why, of all battles, had he participated in that one? She couldn't deny the description of the man who'd killed George fit Levi. Reasoning also told her it fit every other Union officer who was there, but what if Levi was the one responsible for ending George's life? How could she give her heart to the man who may have run his saber through her husband's heart?

After placing the bowl of peas and empty shells on the table next to the porch swing, she stretched her arms and back. The work was tedious, but the promise of Harriet's creamed peas made it worth it. Perhaps she would stay and watch how Harriet made the dish, as long as she promised not to get in the way.

Ever since the fire, Harriet's manner toward Natalie had softened. She didn't seem so distant and even shared jokes with Natalie in a way she hadn't before. It was strange how a tragedy could bring folks together and make them see there really were no differences that mattered. The color of a mother's skin didn't matter when a child was in danger.

With the sun sliding down the western side of the world, Natalie went to gather the slate and books. She and the women hadn't held lessons since the fire. It would be good to get back to them. Making her way to the ancient black walnut tree, she spotted Carolina and Harriet coming around the side of the house from the kitchen. Samuel and Isaac charged past them, obviously racing.

"Is Lottie coming?" she asked when the women reached her.

"Don't know, Miz Natalie." Carolina plopped down on the grass. "Miz Eunice keepin' her so busy we don't hardly see her 'til suppertime."

Harriet joined them. "Poor gal don't have a minute to work on her own sewin'. That chile gonna get here an' have nothin' to wear."

Eunice had taken it upon herself to move into the large suite of rooms Natalie had closed off. Although there were no funds for redecorating, she'd managed to create a space fit for Queen Victoria from items she'd procured from other rooms throughout the house. Natalie despised the woman's audacity, but the mere thought of confronting her cousin left her exhausted.

Lottie hurried from the house a few minutes later as fast as her bulky load would allow.

When she arrived, Natalie smiled. "We haven't started yet. We wanted to wait for you."

A frown drooped the young woman's face. "Miz Eunice say I

can't study the letters with you."

"Surely she can spare you for an hour," Natalie said, irritated with her cousin. Eunice usually took a nap this time of day anyway and wouldn't even miss the servant.

"Ain't that, Miz Natalie." Tears formed in Lottie's eyes. "Miz Eunice say I not allowed to learn 'em. Says Negroes don't have no need to learn to read an' write, and she ain't gonna have no uppity Negro workin' for her."

Natalie's irritation turned to outrage. She glanced at the house, wondering if she should speak to her cousin. While Eunice could dictate what her own servant did and didn't do while they served her, she did not have the say on whether or not Lottie learned to read.

"Lottie." Her firm voice drew all three women's attention. "You are no longer a slave. You may work for Cousin Eunice, but it is *your* decision if you learn your letters or not."

The young woman stared at Natalie, wide-eyed, while Carolina and Harriet grinned.

"I shore do want to learn 'em, Miz Natalie."

"Then sit down. Our lesson will begin right now."

Lottie sat, albeit hesitantly, but the moment she recognized the letter *D* in the book in her lap, the doubt on her face disappeared.

They were so engrossed in their lessons that none of them noticed Eunice arrive until she was upon them. She marched to Lottie, grabbed a handful of the woman's hair, and yanked her to her feet.

"I said you are not allowed to learn your letters!" she bellowed, causing Lottie to shrink into her dress. "No good can come from a Negro learning to read." She turned her venomous glare to Natalie. "I don't know what has gotten into you, Natalie Ellis, but my slave will not participate in this ... this ... *atrocity.*"

Before Natalie could respond, Eunice slapped Lottie, nearly knocking the young woman to the ground. Samuel and Isaac ran behind the thick trunk of the tree.

"Cousin Eunice!" Natalie stood and rushed to Lottie, as did Carolina and Harriet, shielding her from the wrathful woman. "Lottie is no longer your slave. She is a free woman, able to make her own choices. Your behavior is appalling."

"*My* behavior? What would your poor mother think if she saw you cavorting with Yankees and teaching Negroes to read? Why, I'm glad the fever took her long before she had to witness such a disgraceful disappointment." She returned her narrowed glare to Lottie. "You get in that house right now. No Negro of mine is allowed to learn their letters."

Natalie looked at Lottie, willing the young woman to stand up for herself.

"I ..." Lottie's voice came out timid and frightened.

"What did you say, girl? Speak up." Eunice's menacing stare bored into the young woman.

Lottie glanced among Natalie, Carolina, and Harriet before she returned her attention to Eunice. "I want to learn to read, Miz Eunice," she said, more forcefully this time. "I's free now, so you don't got no say in it."

Eunice's face turned scarlet. "How dare you! This is what happens when you give Negroes their freedom. They turn uppity like they were our equals." Her enraged eyes shifted to Natalie. "See what you've done. You've ruined her. Well, I won't have it." She turned back to Lottie. "You either come inside the house this instant, or you can go find yourself someone else to work for."

Tears sprang to Lottie's eyes anew. "Who gonna want me like this?" She indicated her huge belly.

"I guess you'd better get inside that house, then, and leave this foolishness of learning your letters behind." Eunice's lips pinched in a sneer, and she crossed her arms over her own ample belly.

With a look of resignation, Lottie nodded and turned to Natalie. "I best get inside, Miz Natalie. I shore 'ppreciate you wantin' to teach me, but I ain't got nowhere else to go. I gots to stay with Miz Eunice."

"No, you don't," Natalie said before she realized what she was doing. When her thoughts caught up with her tongue, she smiled. "You can work for me, here at Rose Hill."

The young woman and Eunice gasped at the same time.

"What do you think you're doing, Natalie Ellis? Lottie is mine. The judge bought her for me."

"Cousin Eunice." Natalie squared her shoulders. "Lottie no longer belongs to you. She can decide whom she wishes to work for." Turning to the startled servant, Natalie said, "I don't have money to pay wages yet, but like the others, you can work for room and board and a share of the crop. Does that suit you?"

Lottie blinked several times before nodding. "Yes'm, Miz Natalie. That suit me fine."

"This is outrageous!" Eunice practically shook with rage.

"No, Cousin Eunice, your behavior is outrageous." Gathering her courage, Natalie said, "I believe it is time for you to leave Rose Hill."

Eunice sputtered. "You mean to say you're throwing me out? Over a no-good Negro?"

"I'm not throwing you out, Cousin Eunice. I simply believe you'll be happier elsewhere. I won't tolerate name calling or violence on my property. Lottie is a human being and my employee, and you will treat her as such."

The three servants stared at Natalie with rounded eyes. Certainly, they had never heard a white woman stand up to another white woman over a Negro. Admittedly, neither had she.

"You mark my words, Natalie Ellis. You will rue the day you turned your back on your own blood." Eunice stomped back to the house and slammed the door.

It was several moments before Natalie's pulse slowed. When she glanced at the other women, their expressions mirrored her own shock.

"Well." She shrugged and looked at Lottie. "I suppose you'll have time to sew your baby's clothes now."

Harriet was the first to snicker behind her hand. Carolina's brows arched high before she gave in to giggles.

Finally, Lottie, who still seemed stunned by the turn of events, said, "I shore ain't gonna miss that woman's snorin' at night."

Before long, all four women were laughing. And, oh my, did it feel good.

❦

Levi sat at the small desk in his temporary office, writing yet another report for General Granger, this one regarding the stolen cattle. While he didn't like the fact that the thief was growing more brazen and stealing larger quantities of animals, Levi was glad for the distraction. It kept him from dwelling on all that had happened at Rose Hill the past three weeks.

He put the pen in its holder and blew on the page to dry the ink. Granger had not been pleased when he'd learned of the fire and the attack on Natalie. He'd ordered Levi to organize a manhunt, pulling men from the mission of delivering the freedom proclamation in order to catch Jezro. Levi hadn't agreed with the order, mainly because he felt their chief assignment was far more important, but he couldn't deny he wanted Jezro caught and punished for what he'd done to Natalie. When Granger put a bounty on the man's head a few days after the fire, the local patrollers got involved. Their tactics and use of dogs did not sit well with Levi, but he had to acknowledge they had far more experience searching for a runaway Negro than Levi's men. News arrived just this morning that Jezro had been caught and was even now on his way to Austin for trial.

He heaved a sigh. He should go to Rose Hill and tell Natalie the news himself, but try as he might, he couldn't bring himself to face her. Not after little Samuel overheard Lopez's accusation about George Ellis' death. The poor child must be devastated to learn the hero who saved his life might be guilty of ending his papa's. He wouldn't blame Natalie if she never wanted to see him again.

Corporal Banks appeared in the open doorway that led out to one of the side porches. "Colonel, may I have a word with you?"

Levi leaned back in his chair. "Of course."

Banks seemed nervous. "It's a personal matter, sir."

"Come in," Levi said, curious. Banks never got nervous. Not even in battle. It was one of the reasons Levi had wanted the young soldier assigned to him after his promotion to corporal. Banks, for his part, had been relieved to be away from the infirmary where he'd been assigned.

He entered the small room but didn't take a seat. Levi waited.

"I would like permission to call on Miss Carolina." The words tumbled from his mouth, and he seemed glad to have them out.

Levi fought a smile. This wasn't entirely unexpected. He'd seen the looks Banks exchanged with the young servant, but a soldier, even when not in battle, could not afford distractions. And women were most definitely distractions.

"You know how I feel about fraternizing while we have a mission to complete."

Banks gave a firm nod. "I do, sir. I would only use my time off, of course. I wouldn't allow anything to keep me from fulfilling my duty to the Union Army, sir."

Levi couldn't help but feel a twinge of jealousy. Banks and Carolina were free to pursue their attraction to one another with very little to hinder them. Unlike his and Natalie's relationship, which seemed doomed from the moment they met. Why he had allowed himself to seek more, he couldn't say. Especially after hearing where her husband died. Lopez's allegations put everything in perspective … for both of them.

Looking into Banks' expectant face, he couldn't refuse the request. "You have my permission, but see to it this doesn't interfere with your duties."

Banks relaxed his stiff muscles and grinned. "It won't, sir."

"I hope you know what you're doing. You wouldn't want to hurt the young woman. What happens when you leave Texas and return home? Assuming that's your plan."

"I've been thinking on that, sir." He grew sober. "My service with the Army ends soon. I figure we can marry then. She's already said she'd like to see Massachusetts someday."

It seemed as though Banks had considered everything. "I suppose you'll head over to Rose Hill later this evening?"

"I will, sir."

"I'd like you to inform Mrs. Ellis about Jezro's arrest. I'm sure she'll be relieved to hear the news."

"Pardon me for saying so, sir, but I suspect she'd rather hear it from you."

Levi gave the corporal a look of warning. His personal life was not up for discussion. "Just give her the message, Banks."

"Yes, sir." He turned and left the room.

Heaving a sigh, Levi took up the pen again. This was exactly what Levi had warned Banks against. Women were distractions. He had a mission to fulfill here in Texas, and it did not include a romance with a beautiful widow.

An hour later, the last of his reports nearly finished, the inkwell ran dry. Frustrated, he searched the desk for another bottle but found none. A trip to the supply tent in the afternoon heat did not appeal. Surely there was a bottle of ink somewhere in this house.

Levi opened the door that led into the musty interior of the mansion. He hadn't been inside since the day he'd accompanied Natalie while she pointed out the items of worth she was leaving behind. A study with books lining the walls was located on the first floor, and he moved through the silent house in that direction. As he did, he couldn't help wondering what Natalie had been like as a child growing up here. He could picture her running through the rooms, her giggles ringing off the walls.

Shaking the thought away, he found the room and went to the large desk. Muted sunlight came through the curtained windows, aiding his search, but after pulling open several drawers, no ink was to be found. One last drawer remained at the bottom of the desk. It contained several ledgers and a bundle of documents rolled together, tied with string. Lifting them out to see if a bottle of ink might be underneath, the words printed on the face of the first ledger caught his eye.

Sales and Purchases.

Levi stilled, staring at the small book. There could, of course, be all manner of sales and purchases involved in running a plantation the size of Langford Manor. Natalie's father more than likely kept records of how much cotton he sold in any given year, as well as purchases of equipment, feed, and a multitude of other necessities. But something told Levi this book did not hold tallies for the mundane items of plantation life. The book, he felt certain, held the sale and purchase information for one thing.

Slaves.

His stomach roiled with recognition. He should put the books back. There wasn't anything in them that would come as a surprise. Langford owned slaves while he was alive. He bought and sold people at his whim. But driven by years of hearing his parents and their abolitionist friends discuss slavery, Levi had a deep need to see the evidence for himself.

He spread the items on the desk and opened them one at a time. The ledgers did contain records of the slaves Langford owned over the years. Names, ages, and dollar figures were neatly recorded on the lined pages. Thumbing through the books, seeing lives reduced to numbers in a column, he felt nothing but disgust. Next, he picked up the roll of documents and removed the string. The bundle fell open, revealing various sizes of papers, some printed with blanks filled in and some handwritten. Though he'd never seen one before, Levi didn't need to be told he was looking at the bills of sale for Langford slaves.

Sickened, he leafed through the pages, noting names and dates until one caught his eye. After removing it from the stack, he carried it over to the window and held it up to the muted light.

The sum of eight hundred dollars was given to D.E. Boyd for the purchase of a Negro man named Moses, aged about thirty-five years and zero months, this day sold to Calvin Langford, the right and title to which slave I hereby warrant and defend against the claim or claims of all persons whatsoever. Given under my hand and seal this third day of March, eighteen hundred and fifty-two.

It was signed by an official in Galveston.

Moses. Bought and paid for by Natalie's father.

Recalling what Moses said about Langford giving the slave to his daughter upon her marriage, Levi skimmed through the remaining papers until he came to the one he sought.

I do hereby certify that the Negro man named Moses does now belong to Natalie Langford Ellis.

Her father had signed and dated the handwritten note.

Levi stared at the paper, tangible proof that Natalie had owned a human being. While she could foist blame on her father and husband for her part in owning all the other slaves, the document in Levi's hand told a different story. Her father had given Moses to her upon her asking, the way a child asks for a puppy at Christmastime. In her unquestionable selfishness, she had forced the man to leave his family behind and come to Rose Hill to serve her, never once considering his or Harriet's wishes on the matter.

Levi read the date again. Six years ago. She had owned Moses for six long years. A question formed in his mind that would not be ignored.

Could a woman like that truly change?

A noise from the hall drew his head up.

Natalie stood in the doorway, Moses behind her, taking in the scene with unhappy eyes.

CHAPTER TWENTY-THREE

The look of accusation in Levi's eyes nearly took Natalie's breath away.

"Mrs. Ellis."

The warmth she'd grown accustomed to hearing in his voice was absent. She had hoped they would have an opportunity to talk and sort through the confusion Alexander's declarations had left between them. When he didn't return to Rose Hill, despite Corporal Banks' assurances the colonel was well and in residence at Langford Manor, she decided she would go to him. She'd traveled to the plantation under the guise of retrieving an old toy for Samuel. It seemed ridiculous now in light of Levi's cold welcome.

"Colonel. May I ask what you're doing, going through my father's things?"

He glanced at the mess on the desktop. "I was in need of ink and thought to see if I could locate some. Instead"—his cool gaze narrowed—"I discovered these." He held up the paper in his hand.

Natalie looked at the faded document, but it was not recognizable. "I have no idea what that is, but I don't see how anything in my father's desk concerns you."

"I admit it doesn't, but when I found these … to see evidence of the ownership of another human being"—his eyes flicked to Moses then back—"especially a human being you say you care about … well, it is disturbing."

She stepped to the desk and glanced over the jumble of papers. Though she couldn't make out the smaller printed words, the bold letters on one of the sheets became clear in the dim light. She lifted it and read the information, a feeling of regret forming in her stomach. "These are the bills of sale for my father's slaves."

"Yes. And this one is for Moses. Your father paid eight hundred dollars for him. Not exactly worthy of the man standing behind you, wouldn't you agree?"

They stared at each other for a long moment before she reached for the document. The words, although simple in their delivery of information, reduced Moses to little more than a possession.

"And this," Levi said, handing her a second paper, "declares *you* as his owner."

His hard tone told her exactly what he thought of that.

She recognized her father's handwriting. She had a vague memory of him telling her he would deed Moses to her upon her marriage, but she had never seen the document. She looked at the papers on the desk and those in her hand. It seemed a lifetime ago when Papa had bought and sold slaves. Like most daughters, she hadn't been aware of the business practices that were required to keep a plantation running. Only after George and Luther died did she begin to understand the magnitude of what had to happen each year in order to turn a profit. Slave labor was vital to the process, or so they'd believed.

The fact remained, however, that she and her family were party to owning people. The evidence, as Levi called it, was there on the desk. They couldn't go back in time and make things right, but she would do her best to make certain Samuel grew into the kind of man who respected all individuals, no matter the color of their skin.

She turned to Moses, who had remained silent through the conversation. "I'm sorry, Moses. I … I know that doesn't change the things that were done to you over the years, but …"

"You don't need to 'pologize, Miz Natalie. Things was diff'rent then. Now, we all workin' to get on past it. Tomorrow be a new day, and the day after that. Lots'a good can come if we don't keep lookin' back."

Tears welled in her eyes. How many times had the man offered his forgiveness, not only through words but through actions? Seventy times seven, it seemed. "Thank you," she whispered.

"If it be all right, I'd like to see that bill o' sale," he said, his curious gaze on the document. She handed it to him. After scanning the words, he grinned and looked up. "That there says my name. Moses."

She nodded, a sense of wonder that Moses could read at all. Soon, she hoped, his wife and the other women would be able to do the same.

"What these figures right here say?" He pointed to the blank that had been filled in with his age at the time of sale.

"It says you were thirty-five years old when Papa bought you from Mr. Boyd. That was on March third, eighteen fifty-two."

His brow raised. "Thirty-five? That make me 'bout … forty-eight. Well, what do you know? I forty-eight years old." A pleased grin rested on his face while he studied the paper.

"You didn't know how old you were?" Levi asked.

"No, suh, I shore didn't. I's sold away from my family when I's a boy. Never see'd them again. Lots'a years pass after that, and I don't keep track of 'em. Didn't realize I's so old," he added with a laugh.

Natalie's heart wrenched at the thought of Moses, sold as a boy, unaware of the most basic information about his own life: the day he was born.

"Do you mind if I keep this paper, Miz Natalie?"

She shook her head. "I don't mind, but why would you want to have such a thing? Won't it bring back sad memories?"

"Guess it may not make sense to you folks, but this here paper is a part o' me. It tells my story. We all gots a story. Some parts is good, others ain't. I'd like to keep this with my Bible, and maybe show it to my grandchildren one day."

Natalie nodded, wondering if he would ever see the children born to his two oldest sons.

She looked back to the papers scattered across the desktop.

"Could there be something in these documents that might tell us what happened to Moses' boys after they were sold?"

"No," Levi said, sending a look of apology to Moses. "These are the bills of sale from when Langford purchased slaves. They proved his ownership. I don't see any type of receipts from the sale of a slave. Do you have any idea where your sons might have ended up? Perhaps I could send a message to one of our units in the area to help locate them."

Moses shook his head, a deep sadness in his eyes. "Massa George took them an' all the other Langford slaves on down to Ga'veston after the fever killed Miz Natalie's folks. When he come back, he say he has to sell the lot of 'em to the slave broker 'cuz some look sick. He angry 'cuz he didn't get near what they all worth."

Natalie closed her eyes, memories of that terrible day filling her with regret. George refused to listen when she'd begged him to spare Moses' sons. Maybe if she'd tried harder …

When she opened her eyes, she found Levi studying her. What must he think of her, being party to such despicable actions?

She turned to leave, wishing they'd never come. "I want a few things from the attic, and then we'll be gone."

"Mrs. Ellis, wait." When she faced him again, disappointed he'd addressed her so formally, he said, "May I have a word with you?"

"Very well." She wasn't certain her heart could take it if he continued to treat her as though they hadn't shared a passionate kiss. To Moses she said, "Would you please retrieve the rocking horse from the attic? If memory serves, there is also a small chest with baby clothes. I would like that brought down as well."

"Yes'm," he said, giving them a curious glance before departing.

When Natalie returned her attention to Levi, she found him studying her through narrowed eyes.

"You are a paradox, Mrs. Ellis," he said, his voice softer than she'd expected.

She grew nervous under his probing gaze. "How so?"

"I didn't expect you to apologize to Moses. Although I hate

slavery, it was legal. Your father was well within his rights to buy and sell Negroes, including Moses." He looked perplexed. "I thought you'd defend your father."

"Like Moses said, we're all working to put those things in the past." She indicated the papers on the desk. "I'm not proud of what those represent, but I can't change what they are any more than you can change the fact that you were at Manassas Junction."

At her mention of the battle, he frowned. "It was war. What I did in that battle, in every battle, was done because of this." He indicated the papers strewn over the desk. "Men and women were held in bondage right here in our country. It had to end."

"True, but are you proud of everything you did in battle?"

After a long moment, he shook his head. "I'm not."

The simple answer was what she had hoped to hear. "Nor am I proud of everything that was done before you brought the freedom proclamation."

He nodded. "I see your point."

They stood in awkward silence. Natalie was first to speak. "I'd prefer the rest of those were burned," she said, glancing to the papers on the desk. "But I suppose if Moses found some peace in seeing his bill of sale, some of the others might as well. If you'd return them to Papa's desk, I would appreciate it."

"I'll take care of it." He paused. When he looked at her again, the warmth she'd missed returned to his brown eyes. "I should have told you the night we sat on the swing that I was at Manassas."

The soft-spoken words were a soothing balm to her bruised heart. "It wouldn't have been so shocking to hear had it come from you. Alexander said a friend of his was at the meetings with you in Austin and inquired after you."

Levi looked thoughtful. "And it wouldn't have been so shocking had you told me Lopez proposed marriage. I wouldn't have kissed you, had I known."

It was probably wrong to think such, but she was glad he hadn't known of the proposal. "I didn't accept him."

"But you said you would consider it?"

She nodded. "Samuel's inheritance lies in Rose Hill and Langford Manor. I can't run the plantations alone. Alexander promised to make them prosperous again."

"Is that what you want?"

His question resurrected the tangle of emotions that had swirled through her mind ever since Alexander proposed. Was marriage to Alexander what she wanted? Her heart cried no, but she had no other options if she hoped to keep the land. "I want what is best for my son."

"Do you love Lopez?"

"No," she whispered.

He walked around the desk, stopping when they were inches apart. "Come to Pennsylvania with me," he said, his hand moving to caress her cheek. "We'd have a simple life, but a good one. Samuel would have cousins to play with, and perhaps … a brother or two." The smile that played on his lips sent her heart racing.

Her mind could barely focus on what he was saying, so distracting was his nearness and touch. "But Texas is our home. Rose Hill and Langford Manor are all I have left. I can't abandon the plantations." Daring surged through her. His proposal meant he cared for her. "You could stay here, with us," she said before she lost her courage. Her pulse hammered, feeling brazen for voicing the suggestion, but oh, so hopeful. "When the Army leaves, you don't have go with them."

It took a moment, but the passion in his eyes dimmed, and he took a step back. "Natalie, my home is in Pennsylvania. My family is there. I want my children raised with my brothers' children, and with their grandparents. Generations of Maishes have lived in Pennsylvania. Texas has nothing to offer me."

"Except me." Even to her own ears, the words sounded childish.

"You know that isn't what I meant. I am asking you to come to Pennsylvania with me, as my wife and Samuel as my son."

He offered everything her heart desired, but to leave Texas?

"How can you ask me to leave the plantations behind? Rose Hill is Samuel's future, his birthright."

A tense silence filled the space between them. As though a wall had suddenly gone up, blocking out the light and happiness she'd felt only a moment ago. A wall so thick and impenetrable, there was no hope of scaling it.

"Will you marry Lopez?"

The hard tone in his voice cut to her heart and tears sprang to her eyes. "I don't know."

They stood in agonizing silence until Moses' voice came through the doorway. "I got the things from the attic loaded in the wagon, Miz Natalie."

She nodded, drawing herself up. "Thank you, Moses. Please wait by the wagon. I'm coming." When he walked out of sight, she looked at Levi, willing him to change his mind.

But his face remained stony. "I'll need to document the items you're removing from the house." It was as if the past week had never happened. As though they hadn't kissed. As though he hadn't saved her son. He'd become once more the stranger who'd interrupted her life.

She exited the room without a word. He followed her down the hall and out the front door. Moses stood next to the wagon, talking with Corporal Banks, but when they heard her stomping across the porch and down the steps, they hushed.

"The colonel feels the need to document the items we're taking with us."

Moses nodded and removed the canvas he'd thrown over the bed to reveal an old rocking horse and the small trunk she'd requested.

She whirled to face Levi. "Satisfied, Colonel? Does the great Union Army truly care about a child's toy and old baby clothes that were once worn by my long dead brother? They hold no value to anyone except me, but search them if you must. Write them on your list. Do whatever you wish."

She found herself in tears when her speech ended. Aggravated and hurt, she turned to Moses. "Let's go home."

"Natalie." Levi's soft voice was very near. When she wouldn't look at him, he took her by the shoulders and gently brought her around to face him. "I'm sorry for acting like a cantankerous old goat."

She sniffled.

"May I come to Rose Hill this evening so we can talk?"

Looking into his dark eyes, seeing the sincerity there, she couldn't refuse. When she nodded, he offered a slight smile. With the help of his strong hand, she climbed onto the wagon seat. Moses joined her and set the team into motion. She desperately wanted to turn around, to see if Levi stood watching them drive away. Instead, she closed her eyes and prayed, asking God to please change his mind.

Rose Hill and Langford Manor were Samuel's inheritance. Their future lay in this beautiful land.

Somehow, she had to convince Levi that his future was here, too.

CHAPTER TWENTY-FOUR

When the long day of writing reports and meeting with his staff came to an end, Levi made his way to the stable. Not surprisingly, Corporal Banks was there with two horses saddled and ready.

Banks grinned. "I thought you might need your horse tonight, sir."

"You shouldn't eavesdrop on private conversations, Corporal." He gave a mock frown, but the other man's smile prevented it from staying long.

"I was headed over to Rose Hill. Figured I'd wait for you."

They mounted and started off, following the setting sun. The sky was ablaze with reds, oranges, and blues that reminded Levi of Natalie's eyes. He had to admit this country had a rugged beauty to it, but it wasn't home. Not for him, anyway. He missed the green hills of Pennsylvania, and he desperately missed his family. The Maishes were a close-knit bunch. Having all three of her sons away at war had been beyond difficult for his mother. With his two older brothers home, his parents and siblings were eager for his return as well.

But what of his feelings for Natalie? He couldn't deny his deep desire to marry her and claim her as his own. He wanted to be a father to Samuel, especially knowing he may have played a part in George Ellis' death. Despite the vastly different worlds they lived in, despite the many seemingly insurmountable obstacles they faced, he believed he and Natalie could make a good life. In Pennsylvania. Now, he just had to convince her.

After little conversation during their ride, he and Banks arrived at Rose Hill. Levi smiled at the sight that met them. Natalie and Carolina sat on the porch, several lanterns casting a golden glow here and there. A small table held what looked like a pitcher of some sort of drink and several cups. As he and Banks neared, the women stood. Both looked lovely in their finery.

Levi exchanged a glance with Banks, who grinned and kicked his horse into a gallop the last few yards. Carolina hurried down the steps to greet him while Natalie remained on the porch, her eyes fastened on Levi. A look of uncertainty filled her face.

With Banks and Carolina already deep in conversation, Levi climbed the steps, his gaze never leaving Natalie's face.

"Good evening, Mrs. Ellis," he said, adding a teasing note to his voice he hoped would break the tension radiating from her. "May I say you look fetching tonight?"

It worked. Her shoulders relaxed, and she smiled. "Why, thank you, Colonel. Would you care for some refreshments?"

Their polite banter was almost comical, considering the very serious topics that required their attention. He joined her at the cluster of wicker furniture, noticing she didn't settle on the swing. The memory of their time there, Samuel's head resting in his lap, reminded him of his resolve to be completely forthcoming regarding the battle at Manassas Junction.

Levi glanced to where Banks and Carolina had settled on a blanket beneath a huge tree not far from the house. Their laughter and low voices drifted on the rose-scented breeze. "They seem happy."

"Corporal Banks asked my permission to call on Carolina." She looked down at her hands folded in her lap. "My father-in-law sold her mother and sisters several years ago. He was angry when his daughter left with a young man he didn't approve of. I suppose he thought to punish her by selling the slaves she had befriended. I begged George not to let him sell Carolina." Glancing to the young couple, her affection for the servant was obvious. "I hope Corporal Banks will be good to her."

"He will." Levi followed her gaze. "I met him during the battle at Spotsylvania. He was assigned to a medical detail, but when the enemy got too close, he took up a weapon someone had dropped and held them back while the wounded were carried to safety. He earned his promotion that day. When I heard about it, I found him in camp and asked him to be my aide." He gave a chuckle. "I'm certain he is actually a general in disguise."

She smiled briefly before it faded, her nervousness returning.

"Natalie," he said, growing solemn. "I want to tell you about Manassas Junction."

Her eyes widened. "Why?"

"Because you need to understand. To understand me and to understand what I did."

She stared at him for a long moment before nodding.

"War is a terrible thing." He looked toward the darkening fields. Flashes of memory from the past four years played at the edges of his mind. "A man is forced to do things he never dreamed he would do. When we arrived on the banks of Bull Run River, we were already badly outnumbered by Confederates. Our men were green and ill-trained. It was a disaster in the making." He glanced at her, her luminous eyes staring at him.

"We lost hundreds of men almost before the battle began. It was chaos. I remember riding my horse into the fray, swinging my sword, yelling at the top of my lungs." He closed his eyes momentarily. Would that he didn't have to look at her as he confessed his sins. But he refused to take the coward's way out. He opened his eyes and met her gaze. "I don't know how many men I killed that day, but there were many. I never gave them a thought until I met you. Now, I wonder how many husbands and fathers I cut down, all in the name of war."

Moisture filled her eyes.

"We'll never know if George Ellis was one of the men I killed. But we also have to acknowledge it is possible. How can you and Samuel ever forgive me? Even if my sword didn't end his life, I was there." He shook his head and looked away. "That alone would make building a life together impossible for us."

Crickets and tree frogs filled the night with their songs. Banks and Carolina spoke in low tones, occasional laughter echoing in the stillness.

He wouldn't blame her if she told him to leave and never come back.

"You ask how Samuel and I can forgive you," she said, her voice a feather on the wind. When he met her gaze again, tears fell from her thick lashes. "But had it not been for me and all the slaveholders across the South, you wouldn't have gone to war at all. You'd be home in Pennsylvania with your family, not here. It is I who needs to seek your forgiveness."

Stunned by her admission, hope surged through Levi's heart. He moved from the chair across from her to the empty place beside her on the couch. Studying her face in the lantern glow, he didn't see a former slave owner or the widow of a Confederate soldier. He saw the woman he loved. If they could reach this place of mutual forgiveness despite so many obstacles along the journey, surely they could overcome anything that stood in the way of them seeking a life together.

With her gaze on him, her eyes alive with passion, he was sorely tempted to kiss her. The quiet voices of Banks and Carolina, however, reminded him they were not alone.

"We still have much to sort through," he said, feeling more optimistic than he had during the ride to Rose Hill.

"Yes." She nodded, looking at him with such hope, it nearly undid him. "But we don't have to work out everything tonight. Couldn't we just enjoy the evening?"

He could stare into her eyes all night. "We most certainly can."

"Mama?"

They both turned to see Samuel peering around the corner of the porch. He came forward, barefoot and wearing his nightclothes. Levi hadn't seen the boy since the day Lopez announced his guilt in the battle where George Ellis died. If Natalie could forgive him for his role at Manassas Junction, he prayed the little boy could too, someday.

"Samuel, what are you doing out of bed?" Natalie reached toward her son, and he ran across the porch and curled into her side, then peeked up at Levi.

"Hello, Samuel." Levi smiled, hoping he could win the boy's friendship again.

"Hello."

Natalie tipped her son's chin up. "Do you remember what I said about leaving your room after I've put you to bed?"

Samuel nodded. "I'm not 'llowed."

"Yes. You have disobeyed me by coming downstairs."

He peeked at Levi again before ducking his head into Natalie's arms. "But I heard the co'nel talking."

Natalie glanced at Levi. Was she worried his presence had upset the boy? They might have quite a challenge ahead if Samuel refused to accept Levi in his mother's life.

"I'm happy to see you, Samuel," he said.

Samuel looked at him with big eyes the same color as Natalie's. "You're not mad at me anymore?"

The question caught Levi off-guard. "Mad at you? Why would I be mad at you?"

"Because I cried when Señor Lopez said you hurt my papa. Mama said Papa got hurt 'cuz he was a soldier, not because you did anything to him. But"—his bottom lip trembled—"you didn't come back to see us anymore. I thought you were mad at me."

In an act that seemed perfectly natural, Levi stretched out his arms. Samuel didn't hesitate. He crawled onto Levi's lap and wrapped his thin arms around Levi's neck.

Gratitude rushed to Levi's heart. The boy hadn't held his sins in battle against him after all.

The surprise on Natalie's face surely mirrored his own. She smiled, her eyes sparkling with happy tears.

Levi tightened his grip on the boy, relishing the warm little body against his chest. "I would never be angry with you, Samuel."

They sat in peaceful silence for several minutes until Samuel gave a big yawn.

Natalie stood. "It's time for bed, young man."

Samuel didn't let go of Levi. "Can the co'nel tuck me in?"

Levi's brow rose, and he looked to Natalie for her response. When she didn't deny the request, he stood, holding Samuel. "I don't mind."

Nodding, she led the way into the house and up the stairs. On the second level, he followed her down a darkened hallway to a room on the right.

Levi carried the boy to his bed, which was illuminated by a glass lamp, its wick turned low. He carefully lay Samuel down, and his eyes drooped when he touched the pillow.

"G'night, Co'nel." He rolled onto his side and tucked a small blanket under his arm. Levi recognized it as the one he'd wrapped the cats in the night of the fire. "Come see us again."

"I will." Levi watched the boy drift off to sleep.

Natalie stood in the doorway, her arms wrapped around her waist. He joined her. She didn't move but only stared up at him, her eyes dark and rounded in the muted light.

He cupped her cheek, and she leaned into his hand. Levi's heart filled with love for her and Samuel. "I want to tuck him into bed every night."

She whispered, "I want that too."

He had no power to keep from capturing her mouth with his own. Her lips were as soft and inviting as he remembered and held a sweetness he found intoxicating. When she sighed beneath his caresses, he deepened the kiss and wrapped her slight body in a fierce embrace, molding her against him. Her hands explored the muscles on his back with feathery light strokes, and he groaned. The desire he had for this woman was like nothing he had ever known.

All too soon, he remembered where they were—with Samuel sleeping steps away—and reluctantly ended the kiss. He didn't release her, though, but held her in his arms. She pressed her cheek against his chest, a sigh of contentment on her breath.

Eventually, they made their way down the stairs and returned to the porch. If Banks and Carolina had noticed their absence, they didn't let on. Levi knew he should go. Natalie was far too tempting for him to remain after a kiss like that.

"I'll return tomorrow." He took her hands in his. "Perhaps we can take Samuel fishing."

A happy glow radiated from her face. "He would love that." Her eyes grew misty. "I was so afraid you wouldn't change your mind."

"Change my mind?" he asked. "About what?"

"About staying in Texas. I didn't think anything could change your plans to return to Pennsylvania. I'm so happy I was wrong."

Her words sent a chill down his back, dousing the flame his ardor had ignited. "Natalie." His next words would disappointment her, but they must be spoken. "I haven't changed my mind. When my commission in Texas comes to an end, I will go home."

"But ... you kissed me and said ..."

Her eyes widened, and her hand flew to her lips. Choking back sobs, she whirled and ran into the darkened house. He took a step to follow, but what would he say when he found her? Closing his eyes, he silently berated himself. Of course, she would think, by his words and actions, that he'd changed his mind. When he'd said he wanted to tuck Samuel in every night, he'd meant after they moved to Pennsylvania. He had sufficiently made a huge muddle out of an already complicated situation.

Heaving a sigh, he turned to leave. There wasn't anything else he could say tonight.

He found Banks and Carolina standing at the bottom of the steps. Their embarrassed expressions told Levi they'd heard the whole thing.

CHAPTER TWENTY-FIVE

"Miz Natalie?"

Natalie looked up from the tub of sudsy water where the last of her camisoles sat on the washboard, ready to be scrubbed. Ruth, Adline, and Carolina stood behind her.

She straightened and arched her stiff back. "Please don't tell me something else is wrong."

The morning wasn't half over, but they'd already discovered a fox had been in the hen house, and four chickens were missing. After that, Moses found that three of the new workers were gone, taking a good portion of the Army supplies with them. If these women were there to report more bad news, Natalie might crawl back in bed and call the day finished.

"No, ma'am," Carolina said with a giggle.

Natalie waited.

With a glance at Carolina, who nodded with encouragement, Ruth stepped forward. "Miz Natalie, Carolina and Harriet been tellin' us how you's helpin' them learn their letters." She motioned toward Adline, who had never acknowledged Natalie's presence. Now, however, the woman stole surreptitious peeks at Natalie while Ruth spoke. "Adline and me is wonderin' if we could come learn our letters too."

The request came as a complete surprise. She glanced between the women, practically sputtering her answer. "Why, of course you can. I'd be pleased to have you both join us."

Adline met Natalie's gaze. A small smile appeared on her face, the first Natalie had ever seen from her.

"We'll meet under the walnut tree later this afternoon."

With a happy smile, Ruth said, "Whatever you teach me, I gonna teach my man, Wash, and our chillens." Adline nodded her agreement before the women returned to the house.

"It shore is nice o' you to 'llow them to learn to read with us, Miz Natalie." Carolina gave her a studious look. "That freedom proclamation shore done changed things, hasn't it?"

"It has at that."

Carolina eyed her. "You even look diff'ernt."

Natalie shrugged. "I hardly recognize myself these days." She looked at her hands, red and raw from scrubbing laundry with lye soap.

"Seem to me you is more like you 'sposed to be now rather than the way you was before."

The honest words should've offended her, but she knew there was truth in them. "I hope so. It isn't as though I've had much choice."

Carolina returned to the house. Natalie plunged her hands into the soapy water and set to work on the delicate garment, the servant's words playing through her mind as she scrubbed. Was she now the woman God had intended her to be all along? She never would have believed it the day Levi and his men arrived with the proclamation.

Levi.

She closed her eyes, remembering how tenderly he'd put Samuel to bed, and then finding herself in his passionate embrace moments later. It ignited a desire she'd never experienced before. Far deeper than mere physical attraction, she knew she wanted him to be the father of her children. She wanted to make a life with him, to raise a family with him, to grow old with him. But she had misunderstood his intentions and felt the fool for it. He planned to return home to Pennsylvania, with or without her. Why couldn't he understand she must remain in Texas, fighting for her son's birthright?

Tears filled her eyes, and a painful truth became all too clear.

A future with Levi was impossible.

After finishing her chore, she went in search of Samuel, needing the familiar comfort his sweet presence brought to her. He and Isaac were in the barn with Moses *helping* him with one of the milk cows that was due to deliver her calf. Wiping the moisture from her brow as she went, she thought back to the day many months ago when Alexander had brought a bull with him on one of his visits. She'd previously mentioned her concern that their milk cows were not producing as they should. She'd long since sold off Rose Hill's cattle to pay the taxes on Langford Manor, leaving them without a bull to breed and repopulate their small dairy herd.

The image of the handsome *Tejano* came to mind. He'd been nothing but a gentleman throughout the past year, always paying his rent for the pastures on time and even supplying them with beef occasionally. She believed she could trust him to run Rose Hill and Langford Manor, helping them become the prosperous plantations they'd been before the war, thus saving Samuel's inheritance. That was what was most important now. It mattered not that she didn't love him. If she accepted his proposal of marriage, hopefully, her affection, and that of her son, would grow over time.

Putting her troublesome thoughts away, she squared her shoulders and continued to the barn. Samuel's contagious laughter helped soothe her soul. He and Isaac perched on the top rail of a stall. A wobbly calf took hesitant steps through the straw while its tired mother looked on.

"Mama, look! It's a boy cow. Ain't he funny?" Samuel laughed again, and Isaac chuckled beside him when the calf fell flat on its face, its legs giving out from underneath it.

"He nice n' healthy." Moses joined Natalie. "Once he weaned, his mama shore to give us some good, thick milk with lot'sa cream."

Natalie watched the mother nudge the calf up with her wet nose then give him a few licks from her enormous tongue. The caring gesture made Natalie smile. She hadn't witnessed livestock with their young very often. Mama had often reminded her that a young lady's place was in the house learning the things she would need to run the manor someday. Sewing, music, and proper etiquette were of far more importance, especially when one hoped to secure a good marriage. How disappointed she would be to know George had not been the knight in shining armor her parents believed him to be.

She looked at Samuel, and her heart softened.

George had not been the husband she'd longed for, but she wouldn't have this amazing little boy if she hadn't married him.

"Samuel, be sure you and Isaac wash your hands before you come for the noon meal."

"Yes, Mama," he chirped, his eyes on the calf.

She left the barn and went back to the house. Upstairs, she peeked in the door to the rooms Cousin Eunice had occupied. Everything was put back to rights now that the disagreeable woman was gone. Moses, ever the kindhearted man, had volunteered to drive Eunice to town the day after she slapped Lottie. With her wagon loaded and her accusations flying, she left Rose Hill, declaring she would not step a toe on Natalie's property again. Natalie waited for the guilt to envelope her, considering Eunice was her mother's favorite cousin, but it never came. Instead, heaviness lifted as she watched the covered wagon depart her land. When Moses returned some hours later, he said he'd hired a Negro couple to drive Eunice to Rusk County, where another of her distant cousins lived. The couple, he said, was hoping to find family members there as well. Natalie remembered the look of longing in his eyes, and she knew he and Harriet continued to pray that their boys would find their way back to Rose Hill.

After their noon meal, Natalie gathered with the five women under the walnut tree. Ruth and Adline's eyes rounded when she placed a book in each of their hands. They ran their fingers over the hard covers, carefully turning pages as though they held a valuable treasure. A sheen of moisture sprang to Adline's eyes when she glanced at Natalie. A silent message passed between them, and

Natalie nodded, tears of her own clouding her vision.

They spent a lovely hour going over the alphabet. Natalie passed the slate among them, letting each woman painstakingly write the first letter in their name. Lottie, however, didn't seem interested in the lessons. She shifted her position on the soft grass every so often, as though she couldn't get comfortable. When the others stood to return to their chores, Lottie sat with her eyes pinched closed.

"Lottie, are you not well?" Natalie asked, concerned for the expectant mother. If Lottie's prediction was correct, she still had a few weeks before the baby would make its appearance.

"My back's achin' is all." She arched her spine as confirmation. "Couldn't sleep much last night 'cuz it hurtin' so."

Natalie had relieved the young woman of work inside the house as soon as Eunice departed. Instead, she directed the soon-to-be-mother to sew garments for her child.

"Perhaps you should lie down and rest." Natalie helped the young woman to her feet. The moment Lottie stood, however, her eyes widened, and a large stain appeared on her skirt. Her terrified eyes met Natalie's.

Natalie's heart leaped. "Lottie, your water broke. You are in labor."

"I is? Harriet said the pains would be 'cross my belly when my time come. Ain't nothin' but my back hurtin' now."

"Be that as it may, you're in labor." Natalie glanced at the house. "Let's get you inside, then I'll get Harriet."

Lottie hesitated. "I has me a bed in the quarter, Miz Natalie. I wouldn't want to mess up your purty things."

"Nonsense." Natalie took the woman by the arm and led the way toward the porch. "A baby deserves a nice quiet place to enter the world." Neither mentioned that slave babies had always been born in the quarter, noise, dirt, and all.

Harriet met them at the front door.

"Lottie's in labor," Natalie said as the young woman doubled over in pain. "I'm taking her to the guest room."

Harriet's brow shot up, but she simply nodded. "I get some water on the stove and bring up fresh sheets." She hurried away.

Natalie led Lottie to the very room her previous owner had occupied and where Lottie had slept on a pallet. Now Natalie pulled down the covers on the four-poster bed and helped Lottie sit on the edge of the mattress.

"I scared." Tears filled Lottie's eyes.

"There is nothing to be afraid of." Natalie offered a reassuring smile. "Before you know it, you'll be holding your baby."

Harriet bustled in, wide-eyed Carolina following with a stack of sheets and towels in her arms. Natalie stepped back as the older woman went to work, directing Carolina here and there, removing the blankets from the bed and replacing them with several layers of sheets, and finally stripping Lottie down to her underthings. Once she had the mother settled, she looked at Natalie.

"You don't got to stay." She pulled up a chair close to the bed and settled on it. "It may be a while 'fore this little one makes its appearance. 'Sides"—she eyed Natalie—"childbirth can get messy."

"I'd like to stay." She glanced at Lottie. "If it's all right with you."

Lottie smiled. "I'd like that." A moment later, she closed her eyes and clenched her fists.

Harriet leaned over and smoothed the young woman's brow. "It gonna get worse befo' it get better, but you has your sweet lil' baby soon enough."

The hours went by at an excruciatingly slow pace. Moses popped his head in at some point to let Natalie know he was taking the boys fishing. He'd see to their supper too. Lottie's pains grew more intense. Natalie recalled Samuel's birth and how anxious she'd been to have it over and done with. Yet the love that poured from her heart when she'd beheld her son for the first time made all the agony worthwhile.

Evening fell, and Harriet lit a lantern. When the time finally came for Lottie to deliver her child, the overly warm room filled with activity. Harriet threw back the sheet covering Lottie and prepared scissors and string. Carolina rushed in and out carrying hot water from the kitchen, perspiration dotting her face. Natalie wanted to be helpful, but she had no idea what to do. She settled for standing aside so as not to get in the way.

With a great push, Lottie delivered a squalling baby. Moisture sprang to Natalie's eyes, marveling at the miracle of life.

"It be a boy!" Harriet held up the plump little fellow so Lottie could see him. Tears rolled down the new mother's face, and Natalie felt the warmth of wetness on her own cheeks. With deft hands, Harriet cut the cord and tied it off with string before wrapping the baby in a soft blanket Carolina held ready for her.

Natalie thought Harriet would hand the baby to Lottie then, but she turned to face Natalie. "Lottie has some more work to do. Would you hold this little fella?"

With arms more eager than she realized, she took the sweet bundle, cradling him like she'd cradled Samuel. The baby quieted, making the noises only a newborn could make. He looked up into her face as though he knew exactly who she was and didn't mind in the least that a white woman held him.

"Hello, little one." She ran her fingertip across his soft cheek. He turned toward it, and she laughed. Oh, what an amazing gift God had given Lottie.

When the new mother was ready, Natalie placed the baby in her arms.

"He the most beautiful thing I ever did see," Lottie said, staring at her son.

"He be the first Negro chile born on Rose Hill since freedom come," Harriet said, her voice soft, almost reverent.

Natalie stared at her, stunned at the revelation. She turned back to gaze at the little boy, born into freedom rather than into bondage. It was almost as though a heavy darkness lifted from the land. The old ways were gone, the new had come, revealed in the birth of a tiny baby.

"My boy ain't a slave," Lottie said with wonder, looking into the face of her sleeping son. She glanced up at the women, eyes shining. "I gonna name him Jude Liberty. Jude after my pappy, and Liberty 'cuz he be free."

A more fitting name could not have been found.

After excusing herself from the room, Natalie went to her bedroom. She pulled out the small chest she'd brought back from Langford Manor and carried it awkwardly to the guest room. Carolina sent her a puzzled look when she approached to help.

They set it on the floor next to the bed, and Natalie raised the lid. Yellowed paper greeted her, which she tossed aside until she came to what she knew was hidden there.

"These belonged to my brother," she said, a lump forming in her throat as she carefully lifted out a small nightshirt made of soft material. She'd wanted all new things when Samuel was born, so hadn't ever seen these tiny clothes. "They're a bit old and musty, but you might find some things you can use in here."

When she glanced at Lottie, Natalie found the young woman's eyes wide with wonder. "Miz Natalie, I can't take these sweet things. They be yours."

"I want you to have them." She took out another small garment. Lottie's eyes shone with interest. "Jude Liberty needs a wardrobe fit for a free young man."

"Oh, thank ya, Miz Natalie." Lottie accepted the small garment.

Natalie stepped back, and Carolina moved in to see what other treasures the chest held. She picked up a tiny bonnet and made Lottie laugh when she put it on her own head.

Harriet stood beside Natalie while the two younger women chattered and laughed. "That a real nice thing you done. I didn't know your mama had a boy chile."

"His name was Samuel. He died when he was two years old."

Harriet wore a thoughtful look. "Guess it don't matter what color skin a person has. Pain and sorrow find you anyhow, seems like."

Looking at the baby, his skin milky brown and beautiful, Natalie smiled. "That may be true, Harriet, but not today. Today, we celebrate joy and new beginnings."

CHAPTER TWENTY-SIX

Admitting he was wrong didn't come easy to Levi, but the proof stared him in the face.

"Three?" he asked, frowning at Moses.

They stood among Rose Hill's lush green cotton plants, where thousands of pods with puffs of white poking out were nearly ready for harvest. The grand plantation house rose in the distance, giving the whole scene a picturesque look. But all was not well. Corporal Banks arrived back at camp yesterday evening with news of the workers' disappearance. Although Levi's first instinct was to jump on his horse and comfort Natalie, he hadn't done it. Seeing him would no doubt be more upsetting to her than a few missing workers and supplies.

"Yessuh, three. I had me a suspicion them fellows and Jezro was friends, but I shore didn't want to take a job away from a man willin' to work hard." He shrugged. "Guess they figure on findin' somethin' better than what Miz Natalie offering—a place to live with three good meals an' the promise of cash money in they pockets when they's done."

His sarcasm was justified.

"I have to admit I didn't expect this." Levi rubbed his beard. "I assumed men who had only known slavery would jump at the opportunity to work for wages. But first Jezro and now these three have sufficiently proved me wrong."

Moses shrugged. "Don't beat yo'self over it, suh. Men is all the same, no matter what color skin cover their bones. Some is good, some ain't. I known me some mighty fine Negroes, and I known me some that are this side of worthless. I 'spect I can say the same about the white men I known, too." He smiled, seeming to remember something. "That Mistah Brantley that run off with Missy Ellis, he be one o' the good kind." His eyes traveled back to Levi. "You remind me o' him in a way."

Levi had heard enough snippets of the story to piece it together. George's sister ran away with the overseer, helping several slaves escape as they went. He wasn't sure if this Brantley fellow was a hero or a villain, but Moses seemed to think highly of him.

"What happened to them?"

"Who? Missy Ellis and Mistah Brantley?" At Levi's nod, Moses smiled. "They took the folks that run with 'em down to ol' Mexico then headed out West. From time to time, Miz Natalie get a letter from Missy Ellis—guess she be Miz Brantley now—and she says they has a good life, raisin' hosses and such. I brung Miz Natalie a letter from town just the other day from Missy, sayin' Jeptha and Zina and Aunt Lu done moved to Oregon with 'em now that the war is over and we slaves is free. Says Jeptha and Zina has a little boy 'bout Samuel's age." Moses wiped an errant tear that slipped from his eye and rolled down his cheek. "Hearin' they is all safe is shore an answer to this man's prayers."

The story spawned more questions in Levi's mind. "Would you ever consider leaving Rose Hill and going somewhere else to start over? Maybe somewhere up north?"

Moses looked off into the distance before answering. "I 'spect it's crossed my mind some, but we gots to stay here for now."

"Why?"

"My boys, suh. My boys is out there somewhere. Rose Hill be the only place they know to come look for me and Harriet."

Levi understood. Thousands of Negroes faced the same, often impossible, challenge of finding loved ones now that they were free to do so. Inadequate record keeping and the reality of slaves being sold multiple times presented obstacles most could not overcome. Moses' sad tale echoed dozens of others Levi had heard across the state.

"The Army is trying to help families reunite," he said, not wanting to give Moses false hope, knowing the possibility of finding a lost loved one was remote. "We have people all across the South collecting names in the hopes of helping families locate missing members. If you give me the names and ages of your sons, I'll add them to the list."

A spark came to life in Moses' eyes. "That be good news, Colonel. I shore would 'ppreciate you taking down my boys' names. Their mama is mighty anxious to see 'em."

Levi smiled. "My mama's fairly anxious to see me, too."

Moses grinned. A moment later, he squinted his eyes, looking toward the road. "Someone comin'."

Indeed, a rider turned down the lane to Rose Hill. Though he couldn't make out the man in the saddle from this distance, he recognized the horse.

"Look like Mistah Lopez here." Moses watched the rider enter the yard. His frown and tone spoke his displeasure.

Curious, Levi said, "It doesn't sound as though you approve of Lopez."

Moses met his gaze then looked away. "Ain't my place to have an opinion on who Miz Natalie do business with."

"Business? I thought he was her suitor."

"I s'ppose he be both now. But when he first come to Rose Hill a year or so ago, he done it strictly to lease her pastures for his cattle."

Levi stilled, instantly alert. "He has cattle on Rose Hill land? How many head?"

"Don't rightly know. It ain't never the same bunch that stays for very long, as far as I can figure. Ain't even the same kind of critters either. He got all kinds mixed in together. His cowpokes run 'em north after a couple weeks of grazin'. Later, a different bunch o' them animals is here." He shrugged. "Don't make much sense to me. When I asked Mistah Lopez 'bout it one time, he said he didn't want them animals to *overgraze* the land, but there be nigh a hun'erd acre out there." He looked at Levi. "He tol' me to mind my own biz'ness after that."

"Where are the pastures?" Levi had to work to keep his voice level. Inside, his mind whirled. Could Lopez be the cattle thief?

"They sit betwixt Rose Hill and the Langford place. Cain't see 'em from the house nor the road since there be some woods and a low valley. It a real purty place."

Levi turned to look at the house. He couldn't see Lopez and had to assume he was inside with Natalie. That the man could be a criminal sent a wave of panic crashing through his gut. "I can't say more about this just yet, Moses." He cast a glance at the other man, hoping to convey the seriousness of the situation without alarming him. "I don't trust Lopez. I need to do some investigating into him and his business before I make any accusations, but suffice it to say I'd like to you keep your eyes open when it comes to him and his cattle."

"Yessuh, I do it." The unspoken question in his voice would have to wait.

"And keep watch over Mrs. Ellis, too. Especially when Lopez is around."

"I done learned my lesson with Jezro, suh. I ain't gonna let nobody hurt her again."

Levi nodded then mounted his horse and headed toward the house.

He had a cattle rustler to catch.

"Alexander, this brooch is lovely." Natalie held up the gift he'd presented to her shortly after his arrival. With small pieces of colored glass cut to look like gems and set in an intricate design surrounded by gold, it was by far the most ornate pin she owned.

"When I saw it, I knew I had to purchase it for you." He smiled from where he stood near the mantel, seemingly pleased with himself. He glanced at the brooch pinned on the collar of her gown. "Why don't you put it on? The one you often wear is rather plain."

She reached up to touch the blue and white cameo brooch Adella Rose had given her. "This is a treasured keepsake. George's sister gave it to me when she left for Oregon. I will wear yours tomorrow."

The frown on his face told her what he thought of her suggestion, but he didn't argue. "After we're married, I will buy you many jewels and gowns. Anything you want. Perhaps we will travel abroad. I should like to see Europe."

"Alexander." Natalie tempered her voice. His assumptions irritated. "You must give me time to consider your proposal. With all your talk of traveling, I wonder if you forget I have a son to raise and plantations to operate."

His smile did not reach his eyes. "How could I forget, my dear Natalie?" After a moment, he sat on the settee with her and took her hand in his. "Forgive me. I am simply eager to make you my bride and show you off to the world."

George had said something similar to her after they married, as though she were a pretty possession rather than a cherished wife. "We needn't rush into anything." She withdrew her hand. "You thought to court me at first, and I believe I should like that. We don't truly know one another. For instance, I know nothing of your home, your family, or your business."

His eyes narrowed a bit. "Why should those things matter, *mi pequeña*? Has someone put ideas into your head?"

"I don't know what you mean. I simply want to know more about the man who has asked me to marry him. That doesn't seem so unreasonable, does it?"

He relaxed. "It does not. You may ask me anything you wish. And as soon as we are husband and wife, I will take you to see my family's ranch. It is beautiful land with a river running through it. Our cattle graze on the best grasses in Texas." He offered a devoted smile. "Of course, it is Rose Hill and its lovely mistress that have captured my heart."

Uncomfortable with the passion shining in his black eyes, she thought to change the subject. Thankfully, a disturbance in the yard drew their attention to the open window. Ebenezer barked and yelped, followed by Samuel's happy shrieks and bubbling laughter. Curious, she rose to see what it was about.

Her heart tumbled over itself at the scene that met her.

There on the front lawn, Levi had Samuel up on his shoulders, teasing the big dog with a stick. The three of them chased and circled and danced, looking silly and happy and oh, so wonderful. She smiled despite the sheer agony it brought to her heart, knowing they would never be the family she longed for.

"What is he doing here?"

Alexander's irate voice came from directly behind her. She turned to find him staring out the window, his cold eyes focused on Levi.

"I don't know." She returned to her seat lest he see something in her eyes to give away her true feelings. Though it was foolish and there was no future in it, she loved Levi still.

A few moments later, noises on the porch and her son's nonstop chatter told her the playmates were coming into the house. They both appeared in the parlor doorway, Samuel rosy-cheeked and grinning. Levi's face, on the other hand, grew stony the moment he saw Alexander across the room.

"Mama, the co'nel says we can go fishing." Samuel ran to her and clambered onto her lap. "Can we? He says you and Ebenezer can come. Will you, Mama? Please?"

Natalie couldn't help smiling at her son's enthusiasm, and then she looked at Levi. His expression hadn't changed, but his eyes now rested on her.

"Fishing is not something ladies do, Samuel." Alexander moved to stand next to the settee, his scowl imparting his feelings on the subject.

Samuel returned the scowl, his bottom lip poking out. "The co'nel said girls can go fishing."

Natalie didn't relish being in the middle of the squabble. Keenly aware of Levi's gaze, she forced a smile. "You're both correct. While ladies don't normally go fishing, we girls sometimes make exceptions, especially when very handsome young men ask us to join them." She tickled Samuel, causing him to squeal.

He jumped off her lap and tugged her hand. "Come on, Mama. The co'nel said he knows a good place to catch some fish."

She looked up to Levi, the awkwardness of the situation settling around her.

Finally, he gave a slight bow. "I promised Samuel we would go fishing, and I am a man of my word."

Whether the statement had a double meaning or not, she didn't know.

"Natalie," Alexander said, drawing her rather reluctant attention. "Have you forgotten who this man is and what he did?"

She glanced at Samuel, his little ears attentive to the conversation around him. "I have not, but we won't discuss that now." She indicated her son. "Suffice it to say, a trip down to the creek is nothing to worry over. Join us if you like."

All three males in the room frowned at her suggestion.

She rose. "I'll get my hat, and we can be off." Leaving the parlor without looking at either man, she hoped they could get along for the few minutes it would take her to go upstairs.

In her room, she stood in front of her mirror and tied on a wide-brimmed straw hat. A flush high on her cheeks spoke of her anxiety at the prospect of being with Levi all afternoon, but Alexander's presence would serve as a constant reminder that her future was not with the Union officer. That he was kind to her son was endearing. That he'd saved Samuel's life earned her indebtedness. But unless he changed his mind and chose to stay in Texas, there was no hope for anything beyond friendship, passionate kisses notwithstanding.

She joined the three of them outside. Levi held two fishing

poles while Samuel carried a small bucket. Alexander stood a few paces away, his arms crossed and a deep frown on his brow.

"Can we go fishin' now?" Samuel asked as he danced around Levi's legs. More questions tumbled from him in his excitement, wondering where they would fish, how many they would catch, and if they would eat their catch for dinner. A glance at Alexander's dark countenance as he watched, however, reminded Natalie she would need to encourage her son to spend time with the *Tejano*. If she planned to seriously consider his proposal, one of the deciding factors would be Samuel's acceptance.

"We sure can." Levi smiled down at the boy.

"Natalie." Alexander took her by the arm and led her a short distance away from Levi and Samuel. "I do not believe spending time with this man is wise. Your son is too young to understand, but it is very likely the colonel is responsible for your husband's death. Is that really the sort of man you want your son to look up to?"

"The war is over, Alexander." She glanced to where Levi and Samuel knelt, inspecting an insect crawling across the ground. "Colonel Maish and the other Union soldiers are no longer our enemies. We'll never know what happened on the battlefield where George died. I can't hold him responsible without knowing for certain, and even then, it was war."

The muscles in his jaw ticked. "I forbid you to spend time with him. You have consented to my courting you. Surely I should have some say in this."

She bristled at his authoritative tone. He sounded very much like George. "We are simply taking Samuel fishing, Alexander. You will be with us."

"I do not have time for such frivolousness. I am a busy man with many responsibilities." He cast a scornful look in Levi's direction. "Apparently, a colonel in the Union Army is not so burdened."

Something akin to relief swept through her. She had not looked forward to spending an awkward afternoon with two men who didn't like each other. "I'm sorry you won't be able to join us. If it would make you feel better, I'll ask Carolina to accompany me, but I don't want to disappoint Samuel."

"You spoil that boy, Señora," he said, unsmiling. "The child needs a firm hand." Before she could reply—which was probably for the best, considering his comment did not sit well with her— he strode to his horse and mounted. "I'll return tomorrow. I hope you will receive me as a woman being courted should. One of the servants can attend the boy."

She watched him ride away, a knot of unease forming in her belly. His testiness was understandable. He'd come bearing a beautiful gift and had surely hoped to spend time with her. But his indifference toward her son and his demands on her left her more than a little concerned.

"Mama?"

Samuel stared up at her. His cherub face and bright blue eyes erased the unpleasantness Alexander's words left behind. "Let's go fishing, shall we?"

"Yes!" Samuel bounded back to where Levi waited.

When she met Levi's gaze, his eyes held questions, but he didn't voice them. Instead, he took Samuel by the hand and grinned. "Let's go fishing."

They walked to the creek behind the quarter. Several large rocks had been placed along the bank and made the perfect spot to cast into the clear, gurgling water.

Natalie settled on the wild grasses, tucking her feet beneath her wide skirt, while Levi and Samuel hunted worms and grasshoppers. Watching them, she could almost believe Levi had come to his senses and realized that remaining in Texas with them was the right thing to do. Surely his kisses meant he had feelings for her that were more than mere attraction. And it was plain to everyone— including Alexander—that Samuel adored Levi.

Yet she had to accept the reality, not allow herself to be distracted by wishes and dreams. Harvest was only a few weeks away. Once it was complete and the cotton sold, her agreement with the Union Army would come to an end. They would leave Langford Manor eventually, and all the soldiers would return to their homes. Including Levi.

She sighed and closed her eyes. *Father in heaven, I don't know what the future holds for Samuel and me. Help me make the right decisions for both of us.*

Under a hot afternoon sun, Levi patiently instructed Samuel on the art of fishing. They disappeared down the bank after a while, where they were hidden behind shrubs and thick brush. Natalie was on the verge of going to find them when their voices grew closer. Samuel proudly carried two fish, one in each hand.

"Look, Mama!" He held them up, grinning.

"How wonderful!"

"I caught 'em all by myself." Samuel glanced up at Levi, who raised his brow. "Well, the co'nel helped."

"You did well, little man." Levi rested his hand on the boy's bony shoulder.

"Can I show Harriet my fish? She said she would cook 'em for supper if I caught some."

The small fish would not make a meal, but Natalie didn't mention that to her son. "You may. Don't forget to wash your hands after you deliver them."

Her son hurried away, his gait a bit awkward as he balanced the fish. At one point, he dropped one and had to retrace his steps to retrieve it. Natalie wondered what condition the fish would be in when he finally reached the kitchen.

Turning, she found Levi watching her. Her face warmed under his intense gaze.

"Thank you." She looked away, unable to hold eye contact. "Moses is good to take him along when he and Isaac come down to the creek, but I know Samuel enjoyed today."

"He's a fine boy, Natalie. You've done a good job, raising him on your own."

She remembered what Levi had said about Samuel needing a father to help him become a man. "Well." She sent a nervous glance in his direction. "I'm sure you need to return to the army camp, and I have reading lessons to give."

She headed toward the house, and he fell in step beside her.

"How's that coming?"

He truly sounded interested. "Wonderful," she said, unable to keep from smiling. "The women are quickly learning their letters. I thought to start with teaching them how to write their names, as there may come a time when they need to give a signature for something. After that, we'll work on learning to read."

"It's commendable what you're doing." His serious eyes were on her when she glanced at him. "The Freedmen's Bureau will open schools for Negroes throughout the South, but it'll take people like you to help the adults learn to read and write."

She savored his praise. "Lottie won't be able to join us for a while. Little Jude Liberty is a very demanding fellow just now. The poor woman is exhausted simply seeing to his needs."

Levi nodded. "Corporal Banks informed me of your cousin's departure." A smile played on his lips, telling her the corporal had more than likely heard an earful from Carolina and passed the information on to Levi.

Natalie sighed. "I wish I could say I feel badly about asking Cousin Eunice to leave, but the truth is, I don't. The way she treated Lottie was disgraceful. I simply couldn't allow it to continue."

They reached the bottom of the porch steps, where the shade of a great oak offered a brief respite after their walk in the sunshine. She made to ascend, but Levi reached for her hand.

"Natalie," he said, his voice low. She turned to him, afraid of what he might say. Although she knew they had no future together, she hoped he would continue to visit, if only for Samuel's sake. "You need to be careful when it comes to Lopez."

The warning was not what she'd expected. "I don't know what you mean."

"How well do you know him?"

"He's been visiting Rose Hill for a year. He's never given me cause to believe I'm in danger in his presence. Actually, he gave me a similar warning about you."

"You would do well to rebuff his attentions."

Her spine stiffened. "I don't see how this is any of your concern, Colonel. You've made it perfectly clear you won't stay in Texas. Alexander has made me an offer I would be foolish not to consider. Without slaves, I can't manage the plantations. He promises to bring them back to their full potential. I won't jeopardize Samuel's inheritance simply because you don't like the man."

His jaw clenched beneath his dark beard. "Your stubbornness is not your best virtue, Mrs. Ellis."

Natalie huffed and climbed the steps without a backward glance.

The man was impossible.

CHAPTER TWENTY-SEVEN

The fiery sun hung low in the western sky, casting shadows over the narrow valley below. Levi perched on a wooded rise, hidden from view as he observed several cowboys and a herd of cattle grazing peacefully on Rose Hill grass. With a few hours remaining until nightfall, the air around him simmered as though it had escaped from a furnace. A breeze would not only cool his sweat-soaked body but also rustle the too-still landscape. Any movement he made might be seen by the men he was watching. Though his muscles complained, a little discomfort was worth it if he could catch Lopez red-handed. His instincts told him he had his man, but he would need more evidence than a gut feeling to get a conviction in court.

A cow bellowed and ran across the field.

With the vaqueros' attention on the animal, Levi shifted his weight ever so slightly. He could have sent some of his men to watch the herd, but the need to see for himself if his hunch were correct kept him in place. Once he witnessed Lopez with the cattle, he'd bring a company of men to apprehend the culprit. The very thought of the *Tejano* behind bars made him grin.

For a brief moment, he closed his eyes, recalling the fury he'd seen on Lopez's face when Natalie chose to go fishing instead of remaining at the house with him. Levi had wanted to gloat, but goading the man would have served no purpose. He'd have time enough to enjoy seeing Lopez's shocked face once he realized he'd been caught.

Another hour passed. When the men's backs were to him, Levi inched behind the foliage of a prickly shrub. Carefully removing his hat, he mopped his brow with the back of his shirt sleeve. His coat lay on the ground next to him, long since discarded. After replacing his hat, he tipped his canteen to his lips, letting lukewarm water trickle down his throat. He'd sit here until the sun set, watching and waiting, before heading back to camp. By then, Banks would have received the message Levi sent with one of the privates alerting the corporal to a possible break in the cattle theft case. The men would be ready to ride the moment Levi returned.

What would Natalie think once she realized who Lopez really was? Seeing the arrogant man with her in Rose Hill's parlor earlier had nearly driven Levi mad. The *Tejano's* overconfidence about his place in her life—his words and actions oozed with it—told Levi the man was far more certain of a future union with Natalie than she seemed to understand. Promising to restore the plantations to their former glory not only held the key to her considering his proposal, but it was also the reason she'd refused to consider Levi's. Obviously, Lopez knew how to reach the lady's heart far better than Levi did.

Frustration had him squeezing his hands into fists. Were land and cotton so important to her that she would marry an oily snake like Lopez?

No. He shouldn't judge. He couldn't imagine what worries a widowed mother left to raise a son alone might have for the future. On top of that, she was the sole owner of two enormous plantations. It made sense that she would want Samuel to inherit them someday, especially if they somehow became profitable again. Funding enough hired help to make that happen would be impossible on her own.

He glanced at the landscape surrounding him. It was beautiful country, to be sure. Yet her refusal to give it all up and go to Pennsylvania with him hurt his pride. Theirs would have been a tale for the ages. A southern slave owner falling in love with a northern abolitionist and leaving behind the tainted land where men and women had once been held in bondage. But her future, she believed, was here.

A thought crossed his mind as he shifted his backside on the hard ground. Was it *he* who was being stubborn? She hadn't refused his proposal for marriage. She simply didn't want to leave Texas. But he couldn't imagine living at Rose Hill, or even Langford Manor. Her roots might be in the rocky soil of Texas, but his were not. Besides, he didn't relish trying to fill George Ellis' shoes on the very land where he and Natalie had shared their lives. He could still see the sadness that had come to her eyes when she'd learned Levi may have had a hand in her husband's death. It would be far better for them to start their life together in a new place, where neither had to deal with the ghosts of the past.

Rubbing his stiff neck, Levi glanced through the branches of the shrub to the valley where the cattle grazed. Six men on horseback, Mexican sombreros on their heads, were positioned around the animals. Each man had a rifle across his lap and six-shooters strapped to their hips. He'd relay this information to Banks and his men so no one would be caught unprepared for the fight that could ensue once Lopez and his vaqueros realized they'd been found out.

Studying the cattle, Levi estimated there were nearly one hundred grazing there. Although he was no expert on the different breeds, it was obvious there were several mixed in this group. He recognized the famed Texas Longhorns by their enormous spread of horns. There were other animals that looked similar but with shorter horns. There were red and white Herefords, Black Angus, and even some white Brahmans with their oddly shaped humped back. They were all breeds that had been reported stolen, and though he wouldn't be able to get close enough to check just now, he'd wager the animals in this herd bore the brands from those same ranches.

His fists clenched thinking how Lopez had Natalie so completely fooled with his fancy clothes and horse. It wouldn't surprise Levi to learn the beautiful thoroughbred had been stolen as well. The man was smart, he had to admit. Paying a widow to lease her pastures in order to hide his criminal activity was brilliant. Rose Hill was miles from town, with no real neighbors, so no one was around to bear witness to the number of animals he moved through the area. Where they went after they left Rose Hill was a mystery, but more than likely, Lopez had the animals driven all the way to Kansas, where shipping cattle east by train was a growing industry. Putting him out of business would be a pleasure.

The sun soon disappeared. Levi was rising to leave when Lopez himself rode into view. He went directly to one of the cowboys, the man in charge, Levi guessed. He wasn't close enough to hear their conversation, but the men seemed relaxed. Two of the other cowboys rode over, and, a moment later, their laughter echoed in the valley.

Just then Levi's horse nickered. Though he'd tethered the animal some distance away in a copse of trees, the sound traveled on the still evening air. Levi froze when Lopez and his men looked in his direction. After a moment, Lopez said something to the men then nudged his mount and rode across the pasture to the base of the rise, not far from where Levi hid. The three other men trained their guns toward the brush.

Levi didn't breathe. He didn't blink. He sat completely still.

Lopez took a pistol from his holster, aimed, and fired up the hill. The bullet zinged past Levi. He didn't flinch. Lopez fired the gun again, slightly to Levi's left. The bullet ricocheted off a rock. Levi's pulse raced, and he silently prayed his horse would stay quiet.

Squinting into the darkening landscape, Lopez waited another minute before he returned to his men. Levi remained utterly motionless until, finally, Lopez rode away. One cowboy went back to guarding the cattle while another worked to get a campfire started. Levi stayed where he was until the fading light offered him enough cover to get to his horse without being seen. He knew he should go straight to the army camp and gather the men he'd need to catch Lopez, but the strong desire to warn Natalie won him over. She deserved to know the kind of man Lopez was. As the owner of Rose Hill, she also needed to be aware that a company of soldiers would soon descend on her property.

Turning the horse toward the plantation, he kept the animal to a slow walk to avoid any unnecessary noise from its hooves that might travel through the night. When he finally arrived at the grand house, relief washed through him. Yellow lantern light glowed through at least one window. Though his news could have waited until tomorrow after he had Lopez in custody, the need to see her drove him forward. Dismounting, he mulled over what he would say to convince her that Lopez was not the man she thought him to be.

"Good evening, Colonel." She stood in the open doorway.

Her use of his title reminded him they still had many things to work out between them. "I have some news." He didn't relish this conversation.

"Something's wrong. I can see it on your face."

"You're correct." He indicated the wicker sofa. "Let's sit down, and I'll tell you everything."

She settled on the sofa. Levi opted to take the chair across from her.

"Please, Levi, tell me what this is about."

Although happy to have her return to calling him by his name, he couldn't smile. Not when he'd come to deliver such grave tidings. "You must understand, the things I am about to reveal mustn't be repeated, to anyone. At least, not until we've made an arrest."

"An arrest? Of whom? Corporal Banks told us Jezro had been captured and taken to Austin. Does this have something to do with him?"

"No." Levi took a deep breath and plunged forward. "When the Army first arrived in Texas, we received numerous reports of stolen livestock, mainly cattle, although some reported horses stolen as well. We've been searching for the thieves these past weeks, looking into any suspicious activity involving large numbers of stock."

She sent him a look of confusion. "I don't understand what this has to do with me. After the war started, I had to sell off our cattle. That's why our pastures were available when Alexander approached me and inquired about leasing them."

"From what I understand," he said, choosing his words carefully, "the cattle Lopez brings to Rose Hill do not stay long before they're moved again."

"Yes, that's right. I gather he has more animals than his property can accommodate. With our pastures overgrown and unoccupied, it made perfect sense for him to make use of them." Her eyes shot wide. "Has someone stolen Alexander's cattle?"

Irritation rolled through him, although it was not directed toward Natalie. Lopez had her completely duped. "No, the cattle Lopez is grazing on Rose Hill grass are perfectly safe."

She studied him, her fine brows drawn into a V. "Then who do you hope to arrest and for what crime?"

"Natalie." There was no way to soften the blow. "I believe Lopez is the cattle thief."

It took a moment for his words to sink in. Her eyes rounded. "Surely you jest!" Her voice echoed in the still night.

"I do not." He glanced at the darkened house and placed his finger across his lips as a reminder for her to keep her voice down.

"That is preposterous," she said, softer but with just as much fervor. "I've known the man for over a year. He *pays* me to let his cattle graze in our pastures. I highly doubt a thief would do that."

"It wouldn't surprise me if a thief who stood to make thousands of dollars selling stolen cattle didn't mind losing a little money in order to keep a widow in the dark about his crooked business practices."

She stared at him for several long moments. Levi prayed she could hear the truth in his words. Although he didn't have hard evidence Lopez was the thief, he felt it in his gut. And if there was one thing he'd learned in four years of war, it was to trust his gut.

"I know you don't like Alexander." She shook her head, her disappointment apparent. "But to accuse him of stealing cattle is beyond the pale."

He'd feared he would have a difficult time convincing her. "Don't you find it strange that he's constantly moving animals in and out of Rose Hill land? His men are heavily armed with far more gun power than is necessary for simply watching cows eat grass."

"I don't know a thing about cattle, but I'm certain he has a perfectly good reason for both."

"Such as?" He wanted her to think this through for herself.

"Well, he could … perhaps he …" She sent him a look of irritation. "I have no idea, but I simply can't believe Alexander is the thief you claim he is."

"Think about it. A widow with a large plantation is exactly the cover a thief would need to keep his ill-gotten animals safe before moving them north. There was no shortage of Texas beef during the war, which tells me men like Lopez were all too happy to drive cattle north to sell, despite their origin in a Confederate state."

Her brow remained furrowed. "A business associate of my father-in-law sold beef to the Union. He was hanged by Confederate sympathizers. I doubt Alexander would have risked such a terrible fate for the sake of selling some cows to the Yankees. You have the wrong man, Colonel. You would do well to keep searching."

The stubborn woman wouldn't believe him until he had Lopez in chains. "Just promise me you'll be careful should he show his face at Rose Hill. Trust me when I say you will thank me after I've arrested him and sent him to Austin for trial."

"We shall see."

"Yes, we shall. Goodnight, Mrs. Ellis." He stood and stomped down the steps to his waiting mount. Riding away, he recognized that jealousy had been the sole reason for his churlishness. He'd come to warn her, not to win her love. Lopez had been a guest at Rose Hill for over a year. His business was stealing cattle, not harming widows and small children. Still, the thought of Natalie having feelings for the criminal made Levi all the more determined to see that man behind the bars of a Union Army prison.

Turning his mount in the direction of Langford Manor, he slowed the animal to a docile walk. The sliver of moon offered meager light to aid his trek home, and despite Levi's vexation with a certain widow, he wouldn't ride recklessly and endanger his horse and himself. He looked up to the starlit sky, a plan forming in his mind. He would take a full company of men and surround the pastures on all sides, effectively cutting off any escape routes. Catching Lopez with the stolen cattle would be difficult, but Levi would settle for apprehending his men and the animals. A search party could locate Lopez once they had the confessions of his cowhands.

Frustration rolled through him. Why couldn't Natalie see the truth? It was so completely obvious. Did she have feelings for Lopez? Is that why she couldn't admit what was right in front of her face? Well, he would have to—

The cocking of a gun echoed in the still night.

An explosion rent the air in the next moment, and something slammed into the back of Levi's shoulder, knocking the breath out of him. His horse reared and bolted into a gallop. Levi barely hung on.

"Get him!"

Lopez's voice.

The wooded area that lay between Rose Hill and Langford Manor emerged from the shadows ahead. Levi steered the horse into the thick brush, and the terrified animal raced in despite branches that must have torn at its legs. The crashing sound behind him told Levi that Lopez and his men were following.

Clutching the reins with one hand while his other arm hung limp, Levi wasn't prepared when the horse stopped abruptly. Levi flew through the air over the horse's head and landed on the ground with a horrific *thud*. His head slammed into something hard.

The horse tore around the fallen tree that had blocked its path, leaving Levi gasping for air with lungs that wouldn't work.

Dazed and in pain, he could hear Lopez and his men closing in. Had God seen him through four years of war only to let him die in Texas at the hands of a cattle thief?

Though he fought against it, his eyelids slid closed, and the world went black.

CHAPTER TWENTY-EIGHT

Hot tears stung Natalie's eyes long after Levi rode away. Why must men act so foolishly? To come in here and accuse Alexander of stealing cattle was beyond ridiculous. He hadn't mentioned any proof, only speculations and allegations. Perhaps his jealousy went so deep he intended to ruin the only man who stood in his way of having her. Yet even as that thought crossed her mind, she tossed it aside. Levi was not vindictive. Of that she was certain. But to accuse an innocent man of such a serious crime was uncalled for.

She frowned as she peered into the dark night. What had he said about the men working for Alexander? That they were well armed? Why would cowboys herding cattle need so many weapons? Of course, any number of predators lurked in the woods and brush, including bobcats, coyotes, and the occasional bear. They would need to protect the cattle as well as themselves while they moved the animals to … wherever it was they moved them.

Shadows of doubt crept across her mind. Armed cowboys. Cattle moved every few weeks. It did sound rather suspicious, especially when she considered the reports of stolen livestock.

She shook her head. Why, Alexander had proposed marriage to her, and she was giving it serious consideration. Surely she would have sensed something amiss all these months if he were involved in something sinister. His overbearing ways were disagreeable and often reminded her of George, but it didn't mean he was a criminal.

"Miz Natalie, what you doin' up so late?" Moses came around the corner of the porch. "I saw the light an' thought I best come check on things."

"I wanted to get a breath of cool air. The house is rather stuffy." She didn't mention Levi's visit.

"The days shore are gettin' hot. Well, I'll turn in now." He made to leave.

"Moses?"

"Yessum?"

She felt silly for allowing herself even the tiniest bit of doubt regarding Alexander's practices with his own cattle, yet Levi had been so positive. "Have you noticed anything unusual about the cattle Señor Lopez runs through Rose Hill?"

His brow rose, but he turned his head. "I 'spect I don't know much about raisin' cows, but he don't seem to have any particular kind the way your pappy and Massa Ellis used to run. Them were all the same breed, but the cows Señor Lopez brings in has lots'a different kinds all mixed in. I thought that a bit strange."

She nodded. "What about the cowboys he hires? Have you noticed anything about them?"

"The few times I've run across 'em, they ain't too friendly."

"Were they armed?"

"Yessum." Moses frowned. "Miz Natalie, why you askin' all these questions? Is somethin' goin' on with Señor Lopez and his cattle I need to know about?"

She sighed. "I'm not at liberty to say why, but will you keep your eye on them, please? Let me know if you see or hear anything unusual."

"You the second person to ask that of me today. The colonel seemed mighty curious about them cattle earlier."

That didn't surprise her. "Did he mention anything about Señor Lopez?"

"No, ma'am, just said to keep watch on them cows."

She nodded. "Thank you. You turn in for the night now. I'll blow out the lanterns before I do the same."

He regarded her a moment, then nodded. "Good night." He turned and disappeared around the corner.

The conversation left her with more questions than answers.

She went inside and locked the front door. She blew out all but one lantern, then carried the lit one up the stairs, all the while mulling over what Moses had said. He'd noted various breeds in Alexander's herd. While having different breeds of livestock in one herd wasn't evidence of stolen cattle, it was unusual. She recalled the many times Papa bragged on his cattle, declaring them the finest Herefords in all of Texas. He'd prided himself on buying the very best bulls in order to improve the lineage and health of the herd.

She readied for bed. A rose-scented breeze drifted in through the lacy curtains as she crawled under the cool sheet and blew out the light. Glancing toward the darkened window that faced east, she guessed Levi had reached Langford Manor by now. Was their conversation keeping him awake as it was her? Though she had to concede there were oddities about Alexander's cattle business, she couldn't go so far as to agree with Levi. Alexander had been a good friend the past year. The money he paid for leasing her pastures had kept the bankers from taking possession of her land and provided a security she would always be grateful for.

Sighing, she decided that on the morrow, she would have Moses take her to see Alexander's cattle for herself. Then she would convince Levi he was wrong.

❧ ❧

A toad croaking very near his ear awoke Levi.

Gradually opening his eyes to bright stars shimmering through tree branches, Levi couldn't fathom where he was or why he was there. When he tried to move, a searing pain raced through his left shoulder, and memories flooded back.

He gave a humorless laugh then flinched with another wave of pain. Obviously, he wasn't dead. Not yet, anyway. Only the usual night noises met his ears, echoing in the stillness of the wooded area. The toad continued to croak, though not as close.

Where were Lopez and his men, and why hadn't they finished him off?

Taking a deep breath to clear the fog in his mind, he concentrated on remembering. How long had he lain there? He'd fallen from his horse, but nothing seemed clear after that. He'd been certain Lopez and his cowboys were on his tail when he entered the woods. Had they followed his horse without realizing Levi was no longer in the saddle?

Carefully, he inched his head to his right, wincing when a tender spot on the back of his scalp raked across the ground. He must've hit his head when he fell. A dark object loomed in front of him. He spread his fingers and touched something solid and rough. A fallen tree. He guessed he'd landed on the far side of it when his horse shied. Looking overhead again, he searched for the North Star, needing something to give him bearing. But with so many branches obstructing the night sky, it was impossible to locate. He knew he'd turned his horse off the road that led to Langford Manor, but how far they'd gone before he became unseated was a blurry memory.

A sound in the distance brought him alert. Horses' hooves beating the ground. Not close, but near enough to tell Levi he had to get out of there. When he tried to sit up, a wave of dizziness and pain nearly knocked him unconscious again. Breathing heavily, he felt the back of his left shoulder. Warm and sticky. If the wound wasn't attended to soon, he could bleed to death.

Concentrating on remaining calm, he put the skills he'd acquired during the war to work. His best guess was he'd only gone a couple miles when Lopez shot him. Then he'd gone another half mile into the woods before the horse threw him. Langford Manor was still several miles away. Definitely too far to walk in the dark with a bullet in his shoulder.

But he couldn't stay where he was. Lopez and his men would be back soon enough. He lay flat on his back, his life's blood slowly seeping from his body. This was not the way he wanted to die.

Though he'd been in some tricky situations during the war—some he shouldn't have survived—he'd never felt as helpless as he did now.

"God," he whispered. "You've seen me through some tough times. I hope you have more days left for me, but right now, I'm not so sure. Help me, Lord. And keep Natalie safe."

He kept the prayer open-ended. Knowing God was right there, only a breath away, brought on a sense of calm. *The LORD is my rock, and my fortress, and my deliverer*. Ma had reminded Levi and his brothers of that verse before they'd headed off to war, quoting a favorite Psalm. Surely those words rang true in this situation too.

With woods and brush on his left, he turned to his right again and eyed the log. If he could wedge himself up against it and use some of the foliage around him as cover, Lopez and his men might not see him, even after the sun rose. Surely Corporal Banks would send out a search party when he realized Levi had not returned from Rose Hill. It would be up to God which group of men found Levi first.

Bracing himself for the pain he knew would come, he used his good elbow to scoot his body toward the log. He resisted the urge to cry out when fiery fingers shot through his shoulder and down his body. The few inches that separated him from the log seemed like a mile as he dragged himself to it. Once he was up against the rough bark, he closed his eyes for several minutes to let his breathing return to normal, all the while pushing his wounded shoulder into the ground, which he hoped would staunch the bleeding. When the pain gradually subsided to a dull ache, he yanked on the branches of a low shrub and pulled them toward him, again and again, until he had enough greenery to cover himself. The last thing he did was take his gun from its holster and lay it on his chest. He wouldn't give up without a fight.

Having done all he could until daylight arrived, Levi relaxed. He stared up at the starlit sky, his eyes getting heavy. As he drifted off to sleep, his last thought was of Natalie. He hoped he would live to see her beautiful blue eyes and that stubborn set to her jaw again. He might even let her stew in her remorse a few days.

Then, he would take her in his arms and kiss her sweet lips until she agreed to marry him.

❧ ❧

"Miz Natalie? Miz Natalie! Wake up."

Natalie startled awake. Carolina's face loomed above her, the glow of candlelight illuminating her wide eyes. "What's wrong? Is it Samuel?"

Carolina lit the lamp beside the bed as Natalie sat up, groggy.

"Samuel be sleepin'. It be the colonel."

"Colonel Maish?" She glanced out the window where the lace curtains parted. The sky was still dark. What time was it?

"William, er, Corporal Banks is here. Says the colonel didn't never come back to the army camp. Thought he might've come here, but I told him no. He be worried."

Natalie stood, still confused about the conversation. "Where is he? Corporal Banks, I mean."

"He in the kitchen with Moses an' Harriet."

"All right. I'll be down shortly."

After the servant left, Natalie dressed while she wondered where Levi could be. If the corporal was worried, then Levi not returning to camp was unusual.

When she entered the kitchen, four pairs of concerned eyes met her. Corporal Banks stood and gave a polite nod.

"Mrs. Ellis. I'm sorry to disturb you folks so early, but I had hoped the colonel spent the night here at Rose Hill."

Warmth filled her face, although she didn't believe he'd meant to insinuate anything improper. "Of course not, Corporal." She recalled her argument with Levi before he'd ridden out. "He came by last evening to discuss the cattle Señor Lopez has grazing on my

❧ 270 ❧

land, but he left a short time later. From what he said, I gathered he'd just come from viewing the herd."

Corporal Banks' frown deepened. "He sent me a message to let me know he was going to check on some suspicious activity. We were waiting for his return. What did he say about the cattle on your land?"

She glanced at the others in the room. She didn't approve of spreading gossip, but she trusted that when Alexander cleared things up regarding his cattle, the three servants would keep whatever they heard tonight to themselves.

"He believed Señor Lopez to be the cattle thief the Union Army is searching for." At the gasps in the room, she hastened to add, "But I told him he was absolutely incorrect. Alexander is not a thief. He pays me to lease my pastures."

The corporal's grave expression didn't change. "What time did he leave Rose Hill?"

"It was after dark, but I'm not sure of the hour."

"And you say he'd just come from looking at the herd?"

"Yes."

Corporal Banks put his hat on, his face grim. "Ma'am, I didn't want to alarm you, but we believe the colonel is in danger. His horse returned to Langford Manor a short time ago without him." His gaze held hers. "There was blood on the saddle."

Her own blood went cold.

Noises from outside drew their attention. The group moved outside to see dozens of mounted soldiers filling the yard. Corporal Banks drew up next to her.

"We're forming a search party."

"I be glad to help," Moses said. "I get the wagon hitched"—he glanced at Natalie—"in case he too injured to ride."

Fear clutched at her heart. Everyone flew into action while she stood rooted to the porch. Torches were lit, orders were given, and suddenly, the yard was emptied of soldiers. Harriet and Carolina returned to the kitchen to make sandwiches and more coffee. Even the new field workers, aroused by the commotion, volunteered to join in the search. Ruth's tall husband, Wash, climbed up on the wagon seat beside Moses, and they followed the soldiers.

Standing alone, her arms wrapped around her waist, Natalie felt helpless. Clinging to the shred of hope that Corporal Banks was wrong and that Levi was safe, she went upstairs, peeking in on Samuel's sleeping form on her way.

She closed the door to her room. Her bedcovers were a jumbled mess, but she didn't tidy them. Instead, she went to the adjoining sitting room and settled on a chair. Though the sun would not rise for another hour or so, a faint lightening to the sky allowed her to make out silhouettes of furniture and small details in the shadowed room.

She closed her eyes. Was Levi badly injured? Did Alexander have something to do with it? She'd refused to believe it last night when Levi was here, but what if she was wrong? What if her obstinacy drove Levi to do something drastic and dangerous?

Tears sprang to her eyes. "Please keep him safe." She sank to her knees, folded her arms on the seat of the chair, and rested her forehead on them. Her tears wet her skin.

"Father in heaven, forgive me for my stubbornness. I've been a selfish woman, always insisting I know best. I'm sorry I didn't listen to Levi. You know where he is. Please, please, Father, let him be found … alive."

❧ ❦

Voices.

Levi gradually became aware of sounds in the distance, but his head was too foggy to focus on what they were saying. Was it Banks and his men looking for him? Should he alert them to his whereabouts?

Whoever it was continued to draw closer.

A faint yellow light bounced off the tree branches overhead, flickering and moving as it neared. He blinked. Not sunlight. Stars still twinkled in an inky sky beyond. Ah, torchlight. They had torches to aid them in the dark.

Thank God.

He didn't know how long he'd lain here, but he was so weak, he must have lost a fair amount of blood. If he didn't receive medical attention soon, he might not make it. He'd seen enough men bleed to death on the battlefields. Joining them was not a pleasant thought.

A pool of bright light touched the top of the fallen log. Levi took a breath to call to Banks when someone close by said something strange. He couldn't understand the words. Had the knock on his head been worse than he thought? The man spoke again, and someone responded from a few paces away.

Levi's body went cold.

They were speaking Spanish. Lopez's men were upon him.

His heart hammered. Fresh warmth spread across the back of his shoulder. His own fear had caused the blood flow to increase. It didn't matter, though. The moment they found him lying there, helpless as a newborn, they'd put a bullet in his head.

The men drew up next to the log. Levi could see the tops of their heads and the flickering flames of their torches. He knew the few branches he'd managed to cover himself with would not be enough to conceal him if they looked closely. The brass buttons on his coat, the white of his shirt. All would be revealed in the light.

One of the men studied the fallen tree. Levi could see the whites of the man's eyes as he waved his torch over the log.

Levi squeezed his own eyes shut, his finger on the trigger of his revolver. He might be able to take down the one man, but what of the others? He didn't stand a chance once they knew where he was hiding. This was not the end he wanted. He had so much life to live.

Oh, God! Please ...

After several long moments, the men moved away. The voices

faded until only the sounds of night remained.

Many minutes passed before Levi eased his eyes open. His body trembled as if he were resting in frigid snow. No sign of torchlight remained. As his muscles sagged with relief, he wondered how the fool could have missed him.

I am your rock, and your fortress, and your deliverer. I am your strength and your shield.

He stared up at the dark sky for a long moment, stars blinking at him from high in the heavens. The truth of the words swept over him like a warm breeze.

God had delivered him. He had shielded Levi and kept Lopez's men from seeing him. It was the only explanation that made sense.

CHAPTER TWENTY-NINE

Ebenezer's barking woke Natalie.

Morning sunshine filtered in through the sitting room window while a light breeze teased the curtains. She'd fallen asleep with her head on the seat of the chair, praying for Levi. Her neck stiff, she rolled her shoulders before she rose and peeked out the window. The sun was barely over the horizon.

The dog continued to bark.

Hope sprang to her soul. Had Levi returned? Was Ebenezer even now welcoming him? She practically flew down the stairs to the front porch, her heart nearly beating out of her chest with joy. But when she raced outside, the man standing in the yard was not Levi.

"Alexander." A flood of mixed emotions rolled through her. Was he the friend she'd believed him to be all these months, or was he the thief Levi claimed he was? She noted he looked disheveled, a complete contrast to his normal impeccable appearance. Dust clung to his clothes, and at least one small branch stuck out from the cuff of his pants.

"Call off your dog before he takes a piece of my leg," he said, his voice demanding.

"Ebenezer, come." The dog quieted, ran up the steps, and sat at her feet.

Once he was out of immediate danger, Alexander cast a quick glance toward the road then back to her.

"What brings you to Rose Hill so early?" she asked, unease working its way into her gut.

"I thought to check on my cattle, but the desire to see you was too strong." He eyed the dog as he took a few steps forward. "I fear I must return to Mexico for a family matter. I may not be back for several months. However, I could not leave without a proper farewell. I hoped you would do me the honor of accepting my proposal before I depart." His smile was far from genuine. "To know you will be mine when I return would bring happiness to my heart."

He planned to leave Texas. In a hurry. His timing, his early arrival at her home, his disheveled look all confirmed what Levi had said.

Fear sent her heartbeat racing. She couldn't let Alexander see the truth in her eyes. She took a step backward. "I'm afraid I'm not quite ready to accept your offer, Alexander. I wish you well on your journey."

Her voice trembled, as did her legs. Alexander's gaze narrowed, and his false smile faded.

"Let us not pretend, Natalie. I followed the Yankee here last night. I had a suspicion he or the corporal had discovered my unconventional business practices. When I saw him on the road to Rose Hill in the dark, I knew I was correct."

She swallowed. "So it's true. You are a cattle thief."

"Yes." He smiled. "While the stupid *Americanos* killed each other in the war, they left their women and animals ripe for the taking. My only problem was figuring out where to keep the cattle until we were ready to drive them north."

Natalie's stomach dropped. "What about your ranch? You told me your family had a large spread."

His upper lip curled. "My family could never afford to purchase land in *Tejas*. Our own Mexican government would not give my parents a land grant, as they had given to hundreds of greedy Americans, throwing away what rightfully belongs to me and every other son of *Méjico*. My father and mother were forced to labor for Texans until they died, broken and poor. I have only been taking back what should have been mine in the first place."

The confession stunned her.

He was not a gentleman rancher. He was a thief and a liar. What a fool she'd been to trust him.

He chuckled. "Do not feel so bad. You are not the only widow to fall for the ruse."

Her surprise must have shown on her face because he laughed all the harder.

"I have arrangements with quite a few lonely widows, all deeply in love with me and more than willing to let my cattle get fat on their grasses." His gaze narrowed. "You, however, presented a challenge. My charms did not impress you. I truly thought to court and marry you. Owning Rose Hill and Langford Manor would benefit my business very much."

His face grew stony. "But then you agreed to let the Union Army camp on your land. The roads are even now crawling with bluecoats looking for the dead body of Colonel Maish."

Natalie clutched her heart. "No!"

Alexander gave a cruel laugh. "So, you have fallen in love with him, eh? That is a shame. I shot him last night. I suspect the buzzards have found him by now." He sighed. "We could have built an empire together, you and I. But now those plans are ruined. I will have to live out my days in *Méjico* with the fortune I have acquired from selling stolen Confederate cattle to the Yankees. But before I go"—his eyes raked her up and down—"I have come to take what is mine."

She could taste the fear in her throat. "Leave, Alexander." She backed toward the door behind her.

He started up the steps. "Do not flatter yourself, Natalie. What I want are the jewels I know you possess. Now that I can't sell the herd of cattle I have grazing in your pastures, I want compensation in whatever form I can get." He reached the top of the steps as Natalie lunged for the door.

Alexander grabbed her arm and dragged her away from the entry.

"Let go of me!" She struggled, but he wrapped his other arm around her waist and pulled her against him. His fingers spread over her belly, kneading her in an intimate way.

"Perhaps I will change my mind and take you with me," he whispered in her ear. His hot breath sent chills of panic coursing through her. "I will need comfort on the long journey to Mexico."

Before she could scream for help, a fierce snarl brought both of their heads around. Ebenezer leaped into the air, teeth bared. The dog's jaw clamped down on Alexander's arm, and he cried out. Natalie broke free of his grasp and stumbled away. While Alexander pummeled the dog with his other hand, she searched the porch for something, anything, to use as a weapon.

"Hold it right there, mister!"

Carolina appeared in the open doorway. She held a rifle pointed at Alexander.

"Ebenezer, come," Natalie said. The dog released Alexander's arm and came to her, panting but wagging his tail. Blood smeared the fur on his face, but she didn't know if it was his own or Alexander's. She knelt and hugged the dear animal.

"What you want me to do with this varmint, Miz Natalie? Put a hole through him?" Carolina's unwavering eyes were perfectly serious.

"No." Natalie stood and looked at Alexander, bleeding and fearful as he stared at Carolina. With only women on the plantation, Natalie couldn't risk someone getting injured if they tried to detain the thief until Corporal Banks or Moses returned. Besides, as Alexander himself said, Union soldiers weren't far. Surely they would find him. "Leave, Alexander. Go. And don't ever come back."

Tucking his injured arm against his ribs, he gave her one last scornful look and descended the steps. Ebenezer let out a deep growl, and the man hastened his pace. He mounted his horse and raced out of the yard without a backward glance.

As soon as he rode out of sight, Natalie released a sob of relief.

"Good riddance," Carolina said, lowering the weapon.

Natalie met her gaze. "You were so brave."

Carolina shrugged. "Ain't hard to be brave when someone you care 'bout in danger."

Tears sprang to Natalie's eyes, and before she realized what she was doing, she rushed over and put her arms around Carolina in a fierce hug. "You saved my life." She pulled away to find a startled Carolina. "You and Ebenezer."

"I guess I'm mighty glad I come on out here to see why that dog carryin' on like he was." She grinned. "Don't know that I ever been hugged by a white woman."

Natalie sobered. "Alexander said he shot Colonel Maish last night."

Carolina frowned. "Best I tell Harriet so's she can get bandages ready and hot water on."

The servant headed in the direction of the kitchen. Natalie sat on the step and motioned Ebenezer over. With her arm around the dog's neck, she closed her eyes.

"He can't be dead, Ebenezer," she whispered into his fur, the ache in her heart growing. "He can't be dead."

❧ ❧

A ray of sunshine poked through the branches overhead and hit Levi squarely in the face.

He opened one eye and squinted at the brightness. Judging by the position of the sun, it was midmorning. He must have dozed off again. He whispered his thanks to God that he was still alive.

What should he do now? One thing was certain. He had to get off this ground and back to camp somehow. Yet the thought of moving, let alone walking, caused a wave of nausea to roll through him. With the amount of blood he'd lost, he wondered if he'd be able to find his way back. His predicament bordered on impossible.

Another of Ma's favorite verses floated through his mind. *With*

God all things are possible. All things. Even rescue from a bullet-shot shoulder and a murdering cattle thief.

Breathing another prayer, he closed his eyes again, unable to fight the heavy drowsiness that hung over him. Waiting seemed the best—and only—course of action for him to take just now.

"Colonel Maish? You out here, suh?"

Levi woke with a start. The sun was higher in the sky.

"Colonel Maish?"

Was that Moses?

"Over here." His raspy voice didn't carry far. "Over here," he tried again, louder. He lifted his good arm into the air.

A rustling sound came closer. Moses' dark face appeared over the top of the log a moment later.

"Colonel! We's been lookin' for you."

Levi chuckled then grimaced at the pain it created. "I've been right here, waiting for you to find me."

"You hurt bad?"

"Gunshot. In the shoulder." He rubbed a spot on the back of his head that felt as big as a boulder. "Guess I hit my head on my way to the ground, too."

"We get you outta here right quick." Moses stood, turned, and called out, "He over here! He over here! Bring that wagon up, Wash!"

Activity sprang up around Levi. Soldiers and field hands all took a peek over the log while the wagon was brought in. Corporal Banks arrived and barked orders like a general.

He peered over the log. "It sure is good to see you, sir." Emotion hung heavy on each word.

"It's good to be seen," Levi said.

When they lifted him, the pain that rolled through his body sent sparks flying behind his eyes. Groaning as they put him in the back of the wagon, he tried to hang on to consciousness. He needed to tell them about Lopez.

"We take you to Rose Hill, Colonel," Moses' voice told him.

"It be the closest."

He couldn't answer as blackness edged out the light.

❧ ❧

"When is the co'nel gonna wake up, Mama?"

Natalie sat on the porch swing with Samuel on her lap, enjoying the rain-soaked breeze following a brief shower that had rolled through earlier. Supper dishes were clean and put away, and their beds were calling to them after such an eventful day.

"I don't know." She tightened her arms around him. "We have to keep praying for him. The army doctor said the bump on his head is making him sleepy, but hopefully he'll be fine in a few days."

She fervently hoped so. Seeing Levi bloody and unconscious when they brought him in was terrifying. Banks and Harriet set to work on him as soon as the wagon stopped, although they'd sent for the Union doctor as well. Levi now lay in a bed in the bachelor's quarters, his head and shoulder swathed in bandages. He had yet to regain consciousness. The doctor said it could be days before he was aware of his surroundings. Moses volunteered to sit with him and tend his needs so the soldiers could carry on with their duties.

Samuel yawned.

"Time for bed, my love." She stood with him in her arms. He wrapped his spindly arms and legs around her and rested his head on her shoulder.

"I like the co'nel," he said, sleepily.

"I do too," she whispered into his hair.

With her son tucked in for the night, Natalie knew she should retire to her rooms, as exhausted as she felt. But she longed to see Levi. She'd only caught glimpses of him since they'd brought him in.

She exited the house by the back door. A dim light glimmered in the open windows of the one-story building. The two soldiers who'd bunked there had moved into a tent by the slave quarter— the servants' quarter, she corrected herself—to afford Levi some privacy to recuperate.

Carolina's high voice came from the open kitchen doorway, followed by Corporal Banks' even tone. Harriet's deep hum soon joined them. With the aroma of strong coffee drifting out the doorway, Natalie suspected they would all be up for many hours, awaiting word on Levi's condition.

She tiptoed across the grass that separated the bachelor's quarters from the house and peeked through the window. Moses sat in a chair next to Levi's bed. Although it was improper for her to be there, she continued to the door. With a soft knock, she opened it and peeked inside.

Moses smiled. "Miz Natalie." She noted his Bible lay in his lap, open.

"How is he?" She kept her voice low, glancing at Levi's pale face.

"Still sleepin', but he breathin' easier, seems."

That was something. She stepped inside the room, feeling awkward and out of place but needing to see him for herself.

Moses stood. "Why don't you come sit a spell with him? I could use me a break."

The offer was tempting. "I don't know that I should. It isn't proper."

"Ain't nothin' wrong with sittin' at a sick bed," he said, a knowing look in his eyes, "'specially when it someone you care 'bout. Maybe you could read some o' this here book to him." He held up the Bible. "I be back in a bit after I has me some coffee and stretch a bit befo' we all settle in for the night."

She nodded.

Moses set the book on the chair and left, closing the door gently behind him. Natalie stood where she was, watching the covers over Levi rise and fall with his breath. After a long moment, she settled in the chair, clutching the book to her chest while she studied Levi's still face.

How handsome he was, even in slumber. His dark beard and thick brows contrasted with his pale skin, but his lips were pink and full, and she warmed at the memory of their kisses. A bandage covered one shoulder. Oh, how she longed to feel his strong arms around her again, to hear his whispers of love.

A pang pierced her heart. She didn't deserve his love. She'd been a fool to trust Alexander, and her foolishness had put Levi in danger. How could he ever forgive her? He'd come to warn her, and all she'd done was defend Alexander. A cattle thief. A murderer had Levi not survived. She'd been so blind.

After a few minutes of listening to his even breathing, she relaxed back in the chair. Moses had the book open to the Psalms. They'd always been her favorite. She looked at Levi's unconscious face.

"Moses thought I should read to you," she whispered, her voice loud in the quiet room.

Levi didn't move. Could he hear her? The flame of the lantern on the bedside table flickered in the warm breeze wafting through the window.

She turned the pages until she came to the eighteenth Psalm. Swallowing her nerves, she took a deep breath. "'I will love thee, O LORD, my strength.'" She paused and glanced to see if Levi would stir at the sound of her voice. When he didn't, she continued. "'The LORD is my rock, and my fortress, and my deliverer; my God, my strength in whom I will trust; my buckler, and the horn of my salvation, and my high tower.'"

Levi mumbled, and she leaned forward to listen. "'I will call upon the LORD, who is worthy to be praised.'"

Her eyes flew to his, but they remained closed.

"'So shall I be saved from mine enemies,'" he murmured, finishing the verse.

"Levi." She touched his hand. She waited, but he didn't say

anything more. "Levi?" she said louder, but still there was no response.

She read the remaining words of the Psalm, but he didn't open his eyes. He looked exactly as he had when she'd first sat.

Had she only imagined him speaking?

Moses returned a short time later. "You best get some rest, Miz Natalie. It been a long day."

She nodded, glancing at Levi's sleeping form one last time. When she reached her room, she stood at the window in the dark, staring out into the starlit night. The words of the Psalm echoed in her mind. God had indeed saved Levi from his enemy. And her, too. What if she had gone through with a marriage to Alexander? She would have put not only herself in danger, but her son as well.

She shuddered at the thought.

As she readied for bed, the reality of her situation weighed heavily on her. Without Alexander's money for leasing her land, she had no way to make the mortgage and tax payments. As ill-gotten as the funds had been, they'd saved her from foreclosure. Though there might be enough from the sale of the harvested cotton to keep the banks satisfied this year, without workers to plow, plant, and tend a new crop, all would be in vain. She would lose Rose Hill and Langford Manor anyway.

A tear trailed down her cheek.

With Levi lying in the bachelor's quarters, severely injured, worrying over her own problems seemed selfish. Hadn't she confessed that sin just this morning?

"Help me trust in You, Lord," she whispered, crawling beneath the cool sheet. "You are my deliverer, too."

Her eyes slid closed.

God would make a way. She may not like it, but she would trust Him.

CHAPTER THIRTY

Levi opened his eyes and blinked at the muted sunshine coming through a window above his head. The smell of bacon wafted over him, and his stomach rumbled. He glanced around the small room. It looked vaguely familiar, but he couldn't place it in his foggy mind.

"Well, looky there. You's awake."

Moses' face appeared in his line of vision.

"Where am I?"

"You's at Rose Hill, in the bach'lors' quarter. Been here since yesterday when we found you out in them woods."

Levi closed his eyes. Yes, he remembered now. When he opened his eyes, Moses was smiling. "What are you grinning about?"

Moses chuckled. "Just seein' you with your eyes open and talkin' be a real answer to prayer, suh."

"Is Banks here? What happened to Lopez?" He wanted to ask about Natalie, too, but he'd wait and speak with her himself.

"Corporal Banks went on to the soldier camp a few hours ago, but he said he'd be back. Your men is still out lookin' for that scoundrel Lopez, but they was able to catch two or three of his cowpokes tryin' to hightail it to ol' Mexico. I 'spect that where Lopez is headed too."

While the news wasn't what he wanted to hear, Levi felt a measure of peace knowing Banks was handling things in his absence.

"I have my Harriet pour you some broth. She has it nice an' hot, waitin' for you to wake up. That army doctah say you need to stay in bed a couple days befo' you try and get up. Says that knot on yo' head be troublesome if you don't lie still."

Levi frowned. He'd rather be out looking for Lopez, but his head still pounded, and he couldn't move his left arm. "I suppose I don't have much choice."

Moses chuckled. "I be right back."

Levi let his head sink into the soft pillow and closed his eyes. He recalled the events that led him here. He'd need to get a report off to General Granger—if Banks hadn't already taken care of it— alerting the commander to Lopez's identity. That the cattle thief had been right under Levi's nose didn't sit well, but thankfully, he was no longer a problem. Even if he got away, Levi doubted Lopez would show his face in Texas again.

A sound near the door brought his eyes open. Samuel's mop of sandy hair peeked around the opening. A moment later, he stepped over the threshold. He had a streak of mud across the front of his overalls, and his feet were bare. The boy's bright, curious eyes stared at him.

"Hi, Samuel." Levi smiled and motioned him inside.

Samuel glanced toward the kitchen then entered the room. "Moses said you was awake."

"I am."

The boy sidled up to the bed, his big eyes taking in the bandage around Levi's head and the one on his shoulder. "Mama said Señor Lopez was a bad man and that he hurt you. I'm not supposed to talk to him no more if he comes to Rose Hill."

Levi nodded. "That is all true."

"I'm glad." Samuel inched his backend onto the edge of the mattress until he was sitting next to Levi's leg. "I didn't like him. Neither did Ebenezer. Carolina said Ebenezer bit Señor Lopez before he left." The boy giggled.

The sound brought a smile to Levi's lips. "I always did like that dog."

"Samuel, what are you doing in here?"

Natalie stood in the doorway looking as beautiful as ever. Her rounded blue eyes met his gaze, concern shining from their depths.

"Look, Mama," Samuel said, pointing to Levi with a pudgy finger. "The co'nel is awake."

Her eyes never left Levi's. "Yes, I know. Moses told me." A tremulous smile parted her lips. "It's good to see you awake."

Her soft voice warmed him. "I'm happy to be awake, although I feel like I've been chewed up by an ol' grizzly bear and spit out."

Samuel giggled.

Natalie blinked several times. Was she fighting tears? He hadn't intended to make her cry.

Moses arrived with a bowl, steam rising from the contents. "Got some broth here, Colonel." He glanced to Natalie, a question in his eyes.

She shook her head. "Come along, Samuel. Let the colonel rest now. You can come visit him again later."

Samuel hopped off the bed. At the door, he turned to Levi. "Maybe I can tell you a story later. I always rest good when Mama tells me a story."

Levi nodded. "I'd like that." His gaze found Natalie again, but she'd already turned away.

When they were gone, Moses settled into the chair next to the bed. "You think you can manage this here broth, or you want me to he'p you?"

"Maybe if you put another pillow behind me, I can feed myself without spilling it."

Once Levi was propped up a bit, he tried to spoon the liquid while Moses held the bowl, but exhaustion and pain soon had his arm trembling. Ashamed, he let Moses take the utensil. "I guess I can't do it."

"I happy to he'p." He dipped the spoon into the broth and fed Levi like he was a baby. "You been through a lot. Don't 'spect it such a bad thing to let someone else come alongside and he'p 'til you strong enough."

Levi had to admit the warm broth felt better sliding down his throat than dribbling off his chin. When he'd had his fill, he sat back, exhausted from the effort.

"Thank you. I think I'll rest now."

Moses nodded. "I be back after a while to check on you."

Sinking into the softness of the bed, Levi closed his eyes. His belly full of Harriet's delicious chicken broth, he already felt a mite stronger. A few more days and he'd be up and about. In the meantime, he hoped Natalie would come see him. They needed to talk. About Lopez. About the plantations.

But mostly, he grinned as he drifted off to sleep, he wanted to talk about marriage. Facing death out in the woods made him realize life was too short not to go after what a man wanted.

And what Levi wanted was Natalie Langford Ellis.

❦

Samuel's laughter rang out from the bachelor's quarters.

Despite sweat trailing down her back and the ache in her arms as she hung wet sheets on the line, Natalie smiled. Her son's sunny disposition was truly a blessing. He'd taken to spending most of his days in the sick room, entertaining Levi. What they did during all those hours, she didn't know. Levi had yet to send for her, and she didn't feel comfortable visiting the bachelor's quarters uninvited. Not only did her mother's teachings on propriety keep her from it, but her own muddled feelings kept her away.

Nearly losing Levi revealed how much he meant to her. More, she realized, than the plantations she'd fought so hard to hold on to the past four years. But after she'd refused his marriage proposal and then defended Alexander, despite the evidence that seemed so obvious now, she feared she may have missed her chance at happiness with the only man she'd ever loved.

Looking up to the cloudless sky, she heaved a sigh. The army doctor came by that morning to check on Levi's progress. According to Moses, the older man seemed pleased. He'd said Levi would be fit to travel the short distance to Langford Manor soon. While she was happy his injuries were mending, it would be lonely without him. She may not spend time visiting with him the way Samuel and Moses did, but just knowing he was there at Rose Hill brought her a measure of comfort.

"Shore gonna be a hot one when this day get finished with us." Carolina carried out yet another basket full of wet laundry. Ruth and Adline were working the paddles over the hot cauldron, stirring the laundry, so Natalie knew better than to complain about being out in the sun hanging the clean items.

She wiped her brow with the back of her hand. "Days like this make me wish we could dip our feet in the creek, just for a few minutes, anyway."

Carolina eyed her, a mischievous quirk to her mouth. "What stoppin' us? You the boss woman."

Natalie glanced toward the tree line behind the servants' quarter where the creek gurgled through Rose Hill land. Carolina was right. No one was there to prevent them from enjoying a little fun.

"I'll race you!" Natalie tossed a pillowcase back into the basket and took off at a run, going as fast as the bulky skirt of her dress would allow.

Carolina shrieked and soon overtook Natalie. She arrived at the bank first. In no time, they had their shoes and stockings off and waded into the cool water. Holding their skirts high, they laughed and wiggled their toes, with Carolina splashing out into the deeper part of the creek to cool her calves.

"I haven't done this since I was a young girl." Natalie closed her eyes, relishing the feel of water flowing around her ankles and thinking of her childhood maid and companion. "Zina and I used to play in the creek at Langford Manor, but Mama didn't approve after I started wearing long gowns. She said it wasn't proper behavior for a young lady."

"I 'spect it must'a been hard always havin' to follow all them rules," Carolina said, wading back toward Natalie. "Us slaves, we got one rule to follow: obey the massa."

Natalie walked back to the bank and sat, keeping her wet feet away from her skirt and underthings. Carolina joined her.

"I'm sorry you had to endure slavery, Carolina." She hoped her soft words conveyed her sincerity.

Carolina's brow raised when she looked at Natalie. "Weren't your fault, Miz Natalie. 'Sides, you done saved me when Massa Luther wants to sell me when he sell my mama and sisters."

"How did you know?"

"Word travel mighty fast through the quarter 'bout such things, 'specially when Massa Luther breathin' fire, sayin' he gonna get rid of all the slaves Missy Ellis was partial to." She looked at Natalie. "You been real good to me. I won't never forget you."

"You won't forget me? Are you going somewhere?" She had a suspicion she knew the answer.

A shy smile filled Carolina's face. "William—that Corporal Banks' name—he done asked me to marry him. Just last night. Says all this business with the colonel gettin' shot even though the war over has him thinkin' it time to get outta the army and go back home." She grinned, happiness radiating from her. "He want me to go to Mass'chusetts with him. Can you believe it? I gonna go north like all them Negroes talk about doin' before freedom come."

A lump formed in Natalie's throat. "I am very happy for you. When does Corporal Banks plan to leave?"

"He say as soon as the colonel mends he gonna write to that general in Austin and see when his time be up. William say it best to get to Mass'chusetts before winter set in. I guess it get kinda cold up north."

Natalie laughed. "From what I hear, it gets very cold up there, with lots of snow. I hope you won't freeze."

A sly grin crept up Carolina's face. "I'll have me a good man to keep me warm."

"Carolina! You mustn't say such things out loud." But the truth of her words made Natalie smile. Soon they were both giggling.

When their laughter subsided, Natalie sighed. "I will miss you. You've become a dear friend."

When they returned to their chores, Natalie's thoughts were on the future. Everyone, it seemed, was moving forward, embracing the new opportunities that unfurled before them. Moses felt called to preach the Gospel to the Negroes now that it wasn't illegal to own a Bible and read. Carolina and William were making plans for their life together. Even Levi hoped to open his own carpentry shop and settle down once he returned to Pennsylvania.

A longing to be by his side ran so deep it nearly took her breath away. She glanced at the bachelor's quarters. All was quiet now, and she wondered if Samuel had fallen asleep, curled into Levi's side as Moses found them yesterday afternoon. Could she find the courage to march into his room and declare her love for him? To tell him her home was with him, wherever that may be?

Her heart pounded. What if he rejected her? What if her foolish, misplaced trust in Alexander had opened Levi's eyes to the silly woman she truly was? She'd put the plantations and her need to control the future ahead of him, of his love. If she were to go to him now, laying her heart bare, and he spurned her, she'd be crushed. It was cowardly, but she simply couldn't bear that kind of heartache.

Looking west, she wondered if it were perhaps time to accept Adella's invitation to visit them in Oregon. Samuel's half-sister, Mara, was there, and the two had never met. With slavery abolished, the girl could now live without fear of being brought back to Rose Hill as a slave. Perhaps a visit to see family would help Natalie sort out her future.

Laughter came from the bachelor's quarters.

She heaved a sigh. A life in Oregon was not what she wanted. Only one thing—one man—could fill the longing in her heart.

"God, I love Levi," she whispered. "Give me the courage to tell him, come what may."

❦ ❦

Levi scowled. He'd felt grouchy all morning. Endless hours of lying flat on his back were taking their toll. Samuel and Moses and even Banks did their best to amuse him with stories and jokes, but he was ready to get out of this bed and get on with his life. Doc said he could leave for Langford Manor tomorrow, which meant this was his last day at Rose Hill.

And that, he realized, was the source of his surliness. Or rather, it was the mistress of Rose Hill who had him frustrated. Natalie had not been to see him since he woke up. Truth be told, it wounded his pride a bit that she cared so little that she didn't come to check on him from time to time. When he inquired after her, Moses said she was keeping busy helping the servants with chores and tending to Samuel. The big man's answer, however, did not fool Levi. She was avoiding him, pure and simple, and he wanted to know why.

He leaned back against the pile of pillows Moses had crammed behind him earlier. His shoulder still thrummed with pain, but the dizziness and headaches had subsided enough for him to sit up without becoming nauseated.

Mulling over the problem regarding Natalie's absence, he was convinced it wasn't because she didn't have feelings for him. He knew better than that. The memory of their kisses played through his mind and warmed his blood. A woman like Natalie would not return such passion without experiencing emotions that went deeper than mere physical attraction.

So why would she avoid him? One possibility arose in his mind.

Over the past few days, he'd had plenty of time to consider how selfish it was to demand she leave the land her family had lived on for years. The plantations were her son's legacy. He couldn't take that away from Samuel. The reality was that if Levi wanted Natalie as his wife, he had to remain in Texas. And truthfully, the more he thought of going home to Pennsylvania without her, the more he realized he'd be miserable. He'd miss his family if he stayed, especially Ma and Pa, and he wouldn't get to watch his nephew grow into a man, but his life and his future were with Natalie and Samuel.

As soon as Moses returned, Levi decided, he'd have the servant deliver a message to Natalie, asking her to come see him. When she arrived, he'd declare his love and promise to do everything in his power to bring the plantations back to their former glory. As long as he had her by his side, it didn't matter where they lived.

Restless while he waited, he glanced around the small room, looking for something to occupy his time. His gaze landed on Moses' Bible on the table beside the bed. Though the big man couldn't read many words, he seemed to enjoy simply holding the book in his hands.

Levi reached for it and winced when the stitches in his shoulder stretched, but he managed to get the book without tumbling off the mattress. He rested it on his lap, flipped open the cover, and turned pages. It had been a while since he'd read the Bible for himself. There hadn't been much opportunity during the war, although he suspected he should have found time. He thumbed through it until he reached the Psalms. What was Ma's favorite? The one she quoted to her sons as they headed off to war?

He soon found what he was looking for. Psalm eighteen. *I will love thee, O LORD, my strength.*

A fragment of memory flit across his mind. A woman's voice reading those words to him. Ma? No, not his mother's voice. Softer. *The LORD is my rock, and my fortress, and my deliverer.*

The memory cleared. Natalie. It had been Natalie reading those precious words. When? It must have been after he was brought to Rose Hill. She'd been with him while he was unconscious, reading from God's word.

Go to her, the voice in his heart seemed to say.

He didn't need to be told twice. He laid the book aside and eased his legs off the bed, pivoting until his feet were flat on the floor. Using the back of the chair for balance, he rose. A wave of dizziness and stars exploded in his head, but he gripped the chair and fought to stay upright. When his vision cleared, he looked down at his half-naked body. He certainly couldn't go to her like this.

The fresh uniform Banks had brought for his trip back to Langford tomorrow hung on a hook across the room. Though it took an interminable amount of time, Levi dressed himself, mostly. He managed to put his injured arm through the sleeve, but buttoning the garment with one hand proved impossible, nor could he manage his boots. Though not completely attired, his small accomplishment made him smile. Now, if he could just walk to the door without falling.

Pushing the chair in front of him as a sort of crutch, he shuffled to the entry, feeling a little stronger with each step. Fresh air and sunshine greeted him when he stepped out the door. With a deep breath, he filled his lungs. It felt good to be upright.

He glanced toward the kitchen then toward the house. Where would he find Natalie this time of morning? According to Samuel, she had been assisting with nearly every chore there was on the plantation, bringing Levi a smile of pride for her efforts.

Taking a chance he would find her in the house, he stepped off the narrow porch onto the expanse of lawn. He chuckled when his feet hit the cool, prickly greenery. How long had it been since he'd walked barefoot in the grass? When he reached the porch that surrounded the house, he grasped a post and hoisted himself up. Though his shoulder throbbed, his determination kept him going.

Inside, all was quiet.

He glanced up the back stairway and listened. No sound came from upstairs. With a hand on the wall to brace himself, he made his way toward the front foyer. He'd look in the parlor and dining room before checking outside. He moved soundlessly down the hall.

"Ouch!"

The exclamation came from the parlor.

When he reached the doorway of that room, he found Natalie sitting beside the window, her head bent over what looked like a pair of Samuel's overalls. A needle and thread dangled from her hand. He drank in the sight of her like a man at a deep well after being lost in the desert. *Beautiful.* If he weren't mistaken, she was wearing the same blue-and-white striped gown he'd seen her in the first day he and his men had arrived at Rose Hill with the freedom proclamation.

Her brow knit in frustration. She examined her thumb before popping it into her mouth. She looked up, and her eyes rounded.

"Levi!" She stood, the overalls falling to the floor.

He smiled. She'd used his given name. A good sign. "I hope I'm not interrupting." He indicated the small garment on the floor.

"No, of course not." She bent and picked it up. Clutching it to her, her wide eyes met his. "Should you be up? The doctor said tomorrow."

"I managed fairly well," he said. Her concern quieted any lingering doubts he'd had about her feelings. "I could use some help with the buttons on my shirt, however. Accomplishing the task with one hand is beyond my talents, I'm afraid."

Her eyes traveled to his bare chest, and a pretty flush filled her cheeks. When her gaze met his again, he raised his brow in question.

She laid the overalls on the chair and crossed the room. He breathed in the rose scent of her hair, savoring her nearness after the prolonged absence. When she reached to push the first button through the hole, the slight trembling of her delicate fingers gave away her nervousness. Once the job was completed, she released the breath she'd been holding.

"Thank you." A wave of dizziness hit. "I believe I should sit now."

She steadied him and helped him to the sofa. He had to admit, having her see to his needs was rather pleasant.

"I'll call Moses and have him help you back to your room," she said, heading for the door.

"Please don't. I'm glad to be away from my bed, even for a little while. Besides," he said, his eyes imploring her to see his heart, "you and I need to talk."

She swallowed. "Oh?"

"Come." He patted the space beside him.

She settled on the edge of the seat. The sheer fabric of her skirt touched his leg, and she tucked it beneath her.

"Why haven't you been to see me?"

Her face lifted to his, her eyes wide. "It … it wouldn't be proper."

Her answer made him smile. He studied her features. Her creamy skin. The thick lashes surrounding her sky-blue eyes. When she looked away, he put his finger beneath her chin to turn her back to him, sorely tempted to kiss her. "You've been avoiding me."

She shook her head. "I've been busy." She rose and crossed to the fireplace, nervously smoothing the fabric of her dress over her corset. "The work around the plantation never ceases. Harvest is just a few weeks away, followed by the sale of the cotton." She paused and moistened her lips. "Then there are all the necessary preparations for closing the house."

"Closing the house?" Levi frowned. This bit of news caught him off guard. With Lopez on his way to Mexico, taking his phony marriage proposal with him, Levi knew she had no plans for matrimony. What was she up to?

Indecision flickered in her eyes when she met his. She seemed hesitant to answer, but finally, squaring her shoulders, she said, "I haven't mentioned this to Moses and Harriet yet, but I've decided to leave Rose Hill."

CHAPTER THIRTY-ONE

Natalie's legs trembled, and she grasped the mantel for support. She very much needed to sit down, but not beside Levi. His nearness was too distracting, and she had to keep her thoughts clear. Now that the moment had arrived to confess her love, she wasn't sure she had the courage to follow through.

"What do you mean?" His dark eyes narrowed on her.

"I mean just what I said." She straightened the items on the polished mahogany of the mantel. "For years, everyone has told me the plantation is too much for a woman to manage by herself. With the slaves, I was able to keep things going, but now that I'll have to pay workers, it is simply beyond my means."

She glanced at him and found his full attention on her. She moved to the window to keep him from seeing her nervousness. "At first I thought about going to Oregon to visit my family. Samuel's never met his cousins and his half-sister. I'd love to see Adella Rose again. But"—she gathered the nerve to turn and look at him and found he wore an odd little smile—"what I truly want is—"

"Oregon, hmm? That's certainly a far piece from Texas."

"It is, but—"

"You're a stubborn woman, Natalie Langford Ellis."

She looked at him, hurt by the rebuke. "How can you say such a thing when I'm willing to give up everything?"

"You don't have to." He stood, waited a moment to steady himself, then walked to her.

"Yes, I do," she whispered, trembling. "It's the only way to have what I truly want."

A slight frown tugged his brow. "Are we talking about the

plantations? Or something else?"

Her heart beat so hard, she was certain he could hear it. Looking up into his dear face, her eyes filled with tears. "I don't want the plantations if it means losing you. I know I was foolish to trust Alexander. I should have listened to you. I wouldn't blame you if you left Rose Hill and never looked back. But the truth is … I love you, Levi." The last words came out in a sob.

When a tear slid down her face, he wiped it away. "My beautiful Natalie."

Hope surged through her. "Can you forgive me?"

"For what?" He smoothed her cheek with his thumb. "You leased your land to a man who fooled many people with his lies and fancy clothes. You fought to keep the plantations going against all odds. You love your son to distraction and want nothing but the best for his future." He lifted her hand and kissed a dried blister on her palm. "You haven't shied away from hard work, and you've earned the respect and friendship of your former slaves by treating them like the human beings they are."

His eyes caressed her face for a long moment. "You, Natalie, are the woman I love. I want to be your husband and Samuel's father. I'm not going back to Pennsylvania. You and Samuel are most important."

The words were everything she'd longed to hear. "I love you, Levi." She touched his bearded cheek. "But Texas isn't your home. You belong in Pennsylvania with your family. And so do Samuel and I."

He captured her hand and held it against his chest, his heartbeat beneath her fingers. "You'd give up everything? What about Samuel's inheritance? His future?"

She nodded, her eyes filling with joyful tears. "Our future is with you."

The words were no more out of her mouth than his lips descended upon hers, his beard tickling her in the most delicious way. He placed his hand on the back of her head and pulled her close to his body. She wrapped her arms around his waist, lost in the warm sensations flooding every inch of her. Oh, how she loved this man.

She never wanted to let him go.

❦

"Tell me about Penns'a'vaina again, Papa Co'nel."

Seated on the porch swing with the two most important men in her life, Natalie met Levi's gaze, a look so full of love in his eyes, her heart nearly burst with happiness. Together, they'd told Samuel their news before supper. He'd asked dozens of questions about Pennsylvania, about Levi's family, and about whether or not Ebenezer would be allowed to come with them to their new home. One question had brought tears to her eyes—when Samuel had shyly asked Levi if he could call him Papa. Levi, she suspected, had held back a few tears of his own when he'd nodded and said he'd be proud to be Samuel's papa.

Now Samuel sat between them on the swing, bouncing from her lap to Levi's, chattering about his new cousins and his new grandparents and anything else his four-year-old mind could drum up.

"Pennsylvania isn't as big as Texas, but there are lots of trees and streams and lakes. I have a secret fishing hole I'll take you to not far from my brother's place."

The two exchanged a smile that warmed Natalie's heart.

Samuel bounded off the swing and hurried down the steps to where Moses was teaching Isaac how to whittle a whistle. The boys were soon tussling in the grass with Ebenezer.

"It shore is gonna be quiet around here without that chile," Harriet said from her place on a wicker chair. Carolina and Corporal Banks sat on the sofa while Lottie stood near the rail with Jude Liberty in her arms, swaying the wee one to sleep.

Natalie nodded, realizing how dear each of them had become

to her. "He will certainly miss Isaac."

"Guess Samuel gonna need him a brother," Carolina said, grinning.

Levi's smile broadened as Natalie's face grew warm at the bold suggestion. "That sounds like a good plan." He grew serious. "It's still hard to imagine I'll be out of the army soon."

Corporal Banks had delivered a message a short time ago from General Granger informing Levi the end of his service had been hastened due to his injury. He and Banks both would go home in a matter of weeks.

"Are you terribly disappointed?" Natalie asked.

"No." He reached across the empty space Samuel had occupied to take her hand. "My time as a colonel has come to an end. Now I'll be a husband and a father and a carpenter. I like the sound of those titles."

She squeezed his hand.

The setting sun cast shadows across the yard as they talked about the future, their plans, and God's goodness to each of them. Moses and Harriet had agreed to stay on at Rose Hill as caretakers and sharecrop the land. Harriet had decided Lottie and little Jude Liberty were part of their family, so she'd also stay. Natalie invited them to move into the big house, but they said the room above the kitchen had plenty of space for their needs. Lottie would settle into a quarter house once the harvest was complete. When Isaac got older, they planned to set him up in the bachelor's quarters.

Natalie and Levi came to the decision that once the army vacated Langford Manor, she would sell it to help pay the expenses at Rose Hill. Though she'd worried all these changes would bring about a sense of sadness, she felt nothing but peace when she looked at Levi, knowing her future was with this man, no matter where God took them.

As the evening wore on, Samuel and Isaac settled on their papas' laps, their eyelids drooping, while the adults shared stories. It was just before dark when Ebenezer's ears perked, and he rose from his place at Levi's feet. Natalie watched the dog, who stared toward the road. She glanced in that direction, wondering if he'd spotted a coyote or raccoon. She hoped it wasn't the skunk that had tried to get into the chicken coop a few nights past.

In a flash, Ebenezer bounded off the porch and ran out of the yard.

"What got into him?" Levi asked.

Moses, still sitting on the bottom step with his back against the rail posts, craned his neck. "Look like someone be comin' on foot." He set sleepy Isaac on the step and stood.

Natalie strained to see in the dimming light. Indeed, two figures emerged from the shadows of the trees, making their way toward the house. Ebenezer happily trotted beside them.

"My Lord Jesus," Moses breathed, taking two steps forward.

Harriet stood.

With tears streaming down his face, Moses turned to her. "The Lord Jesus done answered your prayers, wife." Harriet rushed down the steps and stared at the two figures approaching.

Natalie stood and moved to the edge of the porch. After laying Samuel on the swing, Levi joined her. He put his arm around her shoulders, and she leaned into him.

She could see the strangers now. Two young Negro men trudged through the dust as though they'd walked many miles to get there. A small pack was slung over each weary back.

Moses took off at a run, and Harriet was right behind. Seeing them, the young men broke into a sprint, closing the gap. When Moses reached them, his wide arms captured both men in a fierce embrace, his cries echoing in the still night. Harriet drew up close, and one of the men broke free from Moses and practically fell into her outstretched arms. Her wails reached the heavens. Little Isaac watched the reunion with wide eyes before running to join his family.

"Oh, Levi," Natalie whispered, tears streaming down her cheeks.

His arm tightened around her, and she buried her face in his chest. How many prayers had Moses and Harriet said, asking for this very thing? How many families were yet praying for the sweetness of being together once again?

When she looked up at Levi's emotion-filled eyes, she touched his face. "You did this. You and Corporal Banks and all the others who fought to end slavery. You gave them freedom. You gave them a new life."

He cupped her chin, smoothing her cheek. "God did this, my love. For them, and for you, and for me, and for Samuel. Freedom isn't just for the slaves." He kissed her forehead and drew her close. "A new beginning awaits us all."

ACKNOWLEDGEMENTS

Thirty years ago when I married my best friend, I could have never imagined all the adventures life would take us on. Thank you, Brian, for loving me and supporting all my wild and crazy ideas. You are the hero of my heart. Forever and ever, amen.

To my sons, Taylor and Austin, as the dedication of this book says, you are my joy, my pride, my heart. Though you have become tall, handsome, and brilliant young men, you will always be my little boys. While writing the final scene of the book, tears rolled down my face, imagining how I would have felt being reunited with you after believing you were lost to me forever. My heartfelt prayer is that we will live out eternity in side-by-side mansions in glory.

Much thanks to my agent, Les Stobbe, for your trusted advice and faithful encouragement. I'm so grateful to have you on my team.

Long before I send a manuscript to my editors, my amazing critique and prayer partner, Paula Scott Bicknell, reads it. Thank you, sweet Paula, for your friendship, your prayers, and your expertise in all things writing. I'm ever so thankful we met at the ACFW conference in Denver many moons ago.

Thank you to my fabulous editors at LPC. Pegg Thomas and Robin Patchen, working with you both on this project has been a joy. Thank you, Eddie Jones, and all the fine folks at LPC who worked on this book in various ways. I'm honored to be a Smitten author.

So many, many friends and family members have supported and encouraged me in my writing endeavors. I appreciate each and every one of you. A few special mentions are Shirley Shocklee, Steve and Chrys Chaparro, Becky Shocklee, and Kim Ulibarri. You make my heart smile.

A huge, heartfelt thank you to all the readers of *The Planter's Daughter*. Your enthusiasm for Adella and Seth's story is every writer's dream. Thank you for the emails, the many five-star reviews, and for waiting patiently for the next installment in the series.

I would be remiss if I didn't acknowledge the hard work and dedication of Union Army soldiers who landed in Galveston, Texas, on June 19, 1865, bearing an amazing proclamation that would eventually free over two hundred fifty thousand slaves still in bondage, despite the war having come to an end. Juneteenth is still celebrated today as a reminder that all men are created equal and should be treated as so.

Finally, without the love and sacrifice of my Lord and Savior, Jesus Christ, I would be nothing. To Him be all the glory and honor.

Made in the USA
Middletown, DE
05 October 2024

62053514R00184